CRAZY B!TCH

BIKER BITCHES, #5

JAMIE BEGLEY

Young Ink Press Publication
YoungInkPress.com

Copyright © 2017 by Jamie Begley

Edited by C&D Editing,
Diamond in the Rough Editing & Hot Tree Editing
Cover Art by Cover Couture
Map by C&D Editing

Connect with Jamie,
JamieBegley@ymail.com
www.facebook.com/AuthorJamieBegley
www.JamieBegley.net

MAP OF TREEPOINT, KENTUCKY

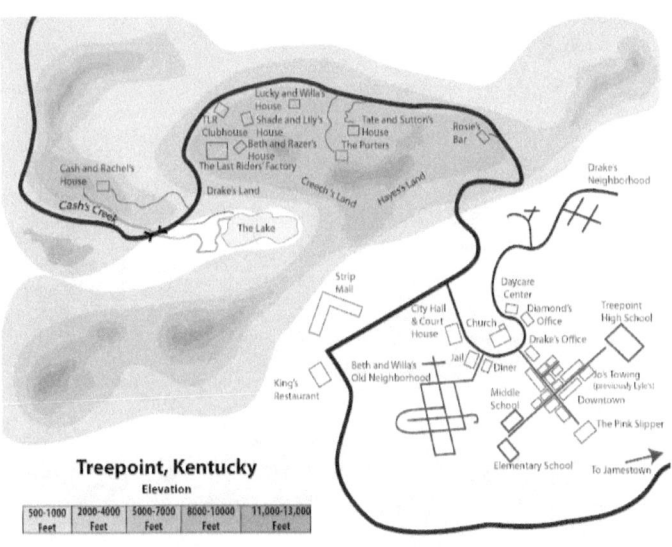

Treepoint, Kentucky
Elevation

500-1000 Feet	2000-4000 Feet	5000-7000 Feet	8000-10000 Feet	11,000-13,000 Feet

"Where's the birthday girl?" Crazy Bitch looked around Sex Piston and Stud's overflowing living room, searching for Star.

Her best friend's living room would make up three of her apartments. Sex Piston had lucked out when she had gotten off her high horse and admitted she and Stud were a couple. The president of the Destructors and The Blue Horsemen hadn't let any grass grow under his feet before marrying her.

The bitch handled his house and her business like a pro. She had even managed to get her stepchildren to love her as much as their own mothers. Meri and Keri had been wary at first, because they were older. To Star, who had been a toddler, Sex Piston was the only mother she remembered, which was a good thing, because Candi, her biological mother, was an addict. Sex Piston never mentioned her anymore, saying she had disappeared after her release from rehab four years ago.

The first years of her marriage had been easily managed with the help of Stud's Aunt Katy, who had lived with them, babysitting Star and then Harley while running Stud's older twin daughters to school and their activities, until she said the winters were hard on her bones and had moved to Florida, leaving them. Sex Piston continued on, managing her beauty shop, her three stepchildren, and Harley with barely a hiccup.

"You want a glass of punch?"

Crazy Bitch juggled the present she had brought. "Yeah." Seeing the large table that had been set up in the corner for the presents, she maneuvered her way toward it, laying it down as Killyama placed hers down.

"Why are you with that loser?" Killyama asked.

"What you got against Sam? At least he has a job." Not only did he have a job, but it was a good-paying one. He drove a car, had money in his checking account, and had a 710 credit score.

Her friend gave her date a phony smile as Sam handed Crazy Bitch a glass of pink punch. "Where's Star?"

"Did you forget mine?" Killyama snapped at the man who looked hapless at how to respond.

"Sam, you mind getting Killyama a glass?"

"Not at all. I'll be right back."

Crazy Bitch waited until he was out of earshot before saying anything. "Cool it. He's a nice guy."

"Then what are you doing with him? You hate nice guys. That's why you told Jonas you wouldn't go out with him."

"I changed my mind." Lofty Crazy Bitch raised her chin on going back on her words.

"Since when?"

"Since I decided I'm tired of partying with bikers."

"That's news to me. You love parties." Killyama gave her a surprised glance.

"Not anymore. I'm turning over a new leaf."

"I give it a week."

Her disbelieving snort had Crazy Bitch raising her chin

higher. "I've been seeing Sam a month. You've just been too busy with Train to notice."

"You pissed at me for standing you up on movie night?"

Crazy Bitch took a drink, making a face at the taste. There wasn't any alcohol in it. The only thing it had going for it was the ice. "I'm not any madder at you than I am at Sex Piston for forgetting my car was in the shop and I needed a ride to work, or Fat Louise for forgetting to bring me tacos for lunch."

Ever since her friends had married, she had become last on their list of priorities, coming right after going to get their yearly pap smears.

Crazy Bitch finally saw Star when she came out of the kitchen with Stud, and Stud's brother coming out behind them.

Dressed in blue jeans and a work shirt from Stud's garage, he looked like what he was—a mechanic. He hadn't even bothered to change out of the grey shirt, while Sam had dressed in nice black jeans and a striped shirt tucked inside.

She never had to wonder who Sam was doing when she wasn't with him. With Calder, it wasn't a whom, but how many.

She had dodged a bullet with him.

When Stud and Calder had hung around the Destructors' club-house while Sex Piston's father, Skulls, was president, she had flirted with him, despite Sex Piston's warnings that Calder was using. Crazy Bitch hadn't cared. If a dude had to take a drug test before she hooked up with them, she would still be a virgin.

She had felt a vibe in her pussy every time she danced with or talked to him, knowing that huge outline of his cock underneath his jeans could get her off, unlike the other jokers in the club she had bedded.

Every time he showed up at the Destructors', she made a beeline toward him like a fucking bitch in heat. Stupid bitch that she was,

3

she assumed he was just as into her as she was him. She danced the night away with him, his cock riding her belly until she decided the night would end with Calder in her bed.

When Stud sauntered onto the dance floor and told him he was leaving, she stared meaningfully into Calder's eyes.

"You want to see my apartment before heading home?"

His eyes shifted away from Stud's, getting her meaning. "You go. I'm good," he told his brother.

"You sure?" Stud questioned.

Another hint she had missed.

"I'm sure. I'll see you tomorrow."

Stud left them dancing. They finished the song then left the floor.

"How far you live from here?" Calder hung an arm over her shoulders, pressing her into his side.

"Close. Let me tell Sex Piston and Killyama I'm leaving. I'll meet you in the parking lot."

"You go ahead. Text me your address, and I'll be there in ten. Wear something hot for me." Calder bent down, rubbing his lips over hers before groaning as he lifted his head. He then handed her his phone, and as soon as she keyed in her number, she gave it back to him then texted her address to him.

"Don't get lost," she teased, patting his ass before leaving him as he turned toward the bar where Dozer was sitting.

"I'm going to fuck his brains out," she bragged to the friends she'd had since high school.

Sex Piston, Killyama, Fat Louise, and T.A. stared at each other from where they were sitting. Crazy Bitch could tell none of them were excited she was about to get laid by the biker.

"I'm outta here. I'm meeting him at my place."

"Hold up, Bitch. Skulls said you shouldn't be messing with him."

Sex Piston's warning wouldn't put out the fire Calder had ignited when they had danced. If she was honest, the fire had started as soon as he walked through the door.

Back then, Calder and Stud didn't come around the Destructors that often. She figured if she didn't fuck him that night, it might be six months before he came back. The itch she had wouldn't wait six months.

"Did he say why?"

"You know Skulls; he doesn't discuss shit like that. When he said to stay away from Calder, that was a good enough reason for me."

Usually, Crazy Bitch would agree, just not that night.

"It'll be cool. Hell, it's not like it's going to be anything serious. We're just going to party a while, then I'm going to fuck his brains out."

"Maybe you should wait." Fat Louise's opinion was chorused around the table.

"Maybe, but I'm not. I'll talk to you bitches tomorrow, if I'm able." She'd snickered.

Crazy Bitch went taut at the memory. She didn't even have the excuse to say she had been naïve. Sex Piston and Killyama had cautioned her about Calder's drug habit.

She usually didn't do dudes who used, but she wasn't Mother fucking Teresa. As long as he kept it under control when he was around her, she had seen no need to stick her nose in his business.

It wouldn't be the first time her pussy had outweighed her conscience. She had been so into Calder that the only thing she'd had on her mind was getting back to her apartment.

He'd wanted her to wear something sexy? Fuck that, she wouldn't be wearing anything but her nipple rings when he got there.

When she arrived home, she took a quick shower, making sure not to get her hair wet. Drying off, she re-teased her hair and put a splash of red color on her lips. When she finished, she confidently went to the living room, trying to think of the seductive pose she wanted to give him. Her eyes went to the wall clock in the kitchen, seeing that fifteen minutes had passed since she had gotten home.

Calder should have been there five minutes ago.

Frowning, she went to her window to see if she could see him in the parking lot. Then she decided to wait a few minutes before texting him.

Flipping the television set on, she flicked through the channels to make the minutes pass faster. Twenty minutes, she was still waiting.

"What the fuck?"

Aggravated that it was taking him so long, she texted him. Maybe he had gotten lost. When he didn't answer, she told herself that he was riding his bike and wouldn't see her message until he stopped. That excuse lasted thirty minutes.

Pissed, she picked up her cell phone, calling Sex Piston.

"Yo!" Sex Piston yelled over the blaring music Crazy Bitch could hear in the background.

"Calder never showed. Is he still there?" If he wasn't, she would get dressed and go looking for him, thinking his bike could have broken down.

"Give me a sec. I'm going outside."

Crazy Bitch nearly hung up the phone. Obviously he was, or Sex Piston would have just answered her question and not gone outside so no one else could hear.

"He's still here," Sex Piston answered grimly when she came back on the line. "He went outside with Dozer, and both of them came back ten minutes later. He's fucked up, dancing with one of the bitches who came along for the ride with the Destructors."

"Which one?"

"Candi. You want me and Killyama to kick his ass?"

"No. If he's fucked up, he's no good for me, anyway." Either in or out of the sack, Crazy Bitch thought to herself. "Thanks for the info. I'll call someone else for company." She hung up, going back into her bedroom to slip on a large T-shirt and panties.

6

Turning out the light, she didn't call any of the bikers who would have beat a path to her door, nor did she answer the door when she heard a knock on it three hours later, knowing it was Calder.

Her pride kept her ass in bed until he left. Next time she saw him at the club, she wouldn't give him the time of day, much less give him another chance of getting in her bed. She didn't give second chances. Second chances were for losers, and she'd had enough of those in her life.

Whoever said party girls didn't get hurt, didn't know what the fuck they were talking about. They could get their hearts broken just as badly as the good girls. The difference was that party girls hid it better.

Crazy Bitch wished there was alcohol in the punch to take the sting away from her stroll down memory lane.

"How'd you meet Sam?"

Killyama's question had Crazy Bitch cringing. "Fat Louise."

"You're dating someone Fat Louise introduced you to?"

"I was meeting her for lunch and Sam was leaving at the same time, so she introduced us."

"What does he do for a living?"

"He bills patients for one of the doctors at the hospital."

Killyama's mouth dropped open. "Who are you and what have you done with my bitch?"

"Nothing is wrong with that. At least he makes a living. That's more than I can say about the last five men I hooked up with," Crazy Bitch defended her choice of date.

"I don't care if he shovels shit. I just can't understand why you would refuse to let me set you up with Jonas. You prefer that pussy over Jonas? It just doesn't make sense to me."

"I want a man I can get serious with, not two."

"That's just a rumor."

"Okay… if you say so." Crazy Bitch rolled her eyes as Sam returned, handing Killyama her glass of punch.

"I miss anything?" he asked, his eyes going from Killy's angry face to her unconcerned one.

"No. Let's get something to eat." She took his arm, nudging him toward the table that held a smorgasbord of food.

"Your friend didn't seem to like me." Sam looked at her worriedly.

"Don't worry about it. Killyama hates everyone."

She wasn't worried about her friend's impression of her new boyfriend. He had a job, a nice car, wasn't bad to look at, and most importantly, he could pay when he asked her out. So far, he only had one failing. He wasn't Calder.

"Who's the bozo with Crazy Bitch?" Calder asked his brother as Star opened her birthday presents.

"Don't tell me you're still sporting a hard-on for that bitch."

Calder shrugged. There was no sense in denying the truth. He had been trying to hook up with her since he got clean.

Seeing Crazy Bitch placing a slice of cake on her new boyfriend's plate had him turning around to watch his niece again. A wrenching pain struck him in the gut when he saw Star motion to Stud, hugging him when he came to where she had unwrapped his and Sex Piston's gift to her. It was the new laptop she had been asking for. He had thought it was too expensive for a kid her age, but Stud had only bragged about how smart she was.

Every time the subject switched to Star when he was with his brother, Stud would give him a look as if he wanted to ask if it bothered him that he had married Candi. He wasn't. He couldn't begrudge Star being a part of Stud's life. He was a standup guy, always looking out for him, even when everyone else had turned their backs.

He didn't blame them. He had fucked over his friends and family for the drugs that never could keep him satisfied for long. The monster inside him had to be fed constantly, gradually increasing his amount of tolerance that had him escalating his use. Stud had tried to pull him back, but he had thought he had it under control.

He didn't blame Stud for getting together with Candi when he was in prison. They had been toxic together. He still had his "Dear Calder" letter she had written to him, telling him she had lost their baby and that she and Stud were getting married.

He wasn't a rocket scientist, but even he could count birthdays. Star was his. Calder had decided before he had even gotten out of prison that he would forfeit any right to be called Star's father.

He had never mentioned it to Stud or Sex Piston, and had no intention of ever telling Star. What kid would want him as her father? A recovering junkie, whose brother had to give him a job because of his record.

Star was staring up at Stud like he had hung the moon.

He then watched as she opened the next present, unwrapping a pink blow-dryer.

"I love it, Crazy Bitch!"

Calder noticed Crazy Bitch wave from the crowd while her date took their empty plates, carrying them toward the kitchen.

Calder squeezed through the crowd until he was standing next to Crazy Bitch. "She's almost finished opening her presents. Let's go for a ride."

"I'm here with a date." Crazy Bitch didn't turn her gaze away from watching Star.

"That lame dick isn't a date. He's an experiment."

"An experiment?"

He finally managed to get her attention on him.

"Yeah, to see if he can make you as horny as I can."

"He might not make me as horny, but at least he doesn't leave me hanging."

Calder crushed the empty paper cup in his hand, wanting to throw it at the man who was heading in their direction. "I was fucked up back then. I'm not anymore. Ask anyone. Hell, I'll even take a drug test if you want me to."

"I don't." Coldly, she curled her arm around the man who came to stand next to her.

"Sam, this is Calder."

Crazy Bitch's date held out his hand, but Calder ignored it, moving away through the crowd to the door. Outside, he unrolled his pack of cigarettes from the sleeve of his T-shirt, took one out of the pack, tapped the tobacco down, and then lit it. Sucking in the smoke, he then blew it out, watching it swirl lazily upward.

Why did he care who she fucked? *Because it isn't you*, he answered his own question.

A headlight turned into Stud's driveway. Coming to a stop, the biker turned off his motor, and Calder squinted through his smoke to see Train getting off his bike, striding to where Calder was standing on the porch.

"Catching a break from the kids, or the bitches?" Train asked as he drew closer.

"The bitches. I take that back—just one of them."

"I hope it wasn't my old lady?" Train's smile faded.

"No. Crazy Bitch. That woman makes me want to run headlong into a rose bush. It would be easier to pull the thorns out."

"I've been there." He gave him a sympathetic look.

"What'd you do to piss Crazy Bitch off?" Calder asked.

"Not Crazy Bitch. Killyama. Hell, all the Destructors had a front seat when I tried to give us a chance."

"I don't have to ask if you thought it was worth it. You married her."

"Killyama might be my wife now, but damn, there were times I could have strangled her. I still want to sometimes. Sex Piston's crew knows how to push buttons that no reasonable man would put up with. Stud, Cade, and I joke that we must be masochists."

"How'd you finally get through to her?"

"Same way Cade and Stud did—let them think they're the boss in the relationship."

"That's not going to work for me."

"I had a hard time with that, too, until I took Stud's advice. Let her think she's getting her way, then show her who's boss in the bedroom."

"My brother told you that? I'm surprised you listened."

"Why not? I figured a man who can tame Sex Piston is a man I'd listen to."

Calder laughingly agreed with him.

"I better get inside, or my new wife will be showing me who's boss for being late. You coming?"

"No. I'm going back to the Blue Horsemen clubhouse." Calder flicked his bud into the dark. "Tell Stud I'm leaving for me?"

"Will do. Take it easy."

Calder was walking toward his bike when he heard Train shut the door. Gripping his handlebars, he swung onto his bike before turning the key. He backed up then rode off, seeing the lighted windows of Stud's house in his rearview mirror.

The wind cooled his temper as he thought about Train's words, but soon, the ride to the Blue Horsemen took his concentration, the road narrow and winding.

He had taken over as president of the Blue Horsemen, since Stud lived closer to the Destructors and to his bike shop. Although Calder still had an hour ride back and forth from the bike shop, he didn't mind. He had finally earned Stud's trust back. His brother had to see him early in the morning, and therefore could see for himself that his hands were steady and his eyes were clear.

The lights were still on when he got to the clubhouse. A few of the brothers were sitting around drinking, while two women were keeping them entertained. Calder hadn't seen the whores before and didn't care.

"You got any ones on you, Calder?"

He stopped as he was about to go to his room, taking out his wallet and taking out what singles he had, handing them to Fender.

Fender grasped the bills. "You want to give her one?"

"No, thanks." With disinterest, he watched as Fender pulled apart the woman's ass cheeks to smash one of his bills into her crevice. Her muscles clenched, nearly making it disappear from sight.

Calder turned back toward his bedroom, passing by Loco, who was watching the women give lap dances.

"Where'd Fender find them?"

"His cousin does porn movies on the side. Those are his co-stars. You want to try one? I'll send one back to your room when Fender and Chief are done with them."

"No, I don't need a case of the clap to go with my morning coffee."

"I'm sure they're clean; movie companies have standards."

"Not when their offices are in Fender's cousin's basement."

Calder left the brothers partying with the two whores. He was sick of coming home from work to see them fucking some whore they had bought for the night. Unlike the

Destructors, they didn't have many female hang-arounds. Not because they didn't attract sluts, the brothers just didn't want the hassle of them hanging around.

In his bedroom, Calder took off his clothes, throwing them into a basket by the bathroom door. He kept his room clean, whereas the other rooms smelled like dirty clothes, sweat, and sex. His had been the same way once, until he had gone to prison and was forced to keep his cell neat. Being an addict hadn't been the only habit he had broken. He had just achieved it too late to claim his daughter, or Crazy Bitch.

Star's birthday party had his old demons haunting him.

He and Candi had been high the night Star had been conceived. He hadn't given a fuck about using a condom or the consequences. He used Candi, because she always managed to keep a supply of the drugs he craved. He didn't care about her or their personalities clashing in a tumultuous relationship they shared for a couple of years. He was never faithful to her, nor she to him.

He wasn't able to care about anyone or anything at that point in his life. His conscience ignored Stud's warnings and concern, unable to fight his way out of the addiction he clung to like a life-saver to lift him out the mess he had made of his life.

Once, he'd had dreams of becoming a motorcycle racer like Stud. When that had bit the dust, nothing else mattered. Especially not a sexy hanger-on he met when Stud took him to meet the Destructors.

The first time he met Crazy Bitch, she was nineteen, and the chemistry between them was immediate on both sides.

Every time he visited the club, he wanted to take her back to the Blue Horsemen's clubhouse, fuck her, and put his jacket on her so both clubhouses knew who she belonged to. Stud stopped him, though, telling him Crazy Bitch was a friend of Skulls's daughter, and you can't walk into another club and take what was theirs. Therefore, he waited.

She was no different than the other women who wanted his

dick, except she was. The more he went to the clubhouse with Stud, the more he wanted Crazy Bitch. The last time he went before his arrest, he made up his mind to take her.

He took enough of a hit before he left the Blue Horsemen clubhouse to feed his monster. It carried him through most of the night, until she asked him to go to her apartment. He planned to talk her into riding with him back to his club, but that was when he screwed up. His monster was getting hungry and needed to be fed. Surely, something was floating around Skulls's club.

There wasn't.

Every second that ticked by made his monster hungrier, until he couldn't think straight. He went outside, texting Candi. Looking at the time on his cell phone, he knew he was blowing his chances with Crazy Bitch. He told himself that she wouldn't mind if he was late, arrogantly believing the jumbled logic that convinced him the nineteen-year-old woman would open her door when he got there.

When Candi arrived, he met her in the parking lot, snorting a line in her car. They stayed outside long enough for his monster to be appeased, and then Candi convinced him to let her come inside the clubhouse.

Forgetting about Crazy Bitch, he danced with Candi while going to the bathroom a couple times to snort more lines of coke. When he came out the third time, he spied Sex Piston and Killyama leaving, only then remembering Crazy Bitch.

He squinted down at his phone for her address. Then, on a drug-induced ego trip, he got on his bike. To this day, he didn't know how he hadn't been stopped on the way to her apartment, or even how he had managed to find it.

He knocked on her door for ten minutes, until one of her neighbors came out and told him to beat it or he was going to call the cops.

Going down the flight of stairs, he saw Candi's car parked next to his bike.

"What the fuck are you doing here?"

"I followed you. I was worried." Candi put her arm around his waist, helping him to her car. "Why are you here, Calder? That bitch doesn't have anything I don't."

"Lay off. I'm not in the mood for your petty jealousy."

"I'm getting sick and tired of you fucking around on me. You didn't want me to come with the other women from the Blue Horsemen, but you had no problem getting me out of my bed to bring you a fix. You think that slut is going to take care of you the way I do? I'm the one who's always here for you. That bitch wouldn't even open the door for you. Baby, let's go to your place. You won't remember her name when I'm done with you." She leaned across the console, placing her hand snuggly between his thighs, cupping his cock.

"What about my bike?"

She reached for her cell phone, making a call. Calder didn't know or care who she was calling. When she finished, Candi turned the car on, taking the choice out of his hands.

He closed his eyes so he couldn't see the opportunity he had missed, not opening them until he was certain they were well away from Crazy Bitch's apartment.

It was better he hadn't met her on time. She didn't need a cokehead in her life. He would have dragged her down in the losing battle he was fighting with the monster that was riding him hard. He had tried to buck it off so many times, but he was tired of fighting.

"I don't even know her real name."

"What did you say?" Candi turned her head from the road.

"Nothing. You got any more coke?"

He handed Stud the socket wrench. "What's Crazy Bitch's name?"

His brother took the tool from him. "Why?"

He nervously took a swig of his cold beer when a brow was cocked in his direction. "Last night, I was remembering when we first met Sex Piston and her crew. Had me thinking I don't know any of their real names."

"Fat Louise is Jane, T.A. is Trudy Ann, Killyama is Rae, and Sex Piston would kick my ass if I told you hers. Same goes for Crazy Bitch."

"I know Sex Piston's."

"Who told you Sex Piston's?"

"Star."

"She wouldn't have gotten that computer if Sex Piston had known. What had you taking a trip down memory lane?"

"Remembering my fuckups." Calder tossed Stud an oil rag to wipe his hands with. He knew his brother was expecting him to bring up Candi and Star, but that was a road he didn't intend to go down with Stud. He was Star's father. She didn't need a loser like himself claiming her. "That dork last night will treat her just as bad as Joker did."

Stud shook his head while opening a beer. "There's no comparison between Sam and Joker."

"They have the same looks in their eyes. I don't care if he works or not; there's something shifty about him."

"And you judge that in the one-second conversation you had with him?"

"Yeah, I did. I'm a better judge of character than you; that's for damn sure."

"What makes you say that?"

"I fooled you, didn't I? Every time I swore I wasn't using, you believed me."

"I didn't believe you." Stud shook his head. "I was giving you the benefit of my doubt."

"Why?"

"Because that's what brothers do."

Calder lowered his eyes, unable to meet Stud's. "I don't know why you put up with me."

"Because I love you, bro."

He bit his lip, forcing his face to remain inscrutable. They had grown hard. At one point, Stud's soul had been just as dead as his, but his brother had never given into the temptation of drugs.

"I love you, too. I won't let you down again."

"I know you won't. You'd have to be crazy as hell to start using again. You hear they found Crank and Ro in their beds, dead as doornails? That's four this month. Last month, it was five. Someone is passing around some hard shit out there."

"I heard. I saw Crank last week. He asked if I wanted to stop by for a beer." Calder took his cigarettes out of his overalls. He lit one, blowing the smoke out of his nostrils. "I used to party with him before I went to prison. Stayed away from him since I got out. I feel bad I didn't go talk to him. Maybe it could have made a difference."

"Stay away from your old buddies. It's not worth the chance of you stepping in that shit again."

"That's not gonna happen." Calder saw the concerned look on Stud's face and reassured him, "It's not gonna happen. I wouldn't do that to myself again. I wouldn't do that to *you* again."

"See you don't. Next time, I'll knock some sense into you the hard way."

"I know you will." He held his hand out, and Stud took it. Shaking his hand, Calder pulled him close until their shoulders bumped. It was as close as a hug the two brothers would allow themselves.

They worked steadily throughout the afternoon. The stifling heat in the garage had him looking forward to a cool shower. After Stud closed the body shop, they walked toward their bikes.

"What are you doing this weekend?" Calder asked as he got on his motorcycle.

"Taking the kids camping. You want to go?"

"It's my turn to stay with Gavin this weekend. Peyton stayed last weekend."

Calder had met Gavin when Killyama asked him and her mother to help through the first couple weeks of his recovery. Both he and Peyton had gone to the rehab, where Viper, Gavin's brother, explained the horrors his brother had survived. They had instantly agreed to help.

"It's cool what you're doing. I know The Last Riders appreciate it."

"Been there. I know what he's going through. So does Peyton."

Calder started his bike, expecting Stud to do the same. He didn't. He just stared at him with a strange look on his face.

He was about to ask what was on his mind when Stud answered.

"I'll tell you what I'll do. Next time Sex Piston gets drunk off her ass, I'll get her to tell me Crazy Bitch's name."

Calder laughed. "How often does that happen?"

"Not often. She's careful when she drinks. She doesn't trust me."

"Why in the hell wouldn't she trust you?"

"One night, she got drunk and I pretended we fucked. She couldn't stand my guts back then. It was right after I made the Destructors a chapter of the Blue Horsemen. Needless to say, she wasn't happy when she woke up."

"When was the last time she got drunk?"

"The Christmas Penni spiked the punch with moonshine."

"Invite her to bring—"

"She's Shade's sister, and she doesn't live in Treepoint. Don't know when she'll be back. That won't work, anyway. It put Killyama in the hospital."

"I could always ask Star. Maybe she would know."

"There's also another way." Stud started his bike. "You could ask her yourself."

Calder made a right out of the parking lot as Stud headed left toward the Destructors' clubhouse, where he would check in with the brothers before riding home.

On his way out of town, he had to pass Sex Piston's beauty shop. He had no intention of stopping, but when he saw Crazy Bitch's car, he found himself signaling a turn.

Seeing the *open* sign glowing in the front window, he shut off his bike and got off.

When he opened the door, a bell sounded that had Crazy Bitch lifting her head as she swept the floor.

"What in the fuck do you want?"

"Is that any way to treat a paying customer?"

"You're wanting a haircut?"

"Why else would I be here?" Calder figured, since direct wasn't working for him, he would give being subtle a try. "Is it too late? You look like you're ready to close."

"Take a seat. I'm not meeting Sam for another hour. It'll pass the time."

Calder passively took a seat in the styling chair she had motioned to.

"What do you two lovebirds have planned tonight?"

Crazy Bitch came up behind him with a black cape, laying it over his chest, then snuggly wrapped it around his neck, nearly choking him, before she snapped it at his nape. "We're going to the drive-in."

"Jamestown has a drive-in?"

"Yes, during the summer months. It gives the teenagers a place to hang out without getting into trouble."

Calder wasn't used to her being so polite. He should have tried this before.

"How short you want it?"

Calder showed her the length he wanted with his finger just above where she had snapped the cape. "It's hot as fuck in the garage."

Crazy Bitch wet his hair with a spray bottle as she ran a comb through the strands. "You want a shave?"

"No, I like my goatee."

Calder tried to think of something to say as she cut his hair, but he drew a blank, his mind turning to mush at the feel of her fingers against his scalp. Under the cape, he tugged it more to the front to hide his burgeoning arousal.

"I see why you're so hot."

Calder met her eyes in the mirror. "You do?" he croaked out.

"Yes. It's too thick. I can shave the underneath off and leave the top length you want."

"Go for it."

"You're going to feel a hundred times cooler when I take it off." She opened a drawer at her station and took out a shaver. "Lean your head down; I don't want to cut you."

He obediently lowered his head, hearing the buzzing sound behind him. Feeling the vibrations on the back of his neck as her fingers waved through his top layer had him beginning to feel worried. If he didn't get himself under control, she would see his hard-on when she removed the cape.

With his head down, he saw thick chunks of his hair falling to the floor.

"You sure you're not taking too much off?"

The buzzing stopped. "I'm sure."

He nearly swallowed his tongue when he felt her breasts against his shoulder as she lifted onto her toes.

"Satisfied?" she asked when she was done.

He took a look at himself in the mirror. "Yeah. I was just worried."

"I might not like you, but I take my profession seriously."

She started the shaver again to finish, and a couple of minutes later, she turned it off again.

"You can raise your head. It'll feel much cooler now. It's long enough that, if it gets hot in the garage, you can tie it back with a band. It'll be even cooler then." Reaching into her drawer, she pulled out a hair tie and demonstrated how to pull his hair to the crown of his head.

Calder ran his hand over the back of his neck. "Damn, that feels good."

"You want me to leave it up or take it down?"

"Take it down. If it bugs me with my helmet on, I'd have to pull over."

Crazy Bitch took off the cape, brushing his shoulders off to remove the tiny hairs.

"You did a great job. Thanks. How much do I owe you?"

"No charge. I've already closed down the register for the night. You can catch me next time."

Calder nodded, becoming tongue-tied. "I wish you would let me take you out some time. We could do a movie or whatever you want. We don't have to hang out at the club if you don't want to."

"No. Sam and I are getting serious. I don't cheat on someone when I'm in a relationship with them."

Calder didn't miss the dig she made at him.

"I admit, I was a fucking asshole back then. We could have had something good, but I was an ass and jerked you around. You didn't deserve it. I wish you would give me another chance."

Crazy Bitch threw the cape in a hamper then started sweeping the hair off the floor. "You know, my dad asked me for a second chance after he begged me to meet him. Never saw the fucker again, even though he lived five miles away. Then my mom told me she quit after every time she used, right up until the night I tucked her ass in bed and she didn't wake up.

"I gave you a chance, although I knew you were using. Instead of meeting me after making me horny as fuck, you gave it to Candi in the parking lot of my club. Then you decided, when you were finally high enough to fuck me, you would come knocking on my door."

"I—"

Crazy Bitch raised a hand to stop him then continued sweeping. "I gave Joker a chance. He decided to quit working after he moved in with me, and he liked to knock me around when I complained about the money he was stealing from my wallet. When I'd had enough of his sorry dick, he nearly killed my crew and Lily. So, you see, Calder, I just don't have any more second chances to give anyone."

He stared at the woman whom he had always assumed

just had a chip on her shoulder and didn't take crap from anyone.

"I can understand." Calder nodded. "I'll leave you alone. See you around." He turned toward the door then paused. "Can I ask you a question?"

Crazy Bitch brought her hand to her hip in an aggravated stance. "What?"

"What's your real name?"

"You really want to know?" she snapped.

Calder had never been a smart man, so he nodded.

"It's fuck you."

T he sound of the bell pealing through the beauty shop as Calder left had her giving up any pretense of sweeping.

"He leave?" Sex Piston asked, coming out from the back office.

"You finally decide to show your face?" Crazy Bitch snapped, resuming her sweeping.

"I was busy."

"Doing what?"

"Counting the bank deposit."

"If it took that long, then I need a fucking raise."

Her best friend smiled, not angered by her snappish reply. "Why don't you just fuck Calder and get him out of your system?"

"I'm done with bikers, especially ones like him."

"What you got against Calder, other than he stood you up all those years ago? Damn, girl, that's ancient history."

"He may not be using anymore, but he fucks any bitch who steps into the club."

"He was a horny toad when he got out of prison, but he's calmed his roll down."

"We've known Calder since we were nineteen; he's always been a player. All the brothers are. I'm looking for something better, like a man who doesn't straddle a bike. Sam's got a car in his driveway. I'm not a kid anymore, and the bitches coming into the club are getting younger and younger. My ass isn't getting any smaller." Crazy Bitch stared at herself in the wall of mirrors facing the chairs. She tugged down her smock that covered her top. "I'm getting a muffin top."

Sex Piston grabbed the broom from her. "Then quit eating out with Fat Louise and drink water instead of beer."

She sank down on one of the spinning chairs. "I'm getting old."

"Bullshit! You're not getting old; you're just fucking depressed because Killyama doesn't hang out with you, and me and Fat Louise's been busy with the kids."

"Kids that I'm never going to have if I don't get my ass in gear."

"You can't settle for Sam just because you're lonely."

"Why not? Sam might not be Mr. Perfect, but sometimes a girl has to settle for Mr. Boring."

"Crazy Bitch, you need to get laid. If you've nicknamed him Mr. Boring, he's not for you."

She watched as Sex Piston swept up Calder's hair and dumped it into the trash. "Why do you think he wanted to know my name?"

Sex Piston rolled her eyes. "Because he's interested in you. He has been since he met you. Calder's been straight a while now—go for it."

"If it doesn't work out with Sam, I'm going on a singles' cruise. If I don't meet someone there, I'm going to ask Jonas out. If none of that works, I'll think about giving Calder another chance."

"What if he hooks up with another woman while you're thinking about it?"

"Then it wasn't meant to be."

"I'm going to call Lucky. You need more guidance than I can give you if you believe that shit."

Crazy Bitch looked out the front window. "Stud's here. You really going camping?"

"Got out of it the last three times. I'm out of excuses."

"You know, if you and Stud break up, I'm going to be the first one in line to steal him from you." Crazy Bitch was only half-joking.

"Aren't you forgettin' something?"

"What?" She stood up, going for her own purse and taking out the keys to lock the shop's door.

"He's a biker," Sex Piston pointed out as they went out the door together.

"I'd make an exception for him."

"If you would make Stud an exception, why not Calder?"

"They might share the same DNA, but that's where the similarities end."

"I can't blame you where Calder is concerned—he was a dick to you that night. But there are more fish in the sea than the Destructors or the Blue Horsemen. How about one of The Last Riders? We can get Killyama to fix you up with one of them. Rider is still single."

"I told you, no more bikers, and he's the biggest biker of them all."

"He's big, not fat," Sex Piston argued back as they went to the RV that Stud had rented for the weekend. "You've never cared about a man's weight before. Joker was carrying that beer gut, and you didn't care."

"Still don't care. I was talking about him owning over twenty motorcycles."

"That many?"

"That's what Killyama says."

"Damn, then Stud is lucky I didn't know that before he married me. I might have given him a twirl or two."

When Sex Piston opened the door to the RV, the sounds of Meri and Keri fighting over which movie to watch, and Star yelling that Harley wouldn't give her the Nintendo Switch she had gotten for her birthday back, had Sex Piston wincing as she went up the steps.

"When you make that reservation for the cruise, make me one. My ass will be sitting on the lido deck in two months." She turned toward her kids. "Rocky, give it back. It's hers."

"Mom!" her son whined from the mysterious depths of the RV. "Quit calling me Rocky. It's a baby name."

"Then give it back before I come back there, *Harley*!"

Crazy Bitch jumped back when Sex Piston slammed the door shut with a hard *thump*. Getting into her car, she drove to the hospital where Sam worked.

Pulling to the front door, she made it with a minute to spare before Sam walked out.

"You sure you don't want me to drive?" he asked as he got into the front seat next to her.

"I'm sure. Mine has a bigger back seat."

"Mine has floorboards."

Crazy Bitch ignored his wary expression of the car as she drove. The apple green paint had turned into a puke green, interspersed with rust, the upholstery inside had metal springs showing through, and the floor had gaps so large that if you weren't careful, you could lose a foot.

"It's a classic. The motor is like new." She gave him an irritated glance at his patronizing attitude.

Sam scooted across the seat with a pained expression, laying an arm over the seat. "I don't mind the car. I just want my girl driving what she deserves."

"What do I deserve to drive?" Crazy Bitch played along as

Sam tried to get himself out of the shit his attitude had dug him in.

"I see you driving a red Miata, or a Mustang."

"I don't have that kind of money working as a hairdresser."

"I could help you out."

"Sam, we've only been seeing each other for a month. I don't want your money, and you shouldn't be offering."

Crazy Bitch found them a parking spot in the back row, pulling the car forward enough so they could hang the speaker on the back window. Sam sheepishly got out of the car as she did, sliding into the back seat next to her.

Damn, she hated it when men pouted. She was terrible at pandering to a man's ego.

Tomorrow was her day off; she might as well start searching for a cruise.

They spent the first part of the movie in silence.

"You want a popcorn or a soda?" she offered when Sam never offered to go to the concession stand himself.

"No."

Crazy Bitch squirmed out of the back seat so the speaker wouldn't fall, tempted to get back in the driver's seat and leave. If she wanted to spend her Friday night with an asshole, she could spend it at the club.

The concession stand wasn't busy. She wished it'd take longer, already planning on leaving as soon as her snacks were gone. There weren't many cars tonight. Some families had spread blankets out, letting the children play as the movie was projected onto the large screen. Even fewer couples were sitting in the back seat like her and Sam were. She hoped they were having a better time than she was.

She awkwardly maneuvered herself back into the back seat and had just managed to take a couple sips from her drink and a few bites of her popcorn before she saw Sam's eyes glittering at her in the darkness.

"Mind sharing?"

Crazy Bitch wanted to tell him to fuck off. Instead, she raised the popcorn in offer.

Her date was becoming a pain in the ass. She promised herself that, once it was over, she wouldn't see him again.

She sat there thinking, not watching the movie. Was it because Calder had come into the shop tonight, highlighting the difference between the two men, that she was now reevaluating her decision to give bikers up? Nah, she was done with bikers. Just because Sam was a wuss didn't mean that all men who weren't bikers were.

"Would you mind getting me a drink? This popcorn is making me thirsty." Sam stared at her.

Crazy Bitch didn't mind sharing popcorn, but there was no way she was going to be trading spit with him when she had decided to give him the heave-ho.

"Why can't you go get it yourself?" she snapped.

"Come on; I'm tired. I had to be at work at six this morning."

He might have been at work, but she could guarantee the jerk hadn't been standing on his feet all day like she had been. At this point, she just wanted to go home.

Handing him her drink, she sidled out of the car again, berating herself along the way for not asking for the money to pay for it.

Every single fucking time she bragged about something, it bit her on the ass.

Taking out her money from her jean pocket, she paid for Sam's drink then went back to the car, giving him a harassed expression as she got back in.

The walk to the concession stand had her thirstily taking a sip of the soda she had just bought.

"That one's mine." Sam tried to take it from her.

"I've already taken a drink out of it; you can have the other one."

"I haven't drunk that much out of it. You have a problem drinking after me?"

She narrowed her eyes on him suspiciously. She only had one rule with men: she never left her drink alone, no matter how well she knew them.

"Never mind, you can have them both. I'm not thirsty anymore." Sam tried to hand her the first soda she had bought.

"You think I got cooties?"

"No! I said I'm not thirsty anymore." Sam's tried to explain at her caustic tone.

The fucker was lying.

"Take a drink," Crazy Bitch ordered, as Sam tried to shrink away when she tried to lift the soda to his lips.

"Fine! What's your problem?"

She might not be able to get a clear look at his expression, but she could hear the worry in his voice.

She rose up, pressing the button on the overhead light so she could see better.

"What are you doing?" Sam stared at her owlishly at the sudden light.

"Watching you take a drink."

"You're being ridiculous."

"I'll apologize after you take a couple of sips."

As Sam lifted the drink to his lips, her eyes stayed on the tip of the straw, seeing the jerk had squeezed it closed so no soda could get up it.

"You bastard, you tried to roofie me?" She snapped her hand out, knocking the cup out of his hand. The top came off, spilling soda all over him.

"You're crazy. Why would I roofie you when any man in town can have you?"

The spineless little weasel was getting brave, knowing he had been caught.

"Cocksucker, there's one man I haven't given it to, and that's you! How many women have you done this to?"

"No one! I wasn't trying to roofie you. You need to go to a psychiatrist; you're just as crazy as everyone says you are."

"Let me show you how fucking crazy I am." Angry, she punched him in the nose, soda still in hand, splattering both of them. Then, furious that he had tried to roofie her, she started whaling on him in the backseat.

His normally good-natured expression vanished at her first hit, turning into the ugly she had seen from Joker when she had broken up with him.

The malice Sam held in his fists that punched her in her face and ribs showed he had been biding his time before showing his true colors. Thankfully, she had been in several fights and was able to fight him off. When his hands went around her throat, she quit playing nice and used her nails to scratch his eyes out.

"You fucking bitch!" Sam shot up from trying to pin her to the back seat. She used the opportunity to lean against the door and kick him in the stomach.

"Get out of my car, or I'm calling the cops!" Reaching for the speaker, she threatened, "I'm going to brain you if you don't get the fuck out."

Sam fumbled for the door handle. When he finally found it, he practically fell out of the car.

Rising up, she slammed the car door shut and locked both doors on that side of the vehicle. With one move, she threw the speaker out the window on her side and locked that door before jumping over the console into the front seat.

Sam hit the window, nearly shattering the glass. "Take me home!"

"You can walk, asshole!" she screamed back at him.

Turning the key, she threw the car into gear and left his ass yelling at her as she drove off.

"Fucking douchebag! The brothers are going to beat his sorry ass to death when I tell them what happ—"

Crazy Bitch cut off her own rant. There was no way she was going to tell them that slimy bastard had been able to get a hand on her and almost roofied her after she had told everyone in the club she was done with bikers. Her pride wouldn't allow her to admit she had been that stupid to be taken in by that little wimp.

She kept her head down as she walked from the parking lot to her apartment. Fortunately, no one was around, so she made it inside without being seen.

Locking the door behind her, she went into the bathroom and got a good look at her face.

"Son of a bitch!" she snarled, gingerly touching the beginning of a black eye, remembering when his elbow had struck her.

Going to her kitchen, she opened the freezer and took out a plastic bag of frozen fish sticks. She held it to her swelling eye as she made her way to her bedroom, hoping the swelling would be gone by Monday so she could hide it with makeup.

Crazy Bitch spent the rest of the weekend holed up in her apartment. By Sunday afternoon, she knew she wouldn't be able to hide her black eye.

Picking up her phone, she made the call she had been hoping she wouldn't have to make.

"Yo," Sex Piston answered after a couple of rings.

"How was the camping trip?"

"How in the fuck do you think it went? I've already told

Stud that shit isn't going to happen again. If I wanted to spend a weekend in a trailer for fun, I could spend it in town where I can at least order pizza. How did your date with Sam go?"

"Okay. I've decided not to see him anymore."

"That mean you're going to give Calder a go?"

"No, it means I'm going to take a cruise when I can afford it. Listen, I ate Taco Hut, and I don't think I'm going to be able to work for a couple of days. You mind if I reschedule my appointments until the end of the week?"

"Why in the fuck you eat there? You hate that place."

"I was craving a taco. Believe me; I've already been blaming myself."

"Next time, make them yourself."

"I will. So, you don't mind?"

"Nope, they're your appointments, your money."

"Thanks. I'll see you Wednesday if I feel better."

"If you need anything, let me know," Sex Piston offered. "I can get Fat Louise or T.A. to get it for you," she joked.

"I'm good. Bye." Crazy Bitch disconnected the call then tossed her cell phone onto the couch next to her.

She mentally calculated how much she would lose from taking the days off. The appointments could be rescheduled, but she wouldn't be able to accept other appointments for the rest of the week. She came to the conclusion that men always cost her money, whether they drove a bike or a car.

Reaching for her cell phone again, she went to her banking app, using her thumbprint when it asked for her identification. She stared dismally at her account balance. Her rent was due today, and she was five dollars short, the five dollars she had spent on Sam's popcorn and drink. She had practically paid for herself to be almost roofied.

She sank back down onto the couch dispiritedly, tossing her phone back down. "Doesn't that say it all?"

5

"That part come in I was waiting for?"

Calder stood up from the motorcycle he was working on, stretching his back. "I put it in your office. It came when you were out to lunch with Sex Piston."

His brother disappeared into his office, coming out five minutes later with the part in hand.

Calder went to the shop refrigerator, grabbing a bottled water. "It's hot as fuck in here," he complained, running the cold bottle across his forehead before opening it and drinking half the contents.

"You should have cut your hair shorter last week."

"I look like I'm sixteen when my hair's short." Reminded about his haircut, he started rummaging in his toolbox. The sound of motorcycles pulling into the parking lot could be heard over the loud fans that weren't alleviating the heat building in the small garage bay.

Stud greeted the bikers who came into the bay.

"Did you leave any Last Rider at home, or did you bring them all with you?" Stud joked, shaking the men's hands.

Finally finding the rubber band he had been searching

for, Calder piled his long hair into a top knot on the crown of his head. Turning, he then went back to the motorcycle he was working on, nodding to Viper, Knox, Shade, Cash, Razer, and Train. His hands were too filthy to shake theirs.

Squatting down, he resumed working on the bike that had come in this morning.

"Since the women are making a night out of going to dinner and the movies, we thought we'd hang out at your club until they're ready to go home, if that's okay with you?"

Calder heard the laughter in Viper's voice and turned to see what he was laughing at, seeing the bikers hastily move their eyes away from him. The only one who didn't look away was Shade, his sunglasses hiding his expression.

"You brothers want to hang out just to keep me company, or because you don't want your wives hanging out after the movie is over?" Stud lifted a questioning brow.

"Nothing wrong with killing two birds with one stone. It's hot as fuck in here." Viper put up a fisted hand to cover his smiling lips.

What in the fuck was everyone laughing at?

Calder stared around the garage, seeing nothing out of place that could put that pained amusement on their faces. Even his brother was acting weird as fuck, not meeting his questioning gaze.

"What movie are they going to?" he asked. Stud hadn't mentioned Sex Piston's crew and The Last Riders' women going to a movie tonight. Usually the women would go out together for lunch once a month.

"It's a double feature for *Fifty-One Shades of Getting It On.*" Stud went to the refrigerator, tossing bottles of water to all the men.

Calder was planning to go back to the Blue Horsemen club after work to sleep before heading out to spend another weekend with Gavin. Changing his mind, he decided to sleep at the Destructors' club.

Calder tuned out what the brothers were talking about, trying to finish his work so he could get out of the hot garage.

He was reaching for a wrench when he saw boots come to stand next to him.

"Brother, which bitch did you let cut your hair?"

Calder looked up at Shade. "Crazy Bitch. Why?"

"She carved the shape of a rat on you." His unemotional voice took him a minute to realize the brother wasn't shitting him.

The silence behind him had him jerking to his feet, his hand going to the back of his head. "I'm going to blister that bitch's ass."

Calder started to leave, determined that Crazy Bitch wasn't going to watch that movie without a fucking donut cushion, only to find a wall of brothers blocking his path.

"Move," Calder grunted as Stud shouldered him back.

"Chill. You want her to know she got to you?"

"She'll know when my hand connects with her bare ass!"

"That's not the way to handle her. She'll just laugh at you harder that you got that mad."

"Why didn't you tell me?" he ranted. "You're my brother; you should have said something before."

"I knew you would be mad as hell and you wouldn't be able to hide it. You only wear your hair like that when you're in the shop. I would have said something before you let her cut it again. She's been waiting for you to find out. Sex Piston told me when she came back to work Thursday. She's being waiting to rub your nose in it."

"I'm not going to disappoint her. When I'm done with that crazy bitch, my nose will be rubbing in her fucking pussy, after I get to smacking that ass of hers," he snarled.

"Can't do it tonight. My wife is with her right now." Shade's forbidding comment sailed right over his head. "She might get upset if you show up angry."

"I don't give a fu—"

Calder was ranting one second, then the next, he was lying down, staring up at the roof of the garage, not understanding how he got there.

Dazed, he felt strong hands helping him to his feet.

"What happened?" he asked Stud groggily.

"Shade knocked you out."

"Oh…."

"No one upsets Lily. You want to have it out with Crazy Bitch, go for it… after my wife goes home."

Calder's temper was already ignited. To be taken down so easily stung his pride.

He narrowed his eyes on Shade. "Your bitch made out of china?" Calder's shoulders stiffened, this time expectantly waiting for Shade to try to punch him again. The menacing biker wouldn't have it so easy the next time he tried.

Stud and Viper moved between the two men, preventing the brewing fight.

"We're all friends, Calder." Stud shoved Calder backward when he tried to move around them to get to Shade.

He hesitated at the warning on his brother's face.

"Lily is sensitive. The Last Riders and the Destructors watch out for her."

Calder turned away, giving the men his back as he tried to cool down. If Shade hadn't told him about his hair, he wouldn't have known, and would have made an even bigger ass of himself.

Turning back around, he gave Stud a curt nod. Only then did his brother move away.

Calder held his hand out. "Sorry. That bitch makes me crazy. I didn't mean to disrespect your old lady."

Shade held his hand out, shaking Calder's. "I've been there. The bitches can drive a man to commit murder then wave you off when they send you down the river to the electric chair."

Viper put an arm around Calder's shoulders. "Brother, there isn't a man here who hasn't wanted to wring that bitch's neck. How about we go grab a beer, and we tell you how we met them?"

Calder reached up, removing the damned rubber band. "I might need more than one to cool me off before Crazy Bitch gets there after the movie is over."

"Knowing Crazy Bitch, he's gonna need something stronger than beer. I brought a couple of bottles of whiskey in my saddlebags," Shade said as they left the garage.

Stud locked the bay and closed the garage. Then the bikers followed Stud as he took the lead, all riding toward the Destructors' clubhouse.

Inside the club, Calder used the opportunity to shower and change his clothes in the room that Stud had given him when he got out of prison. Combing through his wet hair brought back his anger at the sneaky trick Crazy Bitch had pulled on him.

Biting back his anger, he went back to the main room, finding it already full. Seeing Stud at a table, he grabbed a beer from Tanya before joining him where he was sitting with The Last Riders. He silently listened as they talked, not joining in.

Train, he had gotten to know when he had hung out at the club while chasing Killyama. While he couldn't say he was friends with Viper, he had spent time with him during visits to Gavin.

Viper and Gavin had shared the same relationship he had with his own brother, until Gavin had been captured by a rival biker club because of two men. One he had trusted with the club's money to build a factory, and another betrayal from someone much closer—a member of the club.

Killyama had asked for his help when Gavin was rescued. The poor bastard had been forced into drugs, making him an addict to keep him more amicable to his capturer's demands. If he hadn't been rescued, Calder had no doubt in his mind Gavin would now be as dead as The Last Riders had believed him to be for years.

As the men sat around the table talking, several of the club's hangers-on gyrated over, trying to leech on to one of the men. Most of the sluts were too scared of Sex Piston and Killyama to make a play for Stud or Train. The rest of the bikers were fair game as far as they were concerned.

Calder watched five bitches get turned away before they moved on to Cash and Knox, who showed them that The Last Riders weren't there to take advantage of the Destructors' pussy.

"Anyone want another beer?" A hand was placed suggestively on his shoulder and another placed on Stud's as Ginger maneuvered herself between them.

Calder looker up at Ginger, the newest woman who Looney had convinced to take over for Demie and Tanya at the bar.

The two other women had been in too many arguments between Sex Piston's crew and had moved on to other clubs. Stud, nor any of the other bikers, hadn't cared enough to try to convince them to stay. Most of the older Destructors had faded into the background, letting the younger crowd follow Stud after Skulls had stepped down.

The woman staring down at him had red hair like Sex Piston, except hers was more orange. She was at least ten years younger than him. Calder's experienced eye placed her at about nineteen or twenty at the most.

He had also noticed that when Sex Piston or any of her

friends were around, Ginger played it cool, staying out of sight. But when they weren't around, she made sure Stud or he were always within her sights.

She didn't do any of the brothers who were recruits, either. No, Ginger wanted a leader, not a follower.

Calder shook his head. He had no intention of getting involved with the woman. She reminded him of a praying mantis.

At his and Stud's refusal, she surveyed the large table, alighting on Shade as a greedy look entered her eyes.

Her voice dropped an octave. "*You* need anything?"

"No." Shade's curt answer had the redhead blushing as she dropped her hands from Calder and Stud, returning to the bar.

"I think she got your message." Stud laughed, tilting his beer bottle at Shade. "I wish I could get her away from me that fast."

"You give that one an inch, she'll take a mile."

"You know her?" Calder thought the same thing.

"No, and I don't want to. I've dealt with her type before. It would be easier to scrape dog shit off my boot than get rid of women like her."

"I've been keeping my eye on her. So far, I can't complain about how she's hanging around the club. She keeps the beer cold and a few of the brothers satisfied. She'll be gone before too long. None of the bitches stay around for long."

"I wonder why?" Knox wisecracked, whacking Cash in the chest with his elbow. "Can you imagine having to deal with Sex Piston and her crew every time you piss one of them off?"

"I live it." Train's pained expression had the whole table cracking up.

"I don't think they're that bad." Calder had become attached to his sister-in-law.

Even Stud looked at him like he had lost his mind.

"You going to let Crazy Bitch cut your hair again?" Stud stared at him questioningly.

He had forgotten about the rat carved into the back of his head, though the men at the table hadn't. Their laughter renewed at his expense.

Knox ran a hand over his bald head. "I give it three months before your head is as bald as mine."

"Ain't gonna happen."

"Think not?" Knox goaded.

"Next time, I'll go to the Cut and Chop when I want a haircut."

His brother snickered at him. "Let me know when you do."

"Why?"

"Baby brother, sometimes you just have to find things out for yourself where those bitches are concerned."

"One of those bitches is your wife," Calder reminded him.

"I married Sex Piston knowing she's a bitch. I'm not complaining; I'm explaining."

Calder was getting up to grab himself another beer when the women came in through the club door. When he saw Crazy Bitch, he had to sit back down.

Her hair was slicked back into a tight knot, and she had put on red lipstick that gave her skin a creamy complexion. It looked so soft that he wanted to reach out and touch it when she brushed past, going to the bar.

He saw Shade's eyes laughing at him when he caught sight of the whip coiled in her hand.

"Is that a whip?" Calder muttered to Stud.

"Looks like it."

"What's she doing with a whip?"

"With Crazy Bitch, I'd say she's planning on using it on someone."

"Not unless she's planning on skinning them alive," Shade remarked when a dark-haired woman approached him. She smiled shyly around the table as Killyama, Fat Louise, and Sex Piston started barking orders at the brothers sitting at other tables to give up their chairs.

He had met most of the women who were taking the chairs that Sex Piston had forced the men to offer. Diamond sat down next to Knox. A pretty redhead who Cash introduced as Rachel took the seat next to him. The flaxen-haired woman he recognized as Razer's wife.

Crazy Bitch and Fat Louise came from the bar with bottles of beer for the women, except for Lily, who received a can of soda.

"How was the movie?" Shade asked, pulling his wife down on his lap when there weren't enough chairs.

The beautiful woman blushed, not meeting her husband's eyes. "It was good."

"How would you know? You looked away every time something good happened." Crazy Bitch snorted.

"I did not," she argued.

"You did." Beth smiled at her sister.

"It was like seeing Little Bo Peep having to watch her sheep get neutered." Killyama shook her head at Train.

"How'd you like it?" Stud asked his wife.

"Let me finish my beer, and then I'll take you into a back room and show you how much I liked it."

Calder nearly laughed at Stud's expression. Lily wasn't the only one blushing.

"I thought it was bullshit. They make a movie about a man being a Dom; why can't they make a movie about a woman being one?"

"They have. *Wonder Woman* was playing in the next theater."

Calder saw Crazy Bitch roll her eyes at Fat Louise's joke.

"I agree with Crazy Bitch. Do you really think a woman would sign a contract like that?"

Killyama glared at Train as if he had asked her to sign the contract that must have been in the movie they were discussing.

Calder wondered how long the double feature was playing, planning to go see it when he had time. It sounded like his type of movie.

"I bet it's not even legal. Is it, Diamond?"

"Who in the fuck would sign it if it were?" Crazy Bitch answered before Diamond could.

"Depends on the man." Sex Piston shrugged. "I'd sign if I wanted to do a man bad enough."

"You would?" Stud's eyes narrowed on his wife.

"Don't worry, Stud. I'm speaking hypothetically."

"I don't know any woman who would sign a contract like that," Looney said from the next table.

"I do."

Calder's interest was piqued. Any woman who signed a contract that he assumed would make her a submissive was a woman he wanted to get to know. "Text me her number."

The last thing Calder remembered before his chair was swept out from underneath him was Shade's furious face.

Crazy Bitch had been responsible for him being knocked out twice that night, and she hadn't lifted a hand.

6

"Damn, Shade, I was just joking!" Crazy Bitch remained seated, despite wanting to make sure Calder was okay.

The Last Rider who took Calder out with one swing of his fist sat unconcerned that he was a guest in another clubhouse.

She was more furious at herself than Shade. Everyone who knew Shade knew he had a hair trigger temper where his wife was concerned.

"You see me laughing?"

Lily glared at her husband, trying to get off his lap. His club members weren't happy, either.

"Sorry, Stud."

Viper and Knox helped Calder back onto his seat.

"What did I say this time?"

Crazy Bitch lifted her bottle of beer, trying to hide her smile at Calder's question. The man already had one swollen eye. Now the other one was starting to swell.

Her smile disappeared when Ginger came to the table with ice wrapped in a bar towel.

"This will make it feel better," the slut crooned sickeningly.

Crazy Bitch eyed Ginger vindictively, watching her display of concern. He was fine. She didn't need to act like he was actually hurt. Hell, she could take a punch from Shade and not blink an eye.

"Sorry," Shade mumbled at Lily's anger.

"So, you going to tell me what I did?"

"It was my fault for running my mouth." Crazy Bitch wasn't apologizing to Calder but Lily. Every bitch knew that Shade was a Dominant. When they had first met Lily, the poor lamb had no idea of the caliber of wolf that was breathing down her neck. Their marriage had to have been an eye opening experience. That's for damn sure.

She saw Calder looking toward her, and then at Lily.

"You trying to get me killed?" he snarled at her.

"If I wanted you dead, you would be dead." Crazy Bitch made a kissy face at him. "Shade was just giving you a little love pat. If he really wanted to hurt you, your ass would be heading to the hospital."

Train pulled Killyama back to her chair after she went to the bar and brought Calder a beer.

"Dude, what's your problem?" Killyama scolded.

"If Calder needs a beer, he can get it himself, or get Ginger to get it for him."

"Why do you give a fuck that I got Calder a beer? It was one of your friends who knocked his beer out of his hand."

"I guess he wasn't as hard to take down as you thought."

Train's jealousy was ticking off her friend. Crazy Bitch thought about telling Train he was walking a fine line of returning home without Killyama if he made her any madder. Instead, she decided to let the fight she had unknowingly instigated play out. It had been too long since there had been a fight in the club.

"What are you talking about?"

"You remember when we were at the party at Rosie's and you told me I couldn't take Calder with his hands and feet tied behind his back," Train reminder her smugly.

"Number one, you ain't Shade. Number two, Shade hit Calder when he wasn't expecting it. And fucking number three, you aren't Shade."

Crazy Bitch's mouth curled into a devious smile as she watched the fight. "A Last Rider couldn't beat a Destructor in a fair fight." She added more fuel to the fire.

"You trying to start another brawl? Isn't two in one night enough for you?" Calder lowered the ice from his swollen eye.

"Two?"

"Never mind. Quit trying to rile everyone up. We were having a good time until you got here."

She looked down at the table, strangely hurt. What he thought had never hurt her before.

"Don't take it out on my bitch that Shade handed you your ass on a platter. She's right."

Crazy Bitch gave Sex Piston a grateful look for being in her corner.

"That's for sure." Killyama gave Train the cold shoulder when he tried to touch her hand that was laying on the table.

"Knox could take on all the Destructors with his hands and feet tied behind his back." Diamond gave a sickeningly sweet smile that almost had Crazy Bitch vomiting up the popcorn and candy bar she had eaten at the movie.

"Stud could take out Knox like *that*." Sex Piston snapped her fingers in front of her sister's reddening face.

"Only if he was riding on one of those motorcycles he makes and Knox couldn't catch him."

"Maybe we should stop before someone's feelings get hurt," Lily suggested tentatively.

"That's easy for you to say. You're married to Shade."

"I don't understand." Lily looked at Sex Piston.

"No one wants to mess with Shade because he's a mean motherfucker, but Stud and Calder could beat him because they're smarter."

"Are you saying my husband is stupid?" Lily frowned as she leaned toward Sex Piston.

Shade curled an arm around his wife's waist, pulling her back to his chest.

"What's two plus two?" Sex Piston asked Shade with hostility.

"Four."

"Good guess. I bet you had to think a minute, didn't ya?"

"Sex Piston, everyone knows that answer. You're just being a bitch." Stud glowered down at his wife. "The Last Riders and the Destructors are friends; we're not going to know who could win a fight between any of us. Even though I agree with you," Stud said, trying to soothe his wife's temper.

"Really? I agree with Diamond more." Viper winced when Winter hit him on his shoulder.

"I'm not going to watch you, or any of The Last Riders or the Destructors, get in a fight to feed yours and Stud's egos." Winter started to stand. "It's time to go home."

"In a minute. I wasn't thinking of a fight. I was thinking more about a bet."

Crazy Bitch watched as the club members drew closer to hear what was going on at the table between the two clubs.

"What kind of bet?" Stud questioned.

"My jacket against yours. We'll hide them, and whoever finds it can hang the loser's jacket in their clubhouse," Viper explained.

Stud looked at Calder. The brothers were all grinning down at him, wanting him to accept the bet.

"Let's make this more interesting. In my jacket, I'll put the keys of the bike I just finished."

Crazy Bitch had no intention of playing until the bikes were mentioned. She could sell one and have the other to ride. The bike she had now was broken, and she had been without a ride since, unless it was on the back of one of the Destructors' or the car that was on its last leg.

"I'll put the keys of one of Rider's bikes in mine. Since it was my idea, I'll set the rules. The jackets will be hidden by someone impartial. Each club has to have their members searching in groups of two. I don't want anyone stranded out alone or hurt without backup.

"I agree." Stud nodded.

"You can have as many teams as you want, but Killyama and Train, you'll have to figure out who you're playing for before the game starts. Everyone should find their partners tonight. That way, we can figure out if the clubs have equal numbers competing."

"There are more Last Riders than Destructors," Stud said. "Some of The Last Riders won't be—"

"I don't have any objection to letting the Blue Horsemen join with the Destructors," Viper added smoothly, looking toward Calder questioningly.

"The Blue Horsemen accept. I'll add my jacket and the keys to my bike."

"You don't have to. I only suggested because the Destructors are a charter of Blue Horsemen."

Calder earned a trace of respect from Crazy Bitch that he wanted to pay the same price Stud would pay for playing the game.

His bike was sweet. He and Stud had worked a month building it. Crazy Bitch nearly salivated at the thought of winning that motorcycle. If she worked seven days a week, she still wouldn't be able to afford that bike.

"Sounds like we have a bet." Viper held his hand out to Stud, and then to Calder. She watched the three men shake, already planning who she would team up with.

"Who are we going to get to hide the jackets?"

"I have the perfect person in mind, if he'll agree." Viper grimaced.

"Who do you have in mind?" Stud asked.

"Greer Porter."

"Hell, that fucker will keep it for himself." Shade shook his head at his president's answer.

"Shade, call him and ask him to come here. Tell him I'll make it worth his time. While we're waiting for him, let's see how many teams we'll have."

Everyone started talking at once, deciding who was going to ride together. Train and Killyama both started arguing over who they would ride for, while the rest of the married couples quickly stated they would be working together.

Crazy Bitch stood up, going to Bear. "You want to partner up with me?"

"Sorry. I just texted T.A. She said she'd ride with me."

"Fuck." Crazy Bitch started to ask Pike, but saw Ginger had beat her to it. Staring across the crowded bar, she ticked her options off. There weren't many. Fat Louise would ride with Cade. The other brothers were quickly rattling off their names to Viper and Stud, who were making a list.

Looney seemed to be having the same trouble she was having. When his eyes met hers, she glanced away. The biker might be good-looking, but he was a wild card—you never knew how he would react. One day he would partner with you, then forget it the next.

When she glanced away from Looney, her gaze was caught by Calder. *Hell no*, she thought to herself. She would rather ride with Looney.

Giving Calder a haughty look, she started walking toward Looney, only to see him high-fiving Dozer.

"Dammit." Stopped short, she decided to cut to the chase. Grabbing a chair, she climbed onto it. "Any of you fuckers willing to partner with me?" she shouted out across the room.

Dead silence greeted her question.

"Pussies!" she yelled. "Who doesn't have a partner?"

No one answered.

"Warrick? Who you riding with?"

"Puck," the biker shouted back.

"Rolo?"

"Gator."

"I'll ride with you if you leave that whip at home." Calder stood up shakily, holding the edge of the table for support.

Crazy Bitch ignored him, pretending she hadn't heard his offer. "Killyama, you could ride with me, and Train could ride for The Last Riders. Come on; do a bitch a solid," she pleaded, becoming desperate. She didn't want to ride with Calder.

"We decided to pass. We're going to be babysitters. Someone has to stay home and make sure the kids are fed." Killyama gave her a sympathetic glance.

Crazy Bitch couldn't blame her. She wouldn't jeopardize creating hard feelings, either, if Train were in her bed.

"Looks like you're stuck with me."

Crazy Bitch ignored Calder again. "Z, who you riding with?"

"Rooster."

Her shoulders slumped at his quick response. Jumping off the chair, she forced her feet to carry her toward Calder. He didn't look at her when she approached.

"I guess I'll ride with you," she said glumly.

"Maybe I don't want to ride with you anymore. I was

thinking I could help Train and Killyama with the babysitting."

"Fucker, you asked me twice," she muttered, not wanting the rest of the club to hear Calder turning her down.

"And you turned me down twice. The least you could do is ask me nicely."

Crazy Bitch bit her tongue to keep from saying what she wanted to say. "Will you ride with me?"

"If we win, I keep my bike."

She nodded reluctantly, the image of her driving his bike disappearing.

"If we're partners, I won't have to put up with your bitchy attitude?"

Crazy Bitch stared around the clubroom, hoping she had missed someone she could partner with. There wasn't.

"I'll give it a rest until I find the jackets," she agreed.

"Don't you mean, until *we* find the jackets?"

If she hadn't seen the bike that Calder and Stud had built, she would have told him to bite her. Killyama had also told her about the quality of motorcycles Rider owned in his private stash. It was worth taking some shit from Calder to get her hands on one of them.

"Yes."

Calder gave her a satisfied smirk. "Then I guess we're partners."

Crazy Bitch wasn't as enthusiastic. "Whoopie."

7

Crazy Bitch sat at the bar, surveying the occupants of the clubroom. The Destructors were already confidently bragging about what they would do if they won the bikes. The Last Riders just sat talking, cool as cucumbers.

They weren't fooling her. They wanted the bikes as badly as she did. Some motorcycles were made to be ridden on, and then there were a few that were fucking sick. Hell, half the Destructors didn't have the capability of riding those bikes without ending up as road kill.

"Why you sitting over here by yourself?" Calder leaned against the bar next to her.

"I'm waiting for Dozer to bring a case of Miller Lite from the back." She wasn't about to admit her feelings were still hurt that none of the brothers wanted to partner with her.

"Oh, I thought it might be because of something else." Calder shrugged.

"Like what?" Her shoulders and jaw locked belligerently.

"Why do you have to be so confrontational all the time? Jesus, I was just wondering."

"It's a habit."

"Then you need to cool it. You used to be a little fun. All the brothers used to fight over who got to dance with you. Now, you rip their heads off if they look at you too long. Just because you're seeing Sam hot and heavy doesn't mean the rest of us should be treated like horseshit."

"Sam and I are history."

"You are?"

"We are."

"So, you're taking him breaking up with you out on us?"

"Get your facts straight! I broke up with him."

"Then I don't understand, why the chip on your shoulder?"

"You want the truth?" Crazy Bitch turned to stare at him fully, not caring if anyone else overheard. "I'm sick of men. I'm so sick of them I've decided to take a break from them."

"How in the hell are you going to take a break from men?"

"Easy. What am I going to miss, anyway? Their companionship? There isn't any. The only time they give me attention is when they want to get laid, and as soon as they get it, they roll over and go to sleep. My cat gives me more attention. I can't remember the last time a man bought me a burger past the first date. They want to throw out how women are supposed to pay for themselves when they go out with them. I don't have a problem with that. What I do have a problem with is when they want me to buy theirs, too. Men either stand you up"—she couldn't resist that particular dig at him—"or, when they do show up, they give you a drunken kiss that tastes like another woman. I'm tired of the bullshit —have been for a while—so excuse me if I'm not kissing someone's ass just to fill the other side of my bed."

"It's not easy for men, either."

"Really? What problems do you have, Calder? Which slut do you want to spend the night with? Ginger and Gina have been all over you tonight. Take my advice; if I were you, I'd pick Ginger. I saw Gina coming out of Dozer's room half an hour ago."

"Some women can be just as irritating. When's the last time you've seen me take a bitch to my bed?"

Crazy Bitch had to think about that. It had been a while, she had to admit to herself.

"Either they're just using you, or they are accusing you of knocking them up. When Demie couldn't blame her being pregnant on Cade, she accused me. I might have fucked her when I got out of prison, but I was gloved every damn time. I had to spend two hundred dollars on a paternity test, and so did two other brothers. When she left the club, none of us knew who the father ended up being; we just knew it wasn't us. Men are supposed to just take a woman's bullshit."

Crazy Bitch was pretty sure that was a dig at her.

"We're supposed to suck it up as if we don't have any feelings because, guess what? Men aren't supposed to have any of those. And let's not forget, if you fuck up, they never let you forget, even though you've apologized over a dozen times," he added.

Yeah, it was a dig at her.

Crazy Bitch sighed. "All right, you win. I'll cool it with throwing it up to you that you stood me up."

Calder squinted at her from two swollen eyes. "I told you I wanted another chance with you. I can understand you going through a manhater phase, but if you want to win one of those bikes, then we have to come to a compromise."

"Only one? If we win, you can keep your bike and all three of the jackets. I think that's fair."

"How is that fair? We'll let the Destructors have the jackets. I'll keep my bike, you can take your choice of the other two, and we'll sell the one you don't want and split the money."

"I want both bikes," she argued.

"Why?"

"*I* want to sell the one I don't want. I need the money. I don't want to share."

"I don't either, but I will. I need the money, too."

"Fine, but you pay for the gas when we're out looking for clues."

"I can live with that." Calder grinned. "Don't look so angry; it's supposed to be fun."

"It'll be fun when I'm wearing Viper's jacket to the next party we have with The Last Riders."

"I thought you were friends with them?"

"I am. That doesn't mean I can't torture them. They expect me to. I might be able to bribe Rider to take me out on a bike ride the way Killyama did. That worked out great for her. Maybe it will for me, too."

"I thought you were off men."

"I am, but I'd make an exception for Rider."

"You and Rider wouldn't get along."

"How do you know? You barely know the man."

"I don't. Stud does, though, and he said Rider is a big pussy."

"He doesn't say that." Skeptically, Crazy Bitch peered closer at Calder's nonchalant posture.

"Not to anyone else, but he did to me."

"How would he know?"

"A man sees things a woman wouldn't notice."

"Like what?"

"Like that goofball you broke up with."

"You were around Sam for two seconds."

"Long enough to see that he might have jumped at getting a drink for you and Killyama, but he didn't open the door for you when you got to Stud's house."

"How in the fuck do you know?"

"I was outside, smoking a cigarette."

"That doesn't mean shit."

"He didn't let you go first, either, when you got to the door, even though he had never been there before."

"I didn't need him to hold the door for me."

"Just saying, I would have opened the door for you."

She had seen Calder around the club with different bitches. She had also seen him being nice to them. She couldn't see him roofieing any of them, either. Even at the height of his drug use, he had never even offered her a joint.

"So, why does Stud think Rider is a pussy?" All the bitches had fantasies about The Last Riders.

"He said that, when they were searching for Raul, all he wanted to do was go home to make sure the women were safe and Shade wouldn't let him. Everyone knows that you keep your strongest man to protect the clubhouse and the women. Stud said that he whined the whole time to go back."

"Anything else?"

"That's not enough?"

"Have you seen Rider through a woman's point of view?"

"I can't say I have."

"He's sexy as fuck. He may not be Shade's choice of watching the women because he didn't want to leave the fox watching the hen house."

She slapped her hand down on the bar, laughing at Calder's expression. Then she sobered when she saw Dozer carrying in the case of beer. The brothers moved closer to the bar, calling out to him to hand them one. Nearly squished, she started to snap at Looney when he almost elbowed her in the jaw while trying to reach for one.

Before she could, Calder swiveled on his bar stool, his arm going around her waist to pull her snugly between his thighs. With his other hand, he took the beer from Dozer's hand, giving it to her.

"Want me to open it for you? I wouldn't want you to break a nail."

"I got it." She twisted the top off as the other brothers emptied the case before she could take her first sip. "Fuckers, have five other brands to choose from, yet they always finish mine off first."

"You want one, Calder?" Dozer asked, the last one in his hand.

"Give me a Bud. Put that one in the cooler for Crazy Bitch for later."

When the brothers moved away with their beers, she jerked away. "You trying to prove you're nicer than Sam? Don't bother. I didn't break up with him because he didn't hold the door open for me."

"Why did you break up with him?"

"When I want you to know my business, I'll tell you." Dismissing him when she saw Greer Porter coming in the door, she grabbed her beer and returned to the table where The Last Riders and her crew were sitting.

The man arrogantly ignored that he was the center of everyone's attention. "Why did you need to see me in such a hurry? If you're wanting product"—his eyes went from Shade to Knox and Diamond—"I don't sell anymore."

Greer worked part-time as a deputy sheriff. His wife, Holly, was BFFs with Diamond. Diamond had told them that Holly had put a stop to Greer's pot selling, which no one believed he had done, except Diamond and Holly. Stud regularly bought from Greer once a month.

"Holly told Diamond that you're an expert at hiding your stash. Knox said the same thing; that the state police have given up trying to find your plants or your stock."

"The police can't find their ass with their own two hands." He disdainfully sniffed. "But I do take after my pa, and the feds could never catch him moonshining."

"Have a seat, Greer. We want to ask a favor from you. Knox, get Greer a beer." Viper motioned for Greer to take a chair that one of the brothers had positioned at Viper's side.

Greer distrustfully stared at everyone who was staring back at him. "I ain't gonna kill anyone."

Viper leaned back so Knox could set the beer down in front of him.

"Not that I would mind, but Holly wouldn't be happy. I got a kid on the way, and I can't raise it from prison."

"We don't want you to kill anyone. The Destructors and The Last Riders have decided to bet on who has the best club."

"You want me to referee? I'm down with that."

"No, we're not going to fight it out. We want you to hide my jacket, Stud's for the Destructors, and Calder's for the Blue Horsemen. We're each putting in keys to a motorcycle."

"Be easier to fight it out."

"Dude, what are you getting at? This way, no one gets hurt and we can remain friends." Killyama looked like she was about to break Greer's beer bottle over his head.

"Sounds like a pussy way to find out."

Viper and Stud gave everyone warning looks to keep some of the brothers from beating the bastard to a pulp.

"Can you do it or not?" Viper ground out.

"What's in it for me?" His question was the first interest Crazy Bitch had seen in his eyes since he had entered the club.

"What do you want?"

Greer grinned, running his fingers over his temple, his eyes going to Diamond. "Wife's expecting…"

"We know." Becoming irritated, Viper gave Train a side look. "Get me a whiskey."

"Me, too," Stud brusquely requested before Train could stand.

59

"Diamond said Holly can have eight weeks maternity leave. I'm thinking twelve sounds better." Greer stared at Diamond questioningly.

Viper turned toward Diamond. "The Last Riders will pay Holly's salary for the extra four weeks."

"That's fine. I'll be taking my own maternity during that time."

"Then it's a...." Viper's smile vanished when Greer started shaking his head.

"I went to the grocery store the other day. You know how much diapers are?"

"Yes." Viper's face was becoming red with anger. "Since you're Aisha's godfather, you know I do."

"Yeah, well, I didn't have a clue. Might have put off knocking Holly up if I did. A year's supply would come in mighty handy."

"The Destructors will pay for a year's supply of diapers," Stud offered.

"Satisfied?" Viper ominously grabbed his knife from his boot, but Winter took it away before he could open it.

"Seems to me that The Last Riders and the Destructors are donating to pay my fee; I think it's only fair the Blue Horsemen contribute, too."

"What do you want?" Calder shouldered his way to stand beside Stud.

"I got Holly a brand-new truck. Every Sunday, she makes me wash it and gas it up. It's a pain in my ass to spend my time doing it."

"The Blue Horsemen can take care of that," Calder agreed.

"Make sure the tank is filled to the top, too… for a year."

"Anything else?" Calder glared down at Greer, showing his patience was running out.

Crazy Bitch would have to remember the tactics that Greer used to get his demands met. The fucker had three groups of bikers ready to beat him senseless, yet he wasn't even sweating.

"Yeah, don't forget the wax." Greer tilted his beer back, finishing it off. "I better get home. Holly will be waiting for me." He turned his head to look over his shoulder at Calder. "When someone comes to wash Holly's truck Sunday, send the jackets. I'll send an email to Viper, Stud, and you after I hide them. After that, you're on your own. Don't be trying to get me to give any hints. And so you know, it won't be hidden anywhere on my property. I ain't gonna have my backyard dug up to settle a bet." Greer stood up, staring down at Viper expectantly.

Confused, Viper stared back. "What?"

"Shade said you would make it worth my time to get here in thirty minutes. I made it in twenty-five." Greer held his hand out.

"Viper... we don't know the sheriff here. You'll spend the night in jail," Winter cautioned her husband.

Viper's chair scraped back as he stood, removing his wallet. Taking out a hundred, he slapped it down into Greer's waiting palm. Then Greer's palm went out toward Stud, who looked like he was about to have a seizure. Taking out his wallet, he placed another hundred on top of the other one. When Greer's hand went toward Calder, Crazy Bitch nearly howled in laughter. Calder took out his wallet, counting five twenties.

"You can see who has more butter on their bread by the bills a man carries." Greer's fingers snapped closed as he turned to leave, stopping by Diamond. "Let's just keep this to ourselves. She would have expected me to do it for free because she's friends with you."

"All right. It's a good thing she didn't come tonight when I invited her. She said you were under the weather, and she needed to get home and make you some soup. You don't look very sick," she said caustically.

"I'm not." Greer shrugged. "But I wasn't about to let her go to that movie. I don't want her getting any ideas. You dumbasses should take a lesson from me." He smirked as he went toward the door.

Crazy Bitch couldn't hold back her laughter any longer.

"I'm glad you find it so funny." Calder's hand had gone to the chair that Greer had been sitting in as if he was going to throw it at the departing man.

Crazy Bitch laconically stood, making sure she was standing so if anyone threw anything at Greer, it would hit her first.

"You sure he isn't a Last Rider? He fucked all of you and left with a smile on his face."

8

He sat, staring out at the green grass and the flowers that had been planted in a circle underneath the trees. The rehab center Gavin was in was nothing like the one the court had decreed he had to stay at. There were no bars on the windows, and each room was private with its own backyard.

"You're not going to eat your lunch? Bro, you're looking like a bag of bones." Calder had been trying to coax Gavin out of his silence since he arrived this morning.

Peyton had left when he arrived, warning him that Gavin hadn't said a word during the week she spent with him, and he refused to take any visitors, other than him and Peyton.

"Viper called when you were taking a shower. He wanted me to call when you got out. He's not going to be happy I didn't."

Calder looked over at Gavin then returned his eyes to the trees.

"I don't blame you for staying out here all the time. When I was released from prison, I couldn't stand to be cooped up. I still sleep with my bedroom door open at night. You have a sweet deal here. If I had this area attached to my bedroom, I'd sleep out here, too."

Calder raised up from his position on a chair he had carried out from Gavin's room. Taking half the sandwich that remained untouched, he settled back down on his chair. "Did I tell you that I saw Viper and Winter last night? Shade, Train, Cash, Razer, and Knox were there, too. They all asked about you." He took a bite of the sandwich.

Gavin rarely talked to him, just listened in silence until Calder would leave Sunday night. Calder didn't let it bother him, filling in the silence by talking about anything and everything, trying to pull Gavin back to The Last Riders, who wanted him so desperately to rejoin the land of the living.

"They all had their wives there, too. Those women are fine. Not as fine as the woman I have my eye on, but they're smokin' hot."

"Did anyone else call when I was in the shower?" Gavin distracted him from his lone conservation.

"No, Taylor didn't call. You want me to call her?" Viper had explained that Gavin had been engaged to Taylor when he was kidnapped. After he was rescued, he found out she was now married and expecting. It was a raw wound for him.

"So she can ask if she can come and see me again? No thanks."

"Then why you asking if she called?"

"No reason."

"Bullshit. Why won't you see her?"

"I don't want her to see me until I'm back to normal."

"You want to get back to normal, start eating again and hit the gym."

Gavin went back to the silence he hid behind whenever anyone told him what he didn't want to hear.

"You don't want to see her because Viper told you she is

married. Call a spade a spade, but don't lie to yourself or me. It's a big step in your recovery."

"What do you want me to say? That if I see her, I'll beg her to get a divorce? I know the man she married. Taylor's better off with him."

"Is that why you're slowly killing yourself?"

Gavin's harsh features would make anyone proceed with caution, but Calder had been in prison with men who were just as menacing and who had nothing better to do with their days than work out. Gavin was so gaunt and weak that he wouldn't be able to fight himself out of a paper bag.

"I'm not trying to kill myself. I just don't care if I do or don't die anymore."

"When you were held captive by the Road Demons, did you just give in, or did you fight the bastards?"

"I fought."

"Then why give up now?"

"Have you ever loved a woman?"

"Can't say I have. I came close once."

"The one who won't give you the time of day?"

"I never even dated her, and she hates my guts. Can you see how much she would hate me if I had?"

"What's her name?"

"I don't even know her real name. Her nickname is Crazy Bitch."

"If you're hung up on a woman called Crazy Bitch, you're the last one I'd take advice from."

"I'm not giving you advice. You have counselors here who get paid to dish out advice. I'm just saying that, if you want to get Taylor back by making her feel sorry for you, go right ahead. I don't blame you for preferring her to me. The only problem with that is you're going to be the same pitiable mess until your body gives up and you get your wish, and you'll be as dead as a doornail. Or you regain your strength, she will see you no longer need her, and she goes back to her husband."

Gavin struggled to his feet. "I'm going down for a nap."

"Or we can go work out for a while. Then you eat an early dinner and have a good night's sleep."

Gavin went inside his room, shutting the sliding glass door behind him.

Calder remained where he was, giving Gavin time alone. He knew the man had more going on in his mind than a woman. He was fighting off the depression of coming off the drugs. Until Gavin was ready to admit what he was really missing was the high coursing through his veins, he wouldn't get better.

The rehab center had been weaning them off him, but it was a slow process so his blood pressure and heart could be monitored. Each week, the amounts would decrease until he had the willpower to not depend on it. Only someone who had gone through it themselves would be able to understand with hindsight. Calder still remembered the agony of wanting the drugs that had become the only friend he had left.

He shook his head at himself. If he hadn't gotten caught and been forced into rehab, he would have still been using. It was only when his ass had been locked up for a couple of years had he kicked his dependency. Now he would take a loaded gun to his head before doing them again.

Gavin might have become dependent on them because the Road Demons had used every means possible to keep him under control through years of captivity and abuse, but it wasn't the club who kept him prisoner now; it was the drugs. They had taken control, and unless Gavin realized which enemy he was fighting, The Last Riders would soon be burying him.

Calder got up and went into Gavin's room, silently

opening the door, not wanting to disturb him if he was sleeping. He wasn't. He was staring at a picture on the wall.

"Why didn't Peyton include you in the picture?" Calder asked, sitting down beside him on the bed.

"I told her not to."

Calder stared at the men in the painting. Once a week, each of them visited Gavin. Viper came once during the middle of the week, and then again on Sundays when he would bring Winter and their daughter, Aisha.

"It's hard to see them so happy while your life is in the toilet bowl."

"I'm glad they're happy."

"You're jealous as fuck." Calder wryly shook his head. "Stud sent me letters with pictures when I was in prison. I ripped most of them into shreds. I didn't want to see Stud so happy while I was so miserable. It's not The Last Riders you're in here for any more than Stud was responsible for me."

"I only blame four people: Memphis, Crash, Vincent Bedford, and myself. I was a naïve fool."

"You weren't naïve. You were a grown man who had served your country and thought that you could handle yourself. Damn, bro, two men you thought were brothers took you down. Nothing to be ashamed of there."

Gavin's face cracked in agony at his memories. "You don't know the shit I did. If you did, you wouldn't be sitting with me. None of them would be." He pointed at the painting then let his hand drop to his side.

"Gavin, I told you, as your sponsor, anything you want to talk about, I won't repeat. It's just between me and you. I wouldn't want anyone spilling the shit I did when I was using, and I willingly took that crap. You didn't take it will-ingly. It won't make it easier to bear what went down, but cut yourself a break here."

"I went into the Navy to help people. To defend and protect the weak from others who would hurt them. I became what I fought against."

"You might think that, but you didn't. I've done time with hardcore felons. Do you think they're sitting on their beds, slowly starving to death because they feel bad about their crimes? Fuck, most of them are planning what they're going to do next when they get out and how to do it better without getting caught."

"I should be locked up with them."

"Will that make you feel better?"

"Yes. It's where I deserve to be."

Calder ran his hand along his jaw, thinking. "Why don't we go about it this way? Let's get you stronger, and you open up to me about why you think you deserve to go to jail. Then we'll ask Diamond to come talk to you."

At the mention of telling Knox's wife, Gavin started shaking. "No!"

"You think the police will arrest you without you confessing to a crime, that a jury will convict you without hearing the charges? Even if you don't want it, the court will appoint a lawyer for you... unless you're going to defend yourself?"

Gavin ran his hands through his hair. "I have no defense."

"You weren't in your right mind. If you don't want to talk to Diamond, that's cool. We can find someone else to talk to. But I think that's a mistake. Diamond is pretty cool, and as a lawyer, she won't talk to Knox about anything you discuss with her."

"I'll think about it."

"While you're thinking about it, I'll go ask your nurse for some more soup and another sandwich. While I'm doing that, when I come back, think of one thing that you want to tell me, and then we'll go for a walk. How's that sound?"

"I don't like turkey sandwiches." He didn't say he wasn't hungry or that he was ready to talk, but he didn't say no either.

Taking it as a yes, Calder stood.

"Who's coming today?"

"It's Saturday, so Train and Killyama should be here in a few," Calder replied.

Gavin's face brightened when he heard Killyama's name. "Do you mind if we wait for the walk until they get here?"

"No."

Calder went to the front desk, searching for Gavin's nurse. After he found her and asked for another lunch tray, he took his time returning to Gavin's room, giving him time to think about what he wanted to share with him.

His hopes weren't high when he returned. Gavin had turned on the television and was watching it fixedly. Calder didn't push, watching the movie with him.

When the nurse brought the tray in and set it down next to Gavin, Calder kept watching the movie, noticing him lifting the mug of soup to his mouth. When he picked up the sandwich, he wanted to jump up and down, but he remained seated.

Gavin was eating the second half of the sandwich before he spoke. "They videotaped me having sex with members of the club."

He threw his sandwich down, running into his bathroom. Calder followed him, wetting a washcloth as Gavin heaved his lunch into the toilet.

When he was finished, Gavin sank down onto the tiled floor, his arm resting on the lid to support himself, as if he wasn't finished vomiting.

Calder flushed the toilet then lowered himself down to the floor, handing the wet cloth to him.

"The Last Riders aren't shy about fucking in front of each

other. I didn't think I could be embarrassed or ashamed about anyone watching me, but they took it to levels I never knew existed, and I've been in some fucked-up situations when I was in the war."

"You were in a war." Calder tapped the side of his forehead. "Your mind and soul were rebelling against them. If that isn't a war of its own, I don't know what is. Just because you weren't on foreign soil doesn't mean it wasn't as traumatic."

Gavin tilted his head to the side. "You think so?"

"Hell yes. I've never been in the military, but I'm sure they trained you to survive at all odds."

"They did."

"You survived; that's what counts."

"Does it? I don't know anymore if it was worth a fight."

"Because of Taylor?"

Gavin nodded imperceptibly.

"Was she the only reason you fought so hard to stay alive?"

"I wanted to kill the Road Demons and the three who put me there. The Last Riders took out the Road Demons. Bedford and Memphis are dead. They're saving Crash for me. I couldn't kill a fly right now."

"So, all you thought about was Taylor and killing?"

"No," he admitted. "I thought about Ton and Viper. I was used to talking to them every day. Not being able to do that was hard."

"Is that why you won't take their calls? Because you don't want to get in that habit again?"

"I'd rather not get used to having them around if I'm going to lose them again."

"Meaning, if you went to prison?"

"Yes."

Calder scooted over, leaning his back against the bathroom wall. "We don't know if you did anything you can be charged with—"

"I did." Gavin started heaving over the toilet bowl again.

"Okay, let's assume you did. You think Viper and The Last Riders won't stand behind you?"

"Yes."

"Even in prison, you're allowed to talk to family and correspond with friends. You won't lose them again, but they'll lose you again if you don't start eating. When Viper comes, take a good look at him. He's suffering without you, and so is Ton. Shit, Ton's living in a hotel near here and comes by every morning to eat breakfast with you, yet you don't say a single word to your father. What if something happened to him? Sooner or later, we lose everyone, whether through age, sickness, or accidents.

"You being afraid to resume those relationships is what I went through with Stud. I never felt like I measured up to him, or the brothers he leads. I still don't. Stud was smart not to take drugs, he beat me at those races we rode together, and he even married the mother of my child when I was too stoned to get my life together. My girlfriend told me she had miscarried. Then, two months later, Stud comes to visit me at the prison and tells me he's marrying Candi. Six months later, he sends me a picture, telling me they had a baby."

"Stud didn't tell you the baby was yours?"

"No."

"Have you talked to him about the kid since you got out of prison?"

"What am I supposed to say? Star is healthy and happy. She believes Stud is her father, and she loves Sex Piston like she's her own mother. She is. Candi is in prison and doesn't get out for another year, unless she makes parole. I don't want Star to know both of her parents are worthless. Stud gives her the stability I can't."

"For a sponsor, you're just as fucked up as I am. At least I don't have the hots for a woman named Crazy Bitch."

"You want to see what she looks like?"

"Sure."

Calder reached into his pocket, taking out his cell phone. Flipping through the photos, he said, "This is my kid." He turned the phone so Gavin could see Star's picture. He had taken it when she had been blowing out her birthday candles. Sex Piston and Stud were standing behind her.

"Cute kid."

"She's beautiful." Calder cleared his voice, turning the phone back around to scroll through his pictures. Then he turned it back to Gavin. "That's Crazy Bitch."

"What's she doing?" Perplexed, Gavin raised his eyes from the phone.

Calder frowned, turning the phone back toward himself. His frown cleared when he saw what Gavin meant.

Usually when he looked at her, he just thought about how beautiful she was. He hadn't paid attention to the hand gesture she was making when he had been taking the picture.

"Oh, that. She's telling me to fuck off."

9

Crazy Bitch pushed down hard on her brakes, parking in front of the Destructors' clubhouse. When the car determinedly kept rolling, she set the emergency brake.

Taking her strong cup of coffee, she carried it into the clubhouse, seeing the men groggily sitting around.

"What are you fuckers up for?"

Rock stared at the large coffee in her hand. "Same reason you are. We're waiting for Stud to get here."

"Go back to bed. I'll wake you all back up when he gets here," she magnanimously offered.

"Like I believe that," he scoffed. "The only one who is gullible to fall for that horseshit is Fat Louise, and she's not here."

"I don't even think Jane would believe it." Cade yawned, staring at the large coffee. "You going to share that?"

"Uh... let me think about it for a second." She sat down and propped her legs on another chair. "No."

"You could have picked us up one when you went through the drive-thru."

"Why in the hell would I do that? I didn't think any of you assholes would be awake." Crazy Bitch moved her coffee cup closer to her on the table. "Where's Calder?"

It wasn't a good start that her partner was still in bed.

Tired, Cade didn't take his eyes off the coffee. "He must still be in bed."

"No, I'm not." Calder came out of the hallway, still pulling down his black T-shirt.

"I thought you might still be in Lexington with Gavin." Crazy Bitch gave him an appraising glance. "You look like shit."

"I rode in from Lexington a couple hours ago. I'm tired." He took a seat at the table next to her, running a hand through his tousled hair.

She nearly blanched. Crazy Bitch didn't want him to see that she had fucked over his haircut before they won the prize. He would be mad enough to blow the prize, or the contest.

Nudging the coffee cup toward him, she said, "I brought you a coffee."

"You did? Thanks."

"Don't mention it. We're partners now. I have to take care of my best bud. Stop by the shop today and I'll trim your hair for you."

"It's fine. You only cut it a couple of weeks ago." Calder took the lid off his coffee, blowing on the rising steam. "It's hot." Calder caught her gaze before she could stop staring at him.

Turning her gaze away, she saw Cade staring at her with a quirked eyebrow. Giving him a death glare, Crazy Bitch jumped when Calder's cell pinged. Straightening, she dropped her legs to the floor.

"That Greer?" she asked, not looking toward the door as Stud came in.

"Give me time to see." He unhurriedly pulled out his cell phone, but Stud beat him to it, reading off Greer's message.

"I see you every day, but I can't see you at night, though I stay in the same spot."

"Huh?" Crazy Bitch snatched Calder's phone from his hand, staring down at the message, hoping that Stud had read it wrong or there was an attachment. "What in the fuck is this? Where's the treasure map?"

"I guess Greer has decided we're going to play it his way." Calder laughed, taking his phone back.

"Call him and tell that cocksucker to email me a map," she snarled.

"If I do that, he'll send me a map leading us to the sewage plant," Stud shut down her demand.

She snapped her mouth shut. He was right, and she was losing time arguing. Switching gears to think of the lame-assed clue, she listened to the others already trying to decipher it.

"What sees us every day?" Rock asked Pike.

"A drone?"

Crazy Bitch rolled her eyes at that answer. Anyone stupid enough to fly a drone over these parts of Kentucky would have it shot out of the sky right after takeoff.

"We see Stud every day." Ginger moved closer to Stud's shoulder, laying a caressing hand on it.

Stud reached up to brush her off absently.

Crazy Bitch reached out, picked up the coffee cup, and flung the contents in Ginger's face. The men stood up to miss the coffee splatter.

"Keep your fucking hands to yourself," she hissed at the woman who took a step back.

"Crazy Bitch!"

She ignored Stud's yell, staring malevolently at the ginger-headed slut. "I see you touch Stud again, I'll cut that hand off. Don't think I won't tell Sex Piston you've been touchy-feely with her man. There're enough single hornballs here to keep you satisfied without you trying to steal someone else's."

"I was just talking to him."

"Bitch, who do think you're talking to? Sluts like you are a dime a dozen, and I've already tossed eleven bitches out of here who thought they were going to get in Stud's britches. You get close enough to let him smell your perfume, and your ass will be riding the pavement instead of the back of a bike."

"I think Ginger got the message." Amused, Calder pulled Crazy Bitch back down to her chair.

Crazy Bitch hadn't even been aware she had stood up while screaming at the woman who retreated behind the bar. She forced her fury down into a slow simmer, running the clue through her mind to distract herself.

"You ever think of taking anger management classes?"

"Why would I pay someone to tell me I have a bad temper?"

"To help you manage it better," Calder advised helpfully.

"I manage it just fine." She angrily gave another evil grin in Ginger's direction.

"Fuck, no one is going to be able to help her." Looney slid his chair away from her. "She has four different personalities, and that's on a good day."

"Look who's talking. At least none of them are named after a duck."

Crazy Bitch paid no attention to the brothers when they started ribbing Looney. Glancing down at her watch, she realized she had promised to open the shop.

When she stood up, the men around her flinched as if they were afraid of what she was about to do.

"Pussies." She snorted. "And you think Rider's a pussy."

"Who thinks Rider's a pussy?" Stud asked.

Crazy Bitch looked down at Calder, who kept his head down, staring at the clue Greer had sent. She made a face at him, losing the effectiveness of it, since the fucker didn't lift his head.

"I guess no one. I have to get to work. I have an eight o'clock coming in." Reaching down, she grabbed Calder's arm, tugging him to his feet. "Be a gentleman and walk me to my car."

She expected him to give her hell once they were outside. Unexpectedly, he sauntered next to her, even opening the car door for her before she could.

"You doing anything tonight?" she asked once she was seated behind the steering wheel.

"You asking me out on a date?" He braced his arm on the roof of her car, bending down until his face was just inches from hers.

"Not like you're thinking. You figure out that clue yet?"

He didn't answer, turning it around on her. "Have you?"

"Yes. You going to tell any of them inside if I tell you?"

He pretended to zip his mouth and throw away an imaginary key.

"I'm not joking. I want that prize. If you're not going to take this seriously, I want to know now."

Calder's expression turned serious. "You're not the only one who wants to win. You're not the only one who's worried about someone sharing information. Have you ever kept anything from Sex Piston?"

Crazy Bitch looked away. She had, but she had no intention of telling him that. She hadn't told her or the others in her crew about Sam. Fat Louise worked in the same building as him every day. She didn't want her to get into trouble if any of her crew hurt him. Truthfully, she didn't want anyone hurt because she had been stupid enough to pick another loser.

"My crew all have motorcycles; I don't. I want that bike. My half of the money will catch me up on some bills I owe, so don't worry about me."

"Same here. I don't plan on losing my bike to anyone else, and the money I'll win will come in handy. You're not the only one who has bills to pay. We're going to have to trust each other, so we might as well start now. Who can see you every day, but can't at night yet stays in the same spot?"

"Look around. A mountain."

Calder squinted up at the mountains surrounding them. "Which one?"

"Greer hasn't given us that clue yet, but I think it's Black Mountain. It's the largest, and it looks down on The Last Riders', the Destructors', and the Blue Horsemen's clubhouses. That's why I want you to spend the night. We can ride to the overlook and wait for Greer's next clue. It's Sex Piston's turn to open the shop tomorrow morning. I can be back before my first appointment at eleven."

"What if it's a waste of time? It could be Pine Mountain. If it's not Black Mountain, we'll have to wait until the next day when another clue comes out," Calder argued.

"Several of the trails on Pine Mountain have been shut down because of the fires last month. It has to be Black Mountain. That's why I want you to stay the night at my house—no one will see us leaving, and we can get there first."

"What time do you want me there?"

"I get finished at eight."

"I'll pick up a pizza and meet you there at eight-thirty."

"What excuse are you going to tell the brothers for you spending the night?"

"Does it matter?" Calder shut her car door as she started the motor.

"No, as long you don't say something happens that doesn't."

"I'm sleeping on the couch?"

"You can have Fat Louise's old room." She put her car in gear, releasing the emergency brake.

"What if I'm afraid to sleep alone?" he joked, hastily stepping back when the car started rolling backward.

"If you get scared, I won't make you sleep alone." She blatantly stuck her head out of the window as she backed up, giving him a sensual smile that had Calder moving toward her car.

"Don't fail me now," she muttered to her old car, its tires squealing as she peeled out of the parking lot, shooting gravel into the air. She left him eating her dust as she drove to work.

Her day was filled with appointments, her last being one she wished she could have avoided. It was a set of eighty-year-old twin sisters who wanted their hair colored and cut exactly alike. Sex Piston had offered to take one of them, but the younger by two minutes wasn't having it.

"The last time I let Sex Piston do my hair, Sharon's color lasted longer than mine."

Crazy Bitch was tempted to tell the woman that her sister didn't have as much grey.

"I tried." Sex Piston came up behind her when she was mixing the color in the back room.

"It's cool." Crazy Bitch absently checked the color chart.

"Did you figure out the clue?" Sex Piston asked, pretending to search for gloves to place at their stations.

"No," she lied. "You?"

Sex Piston flickered her eyes away as she grabbed the box of gloves. "No."

The bitch was lying.

She bit her lip to keep from calling her out on the lie.

They spent what was left of the day staring at each other suspiciously. She and Sex Piston had never been on separate teams before. For that matter, their crew had always stood together against everyone else.

As she gloomily worked, she didn't feel bad for not sharing information with Sex Piston or the others. They had been the ones who had chosen their husbands and boyfriends over her. She had been forced to work with Calder when they had left her with no choice. Even T.A. had chosen dick over her, and Bear had no intention of putting a ring on her finger, despite T.A.'s demands.

She was checking out the twins when Sex Piston left for the night with the bank deposit. All she had to do after they left was turn out the lights and lock the door. Thankfully, Sex Piston had already cleaned.

She tiredly walked to her car, glad it was summer and just now getting dark.

She had just gotten inside her apartment and changed into a pair of shorts and a tank top when she heard a knock on her door.

Opening it, she was greeted with the appetizing aroma of the pizzas Calder was holding.

"Hungry?"

"I'm starved." Crazy Bitch shut the door. "You can set them on the counter." Going behind the counter, she took out paper plates, setting them next to the pizza boxes before going to the fridge to get beers.

Calder had opened the pizza box and was putting a couple of slices on a plate. She handed him a beer before he handed her a plate.

"We can sit on the couch. What movie do you want to watch?"

"What you got?"

Her ass had just sat down when she heard another knock on her door.

"You want me to get it?" he asked, the pizza poised at his mouth.

"I got it."

Opening the door, she instantly regretted not looking through the peephole.

"What the fuck do you want?" She held on to the door-knob, preventing Sam from coming inside.

"You haven't been answering my calls or texts. I wanted to talk to you. You accu—"

"I have company, and if I wanted to talk to you, I would've answered when you called. I have nothing to say to you," she shut him up before he could say anything else.

"Who's here?" Sam tried to look around the partially opened door.

"Sam, get lost and lose my number." Slamming the door, she turned and ran right into Calder's chest.

"Is he bugging you?" He aggressively started to go around her.

She moved to block his path. "No. He's just trying to cover his ass." As soon as the words were out of her mouth, she regretted them. "I mean... he wants to make sure there are no hard feelings after our breakup."

"Why would there be hard feelings?"

"Because men are weenies. Let's eat; the pizza is getting cold."

She sank back down on the couch and picked the first movie that came up on her DVR, unconcernedly eating her food as Calder resumed his seat. She was so distracted she didn't realize what movie they were watching until she noticed it had Calder's rapt attention.

Picking up the remote, she exited out of the movie, choosing another one.

"Why did you stop it?"

"Because I only watch that movie with other bitches, or men I'm going to fuck."

"I'm not a bitch, so it leaves me out of that category. You don't see yourself fucking me? I definitely see myself fucking you."

"In your dreams." She chewed on her pizza, turning on a comedy she had recorded.

She felt his eyes go to her breasts when she leaned over for her beer.

"It could be hot."

"Do you know how many men have told me that? *Oh, baby, it's going to be so hot when I do you,*" she mimicked in a low voice. "*Damn, woman, that's so hot.*"

Calder laughed. "I was trying to be sexy, not lame."

When he laughed, his tough façade lightened.

Her cynical heart started beating faster, reminding her of when she was nineteen and had first met him. She had thought the attraction between them was two-sided until he had stood her up to get lit and laid by another woman. It had hurt her that he had blown her off.

He was the type of man who made you feel feminine by just being around him. You couldn't look at him without thinking what he would be like in the sack. His stormy grey eyes could carry you out to sea, and you wouldn't even care if he carried you back at high tide.

She shook her head, drawing herself back to earth. Crazy Bitch had to make herself remember that the time they would be spending together wasn't for hooking up; it was for money. She had no intention of letting him sweep her off her feet into choppy waters and leaving her stranded and at the mercy of a riptide.

Despite the comedy on the screen, her expression grew serious. "I'm not into one-liners you used to catch Candi and Demie. I don't play games. I expect the men I go out with to do the same."

His laughter died. "You don't think a lot of me, do you?"

"I don't think about you at all."

10

BIKER BITCHES

"The sheets and blankets are in the hall closet. The spare bedroom is by the kitchen," Crazy Bitch said as she came out of the bathroom after her shower, wearing her short blue robe that she had tied at her waist.

"You going to bed?"

"I've been up since six this morning, and I've been on my feet all day. I had to cut, dye, dry, and curl Sharon and Tilly Hines's hair. They each tipped me a buck and told me I needed to go on a diet. So, yeah, I'm going to bed."

She went into her bedroom, leaving Calder watching the ten-o'clock news. She threw her robe down on the bottom of her bed, looking around her room for her cat. Usually the manic feline would attack any male. Crazy Bitch corrected herself—anyone unwary to enter his—again she had to correct herself—*her* apartment. The hellcat was getting old. She was sure he was hiding underneath her bed and would come out when she went to sleep.

Turning off the bedside lamp, she yawned tiredly then, stretching out on her bed, listened to the soft music she had turned on.

Drifting off to the soothing sounds of a lonely violin, she sank deeper into sleep.

A loud yell had her bolting up in bed. Disoriented, she fell as she tried to get out of bed. Tangled in her sheet, she had to extricate herself from the covers before she could manage to get to her feet.

Hearing another yell, she ran to the bedroom door, flinging it open then running into the room she had told Calder to sleep in, to see him standing on his tumbled bed with a pillow in his hand.

"What are you—"

"Get back. There's a snake in here!" he shouted.

"I don't have snakes...." She carefully backed toward the door, peering around the upturned room.

"There!"

She jumped when he pointed at something black that moved underneath the bed.

She started laughing. "That's not a snake. It's Manson."

"Manson?"

"My cat. Well, technically it's Fat Louise's, but she forgot to take him when she moved out."

Red-faced, Calder jumped off the bed, then jumped back on it when a vicious claw raked his shin.

"It bit me."

"He doesn't bite. He doesn't have any teeth."

He jumped off the bed, moving in a walk-run toward her. "Why doesn't he have teeth? Cade knock them out?"

"No, he's old. Most of them were broken off, so the vet removed what was left. Cost me six hundred dollars. You think Fat Louise or Cade paid me back? Every time I mention it, they say it was her sister's cat."

"Did you ask her for the money?"

"She's dead."

"The cat killed her?"

"He's not rabid, just old." She bent down to pick up the purring cat as he rubbed against her leg. "See? No teeth." She lifted him higher so Calder could see the toothless, hissing cat.

"You should have saved yourself six hundred dollars and put him down."

The cat hissed louder.

"Shh... Manson. He didn't mean it."

"Yes, I did." He jerked his arm back from a darting claw that threatened to rip his hand to shreds.

Crazy Bitch rubbed her cheek against the spiked fur as his claws sunk into her night top.

She was carefully trying to lift it when Calder tried to help her and his knuckles rubbed against the globes of her breasts. She sucked in a sharp breath at his touch.

"Girl, you need to get your ass outta here," Crazy Bitch said to herself as she awkwardly turned toward the door, making sure to keep her eyes away from his naked body, still picturing him in all his glory.

He might lack an inch in height compared to Stud, but Calder was broader and more muscular than his loose jeans and T-shirts had shown.

She was so close to him that she could touch him. And if she didn't get out of the close confines of the bedroom, she was going to regret it in about five minutes... after she was done with him.

"Do not lead me into temptation," she chanted to herself, stopping when Calder placed a hand on the doorway, blocking her escape.

"You sure you don't want to stay and watch... another movie?"

"I'm sure." She didn't lash out at him the way she had intended. Instead, she sounded like she was about to cough up one of Manson's fur balls.

She started to barge past his restraining arm when he gave her a quizzical look.

"Are you listening to classical music?"

"What's wrong with that?" she snapped. "You don't think I can appreciate it?"

"I'm just surprised. When we play music at the club, you make us play hard rock or punk."

"That's for dancing, not for sleeping."

His eyes gentled. "You have trouble sleeping?"

"Sometimes." She couldn't believe she was admitting to a weakness she had never confessed to anyone before.

He dropped his hand, giving her space to leave. "Good night."

She nodded, fleeing the room before she changed her mind and threw the sexy biker to the bed. Closing her bedroom door, she laid Manson down on the bed, where he clawed her sheets into a mound to show his dissatisfaction before choosing her pillow to curl up on.

Shooing him off the pillow, she lay down, trying to go back to sleep, but she didn't fall asleep again so easily. She was tossing and turning until her body was so fatigued it gave in to a restless sleep that had her not hearing the alarm that was going off on the nightstand.

"Anna-Kate, wake up."

The use of her real name had her eyes flying open. She hadn't heard it since her mother had died.

"Do you want to sit here and talk about it, or do you want to get on the road?"

She tossed her sheet off, seeing Calder was already dressed.

Going to her dresser, she took out a pair of jeans and a green tank top that she could put a jacket over. At work, it would be hidden underneath her smock.

"Get out. I'll be out in a minute."

"Gee, thanks for waking me up," he said sarcastically, leaving the room.

"Thanks." She slammed her door closed then dressed in a rush, dodging Manson's attempts to swat her when she tried to put her boots on.

"I shouldn't feed your hairy ass." Jerking her jacket on, she hurried to the kitchen to place a bowl of cat food down. "I'm ready."

Calder got up from the couch. "What about breakfast?"

She opened a kitchen drawer, taking out two protein bars, and tossed one to him.

"There's breakfast. Let's go."

"You're lucky I'm a man of simple needs."

The only needs she had on her mind were the ones that had left her unfulfilled and restless the night before. She wanted to find the motorcycles and jackets so she could go back to ignoring the bastard.

"Next time I want you to stay the night, I'll go to the store and buy some Pop-Tarts... and I'll hide my mail so you're snooping ass won't see something I don't want you to see."

"I like donuts better." He grinned, opening the door for her while ignoring her last comment.

"That belly of yours hasn't seen a donut in years."

His body was hard and toned. There was no beer or donut belly to mar the perfection that had her debating what to do to him.

His grin widened. "I saw you looking at me last night."

"Kind of hard to miss... with everything flapping around."

"It wasn't flapping after I saw you in those panties and that white T-shirt."

"Really?" She sniffed, climbing on behind him on his bike. "I didn't notice." She held on to his sides as he backed out of the parking spot.

"You noticed. Anytime you want another show, let me

know. I'm available." Giving her a wink, he pulled out, driving out of town.

There wasn't much traffic as Calder drove along streets that gradually grew darker and narrowed down to a winding road that led to Treepoint.

Crazy Bitch held on to his waist. She had never ridden with him before. When they had gone out as a club, she had always been on the back of another biker's motorcycle.

He handled the powerful machine with ease. She could feel the strength in his body as he held the bike steady through the dangerous curves. Numerous people had lost their lives by getting lulled into a false sense of security when taking the curves at speeds the locals knew to be wary of.

When they reached Treepoint, Calder made the turn that would lead them away from the town and toward the large mountain that was looming above them. The sun was just coming up as they traveled up the inclining road. Several houses were built along the route, but as it reached higher, the homes became sparse.

Crazy Bitch wasn't afraid of heights, but she stopped looking down when she could see the tops of trees. She had a come-to-Jesus moment when a large truck rounded a sharp curve at the same time as Calder's motorcycle.

Closing her eyes, she rested her helmet against his back, deciding not to look anymore. She had confidence in his ability; it was the assholes they had to share the road with who had her terrified.

The sight of the sign with an arrow pointing to a small road that would lead them to the overlook had her eagerness returning.

The overlook was empty when they arrived. As soon as Calder stopped the bike, she climbed off, wanting to kiss the ground.

"I wish I had brought a six-pack with me to enjoy the

view." Removing his helmet, Calder climbed off his bike to look around the tree-studded mountains appreciatively.

"You'd be driving back alone." She walked around the area, trying to get feeling back in her legs.

"If that gas station we passed isn't open, you might be, anyway." Calder took out his phone. "Sweet. We made it with five minutes to spare before Greer's clue."

She gave him a victorious smile. "I bet everyone is in the club…" Her voice trailed off at the sound of a motorcycle. "Son of a bitch, is that…?"

"Stud and Sex Piston."

Their eyes met in disappointment.

"That's fine. We got here first. As long as it stays that way, they can keep eating our dust."

Her friend got off the back of Stud's bike as the brothers stood talking.

"Bitch, I knew you knew the answer." Sex Piston's calling her out on her lie didn't make her feel guilty.

Pasting an innocent look on her face, she stared back unrepentantly. "You could have told me you had figured it out. I didn't until I went to my car after I closed."

"You lying bitch." Sex Piston's lips trembled in laughter.

"Prove it."

The friends shouldered each other as they went to stand next the men, both anxious for the clue.

"I wish he would send it before someone else shows."

"Yeah, that sucks when it happens." Crazy Bitch used her chin to point at the approaching car.

"Who in the fuck is that?"

"Viper and Winter."

"Son of a—"

"Those were my exact words when you and Stud showed."

Again, she had to mask her disappointment as Viper and

Winter got out of their SUV. The small group didn't have to say anything to each other as Stud's, Viper's, and Calder's phones started pinging.

She wanted to grab the phone away from Calder when the men texted the clue to their clubs before reading it.

Calder finished first, reading it aloud.

"If you figured out the first clue, then you know I wear a necklace. You will find the third clue in the clasp."

Crazy Bitch turned around in a circle before turning back to the group. The couples had already pulled apart to talk.

Calder moved to her, turning his back so the others couldn't see or hear what he was saying. "It's the rock."

Her eyes darted to the rock. "How? It's too big to lift."

"Not if I have help."

"Dammit! You sure?"

"Yes, if we're at the right mountain."

"We could go get my car and a chain and move it after everyone leaves," she suggested.

"It would save time. If Viper and Winter have figured out the clue, they'll just wait until we leave, and then they'll have a start on the next clue. We can do whatever you want to do. I'll leave the choice to you."

She furtively glanced toward the other couples.

"Let's do it. I can't afford to miss more work."

Calder gave her a searching look. "When did you miss work?"

"Stud is coming over." She was relieved to be able to skate past the question.

Sex Piston stayed behind, talking to Viper and Winter. Crazy Bitch knew she was trying to distract them.

"The clue is under the rock."

"No shit." She was dying to get at the clue. That Stud and Sex Piston knew it was under the rock showed it didn't take a genius to figure it out. If they knew, then Viper and Winter knew also. Giving a ragged sigh, she accepted the inevitable. "Unless either of you can pull a chain out of your saddlebags, we might as well work together."

"I was hoping you two would be practical." Stud grimaced. "She said to make sure that you know it's not going to be a habit."

"Same goes here," she agreed wholeheartedly. "Let's get this done before some other assholes come along."

Stud didn't look pleased that he was one of the assholes who had come along when they had already been there.

"They know it's under the rock," Sex Piston said as they drew closer.

The men immediately went to the large rock as the women followed excitedly behind them.

"If it's too heavy to move, I have a towing cable." Viper grunted as they tried to move the rock.

"Of course you do." Crazy Bitch rolled her eyes.

"What does that mean? You don't think we already knew where the clue was?"

Crazy Bitch had to give Winter props for defending her man's honor.

"No, I meant it as a compliment, that he is always prepared."

"That's fine, then." Winter gave her husband a look filled with pride and love.

They were trying to knock it over when Shade pulled up with Lily at his back.

Shade threw an arm over Lily's shoulder when they got off. "Need some help?"

"No!" the women yelled out, but the men had already moved to make room for Shade.

Crazy Bitch stopped watching the men struggle with the rock and went to the overlook to see if she could see the road that led up the mountain. Squinting, she watched to see if others were coming, unconsciously moving nearer to the edge.

She felt herself lifted backward.

"We almost had it!" Stud muttered as Calder pulled her farther away from the edge.

"Stay here."

"I was fine. There's a chain—"

"Which you were leaning over! I catch your ass that close again, the only clue you'll be getting are my handprints on your ass," Calder warned.

She didn't scare easily, but his angry visage had her tongue-tied, leaving her only able to nod.

Calder went back to the rock, his anger tangible as he and the others strained, finally turning the rock over.

Stud bent down and pulled out a plastic bag. Unzipping it, he took out a sheet of paper and unfolded it.

"Read it out loud!" Crazy Bitch demanded.

"It wouldn't make any sense if I do. It looks like a grocery list. One pound of potatoes, two cans of diced tomatoes, an onion…"

Crazy Bitch snatched it out of his hand, reading it. "Did he put his grocery list there by mistake?"

"Give it to me." Sex Piston snatched it from her hand, going toward Stud's bike.

"Where are you going with it? I want to take a picture of it before we put it back," Winter berated her.

"I'm going to shove it up Greer's ass. You can have it back when he's done shitting it out."

Stud caught her around the waist, taking the letter away from her. Taking a picture with his phone, he then gave it to Viper, who was standing near him.

"I'll text it to you, Calder," Stud said as he walked his wife toward his bike.

"Viper!" Sex Piston shouted as Stud forced her onto his

bike. "Tell Greer I'm coming for him."

After the others took pictures on their phones, the men moved the rock back into its resting place.

"How did Greer do that by himself?" Crazy Bitch overheard Lily asking Shade.

"He didn't. Tate and Dustin probably helped him." Viper wiped the sweat off his forehead.

"He used that big truck he's so proud off," Shade disagreed.

"The brothers are going to be pissed when they realize the clue is hidden under the rock." Crazy Bitch got on the back of Calder's bike. "None of you better share. Make them move it themselves."

"Why? It's pointless." Lily's soft heart had her wanting to give the clue out.

"Shade?" Crazy Bitch turned her head toward him at the sounds of more motorcycles approaching.

"I'll handle it." He steered his wife away to his bike. Starting it, he gave Lily no chance to talk before riding off.

She waved gleefully as Rider and Jewell, and Cade and Fat Louise arrived.

Squeezing Calder's waist as they rode back down the mountain, she waited until he was filling the gas tank before taking off her helmet, showing him what she had with a wide smile.

Pausing when he saw it, he finally asked, "Do you know the answer to the clue?"

"Fuck no, but did you see who Rider's partner is?"

"I saw her, but I've never talked to her. Why?"

She raised her hand for him to high-five her. "He's riding with Jewell. We can cross him off our list without having to worry about him. He'll spend more time fucking her than searching for the bike we're going to steal out from under his nose."

11

The two regulars who were having their hair done sensed the tension between their hairdressers.

Crazy Bitch ran the comb through Sophie's damp hair as Sex Piston cut Zoey's long curls. The two friends had been friends since high school and were taking a day off work for a girls' day out. Usually, she and Sex Piston would talk as they worked. Neither had said a word since they had returned from the road trip.

She was clipping layers into Sophie's hair when Killyama, Fat Louise, and T.A. stopped inside to see if they wanted to go to lunch.

"Does it look like I can go out?" Sex Piston's refusal had their friends taking seats to wait.

"I can go get takeout," Killyama offered. "What are you in the mood for?"

"For you all to leave me alone so I can work in peace."

Crazy Bitch looked at Sex Piston in the mirror before glancing at the rest of the women. Fat Louise's hurt was palpable when she started to rise.

"Sit your ass down. I'm supposed to be the biggest bitch

here, but right now, you're beating me. The contest was supposed to between us and The Last Riders. Not against each other in the club. Why are you so determined to win?"

Sex Piston dropped the brush she had been using as she confronted her. "Look who's talking. I didn't see you and Calder waiting to share the clue with Fat Louise."

"No, I didn't. I waited until we were at the gas station to text her."

"You did?"

"Yes. I didn't want to share with her in front of Rider and Jewell."

"You should have seen their faces when Cade and I took off." Fat Louise laughed. "They didn't know it was the rock, and neither did we until Crazy Bitch texted."

"Then why didn't you tell me yesterday that the first clue was a mountain?"

"I'm not that generous. You know what I'm driving; I want the motorcycle that Stud built. He can build another one with spare parts—he's got a garage full of them. My bike is shot, and my car may have fond memories, but it would be easier to stop it with my feet than the brakes."

"I don't care about either bike. If we win, you can have it."

Sex Piston's customer was becoming irritated at her stopping work on her hair.

"What do you care about?" Fat Louise asked as she pulled out a candy bar from her purse.

"Stud's jacket."

Crazy Bitch hit the side of her forehead with her palm. "Bitch, if I win, you can have it. Besides, it's supposed to go back to the club whose team wins it."

"You see Ginger doing that?" Sex Piston grimaced, brandishing her hairbrush like a bat.

Crazy Bitch could see the point she was trying to make.

"Yes, after she prances around with it on for a while."

"I'll kill her first."

"You don't have to worry about it. I'm going to win it, and I promise not to try it on before giving it back to Stud," Crazy Bitch promised.

"What if you don't?" Sex Piston started the blow-dryer. "Winter feels the same way. The ones who got there early are the ones who want it badly."

"There you go. Pike and Ginger weren't there this morning," T.A. spoke up over the sound of the blow-dryer. "Neither were Bear and I, but Crazy Bitch saved us the trip."

Sex Piston shut the dryer off. "Doesn't Calder mind you sharing the clues?"

"Not if we've already gotten them. We talked about it at the gas station when I told him I was going to text it to Fat Louise and T.A., but they also agreed to share their clues if they get there first."

"What if they win because of a clue you gave them?"

"Then they win." She shrugged, finishing the layers then starting her blow-dryer. The shop filled with the sound of them drying their customers' hair.

When Crazy Bitch finished, she started curling Sophie's hair.

"I'm sorry. Ginger makes me nuts, always being up in Stud's grill," Sex Piston seethed.

"You want me to take care of her?" Killyama's cold offer had their customers' eyes widening.

"That bitch is mine to deal with. I'm done talking about her. You figure out the next clue yet?" she asked, removing Zoey's cape.

"No. Calder is going to the store after work and picking up the groceries. We're hoping that seeing the groceries together will give us an idea."

"I cook a lot, but that recipe stumps me." Sex Piston went behind the cash register.

Zoey took out her credit card, giving it to her. "If it's a recipe you need help with, you should ask Sophie. She's the best cook in town."

Crazy Bitch took out her phone, flipping to the list that was Greer's clue.

Sophie took her cell phone, frowning in concentration. "It looks like he wants you to make cowboy casserole."

"I've made that before. I should have recognized it from the ingredients." Sex Piston gave Zoey back her credit card.

"You forgot to tell me how much it was."

"No charge. Your cuts are on the house."

The women beamed.

"Sex Piston, I don't know who Ginger is, but you don't have anything to worry about. Greg went to Stud's shop when his bike needed work done on it last week, and he came home saying Stud was showing him pictures of Star's birthday party. Greg said he showed him more pictures of you than Star."

"Thanks, Zoey. And you, too, Sophie. You saved me a trip to the grocery store."

"We'll see you next month." Sophie gave her a tip, which she held in her hand until they left. Going to the tip jar, she dropped it inside.

"I should text Calder and tell him he doesn't have to go to the store."

"Why? I'd let him fix you dinner." Fat Louise put what was left of the candy bar into her purse.

"I would, too," T.A. chorused.

"I'll go get us some burgers while you decide." Killyama left as Crazy Bitch swept both stations and started a load of towels in the washer out back.

She decided not to text Calder. Even though they knew it was a cowboy casserole, it didn't say where they would be able to find the next clue.

"How does Sam feel about you spending time with Calder?" Fat Louise asked as she helped straighten the hair magazines Sophie had looked through.

"I'm not seeing him anymore."

"Why not? I thought you and him were having a fuck fest when you both took the same days off."

It was gratifying to know that her punches had forced him to lose time from work.

Crazy Bitch hadn't wanted to make it uncomfortable for Fat Louise to work around Sam, but she didn't trust the bastard as far as she could throw him.

"I don't want you to say shit to any of the brothers or Killyama, but he tried to roofie me."

Sex Piston took the broom away from her. "Hell no, I'm not going to keep my mouth shut about it. When I tell Stud, he and the brothers will kick his fucking ass."

"I know, and when they are finished with him, Killyama will scrape together what's left and make hamburger out of him."

"Then why not?"

"I don't want Fat Louise to lose her job. Sam might complain that the Destructors beat him up, and everyone in town knows that Fat Louise belongs to the club. You still want that promotion you applied for last month?"

Fat Louise bit her lip. "Yes. It'll give us another five hundred a month, and I can even work from home a couple days a week. It's in the same office where Sam works."

"That's why I haven't said anything. Once you get the job and get past the probation period, then Stud and Killyama can have him. The only reason I decided to say something now is because I don't trust the bastard not to slip something in your drink to get back at me."

Sex Piston clenched the broom handle. "Then let's go to the sheriff's office and report it."

"I don't have any proof. I never drank it. He was just acting weird. I should have saved it and took it to the sheriff's office, but I threw it at him."

Sex Piston's lips thinned into a line. "As soon as Fat Louise gets that job and is off probation, the bastard is dead meat."

Crazy Bitch looked out the window. "Killyama is back." She hurriedly changed the subject. "You think that clue of Greer's was an actual clue or him just wanting us to cook for him?"

They threw ideas around as they ate.

After lunch, T.A. and Fat Louise left to go back to work. Killyama hung around until Sex Piston was finished so they could go to the club together.

She waved them off when they wanted to wait for her, but she was in middle of a perm.

Exhausted, she turned the open light off after she finished and locked the door on the way out. When she turned toward the parking lot, she stopped, seeing Sam leaning against her car. She hadn't seen him drive into the lot while she had been working, nor had she seen it when she had come out the door.

He must have parked on the side, she thought as she walked forward. She would be damned if she ran like a scared rabbit and went back inside.

"What do you want?"

"I want to make sure you're not spreading rumors you can't back up." The mild-mannered man she had dated was gone. The ugly expression he made no effort to hide gave her the willies.

"I don't spread rumors. Fucker, I'm giving you a heads-up; you need to stay the fuck away from me before you discover a world of hurt that you never knew existed."

"I'm not afraid of the Destructors. You're not the only one

with friends. You're the one who should be afraid of me."

"You're threatening me?" she scoffed. "Your idea of getting laid is to roofie a defenseless woman. I'm done talking to you. I see your ugly face come near me again, you won't be missing work; you'll be claiming disability." She shoved him away from her car door to open it, making sure she didn't turn her back to him as she slid into the seat then slammed the door closed.

Sam was walking back to his car when she started driving out.

Safely on the road, she started shaking. It had enraged him that she had dared to shove him away from her. Sam had a loose screw, but she had already found that out when he tried to drug her.

She should go to Stud and tell him what was going on, yet she couldn't bring herself to do that with Fat Louise wanting that job. She and Cade had a kid, and Cade had sunk money into going into business with Killyama's friends, Hammer and Jonas. They were bounty hunters. With Cade joining them, they had been able to guarantee higher bonds. Until they were able to recoup their investment, they needed Fat Louise's paycheck.

All Crazy Bitch wanted was a bath and bed, but she had forgotten about Calder until she saw his motorcycle sitting out front of her apartment.

She smelled the food he was cooking as she climbed the stairs. She had given him a key so he wouldn't have to wait outside for her to get off. However, she hadn't expected him to already be cooking.

He opened the door before she could. Looking flustered, he then turned back to the stove. He had changed from his jeans and T-shirt he had worn that morning into shorts and a tee so faded you couldn't make out the words scrolled across the front.

"You hungry? You're late. I was afraid I would burn it before you got here. I took a shower to clean off after work. I hope that's okay?"

"I told you I didn't care when I gave you my key. I'm starved. It doesn't smell burned. How'd you figure out the recipe?"

"I didn't. I just put it all in a pan."

"It's called cowboy casserole." Reaching for the plates in a cabinet, she held them out for him to spoon the glob he had made.

"Casserole." He gave each of them a generous portion before turning off the stove. "I fucked that up, then."

"I'm sure it'll taste the same."

They took a seat at the counter, both of them experimentally tasting the food.

"It's good. If Greer gives us another recipe, it's all yours," she complimented.

"It's not much of a clue. We still don't know where the next clue is." Calder stood up to get a second helping.

Crazy Bitch scooted her plate across the counter, not bothering to get up. "Hit me again."

Calder smiled, giving her what was left before sitting back down.

"Thanks for cooking."

"Glad to help out. You work some long-ass hours."

"It wasn't as bad when Sex Piston bought the shop, but the days are getting longer, or I'm getting older."

"You're not old."

"I'm not nineteen anymore, that's for damn sure."

"You're not the only one. I wouldn't go back to nineteen if I had to."

"I wouldn't mind having my nineteen-year-old ass again."

Calder put their dishes in the sink with the dirty pan. "I remember your ass back then. It's better now."

She avoided his admiring gaze. "I'll load the dishwasher after taking a shower. Don't forget to leave my key on the counter before you go."

Calder came around the counter, reaching into his pocket and coming out with the key, which he placed down beside her hand. "You sure you don't want me to stay the night in case we come up with the next clue?"

Thinking more about not wanting to be left alone after Sam's threatening behavior, she didn't nix the suggestion.

"Fine, you can load the dishwasher." She moved around him to go take a shower, expecting him to complain about doing the dishes after cooking. He didn't.

Damn, he was looking sexier by the minute. Not only had he looked all house-wifey when she had come in the door, but now the stud muffin was going to do her dishes.

Her good humor vanished when she saw him dodging Manson's batting claw when he crawled out from under the couch in a sneak attack.

"Are you afraid of my cat?" she taunted.

"That cat makes some of the felons I served time with look like angels."

"You're exaggerating."

Manson hunkered down into stealth mode, his eyes turning into gleaming slits. When his tail started waving furiously as his ass went up, she almost felt sorry for Calder.

"Crazy Bitch!" Calder's voice sank to a whisper when Manson's tail moved even faster. "Why's he staring at me like that?"

"I should have warned you. Next time, feed him first. He gets a little irate when he gets hungry."

"What do you feed him?"

"Bikers who are stupid enough to wear shorts around him."

Having a black cat stare at you malevolently as you undressed was unnerving. Calder debated opening the front door and letting it escape. If he didn't think he would have to spend the rest of the night searching for it if Crazy Bitch discovered it missing, he would.

The cat jumped onto the bed and plopped down on his pillow, showing his gums in a feline yawn.

Not intending to move the cat or place his cheek where the cat's ass was resting, he went to the door, intending to sleep on the couch.

The living room was dark, but the light from the bathroom shone, making it possible to see.

He silently walked to the couch and was picking up one of the pillows when he saw a movement at the window. Crazy Bitch was standing to the side, peeking out the window from the side of the curtain.

"Something wrong?"

She jumped, spinning at the sound of his voice and dropping the curtain.

"No. I thought I heard my neighbors arguing."

"They do that a lot?"

"Not often."

"You want me to go outside and check?" He took a step toward the door.

"No! They must have gone back inside."

Calder was a recovering addict, so he was an expert at lying and when someone was lying to him. Crazy Bitch was lying through her teeth. She wasn't meeting his eyes, jerkily moving away to the refrigerator to get herself a bottled water.

His balls tightened when she walked toward her bedroom, using a damp towel to dry her hair, her pale blue silk shorts showing the curves of her ass.

"You have an extra pillow? Manson is being a bitch and not sharing."

"Huh? Sure, I'll get it."

Calder followed her into the bedroom, her preoccupation with what was going on outside sending a tendril of unease down his back.

She sat the water down on her nightstand then went to her closet to reach up for a pillow on the shelf.

"Sweet Jesus," Calder groaned.

"What?" Startled, she jumped, knocking down the pillow she had been reaching for.

"What has you so afraid?"

"What in the fuck do I have to be afraid of with you here?"

He took her arm, preventing her from bending down for the pillow.

Jerking out of his reach, she started to push past him.

"You tell me. But something has you frightened."

"I'm tired and I'm going to bed. Get the pillow and get out."

Calder grabbed the ends of the towel that was hanging

casually over her shoulders, holding her place. The scalloped lace that bordered her blue satin camisole top rose and fell with her ragged breathing.

"Tell me what's up, Anna-Kate."

With her fisted hands, she hit him on his bare chest. "The only thing that is up is your dick. And stop calling me that sissy name!"

Calder twined the towel around his wrists, tugging her closer. "Why? I think it's a beautiful name for a beautiful woman."

She locked her arms, preventing him from pulling her closer. Then she rolled her eyes as she gave a mocking laugh. "I'm too tired tonight to listen to another one of your lame pickup lines."

"I'm not trying to seduce you. I'm being serious."

Calder caught the brief flicker of decision in her eyes before she lowered her lashes, concealing her expression.

"Something has you spooked tonight, and I want to know what it is."

Her lips mutinously curled into a provocative smile as she went up on her tiptoes to press her lips on his. His cock hardened at the feel of her soft belly against it.

"Crazy Bitch... don't start what you're not wanting to finish."

He felt the subtle touch of her tongue as she parted his lips and then slid inside. He had dreamed of her when he was in prison, wondering how she would taste. Would she taste like tart cherries, or have the heat of cinnamon? When he opened his mouth wider, Calder discovered it was neither. She tasted like sweet strawberries.

Using the towel, he tilted her head so he could take control.

The smell of her freshly washed hair couldn't disguise the faint odor of fear she was putting out. The woman was using his lust to keep from admitting she was afraid of someone or something.

He pulled his lips away a hairsbreadth, about to call her out on it. Instead, he went back for more, twining his tongue with hers in a duel he didn't care if he won or lost.

If she was willing to fuck him instead of owning up to what was going on, it would take more willpower than he had to resist her attempt.

He nudged her toward her bed, expecting her to stop him or break the lust-fueled kiss she had begun. She didn't. Crazy Bitch held on to his shoulders as he tumbled with her to the unmade bed.

He was used to seeing her with makeup and her hair teased and moussed to tame her wild curls. Lifting his lips, he was held spellbound by her creamy skin and her mass of riotous curls.

"What are you staring at?"

His gaze softened at the hint of vulnerability in her voice. "I used to think about you in prison—what you were doing, who you were with." He traced her features with his eyes, seeing the strength of character that showed through the makeup. Without the camouflage, it was still there. "Once I was clean, I kept blaming myself for standing you up that night.

"It's not easy for a man to own up to a woman having more strength than him. Even at nineteen, you were stronger than me. Even when I got out of prison, it was easier to fuck the club sluts than face your contempt.

"I'm not Stud. I never will be. I've had the same opportunities he had, but he never got caught in the same bad moves I have. You're more like him than I am. I couldn't face disappointing someone else in my life.

"I can't promise I won't screw up again, but I can promise it won't be for the same reasons. I swear on my soul I'll never touch drugs again. And if you're willing to give me a chance, I can be the man you're looking for."

Calder didn't have to interpret the indecision on her face or the wariness in her eyes. It was plain to see, yet he felt her arms tighten around his shoulders and her fingers caress the back of his neck.

"I'm not going be a sucker and believe anything you say. If you want my trust, earn it. When you do that, then we can go from there."

Nodding, he started to lever himself off her tantalizing body, but before he could move more than an inch, she tugged him back down to her.

"Where you going?"

"I thought you wanted me to leave."

"Where in the fuck did you get that idea? I don't have to trust you to fuck you."

When she parted her thighs so he could sink down over her body, it fanned the embers of the desire that had been riding him since she had been at his back on the road trip.

Holding on to his willpower, he stopped himself from sliding her shorts to the side and sinking his fingers in the honey that he knew was waiting for him.

Calder slid his hand from the side of her breast where it had been bracing him above her to glide it over her silken flesh exposed by her camisole that was now resting below her breasts. She didn't shy away from his touch, or look away.

"You're making me nervous."

"Your dick doesn't feel nervous." She thrust her hips upward, forcing beads of sweat to form on his upper lip.

"You promise you won't give a critique of my performance to your crew or the other brothers?"

"Do I look like Killyama?" She grinned up at him wickedly.

"I wasn't talking about her and Train. I was talking about you and Joker."

"You have nothing to worry about." She moved her hand from his shoulder to his chest, stroking down to his abdomen and stopping at the band of his shorts. "You don't have his beer belly." She rubbed her belly against the bulge of his cock. "And from the size of that dick, I'm feeling you're no limp noodle. Damn, Calder, if I knew you were going to talk me to death, I would have turned on the television."

Her agitation showed she was as nervous and excited as he was.

He lowered his mouth to nuzzle the cleft between her breasts. Her tits were so voluminous he nearly strangled on his tongue when he pulled her top down.

Laving her nipple, he thought he had died and gone to heaven. When she slid her hand under his shorts, he knew he had.

Her eyes darkened as she stroked him while he sucked her nipple into his mouth.

"I know you've had tit since you've been out of prison, so take it easy on me, or I'm going to bar you from titty sanctuary."

He gentled his mouth on her nipple. She might come across as a bitch, but she wanted to be wooed like a woman named Anna-Kate.

He used his hands to smooth over her skin, exploring the cleft between her breasts, then cupping the other one, caressing it as if it was a fragile flower and it would be crushed if it was handled too roughly.

He wanted more than one night with her, and if he wasn't careful, tonight would be the last. He wanted her to crave him like a drug, so when they were apart, all she could think about was having him back beside her. He wanted her to fill the same void that was slowly tearing him apart, as if she was sitting on a mountaintop and the more he tried to climb to reach her, the farther away she seemed.

With one of her hands, she cupped his balls as she pushed his shorts down with the other until he was able to use the friction of his thighs to take them off.

Tilting his hips to the side, he used the momentum to slide down her body, sliding her silken shorts down.

"Damn, woman, your tits are heaven, but your pussy is fire."

He poised his mouth over her waxed pussy before delving between the sweet flesh where he found the honey he had been searching for. He laved her until a moan escaped her. Then she rose up on her elbows to watch him.

He had been with more women than he could count. He had some more innocent than others. Then there were those who were more experienced than he was and had taught him a thing or two. He had to admit that, beyond giving the women cursory looks, he was more into getting laid than just getting enjoyment with how large a woman's breasts were, or how delicately formed her pussy was.

If he had to describe his perfect woman, Crazy Bitch would be her. There wasn't anything about her that didn't turn him on. She wasn't a stick figure that, when he fucked her, their hip bones would bump together. She was softly curved in all the right places. Her belly wasn't flat, and her curvy hips gave him a place to hold as she thrust up against his ravaging mouth.

When he plunged his tongue inside her, Crazy Bitch's elbows gave out and she fell back to the mattress.

He felt her muscles contract. Satisfied that she was on the brink of an orgasm, he drew it out for a few seconds before lifting off her, preparing to sink his hard dick into her waiting cunt.

Her hands went to his shoulders, stopping him. "Slow your big soldier down. You need to bag him."

"My wallet is in the other room."

"I have some in my nightstand."

"Aren't you on the pill?"

"Uh… yeah, but I know where that dick of yours has been. Until I know that boner is clean, the only action you're getting is a hand job."

He always used protection. The only time he hadn't was when he had been wasted with Candi and had believed her lies when she had told him she was on the pill. He knew Crazy Bitch was a straight shooter. If she said she was on the pill, she was.

Finding a condom, he rolled it on then moved back to cover her body with his. He wanted to be able to look down into her eyes and see her first climax with him, knowing he had given her the pleasure he was determined she would find in his arms.

Giving a forceful push, he buried himself in her wet pussy, grinding himself into her until he ended and she began.

It felt so good he had to pull back and thrust forward again, this time going so high she arched her back as her thighs wrapped around him, thrusting back.

She was all bitch, demanding. He gave her more until their bodies were moving in a furious pace.

His cock tightened, a warning he was about to come. Thankfully, he felt the answering spasm of her pussy gripping his cock harder.

His climax played out in a series of explosions that had his mind going blank. When it was over, he could only stare at her stupidly as she shoved him off her.

"Damn, now I have to go shower again."

Calder watched as she jumped off the bed crossly, her

bare ass bouncing across the room and leaving him alone in her bedroom.

Removing the condom, he found a small trash can beside her bed before making himself more comfortable. If she thought he would go back to the spare bedroom, the bitch was going to be disappointed.

When she came back in ten minutes later, she glanced at him before she came to the side of the bed he was lying on.

"Move over. I always sleep on this side," she brusquely ordered.

Not wanting to push his luck, he scooted over, making room for her.

Crazy Bitch turned the bedside light off before lying down next to him.

"If your ass snores, you're outta here."

Calder tried to think if any of the women he had slept with had ever complained about his snoring. He was pretty sure he didn't.

When he tried to cuddle with her, she shrugged away from him.

"Hot thang, when I want to cuddle, I'll tell you. When I want to fuck, I'll wake you up. Stick to your side, and as long as you don't snore... or fart, I might let you have another sleepover."

"And if I do?" He tried to keep his laughter out of his voice, glad she wouldn't be able to see the amusement on his face in the dark.

"Then we'll just be fuck buddies," she finished simply.

He released a relieved sigh. At least she was willing to fuck him again. Some battles with bitches, you had to take what you could get.

13

C alder stared down at his cell phone, seeing there were no new text messages. It was nearly quitting time, and Crazy Bitch still hadn't responded to the text he had sent her, asking if she wanted to hang out tonight at the club.

He pulled the motorcycle he would be working on in the morning into the garage bay, seeing Stud was still working on the one he was building.

"I'm done for the day. You need anything before I leave?"

"No, I'm good." Stud didn't look up as he moved to the side of the bay where he was working.

"You and Sex Piston doing anything tonight?"

"Nope, Star has dance class. I'm going to the club until they're finished. They'll pick me up when they're done."

"You talked to Sex Piston today?" He tried to act unconcerned as he questioned his brother.

"No, she texted me that she wouldn't meet me for lunch; said she and Crazy Bitch were slammed today with walk-ins."

"Oh."

"Why?"

"No reason." He shrugged negligently.

"Okay. You going to the Destructors' club or you headed home?"

"If you're going to the club, I'll hang out there for a few before I head home."

"I'll see you in an hour, then. I want to put on the carburetor before leaving."

"You need any help?"

"No, I got it. Save me a beer."

"I will."

Calder left the garage, going to his bike. He rode to the club, his mind still on Crazy Bitch and why she hadn't returned his text. They had rushed out of her apartment that morning before he had time to make definite plans about seeing her that night.

Feeling like a lovesick weenie, he almost changed his mind about going to the club and went home, but his foot didn't brake, nor did he change direction, hoping to see her car in the parking lot when he pulled in. Disappointment filled him when he saw it wasn't there.

Annoyed with himself, he wasn't in a good mood when he took a seat next to Cade at the bar.

"What's up, Calder?" Fat Louise's husband greeted him.

"Not much," he responded. "Ginger, give me a beer."

The woman set the beer down with a suggestive smile, not moving away. "Can I get you something else?" She made it plain what she was offering.

"Nothing I want from you." His voice was clipped and cold, sending the slut moving to the other side of the bar.

"I'll have to give you a call the next time she's bugging the piss out of me."

Calder didn't bother to look toward Ginger. If he wanted a piece of tail like her, he could find one who didn't have the calculating sharpness that the fake redhead couldn't hide.

He watched Bear go behind the counter and start to take out one of the Miller Lites in the cooler.

"How many are left?" Calder asked, stopping Bear.

"Huh?"

"How many Miller Lites are left?" he repeated.

Bear opened the cooler. "Four."

"Put it back. I bought that case for Crazy Bitch. You want one, you know where the liquor store is. Stud buys the club Bud, Bud Light, Coors, and Coors Light. He told you all, if you want something different, you had to pay for it yourselves."

"She never says anything when the brothers take one." Bear doggedly gripped the beer tighter, not putting it back.

"She's not saying shit now. I am. Put it back." His jaw firmed as he gave Bear a threatening glance.

Bear put it back, taking a Bud Light. The biker wasn't happy, but he had given up the beer.

Calder couldn't care less if the large man was angry. Bear might be a brother, but Calder didn't consider him a friend, and he had never considered a man's size before deciding to take them on. He'd had his ass beaten many times in prison because of his reckless attitude, yet he never backed down from a fight. Hell would freeze over before he would. He might not be the swiftest motherfucker in the world, nor the richest, but what he did have was a pair of balls.

Satisfied that Bear would put out the word not to touch Crazy Bitch's beer, he took a drink of his own, turning sideways on his stool. "I have a bone to pick with you."

Cade lifted an inquiring brow. "I haven't touched her beer."

"Manson is Fat Louise's cat; you need to take it to your home."

"No." Cade's prompt refusal had Calder seeing red. He had already been irritated because Crazy Bitch hadn't responded, and now Cade was being a shit, which he had to admit, he didn't like that the man was refusing to take the devil cat.

"It's Fat Louise's."

"Brother, I'm not arguing that fact, only that I'm not letting it in my house. I got a kid I have to protect."

"If you were a brother, you would get rid of that cat for me. He's making me look like a pussy in front of Crazy Bitch."

"He sprayed your boots yet?"

Calder cringed at the thought. "No."

"Then you're good. He must like you."

"That motherfucker doesn't like anyone, and that includes Crazy Bitch."

"I don't know what to tell you. You're stuck with him. I married Fat Louise to move away from that cat," he joked as Looney came up to the bar.

"I'm not getting married to get rid of that spawn of Satan." Calder's shoulders drooped.

"You talking about Manson?" Looney raised his hand to Ginger, indicting he wanted a beer.

"Yeah." Calder gloomily motioned to Ginger that he wanted another one.

"I thought of whacking that motherfucker a couple of times myself." Looney grinned, opening his beer.

Calder gave him a steely-eyed look. "When have you been in Crazy Bitch's apartment?"

Looney's grin faded. "A couple of months ago. We went out a couple of times."

"I didn't know that."

"No reason you should have."

Calder's eyes narrowed to pinpoints. "I hope you remember it, because you won't be going again."

"Why not? I had a good time."

"Brother, I'd take my beer and go if I were you," Cade tried to ease the escalating tension rising between them.

"Why? He's got no reason to be mad at me." Looney's eyes widened. He hadn't gotten his nickname by playing with a full deck. "Ah… I get it. You must have snored or far—"

Calder didn't remember moving. One minute, he was staring at Looney snickering at him, and the next, he was punching him on the ground. It took Cade lifting him off the man for him to regain his senses.

Looney managed to get to his feet on his own steam and was smart enough to walk away without speaking.

Calder sat back down on the stool, feeling the brothers in the club staring at him.

"Anyone else met Manson?"

"Not me," Bear mumbled into his beer.

"*Me, neither,*" Pike mouthed the words when Calder glanced toward him.

"Rooster, you have something to brag about?"

"Not me, bro."

"Rolo?"

"I don't even know where Crazy Bitch lives, and I didn't even know she had a black cat."

"How'd you know it was black?" he asked with hostility.

"Uh… I…." Rolo glanced back and forth at the men at his sides, seeking the answer.

Cade slapped Calder on the back. "Take it easy. They got your message."

Stud coming in the door had him turning back to his beer. Grabbing a beer of his own, he took a seat next to Calder.

"Why is everyone so quiet?"

"No reason."

"You sure? You look like someone took a leak in your drink."

"That's because I refused to take Manson off Crazy Bitch's hands," Cade answered when it became apparent that Calder wouldn't.

Stud laughed. "That cat driving you nuts like it did Cade?"

"Yeah."

"Skulls offered to get rid of him for Cade."

Stud's revelation had him considering the option. "Cade forgot to mention that."

"It might be easier to neuter him. That would be easier to explain to Crazy Bitch."

"Both options sound good to me. I knew having you as my brother would come in handy one day."

The men started talking about Cade getting his license in Tennessee so he could go hunt with Killyama, Hammer, and Jonas.

Calder only listened with half an ear, glancing at his watch every ten minutes when he wasn't turning to look out the window to spot Crazy Bitch's car. When an hour had passed and she still hadn't appeared, he realized he should have just driven home.

"Who you waiting for?"

Preoccupied, it took Stud waving his hand in front of his face to realize he was talking to him.

"I was hoping Crazy Bitch would stop by for a beer."

"You should have told me. I could have saved you the trouble of waiting. She never comes in on Wednesday nights."

"What goes on Wednesdays?"

Stud shook his head. "You want to know, go find out for yourself. She'll rip my tongue out if I tell you."

"How am I supposed to know if you don't tell me?"

"Go to the beauty shop, and you'll find her."

"I don't want to bug her if she's working late."

"Go and see."

"I'm just going home."

"Sure you are," Stud mocked.

"I wouldn't do that," Cade advised. "That's how Looney ended up on the floor."

"He turning into Shade?"

Calder left before his brother could provoke a fight. When they were younger, they used to go at it to see who could beat the other's ass. He had no intention of not being able to ride his bike if they ever managed to figure out their last clue.

He kept telling himself he was riding home, but when he put on his blinker to turn toward Sex Piston's shop, he knew he had lied to himself.

The lot was almost empty, except for Sex Piston's and Crazy Bitch's cars, and a middle-sized bus.

When he cut off his motor, he could hear music drifting from the building next to the beauty shop.

Calder frowned. The sign in the window of the beauty shop glowed that it was closed. Had they left to go run around with Fat Louise, Killyama, or T.A. and had left their cars there? Maybe they were still inside and just turned on the sign?

Curious, he went to the shop, seeing through the window that, unless they were out back, the shop was empty.

Drawn to the music next door, he strolled to the next window. It was a dance studio. The large room was filled with little girls of all ages. When his attention was caught by Star, his heart started beating in a painful tug of emotions.

The little girl wasn't very coordinated, but she made that up with enthusiasm, trying to mimic her teacher's movements until it was almost painful to watch. The poor kid had inherited his dance skills.

When the teacher said something to Star, Calder glanced at her, ready to barge in if it was a harsh criticism. He felt his mouth drop open.

Star's teacher had her back to him as she moved forward to work with Star. From her profile, though, he instantly recognized Crazy Bitch.

He moved to the side so he could lean forward and watch without being seen.

She patiently worked with Star until she mastered the steps, and then clapped to draw the other girls' attention.

She motioned for them to form a line. "It's time to cool down!"

The girls dropped like flies, rolling around on the floor, giggling. Crazy Bitch pretended to jump over Star then dropped down beside her.

Calder was sorry when the music stopped playing and the girls started gathering in a large circle as Sex Piston and another woman he hadn't met before passed out boxed juices.

He returned to his bike, not wanting the mothers who should be arriving soon to see him lurking around.

The door opened, releasing the girls as the woman Calder didn't recognize led the line, getting them to the opened bus door.

"Uncle Calder!" Star screamed when she saw him.

He stood when Star started running toward him, his hurried long legs meeting her halfway. When she took a running jump, Calder easily caught her.

He didn't smile back at her ecstatic face. "You didn't even look to see if a car was coming."

He was still reprimanding her as Sex Piston was finally able to catch up with her.

"Star! You know better than that," his sister-in-law reproved her.

"I'm sorry, Mama. I'll be more careful next time, I promise." She laid her head on his shoulder, patting his chest. "Did you see me dance?"

"Yes."

"I'm not very good, but Cra—Anna-Kate says I'm getting better."

"You are," Crazy Bitch said after the bus closed with all the little girls inside. She waved at them as it passed by. "Star, did I see you running across the parking lot?"

"I'm sorry. Calder and Mama got mad at me for doing it."

"That makes three of us. You have to be careful. Who would help me teach the class if anything happened to you?"

Calder was amazed at the way Crazy Bitch didn't focus on punishing her, just making Star realize how she could have been hurt.

"Hug Calder bye; your father is waiting."

He kept his face impassive at Sex Piston's reference to Stud being her father.

He bent down to place her feet down onto the pavement. "I'll see you tomorrow, buttercup." He smoothed over her slicked back bun, messing it up until it hung drunkenly.

"Bye, Uncle Calder. Don't forget; tomorrow is pizza night."

"I won't."

He watched her and Sex Piston go to their car, forgetting that Crazy Bitch was watching.

"She's a cute kid."

"All of Stud's kids are cute."

He forced himself to act natural. He would pay the price of the mistakes he had made in his youth for the rest of his life, and he would die before he would let Star be hurt because of them.

"What are you doing here?"

"I wanted to know why you didn't respond to my text."

"I was going to, but I got busy."

"Bullshit."

Her shoulders went back. "Maybe I needed time to think."

"About what? Me and you? You should have taken the time to think," he stressed, "before you let me fuck you. Did I fart or snore last night?"

"No."

"Then what's to think about?" He placed his hand behind her neck, pulling her to his chest. "You want to call all the shots when we're together, call them. I'm a big boy. I can take anything you want to dish out. You want to change the game we're playing, change it. But we're still going to be playing whatever you decide."

"I knew if I put out, you'd be wanting it all the time until the next bitch comes along."

"You don't want to fuck, we don't have to fuck. I just wanted to drink a couple of beers and dance with you for a while."

"Did I say I didn't want to fuck you again? Don't put words in my mouth," she snapped waspishly.

"You're not making sense."

"I got my period, okay?" she snarled. "I kept hoping I wasn't, but it showed up before the dance class."

"You didn't text me because you were waiting to see if your period was going to start?" He tried not to laugh as he walked her to her car. "You want to go out and get a bite to eat before I go home?"

"Where do you want to go?"

"How about Taco Hut? They're pretty good."

"Hell no. Fat Louise burned me out of tacos. How about Charlie's? He grills a mean burger."

"I'll follow you." He pressed a kiss to her lips before

opening her car door as her cell phone pinged. She opened it as she sat down behind the wheel.

He was getting ready to close the door back when she glared up at him.

"What did I do now?"

"You're not chopping my cat's balls off!"

14

The restaurant was so busy Crazy Bitch had to wait for a table, while Calder ordered their food. She had managed to find a booth before he carried their meals back.

Hungry, they ate the decked-out burgers without talking. She was only able to eat half of hers before giving up.

As Calder finished eating, she glanced around the restaurant, seeing the crowd was thinning out. Charlie's was a hole in the wall that, unless you were looking for it, you would miss from the road. The locals swarmed there, and not because of the décor. It hadn't been updated since it had opened when she was in high school, yet it was always packed. On game days, it was practically standing room with the customers watching the large-screen television on the side of wall she was facing. Tonight, Charlie had the local news playing with the sound turned down.

"I didn't know you taught a dance class."

She looked away from the television screen at his question. "Lily suckered me into volunteering. The girls are foster children. Lily teaches a group in Treepoint and bugged me until I volunteered to teach a class here. Dance classes can be expensive, and most foster parents don't have the extra money to pay for them. It gives those in group homes a chance to get out and do something normal."

"That's cool. You're good with them."

She flushed at the compliment, shrugging it off. "I'm not that good. I'm not trained or anything. My mother took me to lessons a few times when she could get clean enough to pay for them. I always knew when she started using because she wouldn't take me to class."

"That must have sucked."

"It did. I loved dancing. I never had enough real talent to do anything with it, but it was fun."

"The girls seemed to be having fun tonight. You're really good with them."

Calder started placing their wrappers on the plastic tray to throw away. They were sliding out of the booth when her eyes were caught by a commercial that flashed across the television screen.

"Turn it up!" Crazy Bitch yelled, uncaring that everyone stared at her and that Calder nearly dropped the tray as he turned to see what she was pointing at.

"You must really want your teeth whitened if you're excited about that sale."

"Not the commercial," she hissed, lowering her voice. "It switched before you turned around."

She grabbed the tray out of his hands, hurriedly going to the trashcan to dump it. Then she grabbed his arm, rushing him out of the restaurant.

Once they were outside, she doubled over in laughter. "That... that son of a bitch!"

"You figured out the clue?"

"Yes, and anyone watching T.V. will, too. Greer made sure of it." She straightened, forcing her laughter back. "It was a commercial for a rodeo!"

"A rodeo?"

She nodded. "The clue was cowboy casserole. What else could it be?"

Calder started laughing, too. "If I hadn't already bet my bike, I would bet it on Viper wanting to kill Greer when he finds out."

"Me, too," she agreed. "I missed the end where it said the date and place."

"It should be simple to google."

As he took out his phone, she moved to the side to watch the results of the search.

"There it is." He thumbed the first result. "Next Friday in Corbin. Shit, that gives everyone time to figure out the clue and plan to go."

"Which sucks out the yin yang for us."

"Especially since we won't know what we'll be looking for when we get there." He closed the screen, tucking his phone back into his pocket. "It'll be interesting to see how many will admit they saw the commercial."

"I wonder how many have already seen it, and how long that commercial has been playing? I usually fast forward commercials."

"Most people do. We might luck out."

"We can hope." She stuck her hands in her back pockets. "I need to get home. I have an eight o'clock in the morning."

"I'll let you get some sleep, then."

He walked by her side as she walked toward her car then gave her a kiss before opening the door for her.

"I'm having dinner with Stud and his family tomorrow night. You want to come? You can keep me from eating the pizza on the way there."

"Throw in some chicken wings, and I'm there," she said, getting into the car.

He tapped on the window before pulling out. "I'll follow

you to your apartment and make sure you get inside before I leave."

"Hot thang, I don't need you doing the protective boyfriend act. Anyone who tries to mess with me will get more than they bargained for. Besides, the only crime rate we have in Jamestown is speeding, or dealing drugs. I don't do either. Go home."

He gave her a searching look. "What if your neighbors are fighting again?"

"Then I'll call the cops." She rolled the window up before he could say anything else.

When she made the turn out of the parking lot, she wasn't surprised to see he followed her.

There was a parking spot in front of her building, so she slid into it, locking the car when she got out and pointedly ignoring him as he watched her go up the metal steps to her apartment.

Unlocking her door, she gave him a finger before going inside and locking her door. She then stealthily peeked through the curtains as Calder left, and then looked at the cars in the parking lot to make sure Sam's wasn't there. When she didn't see it, she went through her apartment, searching each room, including the closets, knowing she was becoming paranoid.

She almost wished Sam would try something. Her apartment building was heavily monitored by cameras on the outside.

Of all the jerks she had dated, she was becoming more and more wary of Sam. Joker had been the biggest loser of them all, but her instincts were telling her that Sam was just as bad, but smarter. That was what had her looking over her shoulder.

She wanted to kick her ass for ever going out with him. She had been blinded by the façade he had put on around others. He had seemed so straight-laced that he had refused to bribe the clerk at the convenience store when she wanted a beer after hours.

Getting undressed, she showered, pampering herself by painting her toenails with a bright red polish. She was admiring them, sitting on her bed, when her phone rang.

Picking it up, she didn't recognize the number, so she dropped the phone down and turned the sound up on the television, hoping the commercial would come on again. She had turned it to the same channel that been on at the restaurant.

Bored, Crazy Bitch picked up her phone again. Whoever it was had left a voicemail.

Listening, she nearly dropped the phone at the vile suggestions coming from her phone.

"You low-class cunt, I'm going to fuck you until you're..."

It didn't sound like Sam, yet she knew it was him. The sick fucker must have bought a burner phone so she wouldn't recognize his number.

"He thinks I'm low class?" she muttered to herself. "He's going to find how low class I am."

CRAZY BITCH WAVED at Fat Louise as she passed her desk but didn't stop, going to the elevator. Pushing the button, she went inside when it opened. Pressing the fourth-floor button, she impatiently waited for the elevator to glide upward. When the doors slid open, she walked directly to Sam's office.

When she opened the glass door, the receptionist and the patients stared at her curiously.

"Hi, sugar, can I see Sam?"

"Uh, yes." The woman stood, going through a side door. A minute later, she came back with Sam following behind her.

His face paled then turned angry. "What are you doing here?"

She pretended to be confused. "I missed your call last night. I didn't want you thinking I was ignoring your calls."

He stepped closer to the counter, lowering his voice so the patients in the office couldn't hear. "I didn't call you last night."

"You sure? It sounded like you." Lifting her hand, she raised her phone and pressed the button she had readied to play the message back. The vulgar filth pouring out of her phone forced shocked gasps out of the women in the room.

"Miss... please." The receptionist tried to reach across the counter for her phone, but Crazy Bitch stepped back.

"That's not me. It doesn't sound anything like me." Sam was angry, spittle hitting the desk.

"Really?" She put the phone in her pocket. "Then I'm sorry. I was wrong. But he sounds the same way when you pronounce *sugar*. The caller said ants will be eating what was left of me after you're done fucking me like sugar."

"A lot of people pronounce *sugar* like that." He tried to bluster his way through, but Crazy Bitch could see the suspicion on receptionist's face and the other employees who had come out when they heard her trying to take the phone away from her.

"You pronounce it that way?" Crazy Bitch cocked her head in the receptionist's direction.

"No."

"Me, either. Most of my friends don't, either. The only one I know is you, and you're from Georgia."

"Get out before I call the police."

"I'm going. I just wanted to give you a chance to tell me

what you wanted to do to me in person, but I guess you're too big a coward to do that."

Turning, she stalked out of the office, going to the elevator. She warily listened for the door in case he followed her, but he had proven her point—Sam was too big a coward to confront her head-on where anyone else could see.

She stopped by Fat Louise's desk, warning her what she had done.

"When I tell Cade—"

"You're not going to say anything to Cade or anyone else. I saw those women's faces. I think most of them believed me. If someone mentions me, just say we don't hang out much anymore and I didn't say anything to you about it. You might get lucky and still be considered for the job."

"I don't care—"

"Yes, you do. He'd be stupid to mess with me again. He'll be too afraid of what I'd do next while he's working. This will blow over if we give it time."

"I hope you're right." Fat Louise gazed doubtfully up at her.

"I might not be Killyama, but I can take care of myself. You know that."

Conceding, Fat Louise gave in with a sigh. "I won't say anything."

"You going to the club Friday?"

"Yes, I managed to find a sitter."

"I'll see you then. Bye."

"Bye."

Crazy Bitch put the incident behind her after she walked out of the hospital.

She barely managed to beat her first customer to the shop. She had just flicked the open sign on when Gail walked inside with a cheerful attitude that was hard to take before Crazy Bitch had her first cup of coffee.

Turning the pot on, she then settled Gail in the chair and tucked a cape around her.

"You want something different, or the same?" Crazy Bitch asked as she combed her hair out.

"The same, but can you go a tiny bit darker this time?"

"No problem. You want a cup of coffee?"

"Please. I didn't want to keep you waiting, so I didn't stop."

She made each of them a cup, giving Gail hers before taking a sip of the scalding-hot coffee as she went to mix the color.

Sectioning the hair, she asked Gail if she was seeing anyone.

"No, I haven't met anyone new, and I'm not interested. I need to broaden my horizons or start looking online."

The twenty-four-year-old school teacher should have men running after her. She was blonde, thin, and had a brain.

"Be careful about broadening your horizons. I tried that, and you don't want to know how well that turned out."

"Who was it?" Gail's curiosity was aroused.

"No one you would know. I could introduce you to some men at the Destructors' club. Some of them—"

"No, that's okay."

"Some of them are really good guys." Well, two or three were.

"Can they read?" she joked.

Her estimation of the woman dropped to zero at her contempt. If she thought of the men in a derogatory way, then she would feel the same about her.

"They can read. Warrick borrowed *Slaughterhouse-Five* from me, and I borrowed *Cat's Cradle* from Z. Have you read it?"

"No."

"When I get finished, I can lend it to you."

"That's okay. I can get my own copy."

Crazy Bitch switched to discussing the weather to keep herself from throwing the uptight bitch out of the shop.

She was finishing putting the color on Gail's hair when Sex Piston came through the door.

"I heard you're coming to dinner tonight with Calder."

"The color needs to set for twenty minutes," Crazy Bitch told her customer, giving her a magazine.

"I was going to tell you when you got here," she directed at Sex Piston.

Sex Piston buttoned up her smock. "You could have texted me last night."

"I was busy painting my toenails."

"You're pulling out the big guns to catch him—painting your toenails. What's next, getting your eyebrows threaded?"

"Why do that when I can get you to do it for free?"

Sex Piston ran a finger over one of her brows. "Remind me to touch them up before I go home."

"We're only going to your house." The woman plucking her brows hurt like a bitch. "You can do it next Friday. Calder and I will be riding out of town."

"You figured out what cowboy casserole meant?"

"There's a rodeo going on next Friday in Corbin, at the fair."

Sex Piston had the reaction she'd had. She was still wiping the tears away when her customer showed up in a wave of toxic fumes that had her nearly gagging.

"Mrs. Carpenter, you're right on time. I have your favorite chair waiting."

The tiny old woman was so small and frail Sex Piston had to raise the chair by small degrees.

"I see you drove yourself."

"I may be ninety-two, but I can drive better than my son."

"Devon just doesn't want you to get anymore speeding tickets."

The old woman waved her concerns away. "I bought myself a radar detector at the swap meet. None of those cops are going to be catching me again. Devon is just being an old worry wart. You'd think a seventy-year-old bachelor would have better things to worry about than his mother who's in better health than he is."

"He's not blind in one eye like you are."

"I can see better with one good eye than he can with two."

"If you say so."

Crazy Bitch hid her grin, starting to take the aluminum foil out of Gail's hair. She was grateful when she was able to move her to the washing station to escape the overpowering perfume Mrs. Carpenter was wearing.

Washing and giving her a scalp massage as she conditioned, she was still angry at her. She was about to wash it out when her professionalism made her feel guilty, massaging for several more minutes.

Moving her back to her chair, she cut her hair and blow-dried it without making the effort to chat, letting Sex Piston and Mrs. Carpenter's conservation fill the room.

As she styled Gail's hair, Crazy Bitch wasn't able to hold back her tongue any longer when she saw Gail condescendingly listening in as Sex Piston invited Mrs. Carpenter and her son over to dinner one night at her parents' house.

"Skulls and Ma would love to see you. I'll cook. We can even go by the club and get a beer afterward. Of course, I would drive you home if you did," she hastened to add the last part.

"I'd love to. We're not doing anything this Saturday."

"I'll call Ma after I'm done and let her know. It'll make her day."

Crazy Bitch wound a section of Gail's hair around the curling iron then moved to another.

"You want me to order the brownies when I pick up the pizzas for dinner tonight?" Prodding the curl the way she wanted it, she started curling another.

"Yes. If the pizza doesn't add five pounds to my ass, the brownies will."

"Star finish that book she was reading?" Crazy Bitch turned the chair to start another section.

Sex Piston turned her attention away from Mrs. Carpenter, gaping at the question.

"What b—"

"I told Star that, when she finished reading *The Grapes of Wrath*, we would watch the movie together and see which was better: the movie or the book."

"Huh…? Are you…?"

Before Sex Piston could say anything, Crazy Bitch started talking to Gail.

"Sex Piston is just being modest. Her daughter is so smart she should be tested for accelerated classes. Have you met Star's father, Stud?"

"No, I haven't had the pleasure yet."

"Of course, he doesn't use his real name. His fans are always asking for his autograph. He races motorcycles, and he's made a name for himself building them. His daughters, Meri and Keri, are going to be seniors this year. They're really smart, too." Crazy Bitch finished curling Gail's hair, brushing it down gently so she wouldn't lose the curl. "Yep, they're smart as tacks. They take after their father. He's the president of the Destructors. Stud and Sex Piston are taking the whole family to France when the girls graduate. They have a personal friend who's invited them to stay. She's a contessa." She took off the cape, handing Gail the mirror for her to see the job she had done. "You been to France?"

"No, I haven't. I love the color, thank you." Gail reached for her purse, taking out a wallet to hand over her credit card. "Schedule me for another appointment six weeks from now."

"Right now, I'm booked up for the next six months. But if I get any openings, I'll phone you."

Gail's hand went to her hair protectively. "But you always do my hair every six weeks."

"I'm so sorry." She pretended a sorrow she didn't feel. "I must have forgotten when I set my appointments."

Gail turned helplessly toward Sex Piston. "Do you have any openings?"

"She's full, too." Crazy Bitch gave her the ticket to sign, knowing she wouldn't be getting a tip.

"Make sure you call me if you get an opening," she said, giving her the ticket back after signing it.

"I will."

This time, she didn't give a fuck what her professionalism was shouting at her. The snooty bitch could go to the Cut and Chop as far as she cared.

"What in the hell was that about?" Sex Piston asked as soon as the door closed behind Gail.

"I offered to introduce her to some of the men at the club, and she had the nerve to ask if they could read."

Sex Piston placed her hand on her hip. "Most of them probably can't."

"That bitch doesn't know that for sure," Crazy Bitch argued back.

"She's a fucking teacher," she said between clenched teeth.

"That doesn't give her the right to act all hoity-toity."

"Girls, calm down," Mrs. Carpenter tried to intervene.

"She's a teacher in Star's school. She's going in the grade that Gail teaches."

"Maybe she won't get Star." Crazy Bitch started to feel a glimmer of regret.

"What if she does?"

Crazy Bitch snapped her fingers. "Don't worry; I'll buy her the Cliff's notes, and I'll read it to her."

"Why did you even say she was reading *The Grapes of Wrath?*"

"It was on the book list Winter kept trying to get me to read when I was getting my GED."

"Did you read it?"

"Fuck no. And I didn't read the other ones she kept bugging me about, either. Why read it when I have two perfectly good television sets?"

"I wouldn't worry about it, dear. That young woman probably forgot about it before she was out your door."

"See, you're always complaining on something I said..." Crazy Bitch mimicked the same snotty air of the bitch who had just left.

"She's probably wondering why a contessa is living in France. They're Italian," Mrs. Carpenter informed her.

"Mrs. Carpenter." Sex Piston set her hairbrush carefully down at her station.

"Yes, dear?"

"Cover your ears."

15

"I don't have to read it, do I?" Star complained, setting the table off in another round of laughter.

"No," Sex Piston told the girl as she helped pick up the dirty plates on the table. "You can wait until you're in high school."

"What do I do if Miss Williams asks me a question?"

"Tell her you haven't finished it yet, and you don't want to talk about it until you're finished. That always worked for me." Crazy Bitch snagged the last piece of pizza before Meri could take the box away to clean the table.

"How did it work for you? You never graduated from high school, and you didn't get your GED until you were thirty."

"I got it, though." She gave Star a wink. "And you can, too. Anything is possible; remember that, Star."

"Bitch, are you trying to say she won't be finishing high school like you?"

She barely had time to snatch her pizza off her plate before Sex Piston angrily took it away.

"I'm still eating here!" Placing a possessive hand on her

soda, she gave Keri a glare when she tried to take it. "Harley, make your ma and sisters quit bugging me."

Stud's only son shook his head stubbornly. "You stole my brownie when I went to the bathroom."

"I thought you were done with it."

"I told you I wasn't when you asked for it before I went."

She motioned the little boy to come closer. "I'm going to tell you a secret. You promise you won't tell?"

He solemnly nodded.

"Boys are always supposed to give up their chocolate when a girl asks for it, especially your aunt."

"Dad didn't tell me about that rule." Harley lifted questioning eyes toward where his father was sitting.

"He wouldn't. He's stingy with his chocolate. Did you see him sharing with your ma?"

"No, but—"

"There you go." Patronizing the boy, she patted the top of his head. "Now you know."

"But Ma had her own brownie; why would Dad give her his, too?"

The little boy wasn't about to be detoured from losing his fucking brownie. It wasn't even that good. It was too dry.

"Because he is a boy; he's supposed to."

"But why?"

"Harley, remember the last lesson I taught you when I came over? Your aunt is always right."

"Quit messing with my kid's mind. Ready for your bath?" Stud bent down, lifting him onto his shoulders and pretending to drop him. "You're getting too big for me to carry you."

"It's all those brownies he's eating!" Crazy Bitch yelled after them as Stud and Harley left the dining room.

"You're making me feel guilty I didn't give you mine." Calder's amused voice drew her gaze back to him.

"I noticed that." She grinned.

Standing up, she gave Star her empty plate then went into the living room and plopped down on the couch.

"Lord, I'm tired. Being obnoxious takes too much energy."

Calder sat down next to her, placing his arm on the back of the couch. "You never relax and take it easy."

"I will when I'm dead. Life's too short not to have fun. Take bullshit, or live life. I'm not going to have any what ifs when Jesus takes my soul, if He does. My mother had enough of those when He took hers."

Sex Piston and the girls came in from the kitchen, drawing her out of the dark thoughts about her mother.

"Why can't we go to the rodeo?"

"I told you why, Meri. Stud and I'll be looking for a clue. The rodeo is there for two days. You and the others can drive up with us on Friday. We can get a hotel room if you and Keri are willing to babysit Star and Harley. Then all of us can go together Saturday." Sex Piston threw herself down on a chair and propped her legs onto the coffee table.

"I guess we can babysit."

Meri didn't seem happy, but when Sex Piston gave her a sharp glance, the seventeen-year-old was smart enough to appease her by leaning down to give her a quick hug before releasing her.

"I'll go tell Keri. Thanks. You're the best." The teenager took off up the stairs.

"Thank God I don't have kids." Crazy Bitch slid down from the couch onto the floor, taking one of her friend's feet and started to deftly massage it. "If she had talked to me that way, she would have gotten her car keys taken away for a week."

"Sure you would." Sex Piston rolled her eyes. "You would have taken them and searched for the clue on Saturday."

Crazy Bitch didn't try to deny it. She was about to offer

to take them when Sex Piston had come out with the solution to make her kids happy.

"I'll ride up with Calder. He can ride back alone. I'll get a hotel for Friday, go with you and Stud to help with the kids on Saturday, and come back in your van."

"I can stay. You can ride back with me."

Crazy Bitch shrugged. "Whatever." She put the foot she had been massaging back on the table, taking the other to give it the same treatment.

Star sat down on the arm of the chair, laying her head down on Sex Piston's shoulder. "You want me to run you a bath, Mama? I'll put in one of those bath bombs you gave me for my birthday."

Her stepmother laid her cheek down on the top of Star's hair. "That would be nice. Thank you. Save the ones that smell like bubble gum for you. You can put the one that smells like flowers in mine."

The girl jumped up, giving her a kiss on her cheek before going upstairs.

"I take it back; you got a sweet deal going on if they're running baths for you."

"The trick is to train them young, but not young enough that they'll start playing in it."

Crazy Bitch watched as Sex Piston took out her phone, wondering who she was calling and unashamedly listening as she kept massaging her foot.

"Stud, Star is filling my bath. Keep an eye on her. I'll be up in a minute."

She looked at them when she ended the call. "Okay, I admit it; I'm a little paranoid where the kids' safety is concerned. Accidents happen, and I don't want something stupid happening because she wanted to be helpful."

"Aw, that's so sweet."

"Fuck you. Calder, Star made me promise that you would

play a couple of games with her before you left." She arose, getting up. "I'll send her back down. Bitch, I'll see you in the morning."

"Night, Sex Piston."

She climbed back up to sit on the couch next to Calder.

"You and Sex Piston are still as close as when I first met you, even though you spend five days a week together."

"All of us are close. When we were younger, we all swore we would live on the same street that Sex Piston's parents live on."

"Were you all disappointed she moved here when she married Stud?"

"I was, kind of. The crew is all I have. But Sex Piston still works in Jamestown, and she goes to visit them. Fat Louise and Cade were able to buy a house next to them. Killyama will be living in Treepoint. T.A and I both say we're keeping to the plan."

"What if you get involved with someone who lives in… say, West Virginia? I drive to work every day to Stud's shop."

"Are you still going to be doing that in a year or two? Aren't you getting tired of the drive?"

"No, I like it, and I like building bikes." Calder shook his hair back from his cheek, reminding her of the rat she had shaped on the back of his head.

"You should come by tomorrow and let me trim that for you."

"I like it long."

Star jumped onto the couch. "You ready to play, Uncle Calder?"

He turned the machine on, giving her the controller. They were on their second game when Stud came down with Harley. The boy squished himself between her and Calder.

Rising, she went to sit in the other chair, giving them

more room. She curled up on the chair, putting her chin on her hand as she watched them play.

Harley was the spitting image of Stud. Hair color, eyes, even the arrogant tilt of his head when he wasn't happy. Star, on the other hand, took more after her mother. She was going to be dainty and petite, but her hair color was more the color of Calder's, and so were her eyes.

She hastily turned toward the television when Calder noticed her staring at them, pretending amusement at the kids' reaction to the game.

Her mind went back to when she had found out Candi was pregnant and was married to Stud. It hadn't been long after Calder had been sent to rehab. That had been before Skulls had handed the Destructors over to the Stud. She still remembered how shocked she had been when Skulls had mentioned that Stud and Candi got married and she was pregnant. She had even jokingly suggested to Joker that he should have taken a paternity test before marrying her.

Candi was one of the biggest sluts she had ever known. She still had been when she was arrested the night she had kidnapped Star. The woman fucked any man who filled her needs for drugs. The only person she had ever seen her care about was Calder. It was an obsessive love. Even Crazy Bitch had seen that, what little she had been around them together. Candi had used the drugs to keep Calder within her control.

Stud let Star play another game before asking her to let Harley play. Star handed it over. When he lost, Stud told them it was time to go to bed.

Her suspicions that Star was Calder's receded when he gave the kid a brief hug before turning off the television.

They said good night to Stud then left.

"Those kids love spending time with you."

"I love them, too. Stud and Sex Piston are great parents."

As they reached her car, she was glad she had told him she would follow him with her car.

The driveway light showed his somber expression. She didn't immediately get in her car, caught off guard at the inflection she had heard in his voice.

"Stud and I were raised by our father. He was a racer like Stud. He raced in any state or country that had a track. Our mother tried to get custody of us, but our old man stayed one step ahead of the law. Just when they were about to catch up with him, she was killed while coming to pick us up at the police station. Ironic, isn't it? If she hadn't tried so hard to get us, she would probably still be alive. Our dad didn't care. He was just happy he got what he wanted."

She sadly watched him reliving his childhood.

"Stud started racing when he was fourteen. Every mistake he made, our father would go ballistic, forcing him to practice the maneuvers over and over again. He didn't give a shit he could be hurt. He just wanted Stud to win, and he did."

A bitter smile played across his lips. "When he tried to get me to race, I was smart enough to make myself scarce. There was no way I was going to put myself through that hell.

"A couple of the riders showed me how to work on bikes. They started coming to me when they wanted help. It gave me spending money, and when I was able to keep his and Stud's bikes in good repair, he got off my case about not riding.

"He was winning every race, and so was Stud. When Stud told him that Reese was pregnant and they were getting married, I thought he was going to have a heart attack. He had been keeping Stud's winnings and only giving him chump change. Our father knew that was going to stop now that Stud was getting married and had a kid on the way.

"It was before a big race. Dad told me he wanted his tires changed. It had rained that morning and he wanted another set that had better traction. I was changing them when he and Stud were arguing. It was so bad I had to break them up." He gave her a self-deprecating smile. "I forgot to recheck the nuts before the race. He was coming out of the last curve when his front wheel came off."

"God!" Crazy Bitch muttered, reaching out to touch his arm, but he took a step back, avoiding her touch.

"He died because I made a stupid mistake, like I always do."

She shook her head, trying to get him to see reason. "It was an accident."

"A fatal one." He sat down on the seat of his bike, staring up at her grimly. "It made the news. It even made the news that I was the one responsible for changing the tires.

"Stud and I had Dad's body brought to West Virginia. After the funeral, we went to the Blue Horsemen's clubhouse for a drink. Dad had belonged to the club before he started racing.

"I didn't leave with Stud the next day. I told him I needed time to let the news cool down before going back to the circuit. Stud only left after I promised I'd meet up with him in a month. He kept calling me, wanting me to come back, but I didn't. I quit taking his calls and ignored him. He couldn't drop everything to fly back. Besides, the brothers had lied to him, telling him I was fine, that I just needed time. Reese was having Meri and Keri, and he had commitments to his sponsors.

"It was three months before I woke up to find Stud standing over me. I'll never forget the look on his face."

The agony on his face had Crazy Bitch's eyes tearing up. "You had started using."

"I was fucking addicted. When he tried to take me out of there, I fought him. Told him if he didn't leave me alone, I would disappear and never see him again."

"He didn't leave."

"Not my big brother. It would be easier to break iron when someone he loves needs him. That's why he had put up with our father for so many years. He used what money he had to build this house and moved Reese and the girls into it. That was when he started hanging out at the club. When he gained enough power, he took over.

"It was dirty and brutal, but he did it. He got rid of those who were dealing and supplying me and tried to get me in rehab. I refused. I didn't want to feel better, and I damn sure didn't want to take the drugs away that kept me from seeing how low I had sunk. As hard as he tried, I was able to get the drugs I needed."

"Candi." Disgusted, Crazy Bitch was glad the bitch was behind bars.

"Among others," he confirmed. "All an addict has to do is look around. It's easy to spot someone else using. Stud, on the other hand, didn't, so he couldn't spot them as easily as I could." His head fell back as he gave a tragic laugh that was filled with self-reproach.

"I was so out of it. Meanwhile, Reese started hanging around the club. Stud found her with one of the brothers. She had fucked around on him a few times on the circuit, but she must have liked what he was giving her because they both left the club, and she gave Stud custody of the girls. If it wasn't for me staying at the club, Stud and Reese would still be together."

"You don't know that. You said she had fucked around before, so they would have broken up, anyway."

"Maybe, but it wouldn't have been my fault." He punched his chest. "Dad's death, Stud's riding career, Reese leaving him—that's all on me. Stud's a standup guy; that's why Skulls turned the Destructors over to him, and that's why The Last Riders trust him, and those bastards don't trust anyone. You saw their kids at Star's birthday party. They watch those kids like a hawk, but the men sent the women alone with only Razer to watch over them. That shit wouldn't have happened with anyone else. I can guarantee that. When Viper, Winter, and Aisha visit Gavin, he brings four men with him."

"I noticed. I also noticed they trust you with Gavin."

He shook his head, as if shaking away old memories. "I didn't tell you all this shit so you could make me feel better."

"Then why did you tell me?"

"To give you fair warning. I may be Stud's brother, but the similarities end there. I'm not the same man who stood you up or who has been fucking any hole within reach. I've been getting my act together, but I'm far from measuring up to Stud. I guess, what I'm trying to say is, I may not measure up, but there is no way I'm going back to the way I was."

"I don't think Stud expects you to measure up to him, and I don't expect you to, either. Hot thang, I honestly don't know what I'm expecting from you, but I can definitely tell you, comparing you two isn't on my mind."

His grin flashed when he leaned forward on his seat, pulling her toward him.

"You giving me a hard time by calling me that? You really think I'm hot?"

With her hand on his chest, she pushed herself away. "I have to get home; I have that early appointment."

"You always have early appointments."

"I have shit to do at night."

"Since I'm going to be spending most of the weekend with you, I'm going to get a couple hours sleep then go stay with Gavin. I won't be back until Friday."

"If you want to crash at my place, you can. You can get an extra thirty minutes of sleep. It will save you time by not backtracking in the morning." She didn't like the idea of him riding when he was so tired.

"I wish I could, but I need fresh clothes."

"Suit yourself." She went to get in her car.

"Anna-Kate!"

She poked her head back up, almost blasting him for using her sissy name. However, the concern on his face stopped her.

"Stay safe until I get back."

"You're going to be out of town. What trouble can I get into?" she teased, getting inside her car.

They pulled out of the driveway, leaving the house that had grown dark, all the occupants already in bed.

A CURTAIN CURLED INWARD as a breeze sent it fluttering over the master bedroom.

"You miss it?" Sex Piston laid her cheek across her knees. She had sat up to eavesdrop on the voices coming from outside. "Racing?"

"I still race." She felt Stud turn over to face her in the darkness.

"Be real with me. There's no comparison with the races you're competing in now than what you used to. There are no television cameras, no big sponsors."

"I have sponsors."

"Combs Reality might be a sponsor, but they can't get you the money like a name brand competitor would."

"I don't have to kiss their asses, either."

"Would you and Reese have still been together?"

Stud pulled her back down the bed, leaning over her. "She was fucking around on me long before I became president of the Destructors. We never married because we were in love; we married because of the girls. We get along better divorced than we ever did when we were married."

147

"I love you." She buried her face in his shoulder. "You should talk to Calder."

"I've tried. He changes the subject." He ran his hand down her silky back to twist her gown up to her waist. "He's apologized to me several times for how he acted when he was on drugs. Obviously, he's still carrying a lot of blame. He knows I've forgiven him, but he still hasn't forgiven himself.

"Dad always made him feel worthless because he wouldn't race. He constantly threw me up to him. Hell, I didn't blame him. I put up with him because of Calder. We had been dragged through the courts between Mom and Dad. As bad as I hated Dad, I didn't want to put Calder through that again. As soon as he was eighteen, I planned on us going off on our own."

"He died first."

"He's blamed himself ever since. He still does."

"That's not the only thing he's blaming himself for. He thinks you're settling for second best."

"I'm not settling for second best." He raised her face from his shoulder. "I could have left when Calder was sent to rehab. I had enough of my contacts left that I could have started over in the circuit. Once Candi agreed to give me custody of Star, and we got a divorce, I didn't have to stay."

"Why did you?"

"By then, I had met you."

"Does it make me a bitch that I'm glad you and Reese didn't work out?"

"You wouldn't be the bitch I know and love if you didn't."

"What the fuck?" Calder walked into Gavin's room, seeing him struggling with an orderly.

Peyton was watching the struggle with a pale face, as a nurse held her back from getting involved.

"Get off me! I'm leaving! You can't make me stay!" Gavin managed to get away from the restraining hold of the burly orderly.

"Don't touch him!" Calder pulled him back when he tried to grab Gavin again. "What's going on, Gavin?"

"I tried…" Gavin heaved, panting for air. "I need it, Calder. Jesus, I *need* it."

Calder turned toward them. "Get out. Leave us alone."

They looked like they were going to refuse, but thought better of it at his glare.

"Peyton, take the next two days off. I'll call if he needs you."

"All right." Peyton went to where Gavin was pacing across the room, stopping his momentum. "Gavin… call me if you need me to come back sooner."

He nodded abruptly but didn't stop the frantic pacing. As

soon as the door was closed behind her, though, Gavin stopped.

"Help me get the fuck out of here. I'll pay you anything you want."

"You wouldn't get out the front door. Viper has men guarding you. Moon is out front, and Lucky is out back."

The man crumpled to the floor, rocking back and forth. "Okay, okay, you can go and score me a hit. I'll pay you anything you want."

"That's not gonna happen," he shot the suggestion down. He had to keep his face impassive as his heart tore in two.

When Gavin started crying, he sank down next to him on the floor, placing an arm around his shoulders. "Breathe through it. Take a deep breath in through your nose. Now let it go slowly through your mouth." He started rocking the broken man through the withdrawal that had sent him over the edge.

"Do it again." He kept telling him to breathe despite Gavin's pleas that kept barraging him over and over until Gavin went silent and slumped against his shoulder.

Seeing he was asleep, he managed to turn them so he could rest against the bed.

When the door squeaked open, his eyes met Peyton's as she quietly came back into the room.

"What set him off?" Calder whispered, not wanting to wake Gavin.

"They decreased his medication to wean him off. Then Taylor called. She wants to see him."

He wouldn't want the woman he loved to see him in the shape he was in.

"The nurse called Viper. He's on his way."

"Call him back. Tell him to stick to the schedule. Tell him I got it under control."

"Thank God you showed up early. They wanted to give him a sedative."

"The last thing he needs is someone coming at him with a needle."

She straightened the room as Gavin slept.

"You want me to help you get him on the bed?"

"No, he needs the sleep. When he wakes up, I'll get some food down him."

"He ate much better this week. The doctor said he gained two pounds."

"That's good. Go get some rest. You look like you need it."

"I will. Thanks, Calder." She left them alone.

Laying his head back on the side of the mattress, Calder was able to snag a pillow to rest his head on. Bunching it under his head without disturbing Gavin, he closed his eyes.

He didn't know how long they slept, but he felt it when Gavin started to move. Calder lifted his eyelids to see Gavin using the side of the bed to get off the floor.

"Sorry to wake you, but waking up in your arms wasn't what I was ever hoping for."

Calder laughed. "I can't say I blame you. You wouldn't be my first choice, either."

He groaned. Every muscle in his body hurt from the position they had been in.

"One of those orderlies punched me when I was out." Gavin's groan echoed his own.

"Not unless they got me, too." He had to use the same method to rise as Gavin had, moving around with stooped shoulders until they could move freely again.

Calder pushed the call button. "I hope you're hungry. I'm starved." He requested two trays from the nurse who answered.

"I'm ready for lunch. I'm surprised they haven't brought it yet."

"They could have come in while we were sleeping and didn't want to interrupt our beauty nap."

"More like they wanted a break from my shit." Gavin gave him a shame-faced look. "It hit me hard. I would have shoved it in me if I could have gotten it."

"You wouldn't have."

"You don't know that shit," he seethed. "I would have!"

"This rehab center isn't on Mars. Drugs are floating around here, just like there was in prison. You're on a battle-ground wherever you are. You won a battle today. Be proud of yourself."

"Because you were here."

"You wouldn't have given in. You would have just asked for your dosage to go back up."

"I hate that shit."

"I know. You're almost off it. Next week, it will be on you whether you can do without it or not."

"You going to be here?"

"I'll be here. Peyton will be here this weekend. They normally lower your doses on Monday, so I'll be here with bells on. We'll do something to celebrate."

"Like what?"

"I don't know. You tell me. Anything you've been want-ing? I'll see if I can make it happen."

"I want to see Taylor."

"I don't think that's a good idea."

"I need to see the woman I fought so hard to stay alive for."

"That's why I don't think you should see her. What if it sets you off the way it did today?"

"You said yourself my recovery is a battleground. It's another battle I'll have to get through. Might as well be now instead of later. That way, if you're here, you can keep me from going for those orderlies' jugulars."

"You know the biggest mistake an addict can make? Lying to yourself. Brother, I smell the bullshit from over here." Calder saw the determination on his face and knew there wasn't a way to talk him out of it. "I'll talk to the doctor and see what he has to say."

"Thanks."

The nurse came in with two trays. The woman gave them an intent glance before leaving.

"She saw us sleeping."

Gavin grinned. "I bet she tells everyone in the nurses' lounge."

"Could be worse. At least you're not ugly. Those two pounds look good on you," Calder wisecracked.

"Fuck you."

After lunch, they walked around the grounds. Calder was glad Gavin's stamina was improving. He was walking longer distances without resting as long. They even worked out thirty minutes in the gym before Gavin was ready to go back to his room.

When it grew dark after dinner, they went to sit on his back patio. Calder unrolled his smokes from his shirtsleeve, taking one for himself and giving one to Gavin.

"You ever miss them?"

"The drugs?" Calder flicked his ashes away, staring down at the burning tip.

"Yes."

"It used to be every minute, then every hour. Now I can almost get through a day."

"That's disheartening."

Calder gave a low laugh. "I told you I wouldn't lie to you. That's why so many go back to them. That's why you count the number of days you've been clean."

"How did you keep yourself from using again once you were out of prison?"

"I figured I had disappointed Stud enough."

"Viper is used to me disappointing him."

"Bro, there's a big difference between me and you. I chose to do drugs; you didn't have a choice. Viper isn't disappointed in you. He would trade places with you in a fucking second to keep you from getting hurt again.

"When I was at my lowest point, Stud tried to get me help. I threatened never to see him again if he interfered in my life. It took me going to prison to see that I was stupid enough to think that I could avoid falling into quicksand. I thought I was too smart, that I was Superman and could move so fast my feet wouldn't touch the stuff. As my use grew worse, I grew so arrogant I thought I could walk right over it and not get dragged down." Calder shook his head at his stupidity. "Then, when I was caught, I was too stupid to reach out and let Stud help me. Don't make that mistake. If I had to do it over, I would do things differently."

"What if I drag him down with me?"

"You really think you're going to be dragging Viper down? That man is solid. Not only do you have Viper, but you have all The Last Riders."

"You're right. So, what's going on with you and Crazy Bitch? She still hate you?"

"No, we hooked up the other day."

"Was it as good as you thought it would be?" Gavin's envious smile gleamed at him from the light inside.

"Better. We're spending the weekend together." He didn't mention the game the clubs were playing, not wanting him to feel left out.

"I guess I can do without you for the weekend."

"I'm a phone call away if you need me."

"I know." Gavin stood up. "You mind if I go to sleep? It's been a long day. I'm going to call Peyton and tell her good night." Despite his words, he made no move to leave. "I don't know what I would have done without you today."

"You would've fallen asleep on your bed."

"Do me a favor?"

"Sure."

"You don't want to know what it is?"

"Don't need to. What do you want?"

"Bring Crazy Bitch here. I'd like to meet her."

"Then I'll bring her."

"Night."

"Good night."

Calder stayed outside, smoking his cigarette and giving Gavin time to fall asleep. He was about to go inside when he saw a dark figure slip out of the room.

"Checking on him?" Calder asked Viper when he took the chair next to him.

"Peyton said he had a bad morning. Since I was on my way, anyway, I hung around to speak to you. The doctors say he's doing better. What do you think?"

"He's eating and growing stronger. That's about all I can tell you."

"That's the same thing the doctor said."

"Sorry."

"No, you're not. I want to bring him home."

"I know you do, but he's not ready yet."

"Ton is getting married to Winter's aunt. He wants Gavin to come."

"Either they wait or get married without him there. Gavin being there isn't going to be good for anyone. He has to face one person from his past before he can move on and face the life he has ahead of him."

"Taylor."

Calder nodded. "He wants her to come next week."

"Damn. If she comes down, it won't go well. She's seven months pregnant. It might send him over the edge."

"No might about it," Calder said grimly. "But at least he'll be in a controlled environment, versus you and Shade dealing with it."

"Don't underestimate Gavin. Any other man would be dead with the concoction of drugs they were giving him. His nickname in the service was Reaper for a reason. The only other person I've seen go off like Reaper is Shade when he gets pissed off. When Shade goes off, he can take out six or seven men. Reaper can decimate whoever he comes into contact with."

Calder gave a low whistle. "I'll bring my helmet when I come back on Monday."

Viper narrowed his eyes on him. "You're not coming this weekend?"

He could kick himself for dropping his guard. "Peyton wanted a couple of days off, so we switched," he lied.

"Really. Hmm… you and Crazy Bitch having any luck with Greer's clue?"

"Which one?"

"The one where you have to eat that fucking mess Greer dreamed up."

"Oh… that one. Not yet."

"You're lying. That's fine. I don't blame you." Viper stood. "I need to get home to Winter and Aisha. See you around."

Calder stood. "Tell Greer he needs to take precautions."

Viper grinned, unconcerned. "The brothers thinking of getting even?"

"The bitches. Sex Piston is getting pretty graphic on what she wants to do to him."

Viper gave a vindictive smile. "I've had to eat that recipe two nights in a row, and I'm pretty sure I'll be having it for lunch tomorrow. She can have him."

17

"You miss me?"

Crazy Bitch came out of the beauty shop to see Calder waiting for her.

"Were you gone?" Frostily, she walked toward him. "Did you go to the Cut and Chop to get your hair cut?"

She saw his eyes waver from hers. "I was going to come here, but Stud said you and Sex Piston were slammed."

Her eyes bore into his. "I would have made time to cut your hair."

"Next time, I know. Sorry."

She climbed behind him. "Next time I find out you went there, I'll try my waxing technique out on you."

She felt him flinch at the threat.

"You want to grab a bite to eat before we hit the road?"

"No, I'm good. You?"

"No."

Crazy Bitch was hungry. She had to work through lunch today so they could get on the road after her appointments. Sex Piston had taken off a couple of hours ago to get the kids organized and loaded up. She knew damn good and well she had packed the night before. She bet she and Stud were almost to Lexington.

They had to stop for gas a couple of times. She went inside and grabbed a hot dog, eating half of it before coming back outside.

He was putting up the hose when she handed him the one she had bought for him. Calder stared at it strangely before taking a large bite.

She sat down on the bike, taking the last bite. Taking the soda out of her pocket, she then took another can out of her jacket, popping the top and handing it to him.

He took a drink.

"I've never had a woman do that for me before."

Her hand holding the soda paused. "What, buy you a hot dog?"

"Yes. Thanks."

After she finished her drink and tossed what was left in the trashcan beside the pump, she twined her arms around his waist. "I need you to keep your strength up. Crazy Bitch needs a new bike."

As they pulled back onto the road, she searched her memory for when any of the women at the club had done something special for him, and couldn't come up with one instance. She had seen them go into his room, but they would always come out an hour later. Even when he had been with Candi.

Over the last six months, she hadn't seen any of the bitches make their way to his room. She had seen Ginger make a quick meal for some of the other brothers, but unlike the others, Calder had never asked, limiting his interactions with the women to only asking for a beer.

He was probably getting some from one of the bitches at the Blue Horsemen's club. He spent most of his nights there when he wasn't in Lexington with Gavin.

As they drew nearer to Corbin, Calder made the turn from a four-lane road to a two-lane that was as curvy as the one toward Treepoint. It was also narrower, and Crazy Bitch would be glad when they reached the fairgrounds.

The traffic was starting to become backed up. A guy in a red truck was laying on its horn in front of them, his truck stopping and starting with the sound of the powerful engine. The truck was so large that she couldn't see what kind of vehicle was in front of it.

"I'm glad we're not in front of him." She lifted her visor to talk to Calder, since they were sitting still. Calder did the same.

"If he were behind of us, I would have already moved to the side of the road to let him by. He's being a jerk."

The truck horn started honking incessantly. Then, as the driver started to go around the car, she heard the sound of metal scraping as the truck side-swiped the car, pinning the driver inside.

"This is going to get ugly." Calder gave her a warning look from over his shoulder. "Whatever goes down, your ass doesn't come off my bike."

She didn't have time to respond before the truck moved forward again, not enough to let the driver out, but enough room for the passenger in the truck to get out and climb onto the hood of the car, jumping up and down on it.

Crazy Bitch felt the tension in Calder's body, yet he stayed on the bike, watching as the passenger started trying to kick out the car's windshield.

Leaning to the side, she saw the driver of the car finally manage to get out of their car through the passenger door. They were frightened and told the men to stop.

"I called the police."

The man on the car jumped down and started mercilessly beating on the driver, who only stood there, trying to block the punches coming his way. Meanwhile, the driver inside the truck egged his partner on.

"Hit him again, Ray. Teach that cocksucker to move when someone blows at him!"

Calder removed his helmet and got off his motorcycle. Crazy Bitch expected him to help the car's driver. Instead, he went to the door of the truck, jerking it open, then jerking the man out.

"This ain't no business of yours!"

Calder pushed the man against the side of his truck, pinning his arms behind his back. "Make him stop." Calder shoved his elbow into the back of the man's squirming neck.

"Fuck you! *Ray!*" the man Calder was holding shouted for his friend.

The car's driver collapsed to the pavement as Ray dropped him to go to his friend's aid.

Drivers in front and behind them got out of their cars to watch, but no one made a move to help Calder get the two men under control. Some watching had their phones out, recording what was going on, while others were calling nine-one-one. The road was so congested she knew there wasn't going to be a way for the police to reach them in time.

She started to get off the bike, but Calder saw her and gave her a warning glare that had her ass sinking back down.

Her attention was focused on Calder as Ray ran behind the truck, momentarily stopping when he saw his friend pinned against the truck by Calder. "You're dead!" he yelled as he drew closer.

Calder threw the man he was holding at the larger one. Then he shifted on his feet, planting them slightly apart as he raised his fists in the air, preparing to meet the two men who didn't have the balls to attack him on their own.

Their sarcastic chuckles were cut off when the burly one swung at Calder.

Ducking, Calder swiped his leg out, hitting both the men's legs and making them stumble. Calder then straightened in one motion, planting one fist in the large man's face and using his other hand to stop the driver from hitting him, pushing him back.

The man that Calder had struck gave a groan of rage and caught Calder in a bear hug, lifting him off his feet.

Crazy Bitch's jaw dropped when Calder slapped his hands over the man's ears so hard that he dropped him. Calder then swung the other man by the hand then grabbed him by the belt. He threw him over the side of the truck into the bed.

She grinned when she heard the slam of the man's body on the hard metal.

Before the larger man could regain his equilibrium, Calder threw him into the bed on top of the other one.

"You okay?" Calder shouted to the driver who had been beaten.

"Yes, I think so."

When the men started to raise their heads again, Calder turned his attention back to them.

"You want more?"

"No. We were just kidding around."

"Then you're in luck. I like kidding around, too." Calder climbed into the truck, slamming the door closed.

"What are you doing?" The men started pounding on the back window.

Calder stuck his head out the window. "Having fun," he answered as he maneuvered the truck into a grassy bank.

She expected to see him brake as it started rolling down the hill. He didn't.

He opened the door and jumped. Onlookers went to watch the truck come to a stop as Calder came back to his bike.

"Hold on."

Her smile slipped at his warning as he passed the car then went onto the grass to pass the line of cars.

She had known he was a good rider, but the skill he used to weave on and off the road surprised her.

When the shoulder turned to gravel, she felt the wheels skidding onto the road. He skillfully pulled the bike out of the skid to ride smoothly as he passed vehicles trying to get into the fairgrounds.

She jumped off the bike as soon as he found a spot, filled with unspent adrenaline. Making pretend karate chops, she said, "Those pussies are lucky you made me stay on the bike. I would have"—she gave a swish of her hand in a downward arc—"kicked their asses."

"Whoa… Bruceina Lee, you don't even know karate."

"Those big bullies wouldn't have known the difference when I was done with them," she declared, giving another of her swishes that had Calder leaning his head back to avoid getting inadvertently chopped in the throat.

"If I'd known you would get so excited about men getting their asses kicked, I would have done it before."

"Hot thang"—she jerked him toward her heaving breasts by his T-shirt—"you have no idea how hot it makes me." She pressed a passionate kiss to his lips, thrusting her tongue into his mouth. She tongue-fucked him as if there weren't people walking past them.

"Get a room!" one outraged woman yelled scornfully as her family passed.

She tore her mouth away from Calder's, but didn't release him from her grasp. "I will when I check out the rides here." She gave the uppity bitch a brazen wink.

Turning back to Calder, she kissed him again before breaking away. "I'm going to fuck your brains out when we get to the hotel."

Letting him go, she started in the direction of the entrance. She made it two steps before she found herself swept off her feet and flung over Calder's shoulder.

"Fuck the clue. Let's find the hotel."

She playfully started hitting him on his back, trying to wiggle off his shoulder.

"Need some help?"

Crazy Bitch got a head rush when Calder set her back down at Winter's offer. She tugged down her T-shirt under her jacket as The Last Riders stared at her in amusement.

"I guess you figured it out."

At the sarcasm in Calder's question, she turned as the men eyed each other.

"I guess you did, too." Viper's lips quirked in a smile. "I thought you would have beaten us here. We would have already been here, but some asswipe had the traffic stopped."

She had been so busy watching Calder she hadn't realized they had been in the line behind them.

"We took the same shortcut you did. Of course, a couple of the newbies are going to have to call Train to come get their bikes out of the ditches."

They started walking as they talked. Usually, she would fall back and walk with the women. However, still feeling as if she had drunk two shots of espresso, Crazy Bitch bumped Calder with her shoulder until he lifted an arm around it. Content, she walked alongside him.

Once inside the gate, they all stared at each other, trying to determine if one of them knew what to do next. Then they each started to slip away.

Shrugging, Crazy Bitch suggested to Calder, "We might as well just walk around until we see something. The rodeo doesn't start for another hour."

Out of the corner of her eye, she saw Shade maneuver Lily to the side and into the crowd that was heading toward the arena. Meanwhile, Viper and Winter were practically breathing down their necks as she scanned the amusement rides.

Slipping her arm under Calder's jacket, she sped up her steps so they could get away from any of The Last Riders following them. "Let's ride the Ferris wheel."

"You want to ride the Ferris wheel instead of looking for the clue?"

Raising the volume of her voice so they would be able to hear each other, she looked up, giving him a provocative pout. "Sex Piston and Stud will text us when they find something. So will Fat Louise and T.A. Why not have some fun?"

"I'm game if you are." He turned them toward the line for the Ferris wheel.

Pretending to stare up at Calder as if she wanted to fuck him there, she watched The Last Riders move away.

"You know, this is a side of you I haven't seen before; I'm digging it." Calder lowering his head to nuzzle the side of her neck had her absently going on her tiptoes to look over his shoulders, relieved when she saw Viper and Winter backtracking to go in the direction Shade and Lily had gone.

"Mmhmm, later, hot thang. Let's go before they come back." Her attitude changed in the blink of an eye. "Let's find the barn where they're keeping the horses and bulls."

She didn't miss the crestfallen expression that crossed his handsome face.

Crazy Bitch toned down her excitement at the thrill of trying to beat so many to the clue while keeping them moving briskly through the crowd.

"After we find the clue, I'll fuck you all night. But first, we need to find it."

"I don't need all night. Right now, I'd feel pretty good with ten minutes."

"Ten minutes wouldn't get me started."

"Try."

Crazy Bitch saw the roped-off area she was looking for, ignoring the smoldering flames in Calder's eyes. Ducking underneath the rope, she raised it for Calder so he wouldn't have to bend down so far.

"Thanks."

"You're welcome." Grinning, she took off before they could be stopped by any of the workers.

When she nearly stepped in a pile of horse shit, she mentally cursed Greer. If she wrecked her boots, he would be the one cleaning the crap off, right after she used one to kick his ass.

"Watch where you step," she warned Calder.

He wasn't any happier than she was at the sight and smells of the animals that had been brought to the fair for the rodeo.

"How in the fuck are we supposed to know what we're looking for?" His nostrils flared as a horse on the side of the fence crapped. He hurried away so fast she had trouble keeping up with him.

"Slow down," she laughingly called after him.

Indignantly, he turned around to face her. "I'm about ready to call it quits and build myself another bike. And if I hadn't bet my jacket, I would."

"Calm down. It's only a little shit and piss." She sniggered.

As they turned a corner, her laughter died. Shade and Lily were walking in front of them.

"Hide." His whisper had them searching for a place to keep from being seen.

"There." Crazy Bitch pointed at a stack of hay.

The two of them managed to hide before Shade or Lily were able to see them.

"Excuse me, do you have a pass? This area is off limits." A tall man wearing a hat stopped Shade and Lily.

"I just wanted to see the horses."

Crazy Bitch rolled her eyes heavenward at the man's face when Lily smiled up at him.

"Would you like me to show you around?"

"I wouldn't want to take up your time."

"No trouble. I have twenty minutes before I need to get ready. My name's Reno."

"I would have bet a twenty on that being his name," Crazy Bitch muttered.

"Shh… Shade will hear you." Calder pushed her head down when Shade turned to look toward them.

"He's probably trying to find a place to stuff Reno's body."

"My name's Lily, and this is Shade, my husband."

The man's face had Crazy Bitch putting a hand over her mouth. Poor Reno couldn't hide his disappointment.

Neither man made a move to shake each other's hand.

"Like I said, no one is supposed to be back here without a pass." The cowboy gave a shrill whistle that had several men coming toward them with bright yellow shirts.

Shade went taut. "My wife just wanted a chance to get a look at the horses. Horses frighten her, and I was trying to show her there wasn't any reason to be afraid." The protective arm that went around Lily's shoulder had the security hesitating. "I promised her when my unit was no longer on call that I'd take a vacation out west."

Reno gave Shade a speculative glance. "You're in the service?"

"Yes, I'm in the Navy."

"Why would you have to take her out west to see horses? Kentucky is known for their horses."

"Kentucky doesn't have cowboys."

Shade's response had Lily blushing and trying to tug her husband away.

"No, they don't." The cowboy's laughter had Lily turning

violet, stormy eyes on her husband, promising him retribution when she got him alone.

"Clint, give Lily and Shade a quick tour." Reno touched the brim of his hat. "Ma'am, nice meeting you both."

As Reno and the rest of the security walked past them, Crazy Bitch didn't miss the look Lily gave the cowboy. Neither did Shade.

Crazy Bitch wished she could be invisible in their bedroom that night. Both of them would be out for payback.

A lanky young man introduced himself before leading the couple down the long row of horses.

"These are the horses that are used for the trick roping. That's Sunset, Blaze, and Sapphire. These two horses are used for the barrel racing." Clint ran a gentle hand over a brown nuzzle. "This is Buster and Dusty."

They moved farther away so it became difficult to hear him. Crazy Bitch was about to tell Calder they were wasting their time when Lily and Shade's guide stopped at a solid black horse.

"And this is the star of the show. He's Reno's Cactus."

Crazy Bitch and Calder sharply turned toward each other. She was so excited she wanted to jump up and down. Calder, seeing her reaction, grabbed her arm, holding her in place.

"Hurry. They aren't watching." He jerked her up from their hiding spot.

They were so intent on getting away before Shade and Lily saw them that they almost ran into Sex Piston and Stud. The couple took one look at their excited faces and turned back in the direction they had come from.

"You found the clue?" Sex Piston shuffled forward, trying to keep up with them in her high heels.

"Let's go. We can talk about it outside in the parking lot. I don't want any of The Last Riders overhearing us."

"There are thousands of people here. They aren't going to hear anything over these loud speakers."

"We need to go to the parking lot, anyway." Crazy Bitch didn't break her stride, forcing the other three to follow behind her. "We need to hurry. Shade and Lily will be behind us, and when they introduce Reno and his horse, all three clubs will be going there, too. If we're lucky, we'll get there first."

Once they were outside, they took a second to catch their breaths.

"The star of the show is a horse named Cactus. Look around at the names of the sections of the parking lot." The one closest to them was a wooden barrel, the next over was a cowgirl grinning down at the parking lot with a lasso swinging over her head.

Sex Piston and Stud grinned back at them.

"Guess which section we parked in?" Crazy Bitch proudly beamed as if they had planned it that way.

"Quit bragging. It's not like you knew that when you parked." Sex Piston reached down to take her heels off so she could keep up with them.

"It's a lucky charm. We're going to win this son of a fucking game!" Her jubilation came to an abrupt halt when they reached the section where Calder's bike was parked.

"What now?" Stud looked around the rows of vehicles.

"I don't know." Crazy Bitch started to walk down the row then stopped. Gazing around, she went to the lamppost. "Calder, lift me up."

"What?"

"Lift me up. I'll shimmy up and see if I can spot anything."

He looked like he was going to argue.

"You might as well. If she doesn't do it, they'll make one of us, and I don't know about you, but I don't want to get my balls burned sliding down that pole."

Calder lifted her up at Stud's reasoning. He had plans for when they got to their hotel room, and that didn't include getting an ice pack.

She would have made a joke about it, but she was too busy climbing up the pole.

Staring around their section, not knowing what she was searching for, she was about to slide back down when she saw it.

Sliding down, she felt Calder's hands circle her waist when she came within reach.

"There are construction barrels at the end of the rows that have little different-colored flags tied to another light pole. I don't know if that's what we're looking for, but we should check it out."

When they reached the construction barrel, they saw it was flat on top so no clue could be hidden inside. She and Sex Piston stepped back as Calder and Stud tried to turn it over without success.

"Fuck!" Calder groaned when the barrel couldn't be moved.

"It's filled with water," Crazy Bitch informed them.

The others turned to look at her.

Calder tried to move it again, exasperated. "How in the fuck do you know that?"

"Road crews fill them with water so the wind from passing motorists won't send the barrels flying."

"Who told you that?"

Crazy Bitch stared down at her fingernails to avoid the curious gazes of her friends. "Remember when I used to have that sweet little firecracker red Jetta that I bought used? Saved four months for that ride."

Sex Piston's brow furrowed. "I thought you said you totaled it when you hit a deer on the way to work."

"I might have lied about that." Shrugging, she circled the

barrel, thoughtfully trying to figure out where Greer could have hidden the clue. If Greer's wife hadn't told Diamond about how diabolical he was about hiding his pot, she would have started over to look somewhere else.

"Maybe we should spread out and see if he spray-painted something under one of the cars," Sex Piston suggested.

"He could want us to look at the numbers of the parking spots." Stud bent down to peer at the number next to them.

"I don't think so. Greer isn't smart enough to add past ten," Crazy Bitch said, only half-joking. She was becoming frustrated as she tried to shove the barrel herself.

Just then, a gust of wind sent the small plastic flags waving, one hitting her cheek. Irritated, she smacked it away. Lifting her eyes, she pulled her head back so she wouldn't be hit again. Then she narrowed her eyes at the one closest to her.

Each one of the flags was a different color. Crazy Bitch had thought the flags were there to draw attention to the barrel. However, as she reached out to grab one, examining it carefully, she saw the flags had a strip of Velcro keeping them attached to the thin rope.

Ripping the flag off, she used her finger to trace the seam of the nylon fabric, pulling it apart. As it did, a slip of paper fell out into her hand. She read it aloud.

"The ground beneath me is frozen. No kings or queens live here. You can enter my gates, but unless you have an invitation, you won't be allowed to stay and rescue the damsel."

As soon as she was finished reading it, she put the flag and the clue in her pocket.

"You're not going to put it back for the others to find?" Stud gave her a disappointed glare.

"Chill." She reached out, pulling off another flag and giving it to Sex Piston. "I was wrong. Greer can count.

There's a flag for each of the teams. Who knew the fucker could count that high?"

"I did." Shade came from behind a truck to take the red flag. Lily came out of hiding, giving them a guilty expression.

"How long have you been listening?" Crazy Bitch drilled with accusation as Viper and Winter also came out.

"Since you climbed the pole." Viper tore one off for him and Winter. "Didn't see the need for all of us having to do it."

"I see how you are—doing sneaky shit to try to win. It's just a game…" Feeling self-righteous, she was about to read them the riot act when Shade cut her off at the knees.

"You mean sneaky shit like when you and Calder hid behind the hay?"

The arrogant biker actually gave her a smile she had never seen on his cold face before.

Damn, if she wasn't so into Calder, and if he wasn't married, she would do him.

Calder snapped his fingers in front of her face. "See something you want?"

His masculine pride had been offended; she could tell by the hurt in his eyes.

Shrugging, she raised her arms to twine them around his neck. "FYI, I was just admiring Shade's tattoos."

"You weren't staring at his tattoos." Calder didn't respond to her hug. "I have tattoos. I don't see you staring at mine like that."

"Don't have to. I have yours memorized."

"Really?" His face softened and he wrapped his arms around her waist.

"Sure, hot thang."

"You okay, Sex Piston?" Stud asked in concern when she placed a hand over her mouth.

"I'm fine. I'm just trying to keep from barfing."

18

"You going to pout all night? We could be getting it on instead of me watching you watch the news. I even packed my new nightie." She bounced off the bed where she had been posing without success to get a rise out of the still peeved biker.

"Sex Piston was just joking. I never figured you'd be so fucking jealous-natured. You don't see me all torn up because you looked at Lily." She took off her sexy nightie, throwing it down on her suitcase before rummaging through the contents for her favorite shorts and tank top.

"I wasn't looking at Lily like you were Shade. Why are you changing your clothes?"

"Because I was tired of waiting for you to notice that I was looking damn fine. You put me in a bad mood. I don't want to fuck anymore." She went to the side of the bed he was sitting on. "Roll over."

"What if I want to fuck?"

"Then you should have thought of that before I changed my mind. You snooze, you lose. Roll over."

Calder scooted over in the bed, giving her room to get in.

"I didn't know there was a time limit."

"What you didn't count on"—she lay down, pushing the pillow under her head after giving it a hard whack—"was that I wouldn't kiss your ass to make you feel better. Turn out the light." She yawned. "I told Sex Piston I would have breakfast with them in the morning."

"That's another thing that hur—pissed me off. Why didn't you include me when you mentioned having breakfast with Stud and his family?"

She gave a louder yawn. "She wants to eat at eight because Star and Harley wake up early. I had planned for you to be unable to move in the morning, much less drag your ass out of bed."

The television was turned off, but the light wasn't.

"I'm sorry."

Crazy Bitch felt the bed dip as he slid closer to her, settling his chin on her shoulder.

"S'all right. Good night. Turn off the light." She shrugged her shoulder out from under his chin.

"I mean it. I took the fun out of us finding the clue. Let me make it up to you." He caressed his hand down her spine to cup her ass.

"I'm not in the mood anymore."

"But I'm really, really sorry." He kissed the curve of her shoulder that met her neck, sending goose bumps down her back.

"I even bought you a present when I bought my nightie." She carefully poured more guilt on him. "I had planned for us to have a lot of fun with it." She turned her head farther into her pillow to keep him from seeing her smug smile.

Men were such suckers. Give them what they want, and they don't want it. Take it away, and they will beg for it. She had no intention of going to sleep without getting a little something, something.

"I really liked that nightie. Where'd you get it from?"

Her desire to play it cool hit a snag when he started massaging one of her ass cheeks through the soft material of her shorts.

"Shade's sister Penni had a lingerie party when she came for a visit a couple of months ago."

His hand stopped moving. "How did you buy me a present when you bought it two months ago?"

"I didn't technically know it was you I was buying it for."

"It can't be called a present if you didn't buy it for a particular person."

Shit, he was getting angry again. Calder had more mood swings than a woman on PMS.

"Yes, it can, if it's still brand-new and in the wrapper."

"What is it?"

"Something you damn sure won't be unwrapping tonight." She jabbed him in the stomach to make him start massaging her ass again.

The soft laugh he gave as he used his chin to move her hair away from the nape of her neck had her thrusting her butt back toward him until she felt the rigid length of his cock nestled against her.

He curled his arm around her waist to cup her breast and push her back farther.

"I have a present for you, too, and I didn't buy it two months ago." He groaned, using his body weight to pin her down to the mattress until she was lying facedown.

She curled her fingers into the pillow. She wasn't crazy about this position. In fact, she hated it. She hated not being in control and felt like she was being smothered.

"Get off!" It was everything not to scream at him. Luckily, he moved away immediately.

"What happened?" Calder sat up next to her, staring at her worriedly.

"I felt like I was being smothered."

He frowned at her as she tried to gather control of her breathing. "Did someone hurt you?"

"No, it's weird. I've never been able to enjoy that position. I don't know why."

"You didn't have trouble when I laid on top of you when I fucked you last time."

"Because I could see and know what you were going to do next."

Calder fell back on top of the bed in a burst of laughter. "You're a Dominant."

"You're crazy if you think that."

"Don't worry; it doesn't bother me. As long as you don't use a whip on me." He playfully pulled one of her nipples into his mouth. Giving it a swipe of his tongue, he released it. "Or a paddle." His mouth went to her other breast, sucking her other nipple into his mouth. Her hands went to the mattress above her shoulders.

"I… am… not… a… dominant." She had trouble getting the words out of her thick throat. Her large breasts had always been as sensitive as her clit. That Calder was playing with them by tugging and nipping had her nearly ready to climax.

When he released her nipple to seek the curve of the one closest to him, she felt him bite into the plump flesh.

"You still want to go to sleep?"

"I'm reconsidering it."

He laved the small indentions he had made in her skin. "I used to think about your tits every night when I was in prison."

"That must have made for an uncomfortable night."

"It was the only way I could get to sleep—thinking of you. Did you think about me when I was gone?"

She didn't want to admit the truth, but she had heard the vulnerability in his voice.

"Yes." She slid her fingers through his silky hair before sliding down to his neck. His powerful muscles were so thick she could trace each one with her fingertips.

"When Stud wrote to me that you had hooked up with Joker, I spent three days in solitary confinement. I was so jealous I picked a fight with the worst motherfuckers in my cell block."

"Who won?"

"Who do you think won? There were three of them."

"I think you did." She moved her hands back to his hair, using it to tug his head back so she could kiss him. He opened his mouth, letting her sink her tongue inside and explore.

"Take off your shorts," he demanded, twisting his mouth away.

Lifting her hips up, she took off her shorts, throwing them over her shoulder.

"I want to taste you."

She bent her head, expecting him to kiss her mouth, and was surprised when he spanned his hands across her waist, lifting her up and raising her over him until her pussy was straddling his face. When she held on to the headboard, he lowered her to his waiting mouth.

The first feel of his tongue sliding between her damp cleft had her moaning. Engulfing tides of lust stormed her body.

She hadn't fucked a man since Joker, too afraid of making another mistake like he had put her through.

Calder scraped his teeth over her clit, making her jump. He held her in place as he worked feverishly to build her desire that was already sending climaxing tingles through her body.

When he thrust his tongue inside, she lost it, giving in to

the orgasm that had her giving a startled scream at its intensity.

She started to move off him, but again, the strength in his arms held her as he started rebuilding her passion, driving his tongue through her pussy as if he was searching for liquid gold that only he could find.

Racked with the aftermath of her orgasm, each movement sent her sensitized muscles quivering again until her thighs trembled as they grew tired of holding her poised over his ravaging mouth.

Calder didn't just go down on a woman; the man went to town, not leaving any part of her neglected.

"When you come this time, I want you to say my name."

"Huh?" Foggy-headed, she could barely remember her own name. Every twist and turn of his tongue had her breasts heaving while she tried to catch her breath.

"I want you to say my name when you come." Each word was like a lash against her clit. The last one sent her into another climax that didn't have her saying his name. She was screaming it to the wall her face was pasted against.

"Calder! Calder!"

She had every intention of sinking down to the bed when she came down, but Calder didn't give her time. No sooner had her ass hit the mattress than he raised her until she was on her knees in front of him.

"You have a problem with this position?" he grunted, placing his cock at her entrance.

"Not as long as you don't pin me down and you have a condom on that bad boy."

"Fucking hell."

Her shoulders shook when she felt him get off the bed to search for his jeans. Then she felt him get back on the bed after putting the condom on.

"Next week, I'm getting a fucking blood test." He rubbed

his cock against her pussy before driving forward into her. It had her shaking as the large head struggled to enter before sliding inside with a lunge of Calder's hips.

"Just so you know, if I find you giving it to anyone but me, and that includes the sluts at the Blue Horsemen's clubhouse, you'll be going back to condoms forever, *if* I give it to you again at all, which I doubt. I gave Fat Louise hell for taking Cade back after he cheated. She'd never let me live it down."

"Jesus, I'm trying to fuck you. Don't warn me about cheating on you when I'm still inside you. It's not like I'm going to fuck you then jump out of bed to go fuck another woman," he complained, driving higher inside her.

"I'm just saying… Oh God, do that again!"

He was pumping his cock into her like a steamroller, surging through tissue that was still sensitive after two orgasms.

"This?" He brought his hands to her breasts, clasping them in a hard grip that held her steady as he fucked her with thrusts that had the large wooden bed rocking on the floorboards.

Jerky movements within her had her calling out his name again as she shoved her ass backward, wanting to catch the climax that was tantalizing within reach.

"Sweet, sweet Anna-Kate."

It was the sound of her name on his lips that sent her tumbling down the winding path of desire he had driven her toward with every sigh, moan, and move of his body.

He finally allowed her to fall to the bed, falling to the side.

Rolling over, she stared up at the ceiling. How in the hell was a woman supposed to get over being fucked by a man like that?

"Damn." She reached over and turned off the light.

"What's wrong?" His hand went to her pussy possessively. "Did I leave you hanging?"

"No, you're on my side of the bed and I'm too tired to move."

He lifted her over him, switching sides with her. "Better?"

"Yeah, now let me go to sleep."

She let him place an arm around her without pulling away.

He should go back to prison. Stealthily, he had crawled beneath her guard until she wasn't sure she would be able to get him out again. Bit by bit, he was stealing another part of her heart. Each part was one she had sworn never to trust another man with.

Her survival instincts were telling her to run, not to allow herself to get closer, but she worried it was too late.

She wanted a husband and kids. She even wanted a fucking dog. She was going to have to risk her heart to get the prize she wanted, and Calder was a prize.

He wasn't perfect, but he was sexy as fuck, made her laugh, and most importantly, he had made her come three times in one night. Men like that were few and far between—she should know. She'd had her share of needle dicks who thought their dicks were made of steel, only to see them wilting like a tulip when the time came for them to perform.

She liked a man who could get it up and keep it up. A man who gave her hope in mankind. Her last dud still rankled with her, but hopefully she had seen the last of Sam after her unexpected trip to his workplace.

Men hated to be embarrassed, and lowlifes like him hated to have their dirty laundry aired in public.

She would never forget when she was nine years old and her mother had loaded her into their car. She had explained how her current boyfriend hadn't been home for two nights and they were out of groceries. Now that she was older, she realized what her mother had wanted was money for her drugs, but back then, she was just a kid and took everything her mother said at face value.

When they had showed up at her boyfriend's work, he had quickly grabbed their arms and led them out of the loading dock and back outside. When her mother started yelling at him that she needed to feed her, he hastily took out his wallet and gave her several twenties without a word.

Of course, he broke up with her that night after he got off work, but her mother was too high to care, and neither did she. She hated the mean son of a bitch. He didn't care that her mother wanted the money. What he cared about was that, when she had gone to the loading dock, she had done it with the shiny black bruise that covered half her face. He had only cared about how his coworkers had gazed at her sympathetically.

One thing she knew for sure was that Calder had never laid his hand on a woman. She had seen him with Candi, and if he had ever hit her, the whole club would have known. There had been a couple times she had wanted to deck her herself. However, Calder had shown his restraint where women were concerned. He hadn't even badmouthed her when she had turned over state evidence to take a plea to get out of jail time, while Calder had done hard time for the drug buy that had landed him in jail.

The only reason Candi was still in prison now was because she had kidnapped Star.

Crazy Bitch was glad she was still in prison. She was far enough away from Calder that he wouldn't be tempted to resume the way of life he had lived with her. Although, she was pretty sure Calder would remain clean. Still, he damn sure didn't need her dangling a carrot in front of him, and Candi would.

"You asleep?"

"Yes," she answered, drawn out of her thoughts by his whispered question.

"You want to order a pizza?"

"I'm sleeping."

"Let's order a pizza and watch a dirty movie," he cajoled.

Crazy Bitch sat up in bed, reaching for the remote. She might be getting too old to enjoy all-nighters like she had when she was nineteen, but she wasn't dead yet.

19

C alder set the orange juice down in front of Star then placed the coffee down beside his plate before sitting, scooting his chair forward.

He was eating his toast when Crazy Bitch showed up at the table, glaring at him.

"You're an hour late," Sex Piston blasted her as soon as Crazy Bitch sat down.

His grin widened when she gave him a harassed look.

"I was sabotaged."

He pretended innocence when Sex Piston caught his grin. "Don't blame me. That extra slice of pizza kept you up all night."

When Crazy Bitch's eyes went to the kids sitting innocently at the table then turned back to his, he didn't miss the promise of retaliation in them.

"Try the blueberry pancakes," he suggested as the waitress approached the table.

"I'll just take coffee."

The waitress left after giving him and Stud covert looks under her false eyelashes.

"You don't want the breakfast buffet?" Calder poured a generous amount of blueberry syrup on his pancakes.

"I'm still full from last night's. How many plates did you eat?"

"A couple," he admitted. "I'm a growing boy."

"Yes, you are." Crazy Bitch leaned over, placing her hand on his thigh under the table while giving him a possessive kiss.

His hand went to the back of her neck, prolonging the kiss before she could move away. He let her go when the waitress left again after placing the coffee cup down.

"Better?" he whispered when he let her go. His bitch hadn't missed the waitress trying to lure him away from the table.

"Yes," she said, straightening away from him but leaving her hand on his thigh.

The intimate touch made him feel as if he was ten feet tall, and he was still seated at the table. The effect she had on him was better than any high he had ever experienced.

"What's the plan for the day?" Clearly satisfied that her possessive touch had been noticed, Crazy Bitch turned back to Sex Piston.

"Sit still, Harley. We'll go to the pool when we're finished eating." The fidgeting boy resumed his seat at his father's order. "We promised the kids the whole day and night. Any luck with the clue last night?"

Calder linked his hand with Crazy Bitch's. "I googled several castles in Kentucky. I knew about the one in Versailles. I've passed it when I've gone to see Gavin and wanted to take the scenic route. There are two in Louisville, one in northern Kentucky, and one in Guthrie."

Stud nodded. "We should split up tomorrow. Sex Piston and I can take the one in Guthrie, T.A. and Bear can take the one in northern Kentucky since it's the farthest away,

Jane and Cade can take the two in Louisville, and you and Anna-Kate can take the one in Versailles. What do you think?"

Calder knew Crazy Bitch wasn't happy with the suggestion. She wanted first dibs on the clues, even though she hadn't minded sharing up until now because the clues had been just leading them to other clues. As they were hopefully drawing closer to the end of the game, she wanted to be able to find the next clue first in case it was the final one that would lead them to winning the motorcycles.

He looked toward Crazy Bitch, giving her the option to refuse. He was willing to play it any way she wanted.

"We can hang out with them today. I'll call and see if the Versailles castle is open tomorrow."

"We can stay the night if they have any openings. I promised Gavin I would see him on Monday. If it's okay with you, we can go see him together. He wants to meet you."

"I'd like to meet him, too. Mondays are usually slow. I can reschedule the two I have, unless you need me?" she asked Sex Piston.

"No. Go for it. Stud and I are going to take the kids to the pool for a while. You want to come, or you just want to meet up when we're ready to go to the rodeo?" Sex Piston asked as she gathered her purse and Stud took care of the check.

"You have Meri and Keri to help you at the pool. Calder and I will catch up on our sleep until it's time to leave."

Sex Piston waited until Stud left with the kids before giving him and Crazy Bitch an envious look. "Next time I go on a road trip, I'm leaving the kids at home so we can fuck our brains out. Enjoy it while you can." With that, she took off to catch up with her family.

Calder became amused when Crazy Bitch turned red with embarrassment at Sex Piston's mention of the two of them having a family in the future. He thought she would have laughed it off. Instead, she turned serious as they walked back to their room.

"You ever think of having kids?"

Calder tossed the key card onto the dresser below the television then emptied out his pockets to give himself time to think. He wanted to tell her about his suspicions that Star was his child, but he was worried she would say something to Sex Piston. They were as close as sisters—all the women in the crew were. Until he was ready to broach the subject to Stud, he thought it would be best not to say anything.

"I think about it all the time," he answered honestly. "Every time I see how Stud is. I used to think I wanted at least three or four. As I get older, the number goes down to one or two." He watched as she sat down on the end of the bed.

"I want two. A boy and a girl. I want a dog, too."

Calder leaned back on the dresser, folding his arms across his chest. "What kind of dog?"

"I thought I would let the man pick the breed since I'm going to make him get one." She reached down to take her boots off, avoiding his eyes.

"I like dogs, too, and I wouldn't mind having one of each, either." He dropped his arms, pushing her back on the bed and placing a hand on each side of her.

"You want one of each breed?"

"No. One dog, one boy, and one girl." With his thumb at the corner of her mouth, he parted her lips. "I want to fuck you again. All this talk of babies is making me horny."

"Whoa... not so fast, hot thang." She waved her hand in front of his face. "I'm going to have a ring on my hand before I get a baby in my belly."

He raised himself up, unbuttoning her jeans and pulling them down her legs. Her tiny panties were so small they barely covered her waxed mound. He decided to leave them on as he took off her top, exposing the bra that just covered her nipples.

"Woman, a man could come just looking at you in your underwear." He stuck one of his fingers in his mouth then took it out before he slid the brief thong to the side to play with her clit.

He watched as she twisted on his finger, grinding her pussy down onto his hand. It was fucking beautiful watching her give herself to him without embarrassment. She was a desirable woman who enjoyed sex.

Crazy Bitch didn't fake an embarrassment she didn't feel, nor did she pretend to be something she wasn't. She had the healthiest attitude toward sex that he had ever seen in a woman.

He looked down at her tits spilling from her bra, muttering underneath his breath.

"What did you say?" She lifted liquid pools of desire to his.

"I said, thank you, God." He removed his finger to take his clothes off, not forgetting to grab a condom this time.

"You're not going to need that." She seductively got off the bed to take it out of his hand.

"I've died and gone to Heaven."

She laughed, shaking her head as she pushed him back on the bed.

His cock was already hard after finger-fucking her. At her show of dominance, he splayed his arms on the bed.

"I'm yours, baby. Do what you will with me." He enthusiastically waited for her to sink down on his dick.

The smoldering gaze she gave him as she went to her luggage sent his arousal pointing toward the ceiling.

Thinking she was grabbing a lubricant, or one of those gels that were advertised on the television, he felt a drop of pre-cum slide down the head of his ready cock.

The package she pulled out of her suitcase had him lifting onto his elbows to stare.

"What's that? If that's an anal plug, we're going to have a real problem."

She rolled her eyes at him as she finally succeeded in opening the package. "Hot thang, let's both agree that both of our backdoors are off-limits for butt plugs."

He instantly agreed, becoming even more worried about the strange object she was fiddling with at the bottom of the bed when she took out her phone.

He grabbed a pillow, covering his dick. "I'm not into pictures, either."

"Sexually, you're a wimp; you know that?"

"I can live knowing that." He pressed the pillow farther down onto his lap as she determinedly moved closer.

Her hand on her hip, she said, "It's not going to hurt." She lifted up what she was holding for him to get a better look.

"What is it?"

"Haven't you seen a vibrator before? This is male version of one. Penni developed it after she and Jackal were using a feminine one that can be electronically controlled. She said they had so much fun that she drew up the design for a male version."

Calder kept one hand protectively over his crotch as he took the device from Crazy Bitch's hand to examine it. It looked like a thong with a pouch attached to the front. He rubbed the strange material between his fingers; it felt like spongy rubber.

"Try it on." As she tried to take his pillow away, he tried to give the contraption back. "Come on... pretty please?" She sat down next to him on the bed, rubbing her breasts coaxingly against his arm.

"Did Jackal like it?" he asked suspiciously.

"She said he hasn't tried it yet. It's in the testing phase. She had one of The Last Riders make it from her drawings."

"My dick is not going to be a guinea pig for that contraption."

"I'm sure The Last Rider who made it tested it out."

"Which one made it?"

"She wouldn't tell me, but I know it wasn't Shade. Penni said she was too afraid he would set the setting to stun if he knew she wanted it for Jackal."

"Penni's the same one who tried to kill Killyama twice?"

"She didn't mean to. They were accidents." She explained before going back to their original topic. "Knox made the app to control it by phone. It wouldn't do anything that hurt anyone; he's a sheriff."

"No." He shook his head for extra effectiveness.

"Come on. If you don't like it, you can take it off."

He kept telling her no, but she wouldn't stop trying to whittle him down.

"Look… I'll set it on the beginner's mode."

Calder flushed at being called a beginner. "What if I…? You know… What if…?"

Crazy Bitch stared at him without comprehension when he couldn't come out and say what he was worried about happening.

Calder cleared his throat. "What if I… get…? What if I… come?"

When she laughed, she pressed her breasts tighter against him. "It's leak-proof and washable. Please?"

"Jesus… Just once, and you damn sure better not tell anyone. And the next gadget you bring into the bedroom better be meant for you."

"Yeah, yeah. You're such a whiney baby."

Reluctantly, he let her remove the pillow, seeing the disappointment on her face.

"What's wrong?" He looked down at his lap to see he had lost his erection.

Her face brightened as she handed him the toy. "Maybe it'll make you hard again."

"Don't count on it." Feeling ridiculous, he put it on while inwardly blasting himself for giving in. There wasn't a woman on earth he would wear it for, other than her.

"Lie back and relax." She prodded him farther up on the bed. "Ready?"

She picked up her cell phone. He didn't like the way she was grinning at him.

"Wait! What setting is it on?" Becoming panicked, he moved his hand to cover his dick.

"Calm down. It's on Beginner. This is supposed to be fun. You look like I'm about to chop your dick off."

"Wait! You sure you're still not mad over me standing you up?"

"I told you I was."

"Wha—"

He broke off at the feel of the vibrations going through his cock. It felt like a gentle mouth sucking him. It wasn't half-bad. In fact, it was better than some of the halfhearted blowjobs he had received.

"You like it?" Crazy Bitch jumped on the bed beside him. "Never mind. I can see you do!" She chuckled.

He lifted his arms to support his neck, surprised to see his cock start to fill out the rubber glove.

Crazy Bitch lay down next to him, running her hand back and forth over his chest, aiding the stimulation he was experiencing.

"It's not bad."

She raised her head off his chest to lick his nipple. "You ready to go up a level?"

"Sure."

"It has four levels: beginner, intermediate, advanced, and expert. Which one you want to try?"

"Since it's experimental, we should try them all. Don't you think?"

"Absolutely. Here comes intermediate." She swiped her finger across the screen of her cell phone.

He stiffened when the glove tightened around his cock. His erection stiffened further as the vibrations became more intense until he could feel it on his balls. It felt like a more dedicated cocksucker.

Crazy Bitch climbed on top of him, rubbing her tits against his chest as she placed her hands on his shoulders to steady herself while she kissed him.

She slid her tongue between his lips, heightening his arousal. He would rather be fucking her pussy, but it wasn't bad.

"You doing okay?" she mumbled against his lips.

"Yes." He held her closer. "Go to level three."

She grabbed her phone, switching settings, and immediately he started sweating.

This setting had the glove tightening even more. It wasn't painful, but it was tight. This one felt like a cocksucker who didn't like sucking cock. He fucking loved it.

He brought his hand to her neck, increasing the pressure of her mouth on his.

He tried to gather his control, determined not to come in the toy. He tried to think of the alphabet backward so he wouldn't.

"You ready for the last level?" Crazy Bitch raised the phone as if she was about to swipe the screen again.

"No. That's enough for now. Let's save the last level for another time," he choked out, seconds away from coming. "Move so I can take it off."

She moved to the side to give him enough room to take the toy off, dropping the phone onto the bed.

"Come on, hot thang." Parting her legs, she stared up at him expectantly.

He moved to tug the toy off when he saw her accidently hit the phone with her hand.

Groaning, his knees buckled as he fell backward on the bed. His mind went blank, unaware he was yelling her name. It took several minutes for him to realize that Crazy Bitch was saying something he couldn't hear.

A sharp smack on his cheek had his senses returning.

"What'd you hit me for?" Rubbing his cheek, he stared at her accusingly.

"It was either that or call nine-one-one. Are you okay?"

"I'm better than okay. Tell Penni if she needs investors, I'll have a couple thousand saved."

"So, you like it?"

"She'll become a millionaire with that toy. Do you know how many men have to beg their honey to suck their dick? This is better than any blowjob I've ever had, and I didn't have to ask for it."

Her enthusiasm for the toy started waning when he asked to look at the app.

"You can even synchronize it to a particular song. Next time, I'm downloading the song I want—"

"Go get cleaned up," she interrupted his future plans with the toy. "You can show me how much you like my present when you come back."

"Oh... okay. I'll be right back."

As he climbed off the bed, his legs felt like jelly. Bracing his legs, assuming it was a side effect of his orgasm, he took a small step forward. He was able to hold his weight, but his cock felt as if it was on fire.

Rushing into the bathroom, he removed the toy then got into the shower, turning the water to as cold as he could get it. Leaning his forehead against the wall, he shuddered as the cold water doused the flames on his cock. It took ten minutes before he felt capable of getting out of the shower and drying off.

Wrapping a towel around his hips, he slowly hobbled out of the bathroom to see Crazy Bitch sitting on the bed, naked and provocatively posed.

Warily, he stopped when she gave him a smoldering gaze, patting the mattress next to her.

"What took you so long, hot thang? I was about to go in there after you."

"Who else bought that toy from Penni?"

She frowned, sitting up. "Technically, I didn't buy it. She gave free samples to me, Sex Piston, T.A, Killyama, and Fat Louise."

"So, you gave me a present you didn't have to pay for." He clenched his hands into fists around the towel, flinching when the movement sent another surge of fire through his dick.

Without a word, he limped back into the bathroom, turning the water back on before getting inside.

He felt the rush of cold air as the shower door opened.

"Shhhhittt!"

Turning, he saw Crazy Bitch staring at his abused cock.

"Get some shorts on. I'm taking you to the hospital." She started to turn the water off, but Calder caught her hand, leaving it running.

"I am not going to the hospital," he grated out through chattering teeth. "I'd rather die."

"What if it rots and falls off?" She started pacing around the bathroom, nearing hysterics. "I don't know if I can marry a man without a dick."

"I don't know if I can marry a woman who wants to make me a eunuch!" he yelled.

"What's a eunuch?"

"Google it!" he shouted then started counting to ten.

His fucking cock felt as if it had been torched. If she didn't leave him alone, he wasn't going to be responsible for his actions.

"Quit being such a drama quee—"

Screeching, she ran out of the bathroom when he made a threatening move toward her, slamming the door behind her.

He remained standing in the shower until he felt the pain was at a manageable level. He held on to the shower door as he got out, moving slowly, afraid the excruciating pain would return.

"Can I come in?" He barely heard Crazy Bitch's request from the other side of the door.

"No."

"I have something I think will make it better. Please?"

He reluctantly opened the door.

"I called Killyama, and she gave me Dr. Price's number."

"*You told Killyama?*" He scowled at her as he tried to move past her.

"I didn't tell her what for. Cool down before you hurt yourself." Taking his arm, she helped him to the bed, raising his feet to the bed when he couldn't.

"Dr. Price says it's a friction burn. He suggested leaving it exposed to the air, but that if you want, I could put some Vaseline on it."

"I didn't pack any in my suitcase." His jaw locked when she sat down on the bed, jiggling his cock.

"I found some in the package with the toy. I'm sorry… I should have read the directions."

Calder angrily turned his face away from her. Even her rubbing his leg soothingly didn't lessen his anger.

"I don't need the Vaseline. I just want to take a nap and forget it happened."

"That might be a little hard to do... at least for a little while. Dr. Price said not to have any sex for a week."

His face jerked back toward her. "That's not going to be a problem!"

"Aw, come on, Calder. I said I was sorry. You enjoyed it. I know you did."

"I might have, but the experience wasn't worth the pain I'm going through now."

"Next time, we'll stop at the third setting."

"There isn't going to be a next time," he snarled. "I threw it away."

"Are you crazy? I told you it was my fault. The Last Riders wouldn't make anything that would hurt anyone."

"How do you know? They could be trying to take us out one dick at a time."

"Now you're being crazy. I don't even know which one helped Penni make it. But don't worry; I'm going to call that bitch. She could have stressed the importance of using the lube."

"When you talk to her, ask which Last Rider helped her develop it. I have a little feedback I want to give him," he snarled, leaning his head back and closing his eyes.

"I will. I promise. Just relax and go to sleep. I'm going out for a few minutes. Here's your phone if you need me before I get back."

He didn't respond, trying to escape the pain by nodding off to sleep.

He heard Crazy Bitch leave the room, thankfully already drifting off.

He was so tired he didn't hear her come back, waking to the steady hum of cool air bathing his body.

Opening his eyes, he saw one large fan blowing on his cock and another small one was on the dresser, aimed at that part of his anatomy.

When he started to rise, he felt a cold cloth slipping off his dick. Before he could pick it up, Crazy Bitch was there, dousing it into a bucket of ice water, then twisting off the excess water before placing it gently back on his lap.

He was able to raise himself without feeling as if his skull was going to explode.

"You did all this while I was sleeping?"

She nodded. "Do you feel better?"

"Yes, thank you."

"I'm sorry, Calder. I promise I'll make it up to you. I've only given you one blowjob, and I admit, I might have half-assed it, but a girl's jaw gets tired—"

"It's okay," he cut her off, not needing the particulars of why he'd had to coax her into the blowjob she had given him the first night they were in the hotel. Her healthy attitude toward sex was too much to take when he was nursing a dick he wasn't sure would ever work again. "Where did you get the fans?"

"I had Stud drive me to the store." When she saw his dark frown, she added, "I told him the air conditioner was out in our room."

"Did he believe it?"

"I don't think so, but he didn't ask any questions. Are you still mad at me?"

His anger slipped away at her show of remorse. "It's a lot better. Don't worry; if we ever decide to get married, I'll be able to perform up to your standards." He hoped.

"What standards?" she teased, lying down next to him and

snuggling against his side. "The only standards I have is that they're breathing."

"That wasn't what you told me in the bathroom."

"Okay, that may be true. Sex is important to a marriage, you know?"

"It's important, but you do know that men do have trouble getting it up when they get older. You going to divorce me if I can't?"

"You're not going to get old. Besides, they make pills for that, so we're good."

He gazed down at her. Joking around about them getting married gave him a fuzzy warmth in his stomach that he had never felt with another woman. He had also never been so comfortable with another woman whom he had actually spent a great deal of time alone with. She came across with an attitude that was in your face, tough enough to grind men under her boot, and was a smart-ass who could rip a man's pride to shreds with one sharp word.

He had also seen her teach a group of little girls to dance gracefully, let Star and Harley call her Aunt Anna-Kate, and wasn't embarrassed to hold a cold compress on his dick.

Taking everything into account, including his sore dick, he came to the firm conclusion she was his kind of woman.

" Are you sure you don't want to go back to the room?" Crazy Bitch asked as they took their seats in the stands.

She smiled, relieved when he took her hand, as the speakers blared, announcing the entrance of the cowboys.

"Mom, can I learn to ride a bull?" Harley asked excitedly from his seat, watching the bull throw a cowboy off its bucking back.

"No." Sex Piston repeated the same answer she had ever since they had taken their seats and the little boy's fascination had built with every skillful maneuver the cowboys were exhibiting for the *oohs* and *aahs* of the crowd.

"Can I buy one of the stuffed horses?"

"You're too old for stuffed animals. You made me give the ones I bought you for Christmas last year away." His disappointed reaction had her relenting. "We can buy one of the tumblers with the picture of the bull."

Harley's face brightened. "Cool."

She and Calder shared a smile at the little boy's happiness.

Meri and Keri were just as enthralled with the cowboys as their brother, but for another reason. They whispered between themselves who was the better-looking and wondered if they had girlfriends.

"Mom, can we go stand at the fence?"

"No." Stud's firm voice had the teenagers' faces falling.

Crazy Bitch couldn't blame them. The men drew the gazes of all the women in the crowd. The ability to best almost two thousand pounds of raging bull that could crush them under their hooves even managed to get her attention.

She was relieved when the two-hour show was finished, noticing that Calder was shifting uncomfortably in his seat. They waited until most of the crowd had left before going down the steps.

"Can we get their autographs?" Meri pleaded, while Keri looked at their parents with silent entreaty.

"I'm not going near that bull poop with my heels on," Sex Piston told Stud when he looked toward her. "You and Calder can take them, and me and Craz—Anna-Kate can wait by the fence."

Crazy Bitch winked at Star and Harley when Sex Piston almost slipped and used her nickname in front of them. Ever since Star had gotten in trouble at school for talking about her to one of her friends, she had started using her given name when she was in public.

"I don't mind. I wouldn't mind getting a few of their autographs, too. Calder can stay with you, and Stud and I can go with them," Crazy Bitch hastily offered, not wanting Calder to walk farther than he had to. She had tried to get him to take a couple of pain relievers, but he had refused.

"You stay here with Sex Piston," Calder said. "You two can go buy the tumblers and meet us back here."

She wanted to argue, but didn't, remembering her promise not to say anything to Sex Piston about his dick. She couldn't understand why he was so uptight about it. It wasn't like Sex Piston would ask for a picture of it.

They found one of the vendors pushing a cart, selling the tumblers near the gate where the cowboys entered the arena. Star and Harley started climbing the fence, watching as the workers began rolling the barrels toward a small truck.

Several children ran out to race alongside the cleaning crew, who were tossing them what was left of the bandanas that had been lobbed out to the crowd earlier in the show.

"Can we go get one?" Harley asked, already climbing down from the fence.

"Go ahead," Sex Piston told them as she paid for the tumblers.

Crazy Bitch watched them run off, deciding to buy two for Meri and Keri.

"Trying to make Calder jealous?" Sex Piston smirked as she took out her wallet.

"They're for Meri and Keri." She held them tightly as she reached for the money she kept in her jacket pocket.

"You going to tell me why you needed Stud to drive you to the store to buy fans?" Her best friend turned so she could keep her eye on Star and Harley and still question her at the same time.

"I told you; our air conditioner went out. The hotel was booked and didn't have another room they could put us in."

"Bitch, Killyama called me and wanted to know why you wanted Dr. Price's number. So, you need to come up with another cock-and-bull story."

She mentally winced at her choice of words. Crazy Bitch knew Sex Piston wouldn't let it drop until her curiosity was satisfied.

"Calder and I got a little carried away last night and this morning when we went back to our room. The man has too much for me to handle, if you know what I mean. I was so sore that I called Dr. Price to see if he could suggest something."

Her lie had Sex Piston gaping at her in astonishment and curiosity.

"How big is he?"

"Big. *Really* big." She wiggled her brows. "The biggest I've ever seen," she boasted, her lie growing with each word.

"Doesn't matter how big it is if he doesn't know how to use it. I bet Stud's is bigger... and better."

Crazy Bitch shook her head, going all-in with her lie. "He knows how to use it. I came four times last night and three times this morning."

"You're shitting me!" Envious eyes stared back at her. "How come the bitches at the club haven't said he's packing heat?"

She shrugged. "Jealous bitches wanted to keep him to themselves."

"Bitches," Sex Piston said, showing her a new respect Crazy Bitch hadn't seen from her before. "It's that big?"

"Bigger."

"Damn. Stud's big, too." Sex Piston elbowed her conspiratorially. "They definitely must be cut from the same cloth." she joked as they started toward the fence to watch Harley and Star get the bandanas.

Terrified screams had them turning toward where Stud and Calder had taken Meri and Keri. The sound sent a chill of fear down Crazy Bitch's spine, especially when she saw a large crowd of people running frantically.

"Fuck!" Crazy Bitch screamed when she saw what they were running from.

Her head spun, trying to find a way out from under the trampling crowd and a pair of bull horns that were hysterically throwing people out of their way. One was heading directly toward them. The other had gone so crazy it was trying to climb the bleachers. The cowboys were running after them, trying to throw ropes over their heads to steer them away from the crowd.

"Get on the bull shoot," she yelled at Sex Piston, taking her arm and starting to run toward it. *"Run!"*

While she was screaming, her foot had slid from the first board. She righted herself then quickly managed to climb up, pulling Sex Piston up with her.

"Do you see Stud? Meri and Keri?" Sex Piston panted, gripping the top of the wooden shoot. They were so focused on the girls being in immediate danger that they took their eyes off Star and Harley for a split-second.

"No... Wait, there they are!" Crazy Bitch yelled when she saw the two men shoving the crying girls through an emergency exit to the left of them.

Hearing a hair-raising scream coming from Sex Piston, she turned toward her to see what she was staring at, afraid the bull they had barely missed had come back. Sex Piston was already climbing down from the shoot.

It was then that Crazy Bitch saw that the bulls had managed to tear down a portion of the fence that the workers had left open to bring the truck inside and were heading toward the group of children. She was watching a nightmare come to life before her own eyes. Sex Piston in her heels didn't stand a chance of reaching Star and Harley.

The rolling eyes of one of the bulls turned toward her as she started down the shoot, holding her in place. She felt death staring her down, freezing her where she stood.

"Get back on the shoot!" Calder shouted as he and Stud ran past them.

Sobs tore through her throat as she was pushed back toward the shoot, forcing Sex Piston to go with her and getting them out of the way of the cowboys who were frantically trying to corral the bulls.

She recognized Reno from the night before, his rough and hard features concentrated on the largest of the bulls. Her eyes went from him to Star and Harley.

The children had scattered when they had seen the bulls, calling for their mothers and fathers. It was heart-wrenching to see many parents running toward them, risking their own lives for their children.

Sex Piston's cries had her covering her hand, holding her back.

"Calder and Stud will get them!" she told her, trying to give her hope. She knew that letting Sex Piston go would make matters worse for the two men.

Star had been knocked down by one of the older children. She was lying on the ground, screaming for Stud.

"Daddy!" Her scream pierced Crazy Bitch's soul as she could only watch helplessly.

Harley bravely helped Star to her feet, only to have the other children push them apart. Harley was being pushed toward Stud and Calder, but Star remained frozen in fear as the bull stomped toward her.

Calder was running so fast he overtook Stud. She heard his yell to Stud to get Harley. Then, with a burst of speed, he darted past the bull, barely missing a flying hoof as Reno ran around the bull, trying to get the its attention away from Star.

It didn't work. The brightly colored red shirt that Star was wearing had the bull's focus on her.

Calder didn't hesitate as he sprinted toward Star without care that his own life was in danger. When he reached her, he didn't stop, scooping her up into his arms as he continued running.

She couldn't understand why Calder didn't run to the fence. Then she figured it out. The bull was too close.

Calder ran toward one of the barrels that hadn't been

stacked onto the truck yet. He practically threw her inside then turned back toward the bull, protecting the child within with his life.

Her breath caught in her throat, her mouth open in a silent scream. It was the same terrified expression that was on Stud's, Sex Piston's, and the parents' faces who were trying to get their children out of danger.

The bull was inches away from him when a rope settled over the bull's horns, turning it from Calder to Reno.

The screams of the adults and the children faded into the background as two shots rang out, dropping the bulls onto the ground.

Her jaw dropped as she looked around, trying to see where the shots had come from, seeing Shade sitting atop the fence on the other side of the bull shoot.

"Give me that back!"

Shade tossed the tranquilizer gun to the man he must have taken it from before jumping off the fence with an impassive face.

She and Sex Piston climbed down, running toward Stud and Harley as Calder helped Star out of the barrel, holding her tightly as he carried her toward them also. Star was crying frightened tears in his arms.

When they drew closer to Sex Piston, she reached out to take Star. It took a long wrenching second for Calder to release Star to her stepmother's hold.

It was hard to miss the twisting agony of Calder's expression, or the fact that he turned away when Star held her arms out for Stud, crying for her father.

Harley's head was on one of his shoulders, crying, and Star buried her face in the other one, both holding him so tightly that Sex Piston wasn't able to pry one away.

"I got them." He moved closer to Sex Piston so she could enfold all of them in a heartfelt hug that moved Crazy

Bitch to tears at the love the family felt toward one another.

"Everyone okay?"

Shade's cold voice broke through the spell of witnessing the family being reunited after they could have lost one of them.

Stud gave Shade a look of gratitude. "Brother, if I can ever…." His clogged emotions had him holding Star closer, burying his face in her hair.

Shade's eyes shifted from Stud to Calder. "The Last Riders always pay their debts." His voice was flat and emotionless as he gave him a brief nod before walking away while the cowboys shouted at everyone to leave the arena.

"We need to find Meri and Keri." Sex Piston walked closely next to Stud as Crazy Bitch and Calder lagged behind them, giving them the opportunity to be alone.

They went through the same door the girls had exited the arena, finding a large crowd milling around. Meri and Keri jumped up and down, waving at them to get their notice. They were standing with Lily, who was holding John's hand, and Razer and Beth were on the other side of them with their children, Noah and Chance.

"I didn't know half of Treepoint was inside," Crazy Bitch said as they approached the small group.

"When Sex Piston told me she was bringing her kids, we decided to make the extra trip and bring ours. Lily and Shade didn't want John to feel left out, so they tagged along." Beth kept a firm hand on her twin boys' shoulders as they talked.

"Where's Shade?" Lily smoothed a trembling hand through John's hair, trying to be calm for her son.

"I thought I saw him come out here." Calder searched through the milling crowd. "I don't see him."

Razer nodded toward the side of the building. "I saw him that way. If he's not back in a minute, I'll go look for him."

When Meri and Keri finally calmed down after seeing Star and Harley were safe, everyone started talking at once.

"What in the hell happened?" Crazy Bitch heard Sex Piston asking Stud.

She had been about to ask Calder, who still seemed shaken and hadn't taken his eyes off Star.

"I have no clue. One second, we were in line for the autographs. Some of the cowboys were posing for pictures by the horse stalls. We were waiting for Reno to finish with the one in front of us in line. And the next thing I know, two bulls come charging down from the back of the building. I assume they were trying to load them on the trailer to leave when they escaped. I didn't stand around to ask. Calder and I just took off running with Meri and Keri."

"How did Shade get the tranquilizer gun?" Crazy Bitch gripped Calder's arm tightly, relieved they had been able to get the girls and themselves away.

"I don't know. I was too busy running toward Harley."

"I saw him taking it away from Clint when he couldn't figure out how to load the dart," Calder answered grimly. "If he hadn't reacted so fast, I would be dead."

Crazy Bitch wound her arms around his waist, laying her head on his chest and feeling the beat of his heart beneath her cheek.

"He probably has experience using one to keep The Last Riders in line," Crazy Bitch joked, trying to lighten the atmosphere. She released Calder to give Harley and Star their tumblers. "Little Stud, I saw you helping your sister up instead of running away like the rest of those sissies. When I get home, I'm going to make you a chocolate cake."

"With peanut butter frosting on top?" He proudly beamed up at her as if she had promised him a gold medal.

Sex Piston aimed a grateful smile at her for stopping to pick up the tumblers she had forgotten about.

"Should we go back to the car and wait for Shade there?" Lily asked when the children started complaining they wanted to go home.

"Shade's coming." Razer pointed, seeing him coming from the side of the building. "Did you find out what happened?" he asked when he got within talking distance.

His expression had her apprehension rising.

"They think one of the crew members didn't check to make sure the bulls' stalls were properly locked before they loaded them onto the trailer. The crew says they did and don't know how they managed to get loose."

"Whoever did it should be fired," Sex Piston snapped. "It was an accident that could have cost someone their life."

"One of the workers is in pretty bad shape. They took him through the back exit so no one could see," Shade informed them. "Lily, you and Beth stay here, while Razer and I get the cars. Stud and Calder, mind staying here until we get back?"

"Not at all," Stud said, giving Shade a perceptive gaze that sent alarm bells going off inside her.

The ex-Navy SEAL was known to be protective of his wife and child, but that he didn't want them left alone long enough for him to get his car spoke of his concern.

Calder must have felt the same worry as her. He slid an arm around her waist and moved her closer to the group, keeping a wary eye around those who were near them.

When Shade and Razer arrived back with their vehicles, Stud told Sex Piston to stay beside their car until he could return with theirs, giving Calder a signal he didn't intend her to see to watch them.

Once they were loaded into Stud's van, they drove back to the hotel. Now that they felt safe and secure, the kids relived the experience, not noticing the adults were remaining silent in thought.

Once they were in the lobby, Crazy Bitch gave each of the kids a hug before saying good night to Stud and Sex Piston.

In their room, she sat down on the bed, taking off her boots. "Your dick better?" she asked as he took off his T-shirt and jeans.

"Yes." He tossed his clothes down next to his suitcase before going into the bathroom and closing the door.

Stung at his abruptness, she undressed as she heard the shower turn on.

Twisting the doorknob, she went inside uninvited.

Opening the shower door, she stepped under the cold water, shuddering at the temperature. She dipped her head under the ice-cold water to give herself courage before turning around to face him.

"How long have you known Star is your daughter?"

His expression didn't show any trace of emotion at her question.

She held her breath, hoping she was wrong, that she had made too much out of the resemblance between them, and that the look on his face when Star had come close to being trampled was just a reaction to seeing his niece in danger.

"Since she was born and Stud sent me a picture of her. She has the same birthmark on her thigh as I do."

That he made no effort to deny his parentage to Star didn't stem the irritation that was swelling inside her.

"Does Stud know that Star isn't his?"

"I would assume so. I'm sure that's why he married Candi."

His matter-of-fact answer settled in the pit of her stomach like a stone.

"What do you mean, assume? You two have talked about it, right?"

"No."

"Why in the fuck not?" Outrage on Star's behalf had

Crazy Bitch raising her voice in the small confines of the shower.

Calder turned the water off, getting out of the shower and leaving her inside alone.

Angry at his dismissive ending of their conservation, she grabbed a towel, following him into the bedroom.

"Hot thang, I don't like the way you're treating me when I'm trying to talk to you."

Slinging his damp towel over his shoulders, he pulled a pair of loose shorts on. "There's nothing to talk about. Stud and I haven't talked about Star because she's better off not knowing I'm her father. You saw Star tonight. Stud might not be her biological father, but he is her father in every way that counts." Reaching for the T-shirt he had discarded, he fished for his cigarettes.

She stared at him numbly as he went to the bathroom, seeing him lay the towel over the shower rail before coming back into the room and going to the balcony door.

Sliding it open, he went outside then closed the door behind him.

"Hell no, you don't!" She went to her suitcase, grabbing the first thing she touched, which was a grey T-shirt of Calder's. The oversized shirt came to the middle of her thighs.

Padding across the room, she opened the door and went outside.

"What is your problem? Why don't you discuss this with me instead of running away?"

"I'm not running anywhere. My dick hurts too much to run." He squinted at her mockingly through the smoke he exhaled.

"Be very careful of the tone you're using with me right now. I'm not one of the sluts at the club or Candi who will put up with your bullshit. I apologized for forgetting to use the lube. Believe it or not, I'm not really experienced at using them. I fucked up. But you're fucking up more now with how you're treating me."

"What do you want me to say? That when I got out of prison, I told Stud that I knew Star was my daughter? That I want her to know?" He gave a bark of bitter laughter. "That I want visitation? Star worships Stud. She thinks he hung the moon. I'm Uncle Calder to her. She knows I've been in prison—Meri and Keri asked me about it. Little kids hear shit; that's why they quit calling you Crazy Bitch in front of her and Harley. She asked me if it hurt when they put the handcuffs on me.

"She already knows Sex Piston isn't her real mom, that Candi is in prison. Let's just fuck her up even more by telling her that I'm her father. I don't even have an apartment where she can go spend the night with me. I live in a motorcycle club. Not exactly a place I want my daughter to be able to brag about in school."

"You make enough money working for Stud. You could afford a place if you wanted to."

"I'm not going to waste my money on rent. I'm saving my money for a home. One that I don't have to kiss a landlord's ass for to keep him happy. One that will be mine, with the woman I want to share it with. One with a backyard that I don't have to share with thirty other tenants."

His pointed gaze had her leaning backward on the rail, staring at the glass balcony door. Her emotions churned at the pain that his face didn't mirror.

"I never knew who my father was until I was in sixth grade. I kept asking my mother, but she would change the subject, or said it didn't matter because he lived too far away." She bit her lip, trying to explain to him how important it was for Star to know the truth.

"At the end of the school year, there was going to be a

father and daughter dance. I wanted to go so badly I dreamed of it at night, imagining getting a new dress, just like all the other girls in my grade.

"I waited for my mom to go to work one day and went into her room. In her closet, I found an old box that had my school records in it. My birth certificate was in there, too. Then I used the phonebook to see if he lived in Jamestown. He did.

"The next day, when my mom went to work, I stole some money out of a jar she would put her tips in every night. That was the money she would save to buy groceries with. What money she made waitressing after she paid rent for the dump we lived in would go to her drugs, so I knew when she found out, she was going to beat my ass when she got home. I didn't care.

"I called a taxi and gave the driver the address I found in the phonebook. The driver didn't want to take me, but I cried and said my dad had a flat tire and was late picking me up after school. He believed me, and when we got there, I had to count out the change to pay him, knowing I didn't have enough to get home. I was dumb as shit, thinking that, when my dad saw me and we talked, he would give me a ride home. Truthfully, I hoped he would let me stay with him." She kept staring into the empty hotel room, her mind going back to that day, while Calder silently listened, smoking his cigarette.

"When the taxi pulled away, I was too nervous to knock on his door. I walked up and down that street, I bet, twenty times before I saw a big car pull into the driveway." She gave a soft laugh, brushing her sweaty palms against the bottom of the T-shirt. "A man got out of the car wearing a suit. I was standing on the sidewalk, and I fucking knew he was my father. I looked just like him. I was so busy staring at him I didn't notice the woman or the girl getting out of the back seat until they slammed the car doors.

"His wife was all dressed up in a matching pant suit with her hair all done up. She was nothing like my mother. My mom wouldn't want to be buried in that outfit. The little girl was handing my father her backpack as if it was too heavy to carry. She wasn't anything like me, either.

"I was too self-conscious of my jeans that were so old they came up to my ankles, and the shirt that was so big on me it hung off my shoulders, that my mom had gotten from the Goodwill. I hid behind a tree until they went inside and then walked home. I took the beating my mom gave me for stealing her money and never told her what I had done."

"You never tried to contact him again, even when you got older?"

"No. When I saw who his little girl was, I never wanted to see him again."

"For God's sake, why not?"

"Because she was in the same grade I was in. You've probably even met her. It's Allison Staff."

21

"I've met Allison. She and her old man came into Stud's garage, wanting to buy a bike. He told them to get the fuck out of his garage. I couldn't believe that he was turning business away. When he told me why, I understood." Calder remembered the woman who had turned her nose up at Stud and him when the couple had come into the garage. "He told me how she helped several girls jump Sex Piston on the school bus."

"She was their lookout."

"Does she know you're her sister?" He saw a faint resemblance between the two, but nothing that would make it obvious they were sisters.

"Hell no. You think my father would let anyone know he fucked the town whore? He did me a favor keeping his trap closed. The thought of Allison being my sister makes me want to puke. The only ones I've told are Sex Piston and the rest of the crew, and they aren't any happier about it than I am.

"He came and saw me once when he found out my mom had cancer. I told him not to let the door hit him on the way out. I hate his fucking guts. That's why I'm telling you. You need to talk to Stud and Sex Piston and find a way to tell Star. If she finds out for herself, Star will hate all of you."

It was his worst fear, right on top of her finding out. Both his fears were on different sides of the fence, but both had consequences that were going to hurt Star.

He ground his cigarette out on top of the soda can he had left outside last night. "I don't know what to do." He looked at her for help, admitting he was at a loss.

"Stud is your brother. You're close. He's never turned his back on you. Ask him if Star is yours and go from there. But what you three are doing is plain wrong. Sex Piston loves Star. She considers Star her own kid, so she isn't going to want to shake the boat and risk losing custody of her. Once Sex Piston sees you're not going to take her away from her, she'll be cool with you seeing more of Star."

"If that's even going to be an option. What if she hates me?"

"You're nuts if you believe that. She's crazy about you. She'll be hurt and confused at first, but the three of you will be there for her, and she will see that all three of you love her and want what's best for her. If you wait until she's older, it'll be too late."

"I'll think it over."

He sighed. The relationship he and Stud shared had weathered so many storms, but what if him confronting Stud about Star being his child put a wedge between them that couldn't be overcome?

He had always looked up to Stud. It was one of the reasons he hadn't wanted his father to know he could ride a bike as good as Stud. Their father had tried to foster a rivalry between them. That was why he had only ridden the bikes when no one was around to see. If the old man had known, he would have pitted them against each other, billing the races as brother against brother.

Stud had been strong enough to make their father back down, while Calder had stayed in the background, letting his brother deal with the demands made on him.

He was in his thirties and still let Stud shoulder the shit that he should, deluding himself that it was for Star's sake when, in reality, he had been too proud to admit how badly he had screwed up.

"I'm sorry for being an asshole. I don't blame you for my sore dick," he sorrowfully tried to make amends with one of the two girls he loved.

She gave him a mischievous look. "Who do you blame?"

"The Last Riders."

A loud whistle from down below had them both looking over the railing. A group of men below who were going into the hotel's entrance were staring at them, their eyes trained on Crazy Bitch.

"Sweetie, if you're needing some company tonight, you don't have to flash the whole parking lot. Just tell me what room you're in, and I'll be right up," one brazen asshole was stupid enough to shout upward, making the others snicker and catcall with suggestive movements to Crazy Bitch, who wasn't making a move to step away from the railing.

Crazy Bitch hung dangerously over the railing. "Woohoo! What's your name?"

"Buck!" The randy bozo proudly looked at his friends as if he had scored a three-point shot.

She turned her head toward Calder, rolling her eyes. "Figures." She snorted derisively before looking back down at the asswipe.

There was something about this that made Calder feel carefree. It felt like hanging out with a good friend who you didn't have to be self-conscious around or always be on your toes at their reaction. She had a vicious sense of humor that was fun to watch.

"Yo, Buck, you get an eyeful? I bet that's the first pussy you've seen that's not in a *Playboy* magazine."

Calder winced at the way she was staring contemptuously down at the man below her.

"Tell you what; if your whittle dick can find room 232, I'll be waiting."

His amusement vanished when she shouted out their room number.

The man pulled his pants up over his sagging stomach. "I'm on my way, sugar britches!"

"You better hurry and get your jeans on," Crazy Bitch told Calder. "You're not going to scare the shit out of them with that dorky thing on."

"I wasn't expecting company," Calder snarled, his appreciation of her sense of humor vanishing when she turned the tables on him.

"Next time, be quicker defending my honor." Her breasts bounced under his T-shirt at her shrug.

Deciding it was better to spank her ass after he got rid of them, he rushed inside their room. He only had enough time to throw his jeans on before he heard the knock on his door.

"She's fucking crazy," he said to himself as he tugged his zipper over his pained cock that was protesting having to go back inside his pants.

"How do you think I got my nickname?" she asked, coming into the room. "You want me to open the door for them?"

"No!" Nonplussed at her looking forward to him getting his ass kicked, he went to answer the door. Opening it, he saw the four beefy men's faces drop when they saw it wasn't Crazy Bitch who had answered.

"Where's sugar britches?"

He took a step forward, letting his body fill the doorway. "You got the wrong room."

"I got the right room." Belligerently, bozo tried to peer over his shoulder. "Sugar britches, Buck's here!"

Calder ground his teeth together so hard he would have to make a dentist appointment when he returned to Jamestown... if he lived until then. The men weren't happy, and they were getting unhappier by the minute when Crazy Bitch didn't answer.

"You gonna move or what?" Buck asked, his beady eyes narrowing on him.

Calder braced himself for the fight he could see there wasn't going to be a way out of.

He was about to punch the smart-mouthed fucker when the door across the hall opened and Shade appeared.

"You need some help, Calder?"

The redneck turned at the question, seeing Shade standing shirtless in jeans that he hadn't bothered to zip, his body heavily covered in tattoos, giving the four men pause.

The door next to Shade's opened and Razer came out, naked and uncaring.

The redneck's jaw dropped open in astonishment.

When the door next to his opened, Calder didn't have to look to know that Stud had joined the party.

Calder grinned wickedly at Buck. "I'm good. They just wanted to introduce themselves in person. Now that they have, they can leave. Isn't that right?"

"Yeah, that's right. Nice meeting you." The men backed away, leaving them alone in the hall.

Crazy Bitch peeked her head out from over his shoulder. "Leaving so soon...?"

Calder took a step forward, shutting the door on her before she could say something that would escalate in a free-for-all in the hallway.

"Thanks, brothers."

Calder couldn't help noticing the myriad of tattoos on Shade's body. He had several himself, but not nearly as many that covered Shade's, even dipping below his unbuttoned jeans. No one could miss the ones on his arms and neck, but he hadn't seen him without his shirt on before.

Shade and Razer gave him a curt nod before going into their respective rooms, leaving him and Stud alone.

"How did you know to come outside?" Calder asked his brother curiously.

"Crazy Bitch sent Sex Piston a text to tell me to get my ass outside. I assume she sent the same text to Beth and Lily. What did you do to piss her off this time?"

Calder thought back, realizing she had given him a warning when she hadn't liked how he had blamed his sore dick on her.

"Apparently, I apologized too late for something I said." Next time, he would be faster, or keep his big mouth shut.

"Brother, you've been around that crazy bitch long enough to be smart enough to fuck her with one foot on the bed and the other one ready to run."

Stud didn't know how true his warning was.

"I'll let you go back to bed. If I'm not at breakfast, you know she killed me in my sleep."

"You should be safe. I saw her peeking over your shoulder at Shade. That always puts them in a good mood."

"Did you know he had that many tattoos?" If Calder didn't like him, and if Shade hadn't saved his and Star's life a couple of hours ago, he would be tempted to throw the dangerous biker off the balcony.

"Jealous?" Stud gave him a commiserating look. "Don't let it get to you. I use it to my advantage."

"I don't want her thinking of anyone but me when I'm fucking her."

"You could get more tattoos?" Stud suggested. "If it bothers you that bad."

"I might do that." He twisted the doorknob to go back inside his room.

"Just so you know, Shade isn't the only Last Rider who gets them horny."

Jealous, he turned back to his brother. "Who else do I have to kill?"

"Knox."

"That's easy." He shrugged. "I'll just work out more if she's into muscles." He scoffed at him having to be worried about Knox.

"It's not the muscles that get their motors running; it's his tongue ring… and the ones he's got on his cock."

Calder's hand unconsciously went to his still recovering dick as he ran the tip of his tongue over suddenly dry lips. "You know, the more I think about it, I don't have a reason to be jealous of them. Shade and Knox are happily married men, right?"

"Keep telling yourself that, brother. That's what I tell myself. It's a hell of a lot easier than getting your dick pierced… or getting a bad tattoo."

"One thing is for sure—it won't be as painful."

Opening the door, he saw Crazy Bitch lying on the bed, watching a movie. Shutting and locking the door behind him, he started to sweat when he saw it was a porno.

Switching from his jeans back to shorts, he carefully lay down on the bed next to her, trying not to flinch when she cuddled up to him. The low moans from the television made him nervous.

"You didn't forget that Dr. Price said I couldn't have sex for a week, did you?"

"Hot thang…"

He swallowed hard when she glanced up with eyes that had turned slumberous with passion.

"He said *you* couldn't have sex for a whole week. Me?" She lifted one of his hands, sliding it underneath her T-shirt to her already hard nipple. "I can have all the sex I want."

———

"HOLY MOSES! How did I not know this was in Kentucky?" Crazy Bitch stared up in awe at the castle.

Calder grinned as he got off his bike. "Probably because, when you go to Lexington, you take the interstate. I only knew about it because I took the back way a few times. We lucked out; they had a cancellation."

He unstrapped the small duffle bag that he had tied to the back of the bike. Stud had taken their suitcases with them in his van. Both he and Crazy Bitch had only kept a change of clothes for the next day.

After checking in, they scouted around the lobby, hoping something would lead to the next clue. Deciding to go to their room to drop the bag off, they went up the stairs.

As they were going up the steps, Calder recognized the man and woman coming down.

"Rider." Calder held out his hand to shake The Last Rider's hand.

"Calder, Crazy Bitch."

He didn't miss the appraising look that Crazy Bitch gave the biker, or the hostile one she gave the other woman.

Last night, when he had watched her give Shade the once-over, he had thought it was about time she had some of her own medicine.

He turned his eyes to the sexy woman by Rider's side, about to introduce himself, when Crazy Bitch took his arm, going up another step.

"Later."

"That wasn't polite," he mumbled as they continued up the stairs.

"I didn't like the way you were looking at Jewel."

"I don't look the way you look at Shade, Knox, or Rider."

Crazy Bitch didn't say anything until they reached their room.

"I didn't like the way you looked at Jewel, so I said something. If you don't like the way I look at other men, say something. I'm not a fucking mind reader."

Tossing his bag onto the bed, he angrily stalked to where she was standing by the door. "I don't like it."

"Then I won't do it anymore. Satisfied?"

He placed his hands on the door, caging her in. "When I'm with you, I'm never satisfied. I always want more. I'm not even satisfied when I'm done fucking you. I'm not satisfied when you come on my tongue and don't beg me for more. I'm not satisfied that, if I walked away from you, you wouldn't give a flying fuck. You know what would satisfy me? You quit playing around with me like you're expecting me to fuck up and give you an excuse to stop seeing me."

"You are going to fuck up—that's what men do!"

"Woman, you act like you're made out of armor. The problem is, it may be protecting you, but it's keeping me away." He traced the line of her stubborn jaw with his thumb. "You don't have to protect yourself from me. I'm so crazy about you that I'm jealous over every man you look at."

"I don't want you jealous."

"What do you want?"

Her eyes shifted sideways. "I want you to say you like me."

Calder was stunned at her simple request. She wanted what no one had given her before. His heart ached that the only thing she wanted didn't cost a dime, yet to her, it was as valuable as gold.

"Anna-Kate, I like you a lot. In fact, I like you so much I'm falling in love with you."

"You are?" The woman whom he had considered to be hard as stone gave him an uncertain smile.

"A hundred percent."

"You can't go any higher than a hundred percent."

"No, you can't. I guess that settles it then. I'm definitely in love with you."

She gave a smile so radiant he had to blink to make sure he was seeing it. It was like a flower that had unfurled in the sunlight, trying to catch the first rays of the morning. There was also wariness, but a gradual openness that let him catch sight of the gentle soul she kept guarded within her. As if one careless step would trample the budding love she was feeling for him.

He embraced her so gently he heard her breath hitch in her throat.

"Do you know how long I've been in love with you?" she asked.

"How long?" he asked huskily.

"When I looked over the edge on Black Mountain and you pulled me back. I've never had anyone do that for me."

He frowned. "What, keep you from falling off a mountain?"

"Usually, people want to throw me off them, not hold me back."

"That's what makes me different. I would have gone over the cliff with you before I would have ever let you fall."

22

Crazy Bitch stared at Viper's brother, trying to keep her expression cheerful as Calder introduced them.

That Gavin had been through hell was obvious in the shadows of his eyes and the scars on his wrists where they must have kept him chained. It was in the lethal awareness that he was unconsciously watching her as if he didn't trust her movements. He wasn't a man who had survived unscathed. He was waiting for hell to reach out and grab him back into its fiery grasp.

"I expected a woman named Crazy Bitch to be taller and scarier."

"I only get scary the more you know me. I'll take it easy on you until you get to know me better." Prudently, she didn't make any moves to go farther into his room as the tall man paced jitterily across the carpeted floor.

Gavin didn't laugh at her teasing, but his lips did curl in the beginning of a smile. Restless, he kept rubbing his arms as if he was cold.

"I'm looking forward to it, if I ever get out of here."

"Don't rush getting released. My mother did, and both

times she went back to using within a couple days. You can't rush success. I didn't understand that when I was in high school, so I dropped out. I thought the ones who stayed in school were the suckers. Made fun of them for wanting to go on to college. I was a fucking fool because I thought I could skip the steps that would make me a success in life.

"If I had to do it over, my ass would have stayed in school. I could have been a doctor, an astronaut, or a CEO, instead of a hairdresser. I'll never know because I rushed into making a decision that I would regret, and I do.

"It took me years to get my GED, but when I did… Jesus, it was like someone had handed me the Pulitzer Prize or some shit like that when I got my diploma in the mail."

Gavin stopped pacing. "Your mother was an addict?"

"Oh yes, she wasn't like Killyama's ma, who could hide it. My mother couldn't hide her addiction. She lost custody of me a few times. She would swear to the courts and me that she was clean to get me back. She even managed to get through rehab and social worker visits to regain custody of me. Once she did, it would start all over again. She didn't care enough about me or herself not to give in to the drugs again. Rehab gave her the skills to cope with temptation, but they can't help you win the war unless you take advantage of their help."

"I don't need anyone's help anymore." He gravely regarded her.

"I said that about algebra. I flunked it three times before I found a tutor. It's easier to dig yourself out of a hole if you don't fall in there in the first place."

"I'll keep that in mind." He gave her a brief smile that was more of a grimace. "How'd you get your nickname?"

"Most of my friends got their nicknames because they were the opposite of their nicknames. Sadly, I deserve mine. I get a little crazy when I get pissed off."

Gavin lifted a curious brow. "How crazy?"

"I made the news a couple times," she bragged to the men who were looking at her skeptically.

"I don't remember any of the brothers mentioning that."

Crazy Bitch could hear the doubt in Calder's voice at her gloating.

"I was in high school."

"If you were in high school, it doesn't count. We all do crazy shit in high school."

She stared down at her fingernail polish, admiring the color. So far, it was one of her favorites. She should buy another couple of bottles in case they stopped making it.

"Does it count if you have killed?"

The two men stared at her in shock. Then Gavin burst out laughing, slapping Calder on his back.

"If I didn't like you so much, I would steal her from you. She's funny as hell."

She arched her finely arched brow. "You think I'm joking?"

"I think you're trying to take my mind off my Taylor coming, and it's working."

"Glad to help," she said as a knock sounded on the door behind her.

Gavin nervously jumped, hollowed cheekbones flushed when she nodded toward the private yard behind his back.

"Calder and I will wait outside. If you need us, just open the door."

She and Calder went out the back door as Gavin told the person knocking to come inside.

Being nosy, she took the patio chair that gave a view into the room. She couldn't hear what the woman was saying when she came into the room, but when the stunning woman moved toward Gavin, an imaginary hand gripped her heart when she saw that Gavin's visitor was pregnant and his reaction to it.

"He didn't know?" she whispered out of the side of her mouth, wanting to make sure Gavin couldn't hear their conservation.

"I talked to Viper while you were checking us out of the hotel. He said Gavin took the news better than he thought he would. Now, I see why. I think he wanted to pretend the last eleven years never happened."

They sat watching the awkward meeting between the estranged lovers.

"I can see why he's so hung up on her. She's a beautiful woman."

"Yes, she is."

Crazy Bitch wasn't jealous at Calder's compliment.

The pain emanating from the other side of the glass door was tangible. She wanted to look away, but she was spellbound, like waiting for a car wreck to happen and helpless to do anything about it, other than watch it before her eyes.

"What do you think she's saying?" Calder asked.

"I think she's telling him that she doesn't love him anymore, that she loves her husband."

"How do you know that?"

"Because she's twisting her wedding ring and crying."

"Damn."

"Yeah, it sucks getting your heart broken, but it beats her giving him hope." Crazy Bitch turned her eyes away, unable to watch any more. "You want to know what's really sad? I think she's still in love with him. She keeps looking away from his eyes."

"Why would she lie about something like that?"

"She's married." Crazy Bitch shrugged. "Some women take that shit seriously, especially when they're knocked up."

"She's leaving."

Crazy Bitch didn't turn back to watch, finding it too painful. You could put a Band-Aid on someone who was cut, but there was no way to help someone who was having their heart ripped out.

When she heard Gavin calling Taylor's name, she still kept herself turned away, giving him privacy. Her hands clenched into fists at the ragged plea for her to come back and not to leave him. A tear slipped down her cheek at the guttural moan that next came from Gavin's room.

She heard Calder take off when the sound of glass exploding came from inside.

Standing, she saw Calder trying to hold Gavin back.

"Taylor, *come back!* Let me go, Calder. I don't want to hurt you, but I will if you don't. *Taylor!* God… Please don't leave me."

"Gavin, she's gone. Don't make it harder for her."

"*Hard for her?* What about for me? She's the only reason I'm alive."

Crazy Bitch hesitantly walked into the room as Calder tried to keep Gavin from following the woman who had left with a heartbroken sob. She had thought Gavin would keep fighting Calder; instead, he stopped struggling to sit down on his bed, staring at the wall as if they weren't there.

Calder looked questioningly toward her, neither of them knowing what to do next. Gavin might still have been in his room, but he was no longer with them.

A look crossed his face that had her stepping toward Calder in fear. Gavin's appearance masked the desperation she knew he was feeling at truly losing the woman he loved.

Pushed beyond what his still fragile mind could handle, he didn't move when Peyton came into the room, casting him a worried glance.

"Gavin?"

His eyes didn't flicker as Peyton and Calder moved closer.

"Gavin, are you okay? Can I get you something?" When Peyton laid a hand on his arm, he didn't respond, just continued to stare blankly at the wall. The lights were on in Gavin's mind, but he was no longer there.

Peyton and Calder both tried to say something that could draw him out of his stupor. Then Peyton began crying when the nurse came rushing inside.

"I'll stay with Gavin. You and Peyton go get something to eat," Calder told her.

Crazy Bitch took Peyton's arm, leading her from the room. "Where do you want to go get something to eat?"

"I can't eat."

"Let's go to the waiting room, and I'll get us each a cup of coffee."

Peyton sniffed back her tears, nodding as she looked back at Gavin's door. "I should call Viper. He's waiting for my call at the hotel next door."

"You go ahead while I get the coffee."

She had just handed Peyton her coffee and took a chair next to her when she saw Viper and Ton striding down the hall, going into Gavin's room.

"I tried to tell him to wait before seeing her. He's tried so hard to get off the drugs and put some weight on. I think he really believed she would leave her husband and stay with him." Peyton looked down at her coffee cup, not drinking it.

"When you're lost, you want the one you love to make you feel better. He wanted Taylor to make him feel better, and he crashed when she didn't. He's going to have to regroup and find another reason to keep living."

"What if he doesn't?" Peyton's shaky hand nearly spilled her coffee. Crazy Bitch took it away, setting it down on the small table next to her.

"He will. If he has an ounce of Viper's blood inside him, he will."

JAMIE BEGLEY

They sat for several minutes before Crazy Bitch stood, wanting to stretch her legs.

"I haven't eaten since last night. Calder was in too much of a rush to get here this morning to eat. I'm going to get me and Calder something. You want anything?"

"No thanks. I'll tell Calder where you are if he comes out."

Crazy Bitch went out through the sliding door.

She and Calder had spent most of the night searching through the castle, but hadn't found any hint of another clue. She hoped the others in her crew had better luck.

The restaurant was busy. Taking a seat at the counter, she ordered two burgers and fries to go. When she finished ordering, she absently looked around the restaurant, seeing a couple arguing in one of the booths.

Recognizing the woman as Gavin's ex-fiancée, she saw that the meeting in Gavin's room hadn't just taken a toll on him. Taylor was sobbing into a man's shoulder as those sitting near them nosily looked on.

When he managed to calm her, he stood and went into the restroom.

Crazy Bitch was about to get off her stool to approach her when she saw the bitch's face. Any sympathy she had for the woman died.

The bitch had reached inside her purse and checked her makeup with an expression that she had seen on too many women's face.

She wasn't surprised when she saw Taylor hastily put the mirror back inside her purse and her lovely eyes once again swam with tears when her husband came out of the bathroom.

Crazy Bitch swung back on her stool. "Fuck me."

"Pardon me?" the waitress asked, setting the bag of food down in front of her.

"Nothing." She stood, throwing a twenty down on the counter. "Keep the change."

"Wow, a whole dollar. You sure you don't need it more than I do?"

She was angry at herself that she had her mind on what was going on back in Gavin's room that she hadn't paid attention to the total of the ticket. As a woman who worked hard for her tip money, she always made sure she gave a good tip. On the other hand, when her customers didn't tip well, she didn't get in their faces.

"Now that you mention it, I do." She patiently held out her hand for the dollar, glad her food was already bagged and in her other hand.

Taking the dollar that was thrown down on the counter, she reached into her back pocket and took out her wad of pocket money. She took out a ten and two more twenties, handing the bills back to her waitress.

"The ten is for you. The twenties are to pay for Pollyanna's lunch over there in the green top. Tell her that was the best performance I've ever witnessed."

Crazy Bitch found Peyton still sitting where she had left her. Taking out her hamburger, she ate it, still fuming.

Women like Taylor made her ashamed to be a woman. She was willing to bet a thousand dollars that, when Taylor had found out Gavin was missing, she had soaked up all the attention she could, and when she couldn't get anymore, she had married the sucker who had been sitting next to her in the booth. Now, with Gavin returned, she had waited until she couldn't hold it over the poor sap she was married to anymore, turning the screws until she was ready to put him out of his misery by seeing Gavin.

Gavin would see that bitch again; she would put bank on it. She hoped she was wrong, sweet Jesus, she hoped she was wrong, but experience breeds contempt.

Her mother had shed the same crocodile tears every time she had wanted something. She had watched her cry fake tears every time she had lost custody of her, or one of her lovers had gotten tired of being used for their money. Even their landlords had been treated to them when they had threatened to evict her.

Taylor had the same scheming expression as her mother when her husband had gone to the bathroom. Crazy Bitch could sniff out a fraud five hundred miles away, but she had missed the scent outside of Gavin's door because it had been too hard to watch.

She mentally gave Taylor one point by getting her once. Now she was on her scent. She never involved herself in anyone's personal business, but if the bitch showed up again, she would make sure to introduce herself.

Calming herself, she opened the bag and started eating the burger she had bought for Calder. She always ate when she was mad. It was easier to deal with losing five pounds versus letting the fury that was simmering below her surface out.

"I thought you were saving that for Calder?"

"It's cold now; no need wasting money." She looked at Peyton as she took another bite of the burger.

"How many hamburger patties are on it?"

"Three."

"That's the same as the one you just ate?"

"So?" She opened the bag again, taking out his fries. "I eat when I'm upset, okay?"

"I tend to eat when I'm upset, too, but I don't eat the whole cow."

"I already planned to eat salads for a week to make up the five pounds I'm going to gain."

"I'd make it two weeks and keep nine-one-one on speed dial."

Killyama's mother got her point across. Crazy Bitch wrapped what was left of the burger and fries, putting them back in the bag.

"Peyton, you remember how I used to say I wished you were my mother when I came home with Killyama on the bus?"

"Yes, those are some of my fondest memories." The attractive woman didn't look old enough to have a child Killyama's age. Crazy Bitch prayed she looked that good at her age.

"Today isn't one of those days."

Peyton wasn't upset by her snarky comment.

"I wish Gavin had your appetite. He's so tall that you can't tell when he gains a pound. I found a short-term lease that starts in three days. I promised to make him some home cooking. Some of The Last Riders have been sending food when their husbands come, but it's not the same when you have to reheat it, and Gavin doesn't like leftovers."

"You've gotten attached to him, haven't you?"

"He's like the son I never had. I am so blessed to have both Train and Gavin in my life now. You can never have too many people who give you reason to get out of bed in the morning."

"And Gavin gives you that reason?"

"Oh yes. Killyama comes and visits me all the time, and so do Jonas and Hammer. But Train and Gavin need me. There's a difference." Affection filled Peyton's voice.

"What does Train need you for? He seems pretty self-sufficient to me."

"He needs me to remind him of what it's like to have a family. I think he misses his mother and sisters, and while I could never take their place, I think I fill a space so he doesn't feel as empty inside."

Crazy Bitch laid her hand over hers. "You do more than that. You're what a mother should be. You're home."

She didn't get sympathetic often, but Peyton had been there numerous times for her. She had given her a couch to sleep on many nights when she hadn't wanted to go home to her mother. She was the one she had called when she had found her mother's body, sheltering her in loving arms as the coroner had wheeled the woman out of her bedroom on a gurney. Peyton had pleaded and begged with her not to drop out of high school. She had also been the one to tutor her in algebra. She was an expert at mothering. Gavin couldn't be in better hands.

Both of them were watching Gavin's door when Calder came out. He looked as tired as she felt.

"The nurse gave Gavin a sedative. Peyton, I'm going to stay for a few days. If you want, you can go back to Jamestown. Can you give Crazy Bitch a ride if you do?"

"I'd like to stay in case he asks for me. I can drive her home, but I'm coming right back."

Crazy Bitch shook her head. "It's almost a four-hour drive. I'll rent a car."

Calder frowned. "I hate to put you out, but I don't want to leave Gavin."

"It's not a problem. I'd stay if I didn't have appointments tomorrow."

"If you're ready, I'll drive you to get the car. I want to be back before Gavin wakes up," Calder explained.

Crazy Bitch gave Peyton a hug before leaving.

As they walked toward the parking lot, Calder took her hand. She cast him a surprised glance.

"I've never held a man's hand before. Joker would have laughed his head off if I tried to hold his."

"Joker was a fucking idiot." Releasing her hand, he gave her the keys to his bike. "You want to drive?"

She almost cried. "You'll let me drive your bike?"

"Why not? It's not like any of the brothers will see. I've seen you ride; you can handle it."

She straddled the bike, turning it on and gripping the handlebars as Calder got on behind her.

"You remember when I said I knew I was in love with you when you pulled me back over the cliff?"

"Yeah."

"I may have been wrong."

He settled his chin on her shoulder as he curled his arms around her waist. She leaned the side of her head to rest on his.

"This…" She stared down at the powerful machine beneath her thighs, proud of the confidence he was placing on her. "This is love."

23

Crazy Bitch opened a bottle of beer, seeing Bear eyeing her enviously. Taking a drink, she showed her satisfaction as the cold beer slid down her throat.

"Quit bugging Bear."

"I'm not bugging him. I'm minding my own business."

"You didn't have to tell him that he couldn't have one of the ones Calder bought for you."

"Stud, anytime Bear wants to buy the beer with his own money, or club money, I'll be gracious. Calder bought these for me, and I'm not sharing. If he had given me roses, Bear wouldn't expect me to share. I don't see any reason that it shouldn't be the same way with beer."

"You can't drink a flower," Stud countered. "You're hurting his feelings."

"The big wuss will survive. If I give him one, all the brothers will want one, too. That'll leave me with zip, zilch, nada. So, I'm not sharing. At least until you buy me more beer, or I get paid." She looked across the table to where Sex Piston was watching her and Stud argue back and forth.

"I can't pay her until Friday. Besides, Crazy Bitch has a point. Why don't you just buy more Millers?"

"I did," he reluctantly admitted. "They drank it all."

"See?" Crazy Bitch grabbed a handful of the popcorn she had popped at the beauty shop and brought to the clubhouse to share. "You need to start a factory like The Last Riders, or make the brothers start paying dues. Or, better yet, do what the other clubs do—get involved in illegal shit."

"Like what?" Stud took a handful of popcorn.

"How about gun running?"

"Everybody in Kentucky has guns."

"That's the point. We could steal them and sell them to people in other states who don't have them."

"There's a problem with that. Everyone in Kentucky knows how to use them. The brothers would be dodging lead if they tried breaking into anyone's house to steal them."

"That's true." She nibbled on the popcorn. "I came up with the idea. You're the club president; you can fine tune it."

"Fine tune what? Getting the brothers killed or landing them in jail?" he caustically replied, taking out his wallet and motioning for Bear. "Go on a beer run. Make sure you get a case of Miller Lite. Mark it with my name."

She placed a hand over her chest as if she had been stabbed. "That hurt. I would share my beer with you."

"I don't drink Miller." He didn't react to her mocking exaggeration.

"I have an idea." Sex Piston beamed as if she had solved the never-ending lack of club's money.

"I hope it's better than Crazy Bitch's." Killyama moved the popcorn closer to her. "I'd hate making money just for her to skip out on bail for breaking and entering."

"It is." Sex Piston excitedly slammed her beer down on the table. "Why don't we pool our money together and invest in Penni's invention. Lily said she's looking for investors."

"Count me out," Killyama jeered. "I wouldn't trust her with cooking, much less with my money."

Crazy Bitch coughed out the popcorn kernel that had become lodged in her throat.

"What invention?" Stud turned toward Sex Piston, his interest piqued.

"I haven't shown you yet. I was waiting for your birthday."

"I agree with Killyama. Forget I said anything. I think dues are the way to go." Finally able to talk, she tried to close the discussion before another dick was hurt.

"What kind of investment is it?"

Crazy Bitch's shoulders slumped at Stud's refusal to change the subject. She tried to wiggle her eyebrows at Sex Piston. Either she didn't see or didn't care.

"It's a sex toy."

"And you haven't let me use it on you yet?"

Her heart fluttered at the sensuous smile Stud gave Sex Piston. Damn, where was Calder when she needed him? Then she remembered he wouldn't be back until tomorrow night. The longer he was away, the sexier Stud was looking to her.

"It's for men," Sex Piston explained.

"Really?" His interest racked up another notch. "We can ask your parents if the kids can stay with them tomorrow night, and we can see if it's worth investing in."

The conservation was going from bad to worse. Drumming her fingers on the table, she tried to think of a way to save Stud's dick without breaking her promise to Calder about what happened to his.

Inspiration struck.

"Do you really want your kids to know you're making money off a sex toy?"

"It doesn't bother Willa. She's rich as fuck from a condom company."

Crazy Bitch shot Killyama a dirty look at that revelation.

"Don't forget the one she gave us was a prototype. You know Penni. I wouldn't use it until she gets feedback from the others she gave it to."

Sex Piston waved her suggestion away. "She only gave them to us. She texted me the other day, asking how the men liked it. I told her we hadn't tried it yet. If my parents keep the kids, we can give her all the feedback she wants."

"I haven't used the one she gave me." Killyama snorted. "I'm not letting any contraption of hers near Train's dick."

"It's just a fucking vibrator. You're both acting like it's a drill. We have four kids who need their college educations paid for. If that vibrator is any good, you better believe me, we'll be investing. Isn't that right, Stud?"

When Crazy Bitch turned her eyes toward him at Sex Piston's question, she saw that he had been watching her own expression.

"I think we should wait until Penni gets at least a couple reviews."

She glanced away from his penetrating stare. Then she blinked upward several times, trying to give a subtle hint. "I think twenty reviews sounds like a good, even number."

"The kids need a college fund. They'll need a nursing home before you make up your mind," Sex Piston complained, seeing her imaginary fortune slip away.

Satisfied that Stud wouldn't let the toy near his dick, Crazy Bitch relaxed, enjoying her beer and the music. It would have been better if Calder was there, but a girl couldn't have it all.

"Fat Louise finally got here," Crazy Bitch told the others as Fat Louise waved, making her way toward their table.

"Guess who got her promotion," she said, sitting down.

"That's cool." Crazy Bitch was thrilled for her. She had

worked hard for the job that she had been promised several months ago.

"Not only that, but Sam called in and quit today. They said he missed the last couple of days, and when the doctor called, he quit."

"Thank fuck!" Crazy Bitch shouted out, the burden of keeping the secret of being roofied by him falling off her shoulders. "You all can have a beer on me. You just made my night, girlfriend." She laughed, relieved that Fat Louise wouldn't have to work with the sneaky asshole.

"Does that mean we can tell Stud now?" Fat Louise looked at her questioningly. "I hated keeping the secret. Cade won't be happy that I didn't tell him, but I'll make it up to him. I'll break out that present that Penni gave us."

Her joy at Fat Louise's announcement dimmed.

"I would save that for another—"

"Forget the toy. What secret?" Stud interrupted brusquely.

Sex Piston, Killyama, T.A., and Fat Louise began munching on the popcorn, leaving Crazy Bitch the only one able to answer.

"We can talk about it later."

"Now."

Crazy Bitch swallowed hard. It wasn't often that she found herself on the receiving end of the hard gaze he was giving her.

"There's a reason I quit seeing Sam. He tried to roofie me when we went to the drive-in."

Stud's face grew dark. "And why didn't you want me or any of the brothers to know?"

"I wanted Fat Louise to get her promotion. As soon as she got the promotion and got past the six-week trial period, I would have told you."

"I see."

Crazy Bitch paled at the lethal stillness of those around

them. When the music stopped, she knew the brothers were listening in. Their anger was evident when she reluctantly looked up to gauge their reactions.

"I only told Fat Louise because I didn't want her working with the fucker. She wanted that job. I didn't have the proof he did it. It would have been his word against mine. No one would have believed me."

"I would have."

"You're not the one handing out promotions."

"Tell him all of it." Sex Piston's face tightened when Stud shot her the same glare.

"What else is there to tell?" Crazy Bitch tried to keep from confessing anything else. The man was so furious his eyelid was twitching.

"That he gave you a black eye and that you missed three days' of work because of him. Bitch, I work beside you; don't think I didn't notice that pancake makeup under your eye."

"That didn't matter. I blackened his, too."

"It matters to me," Stud ground out.

"Me, too." Killyama gave them all looks of betrayal. "Why didn't you tell me?"

"I didn't want you to tell Train. He would have told Stud."

"You're right about that." Train maneuvered through the crowd to lay his hand on Killyama's shoulder.

"Is there anything else you forgot to tell me?"

She really didn't want to tell Stud anything else, but the warning glint in Sex Piston's eyes had her confessing the rest.

"He called me one night, calling me names, but I took care of it. I went to his office and played the recording."

His dark expression went from bad to worse. Stud's fury had her regretting having her friends keep the secret. She should have known Fat Louise wouldn't keep quiet.

"You still have the recording on your phone? I would think twice before lying to me."

She apprehensively took out her phone, playing back the message. When filth spewed out of the phone, she flinched as Stud reached out and overturned the table, sending beer bottles and popcorn flying.

Sex Piston's eyes widened at her husband's behavior. She shakily stood up. "Stud—"

"You heard that shit and didn't tell me?"

"She didn't play it for me. I didn't realize it was that bad—"

"It was bad when the douchebag tried to roofie her." He pointed toward Crazy Bitch's phone. "That sick motherfucker isn't rational. I'm going to call Knox, and you're going to make a report."

"Okay." Crazy Bitch bowed her head, acknowledging she had screwed up. "I was worried that if you knew, you or one of the other brothers would hurt him."

"You don't care about that pervert, do you?"

"Hell no!" Aghast, she stared at him at the question. "I didn't want any of you doing jail time because I was stupid enough to go out with him."

"That says a lot about my inability as president that you think I'm not smart enough to keep from getting caught when I kill the motherfucker."

She blanched. "I do not want him killed. He's not worth the trouble it would cost the club!"

Stud shoved the table away, looming over her. "If someone had treated Sex Piston that way, what would you do?"

She tugged at her bottom lip. Crazy Bitch knew what she would do. "I'm not Sex Piston."

"You think you're any less important than she is to the brothers? I'm married to Sex Piston, but I became your president in this club when I accepted Skulls' offer to make this club a charter of the Blue Horsemen. That means I accepted every man and woman as my responsibility. You listening to me?"

"Yes." She blinked back tears at his fierce tirade.

"That includes you! All of you!"

"I was wrong," she admitted when his gaze returned to hers after he was sure he had everyone's attention. "I was only doing what I thought was best for the club."

"That's *my* fucking job." Stud smacked his chest with a fist. "That's Cade's job, that's Bear's job, and that's fucking Train's job—protection. Not for you to take it into your own hands and decide what's best for everyone else. That's why we're a club!"

He turned away from her. "When we call church tomorrow night, the brothers will decide on your punishment. Sex Piston, Fat Louise, and T.A. will also receive their share for keeping your secret."

"Stud, I'll take your punishment. I'll take theirs, too, since I had to talk them into it." Crazy Bitch hated seeing Stud so angry. She hadn't meant to diminish his role as president over the bitch, but by asking them to keep the secret she had done just that.

"Fine," he snapped. "You clean this fucking mess after you go to my office and talk to Knox. I'll count one of the punishments off."

He didn't seem happy about letting her get off with such a simple punishment, but Stud was fair. He had been the one to make the mess because he was so angry at her. He didn't want to punish the other women. She took to heart that the other punishments wouldn't be so easy to accomplish.

She followed him into the office, listening as he Face-Timed Knox and explained what she had told him.

"You threw the drink at him?"

Crazy Bitch took a seat next to Stud so Knox would be able to see them through the phone.

"Yes, I was so angry I wasn't thinking."

"Did you take any pictures of your face, or did anyone see your face with the bruises?"

"No."

Knox shook his head. "I won't say you handled this wrong. I'm sure Stud's already told you that."

"Yes, he has."

Knox looked thoughtful. "I've met the sheriff in Jamestown a couple times. I can understand your concerns. Lucky's had to deal with him more than I have. I stay away from a-holes whose egos are bigger than their badges. He's under investigation with the DEA for a couple of mishandlings of OD deaths in Jamestown in the last four months."

Crazy Bitch shot Stud a sidelong look, hoping Knox's words would take out some of the sting of her not confiding in him. It didn't.

"I didn't call the sheriff here. I called you. I don't trust Eli any more than the DEA does."

"Send me your ex's full name and date of birth. I'll see what I can pull up. We can go from there when I get the results back. Crazy Bitch, if you see him again, call Stud immediately. Don't take any chances."

"I haven't seen him since I went to his office. And Fat Louise said he no longer works there. I haven't gotten another phone call, either. I'm sure he's too scared to try anything else. A man who roofies a woman doesn't have balls, anyway."

"I hope you're right."

The phone that Knox was holding jiggled as it was turned, showing another face staring back at her.

Greer, dressed in a deputy's uniform, explaining why he was in Knox's office. It also explained why Knox had seemed so aggravated when he had answered Stud's FaceTime call.

"A man doesn't roofie a woman because he's afraid of

getting caught. They do it because they're hiding something. Find out what he's hiding, and you'll be able to catch the bastard before he does it to someone else."

"Thanks for your advice, Greer." Stud held his cell phone tighter, trying to settle the picture as Knox and Greer struggled over his phone.

"How are the Destructors doing with my clues?" Greer's face suddenly righted as Knox stopped trying to get his phone back. Crazy Bitch saw that he was just as interested in Stud's answer as Greer was.

"We could use a little help with the frozen one."

Greer looked delighted that they hadn't found the castle clue yet. Each of their teams had returned, unable to find the next clue.

"I'll give you another clue. Use your fucking brain." He sniggered.

Knox must have grabbed his phone back, because the connection went haywire before the call disconnected.

"He's a son of a bitch." Stud stared at his phone as if he wanted to reach out and drag Greer out of the device.

"That's what Sex Piston and I have been trying to tell you." The Destructors were taking bets on who would be the first one to beat Greer to a bloody pulp. The pot was beginning to be worth as much as the treasure he had hidden.

Stud's anger returned in a flash, sobering her as he pulled up his contacts on his cell phone.

"You calling Knox back?"

"No, I'm calling Calder."

Crazy Bitch left Stud's office so fast she didn't bother closing the door, wincing when she heard it slam shut before she made it back to the clubroom.

Going to their table, she saw that they had already cleaned up the upturned table and broken beer bottles.

"Stud's not going to be happy when he finds out you cleaned. I was supposed to do it."

"I'm a big girl. I don't need you doing my punishments for me." Sex Piston brushed off the drops of beer that were clinging to the tabletop.

Crazy Bitch grabbed her purse. "I'm out of here. Anyone need a ride?"

"I got a new dress on. I don't want it ruined by the springs in your car."

Crazy Bitch started to tell her that it would be doing it a favor. The navy blue and white dress made her want to gag. It was suited for one of the uppity bitches who worked in offices who always set her teeth on edge.

"I haven't returned my rental car yet. Calder paid for it for an extra couple of days. It has a sunroof."

Fat Louise gathered her purse. "I'm ready. If I'm lucky, I'll have time to get home before Stud calls Cade."

"If we go now, you'll make it. He was calling Calder when I left him."

Sex Piston gave a low whistle. "You sure you don't want to go home with me? He's going to be pissed."

"The day I get afraid about how a man reacts to something I've done, do me a favor and put me down, besides he's still in Lexington."

"Then what's the rush to get home?" Sex Piston asked.

"I fucking gave my beer away like a loser. No reason to stay. I don't think Stud is going to be giving me one of his."

"I think you're right there. He's so mad right now he'd pour it down the drain before letting you have one."

Crazy Bitch winced. "I really fucked up. I'm sorry I dragged you all into this bullshit with Sam. Where's T.A.?"

"Bear hauled her off to his room. They haven't come back, so she must be making it up to him. She'll probably be the only one getting laid tonight."

"No, she won't." Killyama took the beer that Train was handing her.

Crazy Bitch flipped the lucky bitch off, waving bye to the others.

"What'd you say?" Fat Louise asked, trying to keep up with her as they walked toward the rental car.

She looked over the roof of the car, waiting for her to catch up. "I said, Killyama is the luckiest bitch I know. She was the only one who had a car when we went to high school, she was the only one who had a mother with a brain, she works with two men who are not only hot but they know how to kick ass, and she's the only one who's going to get laid tonight. And she has the nerve to gloat to us!"

"No, she isn't. T.A—"

"Bear couldn't fuck his way out of a paper bag." Crazy

Bitch snorted, unlocking the car door. "Those 'roids he uses to make his arms and neck bigger have shrunk his dick into a thimble."

Fat Louise giggled as she got into the car. "T.A. brags about how good he is."

Crazy Bitch started the car. "That bitch is lying."

Pulling out of the parking lot, she drove toward Fat Louise's house.

"How do you know?"

"I just know."

"Did you and Bear...?"

"Hell no. I might have been drunk one night and accidentally went into his bedroom by mistake. T.A. was trying to get a rise out of his limp noodle."

Fat Louise slapped her hand over her mouth. "Accidentally?"

"That's my story and I'm sticking to it."

She slowed the car, coming to a stop at a stop sign. Turning, she accelerated down the empty street, when the dark interior of the car was suddenly filled with red lights.

"Damn. It's the cops."

Fat Louise turned to look over her shoulder. "Were you speeding?"

"No... or I don't think I was." She was reaching for her purse for her license when there was a tap on her window.

She pushed the button, lowering it to see the grim-faced cop asking for her ID and registration.

"Was I speeding?" she asked, giving him her ID and the rental receipt that Calder had given her.

His lips tightened. "I'll be back." When he strode back to his police car, they turned to look at each other.

"I don't think I was speeding."

"I don't think you were, either."

The red lights highlighted their worried faces. Crazy

Bitch knew it wasn't a good sign when another patrol car arrived, pulling in front of her car and sandwiching them between the two cruisers.

"Passenger, step out of the car."

Fat Louise gave a frightened squeal when the bullhorn shouted instructions to get out.

"Does he mean me?" she gasped.

"Yes, you're the passenger. Be cool. Just get out and leave your purse."

Crazy Bitch watched as Fat Louise opened the door and stepped out, leaving the car door open.

She remained inside until she heard the bullhorn again.

"Driver, exit the car slowly."

She opened the door, getting out and facing the police car behind her. She had no more turned than she felt herself plastered against the side of the car.

"What...? Let me go! You can't handcuff me for speeding."

Obviously, they could. Handcuffs clicked onto her wrists.

Looking up, she saw Fat Louise in the same position.

Neither officer answered their questions. Taking their elbows, they led them to the end of the car, where they forced them to sit down on the curb.

A car with *Sheriff* blazoned on the side of the vehicle pulled up, neatly blocking them from sight of cars driving by.

Crazy Bitch started getting scared. The distant memory of the night that Winter and Lily had nearly been killed by a rogue deputy heightened the feeling that they weren't acting normal.

She had only seen Eli May a few times around town. He had been sheriff since she was a little girl. He should have retired a long time ago, but the town kept voting him in office. Crazy Bitch promised herself, the next time he ran, her ass would be out campaigning against him.

"You been drinking tonight?" he asked, looming over them.

Fat Louise looked up, frightened. "Yes, sir. I had a beer, but I wasn't driving."

The sheriff glanced at Crazy Bitch. "How about you?"

"I had two sips, not enough to register."

"We'll see about that. Doug, give her the breathalyzer. You mind if I check out your car?"

"It's not mine; it's a rental."

"It's rented to a Calder Riggs," the deputy said.

"Why you driving it, then?" the sheriff asked.

"My boyfriend rented it for me," Crazy Bitch answered, meeting his calculating eyes.

Her instincts went into overdrive. The asshole was acting too cocky. She could tell by his demeanor that he wanted to get her for something. He was itching to arrest her.

"Guess I don't need your permission to go search it, then, do we, boys?"

"I'm not giving permission." She glared up at him. "I don't have anything to hide, but I'm not giving permission. I have a friend who is a lawyer, and I know my rights. Either tell me what I've done and write a ticket, or let us go. If you're arresting me, I'm not saying shit until I see my lawyer."

The sheriff laughed down at her. "Send for the canine. If the dog gives you the all-clear, you can be on your way. What'd you pull them over for, Doug?"

"She blew a stop sign."

"He's lying."

"I'm not going to dignify that accusation by explaining myself." The thin, balding deputy looked like a puff of wind would blow him away.

"I bet you won't, since you're lying."

"She's telling the truth," Fat Louise defended her.

"Where's your ID?" the sheriff asked her.

"It's in my purse in the car. My name is Jane—"

"When I want your name, I'll ask for it." The sheriff gave them a complacent smile as an SUV parked behind his car.

"Something tells me this isn't going good," Fat Louise whispered out of the side of her mouth.

"No shit." Crazy Bitch made no effort to lower her voice.

They could only sit on the curb and watch as the deputy opened the back of the SUV, taking out a large German Shepherd. Holding the leash, the deputy led it to their parked car.

The Shepherd was led around the car, and then it sat down by the back door.

"How did I know Killer was going to do that?" The sheriff gave them a satisfied smile as he opened the back door.

"Go for it, Columbo!" Crazy Bitch yelled as he bent to look inside the car. "I don't give a fuck what you find."

"Don't antagonize him!" Fat Louise shushed her, but Crazy Bitch didn't care. The sheriff had been too sure of himself.

When he rose up a second later, she wasn't surprised to see him holding up a baggy as he walked back toward them. "This was under the car mat. You have prescriptions for these?"

"Fuck you! I want my lawyer."

"Doug, put loud mouth in your car. I'll take the quiet one. Mack, secure their purses and call for a tow truck."

"Sure thing, Sheriff."

The deputy took her arm, jerking her to her feet, as the sheriff lifted Fat Louise to hers.

"Sheriff…" She dragged her feet on the pavement. "You hurt one single hair on her head, and you can kiss that badge goodbye."

"You threatening me?" His smirk had her glad her hands were restrained.

"That deputy run my record?" she asked.

"Yes, ma'am."

"You should read it. I don't make threats."

"Add threatening an officer when you make your report," he told the deputy.

"You can shove that report up your ass!" Crazy Bitch snarled, trying to jerk away from the deputy's hold.

"Add resisting arrest," the sheriff said, shoving Fat Louise inside his car.

Crazy Bitch lowered her head as the deputy shoved her into the back of his squad car. Furious, she used her shoulder to keep him from shutting the door.

"You fucking know he planted that evidence on me!"

The deputy quit trying to shut the door on her, putting a hand on her forehead to push her farther into the squad car.

"I didn't run that stop sign!"

The deputy looked over his shoulder, making sure no one was near him. "No, you didn't."

At the admission, Crazy Bitch lost her temper. Her hands might have been restrained, but her feet weren't.

With one foot, she nailed him in the nuts, sending the deputy to his knees. His yell of pain sent the two officers who were still on scene coming to his aid. The deputy who had brought the dog pulled the foot she had used to nail in the other deputy's nuts away from the door of the car so the other one could close it.

Cursing them, she started kicking at the window, wishing it was the bastards' faces. She was still kicking the passenger side window when the deputy managed to get behind the steering wheel.

"You're going to pay for that, you stupid bitch."

"You fucking cocksucker! I'm not afraid of you." She switched sides, trying to kick the wired cage behind his seat, making sure she was hitting the spot behind his head.

"Stop!"

"My lawyer is going to rip you another asshole!"

She used her nails to rip at the upholstery behind her back as she kept kicking the cage.

When the deputy jerked the car to a stop at the sheriff's office, she heard him call for help. Her rage was out of control, yet she didn't care. It took three officers and a Taser to remove her from the cruiser.

After that, it was a blur as she was restrained to a metal chair, each limb handcuffed to the chair. Wheeled into a cell, she caught a glimpse of Fat Louise in the cell across from hers before the door was slammed shut.

She started wiggling on the seat, trying to make it move. Her rage was so overwhelming, adrenaline rushing through her system, that she refused to give up the futile struggle.

The deputy's confession had sent her over a tipping point. He'd had no fear admitting he had pulled her over without reason. If he was so sure enough of himself to drop his guard once, he would do it again. All it would take was pushing the right button. She might not have a college degree, but she had a PHD in making men regret screwing her over.

Visualizing putting her head through the steel door, she felt the metal chair slide a scant inch across the concrete floor, despite the brakes the deputy had engaged before leaving her cell.

"Ha!" she yelled out, proud of her success, wiggling harder as the cell door was swung open.

It was her last thought before another jolt of electricity shot through her body, stunning her senseless and dimming the cell walls as her eyes involuntary rolled upward.

With sheer force of will, she twisted one of her hands in the restraints, visualizing an imaginary hand holding hers, giving her the peace of mind she needed to succumb to the waiting darkness.

"How much longer do we have to wait?" Frustrated, Calder rubbed his hand across the back of his neck, trying to stretch the kink out of it.

He had started driving back from Lexington last night after Stud had called to tell him about Sam. He had every intention of finding that man and beating the hell out of him for trying to roofie Crazy Bitch. Then he had been forced to change his mind when he had stopped to get gas and saw Stud's text about her getting arrested.

Every pit-stop he made after that, the news kept getting worse until he stopped looking at the texts, afraid he would wreck if he rode any faster.

"Calder, calm down. Killyama will come outside the courtroom when they call Crazy Bitch's name." Diamond sat with her briefcase on her lap outside the courtroom, studying the documents in her hand.

"How did Fat Louise get out so fast and Crazy Bitch didn't?"

"Her charges were misdemeanors, and there were no aggravating circumstances. Crazy Bitch has a past history of offenses, though she wasn't convicted of any of them, thanks to me. She's why I moved to Treepoint. I was tired of getting her out of jail. At least she's stayed out of trouble since her mother's death. I was actually expecting worse when Sex Piston called to tell me she had been arrested. It could be worse."

"How could it be worse? She's been charged with drug possession, resisting arrest, destroying police property, and striking a police officer." Calder rubbed his neck harder, the tension making the crick in his neck worse.

"The car wasn't hers. It was rented in your name." Diamond glanced up at him, tapping her pen on the rental agreement where his name was signed on the bottom.

He paled. "I didn't even step foot in that car. I don't want this pinned on me for something I didn't do."

"Don't worry about it. I'll defend you and blame it on her if it goes to court. You have to love the judicial system. When it comes down to it, it can't be proven who was responsible for those drugs being in that car. By the time one of you are convicted, you'll be so old the state won't want to pay for your medical bills."

"What about the rest of the charges?"

"Those she's guilty of. She's looking at jail time or probation, and she'll have to make restitution for the property she destroyed. It's going to be a pretty penny. She ripped the upholstery in the back seat, one of the side windows is damaged, and they have to replace the barrier between the front and back seat. The charge that has me the most worried is striking an officer. The deputy said she hit him in the back of his head when he was driving. She could do serious time for that. Are you sure you know what you're getting into with her?"

"I love her." He felt a muscle spasm at the back of his neck at his admission.

The door of the courtroom opened, and Killyama motioned for them.

Diamond placed a folder back in her briefcase before standing. "I hope you don't want children. If she gets convicted, you can kiss the likelihood of that happening good-bye. You should take some aspirin for your neck. It looks like it hurts."

"You have no idea," he stated, unable to move his neck to look at her. "I don't take aspirins. It'll work its way out in a couple of days."

"You should go to a chiropractor. It'll be less painful than waiting. This shouldn't take long. It's just a parole hearing."

"How are we supposed to pay if it's a large amount? The club doesn't have much money, and Kentucky doesn't allow bail bond companies to post bail. It has to be cash… and none of us have a lot."

"I'll take care of it. Don't worry."

"You have that kind of money?" he asked.

"Enough to pay, unless it's for a ridiculous amount. Don't worry." Diamond went through the door first, coming to an abrupt stop. Turning back, she gripped the door tightly. "You should wait out here. I'll come outside after I get her released."

He lifted his brow. "Why? I want to go inside."

"I have money, but I'm not rich. I don't have enough to get you both out of jail. Do me a favor and go sit down and wait."

He wanted to rip the door out of her hand, but he didn't want to make her angry by doing it. He had promised to be at Crazy Bitch's back whenever she needed him. He had failed last night by not being there to keep her from getting arrested. He wouldn't fail her now.

"I'm going into that courtroom. I won't make a sound, whatever happens. I swear."

"I'm going to hold you to your words."

Diamond released the door, and Calder followed her inside, immediately regretting making the promise.

Finding a seat next to Sex Piston and Stud, he saw they were tightly holding hands. They were just as upset as he was at Crazy Bitch's appearance.

Diamond took her seat at the table in front of the judge where Crazy Bitch was standing, her hands and feet shackled, and her hair that was always styled and teased upward was a holy mess, sticking out in different angles. When she had turned to watch them enter the courtroom, he had seen how the left side of her face was bruised and she had a gash on her forehead. Seeing her in the orange jumpsuit broke his heart, imagining how they had gotten her out of her clothes.

The judge looked over his glasses at Diamond as the bailiff read the charges off. The judge's face grew glacial.

"Ms. Macrae, our police have enough to do without you making their jobs harder. Have you got anything to say for yourself?"

"Yes, I f… Yes, I do, Your Honor."

Diamond covered the microphone so those sitting in the courtroom couldn't hear what she said to Crazy Bitch.

"Mrs. Richards-Bates we're waiting."

"Yes, Your Honor. I'm sorry. Go ahead, Anna-Kate."

From where he was sitting, Calder could see the warning look on Diamond's face as she pulled her hand away from the microphone.

"I was just about to say that I have been falsely accused."

"Of which charge? Resisting arrest?" the judge asked.

"No, I did that," she admitted.

"Destroying police property?"

"No, I did that, too."

Diamond put her hand over the microphone again. This

time, Calder could hear the women arguing without the microphone.

"Do you want out of here? Shut up!"

"I'm going to tell the truth. You're supposed to tell the truth and swear on a Bible, aren't you?" Crazy Bitch whispered loudly.

"Do you see a Bible?" Diamond hissed back.

"No."

"Then shut up!"

"Okay."

The women turned back to the judge.

"Are you ready to explain which charges you have been falsely accused of?" The judge pushed his glasses back up his nose.

"I'm trying, but she keeps interrupting me." Crazy Bitch nodded her head sideways at Diamond.

"So, are you guilty of striking an officer?"

"Not technically, no."

"What do you mean, *not technically*? Either you did or you didn't."

"He was a police officer. And may I state for the record that I do admire and thank them for the job they do, but he stopped being a police officer when he pulled me over without just cause. I stopped at that stop sign, I didn't have a light out, and I wasn't speeding. When he put me in the back of his car, he admitted it to me, so when I kicked that metal cage, I wasn't hitting a police officer. I was hitting a kidnapper."

The longer Crazy Bitch talked, the more the judge's face took on a ruddy hue.

Calder wanted to bury his hands in his hair, but his neck hurt too bad.

"So, you're saying you were falsely accused of running the stop sign?"

"Yes, Your Honor, and the pills. They weren't mine. Do you have a CSI to test the baggie for fingerprints? Mine are on file if you want to match them."

"Ms. Macrae, we don't have a CSI."

"That sucks. They wouldn't find mine if you did."

"Ms. Macrae, I don't find that reassuring. With your history—"

"You see any drug charges on that record?"

"Ms. Macrae, remain silent until you're asked to respond."

"Yes, Your Highness."

The judge's jowly face shook as he pointed a finger at Crazy Bitch. "I'm setting bail at full cash, three-hundred-thousand-dollar bond." The judge started to pound his gavel down.

"Your Honor, Ms. Macrae is a hairdresser. She has nothing of value to meet that bond. She's isn't a flight risk—"

"Your Honor, I don't have any family to run to. I've only lived in Jamestown. I've never been out of the country, unless you count the time I went to Mexico to rescue Fat Louise, and I came right back. I have to feed my cat. He gets lonely without me. The only friends I have are in this courtroom, and they can't afford that bail."

"Ms. Macrae, you should have thought about that before you struck an officer." The judge slammed his gavel down then left with a *swoosh* of his robe.

Calder went to the wooden barrier as Crazy Bitch turned to leave at the deputy's urging.

"Hot thang! You're back!" She tried to shuffle toward him. "I was going to make you dinner."

The deputy took her arm, leading her to the side of the courtroom.

"I missed your smiling face, so I came back early."

"Awe. I might need to start calling you sweet cheeks," she said, blowing him a kiss. Then she gave him a water-filled smile. "Wait for me!" she yelled dramatically as the deputy tried to push her through the door. Then she tried to hop up so she could see him. "Don't let those sluts at the club get you to stray. Remember, you're mine!" she howled as the door swung shut.

"Jesus." Diamond fanned her face with her folder before she went to the row of seats where Sex Piston and Stud were sitting. "I'm pregnant, and that woman makes me want a stiff drink."

"I have five thousand in my checking account." Calder took out his debit card.

"I have twelve thousand, give or take." Sex Piston opened her purse, taking hers out.

"I thought you're broke?" Stud asked, dropping the hand he had been holding.

"It's my emergency money in case our marriage doesn't work out."

"We've been married for six years." Stud reached for his wallet. "I have four thousand. I'd have more, but you're always telling me you're broke."

Killyama reached in her back pocket. "I brought a check for fifty thousand."

"Next time, you're buying lunch," T.A. said, taking an envelope out her purse. "Here's seven thousand in cash. The brothers, me, and Fat Louise put in. I tried to convince Cade, but he's still mad at Crazy Bitch for not letting Fat Louise tell him about Sam. How much is that?"

"It's not three hundred thousand," Diamond said, still fanning herself.

"Ma and Skulls don't have money."

"My mother would give some if she was here." Killyama cast a look at Train, who was trying to avoid looking at her directly.

Giving a hard sigh, he took out his wallet, the chain

attached whipping his leg at the jerking movement. "Where do we pay?"

Killyama's unhappy frown broke into a relieved smile. "How much are you putting in?"

"All of it. You all can keep your money."

Killyama was so happy she jumped on Train, wrapping her legs around his waist and kissing him. "Thank you, thank you, thank you. When we get home, I'm going to do something for you," she promised, dropping back to her feet.

"I'll show you where you pay. Then I'm going to the sheriff's office to be there when they release her. I don't trust her not to do something to screw it up before I can get her out." Diamond fastened her briefcase, standing up.

"I'll go with you. Give me a second," Calder said to Diamond, holding his hand out to Train. "I owe Shade a debt. Now I owe you, though I don't know how I'll be able to repay you."

Train took his hand, not releasing it. "You don't owe me shit. Crazy Bitch won't break bail, so I'll get my money back. What you and Peyton are doing for Gavin is a debt we can't repay."

Calder gripped Train's hand tighter. "I will always be there for Gavin when he needs me."

When Train released his hand, Calder went with a waiting Diamond to the parking lot. Getting on his bike, he rode behind her as she drove her car to the police station where Crazy Bitch was being held.

They waited in the lobby for the call to come through, and when it did, the sheriff and four of his deputies went through a steel door to get her.

Calder heard Diamond mumbling.

"I can't hear what you are saying."

"I am praying."

"She wouldn't really do anything that would keep her from getting released, would she?"

Diamond gave him a look filled with exasperation. "You have no idea. Crazy Bitch is crazy. If she feels that she or someone she loves has been wronged, she goes after them no-holds-barred. Did she ever tell you about the men she killed?"

"I thought she was joking."

"She wasn't joking. She was telling you the truth. Her mother was one of the worst addicts I've ever met, and I've met a few. She'd get waitressing jobs, but as soon as she got a new boyfriend, she'd quit working. To give her credit, she made sure none of those lowlifes ever touched Crazy Bitch. That being said, she spent most of her time going back and forth to different foster homes. As far as I know, most of them treated her fairly well, but I don't know for sure. She really hasn't ever talked to me personally, and Sex Piston and her crew damn sure wouldn't say anything if she did.

"One of her boyfriends had a rap sheet of domestic violence charges. A couple of them were brought on by Crazy Bitch's mother. She kicked him out and managed to get custody back during one of those times.

"One day, Crazy Bitch came home from school and heard her mother in the bathroom, crying for help. When she went to the bathroom, she found her half dead, the boyfriend strangling her. Crazy Bitch went nuts trying to get him off her. She went to the kitchen and got a knife. When she came back, he was still on top of her mother. She stabbed him in the back. They tried her for murder, but she was acquitted."

"I don't remember hearing about that, and I've known her a long time."

"I didn't know about it either until I got my law degree and had to get her out of jail one time for breaking a man's jaw because he had tried to rape T.A. As her lawyer, I was given access to her records. None of the other brothers know because she was underage and her identity had to be protected."

"How old was she?" Calder asked hoarsely.

"Eleven years old."

"Why are you telling me? You wouldn't talk to Stud about my case because I wouldn't give you permission." Calder hadn't been trying to convince Gavin to trust Diamond for no reason. Besides being a hell of a lawyer, she knew how to keep her mouth shut. She didn't talk about other clients' cases.

"Because, when I had an office in Jamestown, all my cases were here. Several of those cases were for the Destructors, and those include Crazy Bitch's." Diamond stepped to the side, motioning for him.

She lowered her voice to make sure no one in the offices could hear them. "When I talked to Crazy Bitch last night, she said she knew something didn't feel right when the sheriff showed up. She said, as many times as she's dealt with the cops, the sheriff has never responded to a call. She's right. I grew up here. I've never dealt with him, either.

"He comes to work about ten and leaves about four. Anytime I've had to come to the station, he's always in his office. Crazy Bitch said that when the deputy put her in his car, he told her that she hadn't blown the stop sign."

"Why would he tell her that?" Becoming indignant at Crazy Bitch's treatment, he warily looked around the room to make sure no one could overhear their conversation.

"I think he did it to set her off. Anyone who has access to her rap sheet would know she has anger issues."

"What kind of anger issues?"

"Nothing for you to worry about." Diamond's mouth closed tightly.

Her discussing Crazy Bitch's record showed she felt he needed to know this to understand that Diamond believed Crazy Bitch's traffic stop had been a setup.

"I agree. I may have seen a few of those issues." Calder thought about the night she had goaded the rednecks into coming up to their hotel room. "Nothing I can't handle."

"I don't doubt you can. You have a few issues of your own."

"That's what makes us the perfect couple."

"I wouldn't go that far, but you two definitely deserve one another."

"You being sarcastic?" Him liking Diamond took a nose-dive at her comment.

"Don't look at me like that." She gave him an encouraging smile. "I meant it as a compliment. There is no perfect couple. They each have their differences, like two pieces in a puzzle that fit together. But when you put them together, they fit. You and Crazy Bitch fit, like me and Knox fit."

He solemnly stared at the door again. "I never felt like this before. I feel whole, as if a part of me has been missing, and now it's suddenly there. I don't know where it came from."

"I understand." Her eyes grew misty as she patted her barely recognizably pregnant belly. "Must be my hormones making me so sentimental." She pressed her fingers to the corner of her eye.

"Do you know what you're having yet?"

"You're kidding, right? I don't need an ultrasound to know it's a boy. It's Knox's kid."

The two of them laughed, breaking the moment of sharing their love for their partners as the door opened and Crazy Bitch was escorted out.

"I'll be seeing you." The sheriff gave her a threatening glare.

"Not if I see you first." She was snapping her head back around when her eyes locked on his. "Hot thang! You didn't forget me!" She ran toward him, her arms out.

Calder couldn't help it; he laughed as she jumped into his waiting arms, wrapping her legs around his waist.

"I only saw you about thirty minutes ago." He stroked her cheek with his.

"You and Killyama need to be more circumspect."

Crazy Bitch turned her cheek away to glare at Diamond. "Don't lift that snooty nose at me, girlfriend. Don't act like you don't jump Knox's bones two or three times a day. All bitches are the same under the sheets."

Calder broke the budding argument. "I see you have a new piece of jewelry." He tapped her ankle as her legs slipped from around his waist.

She snorted. "As if anyone could keep me in town if I wanted to leave."

Calder saw the sheriff fiddling with his handcuffs. "Let's go before you talk yourself into being rearrested."

"I need to get my purse. My phone is in there. How'd you come up with the money to bail me out?"

"Train."

"That's it? Just Train?"

"Yes." Calder couldn't understand why Crazy Bitch was beginning to look irritated.

"That lucky bitch!"

"Who?"

"Killyama."

"I don't understand," Calder stated.

Crazy Bitch's irritation cleared. She reached up to pat him on his cheek. "Never mind, hot thang. I still have her beat. You're better looking."

"Thanks… I think."

"Let's get your stuff. I need a nap." Diamond tapped her foot to speed them up to the counter.

"Jeez, I'm coming. Being knocked up has turned you into a real bitch. Wait." She came to a stop, putting a finger to her forehead. "You already were one."

"OMG! Can we please leave?"

"Okay, okay. It's my stuff." Crazy Bitch leaned cockily against the counter, giving the deputy behind the counter an evil eye as he turned to get her belongings. "I need to get my phone so I can call Train and thank him."

Diamond glanced down at her wristwatch. "I'd wait and call him later," she said, looking back at her.

"Why?"

"Killyama promised him a special surprise for bailing you out of jail."

"Huh?" Crazy Bitch's face scrunched in a worried frown.

"I said…" Diamond repeated. "Killyama promised—"

"I heard you the first time. Hurry up!" Crazy Bitch slammed her hand down on the counter. "I need that phone."

"What's the hurry?" Calder moved closer to her, not wanting her to piss the deputy off.

"I have to save a life!" she yelled hysterically.

"Who?" Calder, Diamond, and the deputy asked as he came back to the counter with a plastic bin with her belongings.

"Penni."

How long did it take to find a key?

Calder bit back the groan at the back of his throat. He had missed her over the last four days, and instead of wanting to come back to her apartment immediately, she had wanted to grab breakfast.

Crazy Bitch had sat next to him, teasing him the entire time, sometimes deliberately, like keeping her hand intimately on his thigh as they ate, or unconsciously when she licked a dollop of strawberry jelly from her bottom lip. On the ride to her apartment, she described what she wanted to do to him in detail. Every time he had to stop because of traffic or a red light had become a sexual torture. Now he had to watch her search for her apartment keys.

"You want me to find them?" he asked, bracing one hand on the doorjamb and laying the other one on her ass, squeezing it firmly.

"I got it." Taking out her keys, Crazy Bitch slid the key in the door, turning it with a sharp twist that had his gut clenching.

Instead of opening the door, she turned around, resting her back against the door.

"How's your dick?"

"Open the door and find out."

Calder wasn't about to ignore the invitation of her waiting lips. Leaning down, he licked her bottom one, tasting the strawberry jam she had enjoyed. Parting her lips, he searched for more, delving into her mouth with lust-filled intentions.

Crazy Bitch buried her hands in his hair; the crick in his neck echoed the pain in his dick.

"You need a haircut."

"That isn't all I need," he moaned against her lips.

"What do you need, hot thang?" she murmured back seductively.

"I need to fuck you!"

"Then go inside!" a voice behind them groused as a woman passed them, going to the apartment next door.

Crazy Bitch's soft laughter filled his mouth as she broke the kiss. "Sorry, Ollie."

Her neighbor didn't bother to say anything, going inside her apartment.

"Something wrong with your door?"

"No, why?"

"You haven't opened it yet."

"You haven't said the magic words yet." She wadded up his T-shirt, pulling him closer to her. He felt the pinpoint of her nipples beneath her thin top.

He swallowed hard, his cock swelling inside his jeans so much that he became worried the zipper would bust, and become a viral video of anyone passing by on the landing. "Please."

"That's not it." She started to languorously rub her breasts against his chest.

Trying to come up with a word that would get her to open the door was beyond his capabilities when all he wanted to do was tear her clothes off and fuck her.

"You need a hint?" She gripped his cock through the denim of his jeans.

"Fuck me!"

"Wow. Give the man a cigar." She twisted the doorknob behind her back, letting the door fall open behind her.

Calder lifted her up by her waist, carrying her into the apartment and using his foot to swing the door closed.

"I have two words for you," he grunted out, turning her around to face her forward as he pushed his hips into her ass. "Bend over."

Toppling her over the back of her couch, he slid his hand to her hips to jerk her jeans and panties down, baring her ass.

When she would have risen up, he smacked one luscious cheek.

"Motherfucker!" she screamed, trying to wiggle out of his hold.

"That's for not telling me about Sam." He placed a firm hand on her back, keeping her exactly where he wanted her. "Diamond said you got that mark on your forehead by trying to bang your head through a steel door. That true?"

"Fuck you!"

Another smack landed on her ass.

"That's in the same spot!" she bellowed.

"Good. That's where I was aiming it." He deftly kept her immobile as a series of smacks turned her cheek a rosy red.

"What are those for?" she screeched.

"For the crick in my neck. I nearly killed myself four times getting here when Stud texted me that you had been arrested and that you resisted."

"I was framed!"

He spanked her again.

"Ouch! That one hurt!"

"Do you know how frightened I was for you? *Do you?*"

She quit trying to get away from him. "No."

"I've been in jail. Do you not see the rips in your T-shirt and jeans?" He leaned over her back, placing kisses down her spine. "How can I catch you if I'm not there?"

"I don't need you to catch me."

Calder wasn't sure, but he thought he heard her voice tremble.

"Maybe I need you to catch me. You think of that when you were hurting yourself?"

"No," she acknowledged.

This time, he was sure her voice was trembling.

"Well, I do. If anything happens to you, it happens to me." He stroked over the curve of her ass before slipping inside the crack to find the heated warmth of her pussy. He expertly strummed her engorged clit.

"Omph!"

"What did you say?"

Crazy Bitch lifted her head from the couch. "I said, do that again!"

"Oh, baby, I am. I'm going to fuck you so hard that the next time a cop tells you to get in the back of the car, you'll say, 'Yes, sir.'"

"That is go—ouch!"

"What did you say?" he asked, lifting his thumb from her clit.

"Nothing! I didn't say a damn thing!"

"I didn't think so." He moved his fingers to another target, sliding roughly inside her wet pussy and fucking her with them until her hands splayed out on the couch, trying to give herself traction so she could fuck back against him. He didn't let her have it. Keeping her off balance, he controlled her by keeping her feet off the floor, holding her farther over the back of the couch.

"You know, about halfway from Lexington... Did I mention the crick in my neck?"

"Yes!"

"Anyway, halfway from Lexington, it dawns on me that I may have given you the wrong impression. You think I am a gentleman, that you can just run over me. Did I give you that impression?"

He listened intently, not hearing a peep from her.

"I see that I was right. Anyway, I made two decisions on the rest of the ride, that if I was going to pursue a relationship with you, I was either going to get a chiropractor, or make you realize that every time you decide to be a pain in my neck, you're going to feel my pain on your ass. Do you feel that's fair?"

"Not really," she mumbled, raising her shoulders up as she tried to look back at him.

He let his fingers slip out of her cunt, letting her see that he was about to spank her again.

"Yes! Yes, it's fair!"

"Good. I'm glad we can see eye-to-your-ass that this will make us both happier."

Calder used the hand he was about to spank her with to reach into his back pocket, taking out his wallet. Still keeping a firm hand on her back, he used her back to open his wallet and take out a condom. Letting the wallet fall down to the couch, he then used his teeth to tear the wrapper while using his free hand to unzip and tug his jeans down.

"You want to know what will make me happy?" Crazy Bitch pushed her ass backward, jiggling her still pink ass cheek.

Finally managing to cover his cock, he aimed his dick at her opening, driving inside with a hard plunge that had him gritting his teeth.

"Fuck!"

"That's it! Oh, God! Do that again!"

It took all his willpower to slide his dick back out of her opening, just letting the tip remain inside, then driving it forward again higher. Repeating the motion, he rhythmically set a pace that stroked the fire in his balls and had her whimpers escalating into moans.

Lifting her higher over the couch, he was able to watch his cock slide into her silky pussy, his stomach clenching at the erotic sight.

The pleasure at seeing his hands holding her ass open as he fucked her made every miserable night he had spent in prison worth every minute. Hell, every minute of his life was worth this moment in time. Having her spread before him as he drove into her depths, trying to reach for something he had never managed to reach before, to catch Crazy Bitch before she could run out of his reach, to reach the point where a mountaintop soared over the land and met the sky.

He thrust deeper and higher, his hips surging forward and backward, trying to slow her down with his hands as he climbed faster. The desire tingled at the base of his cock, traveling along his length until he could no longer tell where he began and she ended, fusing them together as he felt her muscles rippling as she climaxed. He was determined to keep his promise.

He tumbled down, disappearing in a free-fall that neither would be capable of surviving intact.

"Damn. Next time I fuck you, I'll say my prayers."

Calder grinned, helping her off the back of the couch. "It was that good?"

She shakily pushed her hair back from a flushed face. "Hot thang, it was so good you should come with a warning."

"You're the one who should have come with a warning."

"What would it say?"

Calder loved it when they bantered back and forth. It was then she would slip out of that armor she hid behind to have fun.

"Continual use will result in a stiff neck and a sore dick."

She saucily took off her T-shirt, throwing it over her shoulder toward the couch, following it with a wispy bra that didn't quite make it, hanging drunkenly over the back before dropping to the floor.

"I thought you said your dick was better?"

He grinned, taking off his own T-shirt and throwing it toward the couch with hers. "I said continual use, sweet cheeks. We're just getting started."

27

"I thought you were going to make dinner while I showered?"

"I did." She grinned at him. "Voilà." Taking a bite of the pizza, she kept her beer steady that she was holding in the center of crossed legs as he jumped and sat down on the bed.

"You're looking rickety there, old man. You're neck really is hurting, isn't it? I thought you were joking."

"Nope." He slowly moved a pillow to place it behind his back before settling back with a slice of pizza.

She reached over to her side table to hand him a beer.

"How's Gavin?" she asked.

He finished his bite of pizza before answering. "Not good. He eats, works out, and sleeps. He barely talks. I'm worried about him. Viper and Ton are constantly there, but it makes no difference; it's as if he doesn't see them."

"I wish there was something I could do." She chewed thoughtfully trying to think of something that would make a difference. She would go and see him, but thanks to the monitor, she wouldn't be going anywhere until it was off.

"Damn it, I just thought of something. I can't search more clues until this monitor is off."

"It's not like were making any progress anyway. None of the teams have."

Crazy Bitch stretched her arm out to grab a notebook from the drawer of her nightstand, setting it down next to him on the mattress.

"I started a notebook to keep the clues straight."

Calder took the notebook, opening it to read the clues, concentrating on the page that had the last clue.

He read it aloud.

"The ground beneath me is frozen. No kings or queens live here. You can enter my gates, but unless you have an invitation, you won't be allowed to stay and rescue the damsel."

"We checked every floor of the castle we stayed in. I didn't see any damsel in distress or how to save her." Crazy Bitch handed Calder another slice of pizza before taking another for herself.

"Maybe we placed too much trust on the others in being able to recognize the clue. What if they missed it?"

"We could have, too," Crazy Bitch agreed. "The only way of knowing is if we go back and actually go to the other castles. I'm game for a road trip." She used her elbow to tap the ankle monitor. "But until it's off, it will have to wait."

"Or someone else finds the treasure."

"Bite your tongue. I refuse to believe anyone else will win it before us."

Calder stopped chewing. "What if someone else thinks the same thing? We've been ahead this whole game. Maybe someone doesn't want us to get there first. Why would someone plant drugs in the car you were driving? There had to be a reason."

"I have a reason for you. That sheriff was an asshole. You want another slice of pizza?"

"No thanks. I'm full."

Crazy Bitch took her last bite, closing the pizza box as she finished her beer. Carrying the box and empty beer bottles into the kitchen, she then went to her bathroom to wash her hands and brush her teeth.

Leaving the water on to get hot, she filled a cup with hot water before turning it off. Opening her bathroom closet, she searched for a vial of massage oil, putting it in the cup of hot water to heat. Carrying it into the bedroom, she set it down on the bedside table next to Calder.

"Alexa, dim my lights."

Her overhead light went to dim mode.

"If you can do that, why do you ask me to turn the light off?" Calder asked.

"I don't want you to get lazy." She gently took the pillow out from his back. "Now lie down on your stomach." She kissed his cheek when he did. "I thought you would argue with me."

"Any time you want me to lie down, all you have to do is ask."

She broke the top off the massage oil, letting it spill into the palms of her hands. Working the oil into his neck muscles and shoulders, she felt the coiled tension under her fingertips.

"Sex Piston took my appointments today. I told her I'd take hers for the next two days. I also told her we would watch the kids if she and Stud want to check out the castles to double-check that we didn't miss anything."

"That feels amazing," he groaned. "I was going to have a talk with Stud tomorrow. It can wait until he gets back."

"About Star?"

"Yes."

"I think it's the right decision."

"I'm going to talk to him, but I'm going to play it the way he wants."

Crazy Bitch straddled him on the bed, putting her weight on her knees and not on him. She edged her hands down to his shoulder blades, then his sides, working the knots and tension out of him and letting the room go silent to put him in a peaceful frame of mind. She knew when he had fallen asleep; he sank deeper into the mattress and his body became heavier.

She carefully moved over him, not wanting to disturb his sleep. Then, going back to the bathroom, she silently closed the door then showered to remove the oil.

Her sheets would be a mess in the morning. She had already changed them after their lovemaking before the pizza had arrived. The ones on the bed now were her extra set. She hadn't gone down to the basement to do laundry in a while. It gave her the fucking creeps, so she always made sure she did laundry during the day.

Yawning, she turned the water off then toweled off, thinking about how she would wash a load before going to work tomorrow.

Returning to the bedroom, she put on a clean nightshirt then went to the wall to turn the light off. She didn't want the sound of her voice waking Calder. He was exhausted from the ride from Lexington, and she knew he hadn't slept since being back in town. Crazy Bitch wanted to cuddle with him, but didn't want to rouse him.

Her mind went over the clue that Calder had read out. He thought someone was trying to stop her from winning the bikes. She shook her head on her pillow, trying to become more comfortable. Someone *was* trying to stop her. What Calder didn't know was she was trying to win something more valuable than a thousand bikes. She was trying to save a town.

SHE WOKE EARLY the next morning. The morning sun peeking in the blinds had her looking toward Calder to see he hadn't moved.

Dressing, she put on her least favorite stretchy leggings to hide the monitor and slipped on her sneakers she would change before going to work. Picking out a teal off-the-shoulder top, she finished dressing then picked up the laundry basket. Stopping at the hall closet, she plunked down the laundry detergent onto the clothes before carrying it outside to go down two flights of stairs to the laundry room.

The light was out when she opened the door. Turning it on, she walked around the room, making sure it was empty before she hurriedly separated her clothes and started the washers for a quick wash.

Turning toward the doorway, she nearly screamed when she saw a dark figure coming into the room. When he raised his face from underneath his hat, she gave a relieved sigh.

"You nearly caused me to have a fucking heart attack!"

Her sigh might have come too soon.

Lucky furiously strode toward her. "Have you lost your mind coming down here? How are we supposed to keep an eye on you if you keep doing stupid stunts?"

Crazy Bitch folded her hands over her chest. "I made the last man who talked to me that way regret it."

"I'm already regretting your involvement. One more thing goes wrong, I'm pulling the plug."

"You do it, and I'll keep trying to bring that sheriff around myself."

"What's it going to take to make you stop? You going to prison, or worse, being dead?"

"I'm not going to be dead. Your narcotic buddies are watching out for me. I'm not stopping. I told you when my mother died from that OD that I was going to find who was responsible for supplying her with those pills. If I hadn't screwed up by throwing that drink at Sam, we would have been able to use him."

"That wasn't the only way you screwed up. You going to his office had his boss taking another look at him when two women in the office got enough courage to complain about Sam."

She shrugged. "I told you I didn't trust that he wouldn't try that shit on another woman. I wasn't going to have that on my conscience, knowing we could have stopped it from happening."

"The Narcotic Task Force was working on getting a search warrant."

"They get one? Fat Louise said he quit."

"He did. When his boss was looking into the complaints, he discovered numerous prescriptions to patients he hadn't authorized. Sam had."

"So, arrest him. Make him tell you that he's paying the sheriff off, too. I told you when I found his burner phone in my back seat and gave it to Shade that I would do anything necessary to help, and I've done everything you wanted, except when I went to Sam's office."

"What you did was spook him when the doctor started digging, which was what the task force didn't want. You're no longer a credible witness." Lucky moved to the side when the washer stopped to put the wet clothes into the dryer.

"Those weren't my pills, and you know it was bullshit I was even pulled over."

Lucky nodded. "They know, but the drugs were still found, and now you have a list of charges against you."

"I guess your buddies on the task force need to make the charges disappear."

"They can't just make them disappear. It's not that simple. They have to have proof he planted the drugs in your car."

"Then find what you need and quit pussy-footing around. Jamestown is becoming a ghost town. More people are dying every day while the drug task force tries to build a case against the sheriff."

"They're trying. I'm trying. This isn't the first time I've tried to take Eli down. I don't want to lose him a second time."

Crazy Bitch opened the dryers, dumping her clean laundry into her basket and setting the detergent on top.

"You're wrinkling your clothes."

She shrugged, unconcerned. "I need a favor for if anything happens to me. It's a big one. I had to take several hits being an informant—"

"I heard. That must have hurt. We appreciate your dedication."

She shot him a nasty look. "Calder couldn't give a good spanking if he had a gun pointed at his head. It's not in his DNA. Don't make me regret letting you bug my living room to keep me safe."

"So, what's the favor?"

"When the shit goes down, I don't want anyone to know I was the informant. The brothers in the club won't understand."

"That you're not as hard as you pretend?"

"I'm not pretending." Tired of holding her clothes, she set the basket on the laundry table. "I tell Sex Piston, T.A., Fat Louise, and Killyama everything. We even share the clues. I don't want them in any danger. If anything happens to me, I want them protected. That's why I haven't told them anything."

"I can do that." Lucky nodded, starting to leave.

Crazy Bitch grabbed his arm. "Make sure. But that's not

the favor. I want you to personally make sure that Calder is protected, too. No handing it over to any of The Last Riders or any of your buddies on the task force to handle. I want *you* protecting him. Another thing—"

"Don't you have to go to work?"

"I'm going. I need to get something off my chest. Gavin's ex. She's bad news."

Lucky stiffened. "I personally know Taylor. This is a hard situation for her."

"You know everything about me, don't you?" She cocked an eyebrow at him.

He didn't say jack shit in response.

"Who do you think is the better judge of character: you or me?"

He stared back at her. She could see the conflict in his expression.

"I'm saying outright that bitch is bad news. Take it however you want. I'm only giving Viper a heads-up because the Destructors are going to win our bet."

"I'll convey your concerns to Viper."

"You do that." She picked up her laundry basket. "You want to go first?" She motioned to the door.

"No, you go ahead."

She waited until Lucky was at the back of the room before juggling her clothes to open the door.

"Crazy Bitch? Take care."

28

Crazy Bitch reclined on the couch, watching Star, Harley, and Calder play a card game. They sat on the floor as she flipped through a new magazine she had bought at the store when she had picked up food and snacks for Sex Piston's kids.

"Why do we have to stay here?" Keri complained from the other side of the couch.

"Blame the man. My monitor will beep if I leave Jamestown."

"The man?"

Crazy Bitch looked at her from over the magazine. "The man, the police," she explained. "Jeez, kids don't know anything anymore."

"I know enough not to get arrested." The smartass gave her a holier-than-thou look that had Crazy Bitch begging for a setdown. And she was just the bitch to do it if Keri wasn't careful.

"I guess you're just smarter than me." Crazy Bitch flipped another page.

"Obviously."

The young woman was getting too big for her own britches, but Crazy Bitch let it go. Keri knew better than to act like that when Sex Piston or Stud were around.

Calder picked up one of the cards that Star had discarded, not saying anything, yet his stern expression didn't leave Keri.

"Or Calder," Meri added.

"That is unnecessary, and I expected you to act better in front of your brother and sister." Calder slammed his cards down, about to get off the floor.

Crazy Bitch turned another page. "It's not going to work."

The twin girls turned resentful faces toward her.

"Calder and I aren't going to get angry and send you to stay with Skulls and Sizzle. Sex Piston told me, if you act up, to call her and they'd come back, so you're out of luck."

"Why couldn't we stay there, anyway?" Meri argued.

"Because Sex Piston knows you'll sneak out when they go to bed."

"We wouldn't."

"Please… I don't need to show you my GED certificate to know what you two are wanting to do. I used to be seventeen once, and had more hormones than sense. Sex Piston is nipping it in the bud. She has no intention of being a grandmother anytime soon."

"Keri and I are good girls."

"There is no such thing as a good girl. There's only those who haven't been tempted."

"You're so lame!" Meri hit her forehead with her hand, rolling her eyes.

Crazy Bitch let the magazine drop to her lap. She could take a lot from her friend's stepdaughters; being called lame wasn't one of them.

"Does your lollipop that you're willing to get grounded for have a name?"

Meri and Keri shared a conspiratorial look.

"Or names?" Crazy Bitch amended.

Meri gave up pretending to be preoccupied by her cell phone. "Steven and Brandon."

"Those names sound lame to me."

"What do you know? You don't even have a boyfriend." Meri rose to sit on the edge of the couch cushion, rebelliously glowering at her.

"How many you had?"

"A couple."

"When you've had a hundred, we'll talk." Crazy Bitch gave Calder an imperceptible shake of her head to stay out of the argument.

"You're really going to admit you had that many?" Scorn filled the little bitch's voice as Keri gave her sister an approving nod.

The two girls thought they could take her on? *Go for it*, she thought, not losing her temper. The bitches were just sharpening their claws. She was about to teach them her skills of being a real bitch.

"Calder, why don't you take Star and Harley to the kitchen? I promised them an ice cream sundae. The jar of hot fudge is in the cabinet." She patiently waited until the younger children were distracted before she started sharpening her own claws.

"Are they seniors, too?" she asked the twins.

Crazy Bitch knew she had them when their expressions began to look sickly.

"How old, nineteen or twenty? Older?"

"Age doesn't matter. Girls are more mature than boys, anyway."

She grinned vindictively. "Older than twenty? Damn, Sex Piston didn't mention you both have boyfriends older than twenty."

Keri nearly fell off the couch. Righting herself, she stood up. "They're seniors in college. We met them when our class went to Eastern University."

"You got to love higher education." Her grin widened. "How often do they sneak down from Richmond?"

"That haven't. It's the first time—"

"Shut up, Keri." Meri angrily turned toward her twin.

"Don't worry; I won't say anything. This is just girl talk." Crazy Bitch tried to waylay Meri's concern.

"You won't say anything to Stud or Sex Piston?" Meri asked distrustfully.

Crazy Bitch knew which twin was smarter. "No, I'm all about girls getting a little something-something. So, you've only been texting them since you met?"

"Yes. I suppose you're going to tell them that, too."

"I said I wouldn't, and I won't." She raised her hand in the air. "I swear. How about you girls forget about sneaking out? It's not going to happen. I'll get my case and do your nails."

"Since we don't have any other options, I guess so."

Crazy Bitch went to the bathroom and got her nail case, taking out her favorite and putting it in a drawer before going back into the living room.

Opening the case, she settled back down on the couch as Meri and Keri started searching through the colors of polish.

"Where's the one you're wearing?" Keri asked.

"It's empty. I threw it away," she lied without regret. "This one is really pretty." She held a sheer pink color for her to see.

"That'll work." The teenager held her hand out as if she was the Queen of Sheba.

Crazy Bitch worked tirelessly on Keri's nails, enjoying watching Calder and Star eating their sundaes at the counter as Harley made a mess of his, mainly eating the Oreos and sauce on top.

"Those sandals are sharp. They new?"

Keri chewed on her bottom lip. "Yes."

"They look like a new pair Sex Piston bought when we went shopping."

"She let me borrow them." Keri kept her gaze focused on her nails.

"That's nice of her. She never lets me or any of the bitches borrow anything. She even gets pissed if we go in her closet to look."

Neither girl filled the silence.

Crazy Bitch continued talking to fill the void. "You really should stop chewing your nails; it's very unattractive. Older men would consider it a childish habit." She lifted the hand she was working on to examine it closer before lowering it to finish painting it. "It looks like you're starting to get a little wart on your forefinger. I'd get that taken care of before it spreads."

"I will."

"Raise your head; you can look at it later." She finished her pinky with a final swipe of the nail polish before putting the brush back into the bottle and twisting it closed.

"You're next, Meri. You want the same color?"

"No." She reluctantly handed her the color she had chosen.

"You sure you want this color?"

"Why?"

"With your skin coloring, it could make your hand look yellow."

Meri's cheeks flushed. She had picked the same shade of fingernail polish as her top.

The girl found a different color in her case. "Is this better?"

Crazy Bitch let her pained look speak for itself, sending

the girl picking the first one she came to, looking at her in askance at her choice.

"Would you like me to pick one for you?" she offered pityingly.

At her embarrassed nod, she chose juicy magenta.

"That's lovely," Meri complimented her choice.

"I know."

She started filing Meri's nails after she had removed her old polish. "I see you have your sister's habit."

"I'm trying to stop."

"You and Keri both have your licenses now. You should come to the shop once a month and let me do your nails. It looks like a newbie has been doing it for you."

"I do them."

"Oh... that explains it."

She painted Meri's nails as Calder helped Harley get ready for bed then put him in the spare bedroom as Star took her shower and put on her nightgown and robe.

She used the opportunity of Calder being out of the room to swipe at them further.

"You have pictures of your boyfriends?"

"Uh... no."

"Come on, share. I promised not to tell. When I get done painting your nails, I'll show you pictures of some of my old boyfriends."

"All right. Keri, show her."

Keri got off the chair, bringing her phone over to show a picture of one boy who was sitting at a desk.

"That one yours?"

"Yes. This is the one Meri likes." She swiped her finger to show a picture of another boy sitting on a motorcycle that no brother would be seen dead on. The baby bitches made it too easy.

"They're cute. Yours get help for that skin condition?"

"It's usually not that bad. He said it was an allergic reaction to something he ate."

"Then he should stop eating," she said disparagingly. "Meri's is much better-looking. I bet he gets all the girls in college with that picture. Of course, they don't know he doesn't know how to ride it."

"He rides it all the time."

"It's brand new. I bet he's ridden it once."

"How can you tell that from a picture?"

"You can see the sales person behind him."

"That's his brother."

"His brother's name is Jonathon."

Keri's face scrunched as she turned the picture, trying to see the person in the background. She sat back down when Calder came back into the room, ignoring them to clean and wipe down the counter.

"Hand me my phone. I'll show you the pictures of mine." Crazy Bitch held her thumb down as she opened her cell phone, going to her photos. "Scroll through those bad boys."

Keri sat down on the floor next to Meri as they stared at the pictures.

"That's a good picture of Uncle Calder," Keri complimented her uncle.

"He looks damn fine. Keep scrolling.

"That's Sam. I brought him to Star's birthday party." She hated him now, but he was good-looking.

"That's Jace," she continued, smothering a smile at their faces.

"He's one of dad's friends."

"Yes, he is. He's mine, too."

"Who's this?"

Each photo showed men who would stroke any woman's fire.

"That's Joker. He had a big gut, but he was still

smoking hot."

Keri stopped when she came to a face she recognized. "That's Shade."

"That was wishful thinking." She finished Meri's nails, closing the nail polish to put it neatly back in the case. Holding out her hand for her phone, Keri placed it in her hand. "I can show you the rest another time. It's bedtime."

"I wanted you to paint mine." Star jumped up after putting the cards back in the box.

"I'll do yours tomorrow night," Crazy Bitch said, closing her case as Star looked at her wistfully. "Come on; you can help me open the couch."

Star got a kick out of tossing the cushions off. Crazy Bitch then let her pull the strap that would open the full-sized bed.

"Can I sleep here?" Star pleaded.

"No, me and Calder are sleeping here. You're sleeping...."

Meri's face fell as if she had wrecked the sweet used car Stud and Sex Piston had surprised the twins with when they had gotten their licenses. "I thought me and Keri were sleeping on it."

"You're a guest. I can't have my guests sleeping on the couch. Time to go beddy bye. You all have school in the morning, and Calder and I have work."

"That's right. I'll pack your stuff into your room for you." Calder gave her an amused smile as he passed them to get the twins' suitcases that they had deliberately left by the door in the hopes of being able to go to Sex Piston's parents' home.

When the twins huffily went into the bedroom, Calder hooked an arm around her shoulders, pulling her toward him. "Sorry my nieces are being such brats."

"I've dealt with worse." She lay her hands on his chest. "We have any ice cream left? I'm in the mood for something sweet."

"You're sweet enough." He kissed her then went into the kitchen. "Step into my parlor," he teased.

She sat at the counter, admiring his easy familiarity with her kitchen. "You know, you're very sexy when you're waiting on me."

He sat a bowl down, scooping in ice cream then dousing it with hot fudge sauce. "Am I as sexy as the other men on your phone?"

"There's no comparison; that's why you're my screensaver."

"You deserve whipped cream for that answer." He gave her a generous splat on top of her sundae.

She took a generous spoonful of her ice cream, letting the gooey deliciousness slide down her throat. There were two things she was thankful for. Ice cream was one, and beer was the other.

Calder tossed the empty ice cream container away, coming to sit on the stool next to her. "You really not saying anything to Stud or Sex Piston?"

"Of course not. I swore. You heard?"

"They won't be happy if they find out you knew."

"You going to tell him?" She spooned another spoonful of better then sex ice cream into her mouth.

"Yes." Calder eyes narrowed on her rapturous expression.

"Then that solves that problem. I swore; you didn't. It kills two birds with one stone."

"What would you have done if I said no?" His Adam's apple bobbed when she licked her spoon. She loved teasing him. It was like putting out cat nip in front of Manson.

"I would have told Star to tell on them."

"You have a very devious mind. You know that?"

She stared down at her melting ice cream. "Does it scare you?"

"There isn't much in life that scares me anymore. Prison has…"

Her spoon halted halfway to her mouth when his eyes widened. "What's wrong?"

"Where's your notebook with the clues?"

"In my bedroom."

"Get it."

She went to the bedroom door, knocking. "Can I come in?"

A minute later, she set the notebook down on the counter in front of him.

"The ground beneath me is frozen. No kings or queens live here. You can enter my gates, but unless you have an invitation, you won't be allowed to stay and rescue the damsel."

"You think of something?"

"The ground beneath me is frozen, which could mean no one wants to be there, not even kings or queens." His voice rose in excitement. *"You can enter my gates, but unless you have an invitation, you won't be allowed to stay….* We thought the castle Greer was referring to meant buy tickets for tours or booking a room to stay the night."

"It isn't?" she asked, staring down at the clue then looking back at Calder. "What else could it mean?"

"An arrest warrant is a kind of invitation. Or it could be the sentence the jury hands down. What do you think?"

She gripped his strong thigh. "I think you're on the right path." Crazy Bitch pointed at the word *frozen*. "Frozen could mean frozen in time, and no one wants to be there!"

"You have to get approval for some prisoners, too!"

They smiled each other, and then she leaned forward and kissed him. "Killyama may have nabbed the rich one, but I got the smart one!"

"What?" He frowned.

"Never mind. Who do The Last Riders and the Destruc-

JAMIE BEGLEY

tors know in prison?"

Their enthusiasm waned as they started thinking of all the people they knew were in prison.

"It has to be a woman." Crazy Bitch stared at the clue, seeing *damsel*.

"Let's google prisons in Kentucky. I was in the Grange. I can't think of anyone... Candi. The damsel could be her."

"She's no damsel." She snorted. "Let's look at the prisons." She took out her cell phone, putting in *"prisons in Kentucky."*

She scrolled down the list as Calder looked on.

"Fuck."

"What?" Crazy Bitch paused.

Calder laughed. "Kentucky State Penitentiary, it's nicknamed 'the castle.' Greer has sent us chasing our tails, looking for castles, when it was just a nickname."

"It's a maximum and supermax security prison. Who in the fuck do we know who could be there?"

Calder shook his head. "I don't know, but I'll call Stud and tell them to head back tomorrow. Maybe he knows."

"Go ahead and call Stud. I'm going to get ready for bed."

She left him to make the call, showering and getting changed in the bathroom. She had grabbed a nightshirt when she had gone into the bedroom for the notebook.

Calder took over the bathroom when she came out.

She turned out the lights, leaving the light on in the kitchen so Calder would be able to see. Setting her alarm, she then snuggled down under the sheet, seeing the light under her bedroom was off.

"You need anything before I lie down?" Calder asked when he came out of the bathroom.

"Just you."

The light went off, and then she felt the bed dip as he snuggled against her back.

"My neck is much better. I wanted to thank you this

290

morning, but you were already gone."

"I didn't want to wake you up. I knew you were tired."

He slipped his hand around her waist. "It's nice having a house full of kids, isn't it?"

"It's a blast." She yawned, nestling her ass into his cock. "Only boys."

"Star is a girl."

"No more girls," she said drowsily, feeling him smiling against her neck.

"We're going to count Star as our first?"

"Of course," she mumbled, hearing the subtle opening of her bedroom door. Instantly rising up onto her elbow, she said, "Alexa, light on." The kitchen light turned on, shining into the living room. "Can I get you girls anything?"

"Uh… no, we were just going to get something to drink," Meri said as both girls went to the kitchen, coming out seconds later and heading toward the bedroom with bottled waters.

"If you girls need anything, don't hesitate to wake me."

"We won't," Keri said as they were about to close the door.

"Oh, Meri, those jeans are too tight to wear in school. I hope you packed another pair in your suitcase."

"I did."

The door slamming had her lying back down. "Alexa, lights off."

"You could have told me you can do that in the kitchen, too."

"Now you know." She thumped her pillow, scooting her ass backward until she felt a hard body behind her. "Night," she muttered, closing her eyes.

"Good night."

It felt as if she had just gone to sleep when she heard the soft chiming of her cell phone. Sitting up in the bed, she rolled over onto her back, unintentionally waking Calder.

"Something wrong?" He raised up to look at her in the dark.

"No. Go back to sleep. I got this."

"Got wha—"

The creaking of her bedroom door had their heads turning.

"Need more water, girls?" Crazy Bitch asked, not bothering to turn the lights on.

The bed shook with Calder's laughter when the door slammed shut.

Reaching for her phone, she reset her alarm.

"You going to do that all night?"

"They'll give up after a couple hours. You see why I don't want more girls? They give you sleepless nights."

"If we have boys, they won't give us sleepless nights?"

"No, they'll be giving some other girls' parents sleepless nights. I'll be sleeping like a baby."

"Isn't that sexist?"

"Don't know, don't care. No daughter of mine will be a hump post for a randy, hormone-fueled, blue-balled little motherfucker."

"If you do end up having a daughter, are you going to say that to her?"

"Of course. Why not? I have plenty of experience with the little fuckers. Did I ever tell you about the men I killed?"

"You mentioned it, yes."

She tucked her sheet around her, making sure Calder had enough for himself. Stretching her hand out, she double-checked the alarm was set. Those little fuckers from Eastern weren't going to score on her watch.

"You still want to talk about having kids with me instead of going to sleep?"

"No, I don't think I do."

29

S tud had called that morning, telling him that he and Sex Piston were home. Calder hated having to tell his brother how Meri and Keri had acted the night before and about the men they had been texting.

"You and Crazy Bitch mind keeping Star and Harley another night?"

"No. Why?"

"They get upset when their older sisters get in trouble. When Sex Piston gets done with them, they're going to realize the painful reality of making us both angry at the same time."

"No problem. You packed them enough clothes for two days. I'll see you tomorrow at work."

"Thanks, bro."

He disconnected the call, not feeling guilty about the girls being in trouble. They had been disrespectful to Crazy Bitch. He had ignored the way they talked to him, not mentioning it to Stud. He had made his own bed where that was concerned. How could he expect his nieces to respect him when they were aware of his past? Neither Stud nor Sex

Piston had discussed it with the girls. It had been his Aunt Katy.

She had cut him out of her life, and when Stud didn't do the same when Calder got out of prison, she moved away. Stud was hurt and angry, but he still let her see his kids. She had helped them, and he hadn't wanted to punish them for their aunt's decision.

Calder had a couple of jobs he had promised to finish for Stud. When he was done, he decided to pick up carryout for Crazy Bitch's lunch. With Sex Piston being off, she wouldn't be able to leave the beauty shop, and they had their hands full this morning, so he knew she hadn't made herself lunch.

The drive-thru was busy. He edged his bike along after each car in front of him ordered. When it was his turn, Calder paid, taking the food from the worker's hand before riding around the front of the restaurant to put it in his saddlebag.

He was about to get back on his bike when he looked through the glass window inside. The woman staring back at him recognized him, standing to come outside.

"Calder!"

When the woman would have thrown herself into his arms, he shrugged her off, getting back on his bike. "Candi, when did you get out of jail?"

His ex-girlfriend looked good. She had gained some weight during her prison sentence, her snug jeans highlighting her firm body. She had cut her hair, making her look younger and healthier. Her gaunt cheekbones had filled out, making Calder realize how he had been attracted to her when they were younger.

"Last week. I was planning to come to the club tonight to see you."

"Don't bother. You're not welcome there. Not now, not ever."

Her jubilant attitude vanished. "We have some things we need to talk about."

"We don't have shit to talk about. I've done my time; you've done yours. I don't want to talk about old times. They weren't good. Have a good life." His hands went to his handlebars.

"Has Stud told you that Star—"

"That Star is my kid? No. He didn't have to. I saw the birthmark. I may have been a drug fiend when I was with you, but my head is clear now."

"You hate me because I married Stud. Baby, don't be jealous. I never fucked him once."

Calder gave a harsh laugh. "That doesn't surprise me. You're not Stud's type. I couldn't believe it when he wrote to me when you got married. When he sent the picture, I knew why."

"He didn't leave me a choice but to marry him. When the cop busted you for buying and Bobcat implicated me for setting up the buy, I would have gone to prison, too. When I told Stud that I was pregnant and wasn't going to have my baby in prison, that I would have an abortion first, he made me marry him."

That Stud had kept Star from being aborted was another heavy weight that always sat on his shoulder. How could he ask Stud to tell Star she was his when she wouldn't have been born without him interceding?

"I didn't hate you before. Now I do. Stay the fuck away from me and Star. I mean it, Candi. I'm clean now, and I'm not going to let you twist me around your little finger to get a hit."

"You think you can talk to me like this and get away with it?" Candi grabbed his handlebar contemptuously. "I can fuck you over so badly that you'll never see Star again."

"That would be a big mistake. Move." Calder let his bike roll so she would have to step back.

"Calder! Come back here!"

He drove back to Stud's garage, too angry to see Crazy Bitch.

Going into Stud's office, he immediately dialed Diamond's number.

"Hello?"

"We need to set up a meeting for tomorrow afternoon. You available?"

"If this is about Crazy Bitch, we may have gotten a break. A realtor had a video camera pointed at the street where she was pulled over. I sent Knox to get a copy. The realtor just got it installed and didn't realize it was pointed at the street."

"How did you know the realtor had a camera?"

"When I was in town, bailing her out, I drove by where Crazy Bitch was pulled over and took a chance that the camera would see something. I got more than I expected. I'm hoping to get the charges against her dropped. I have a meeting with the DA on Monday. So, keep your fingers crossed."

"I will. I'm glad her case is looking good, but that isn't why I need to meet with you."

"Is two o'clock good for you?"

"Yes. Thanks, Diamond."

"You're welcome. I'll see you tomorrow."

After he disconnected the call, he reached for a sketchpad that Stud used to make drawings of motorcycles. Stud's motorcycles were customizable. He would work with the riders until he drew their dream bike, and then build it.

He had an idea he had been thinking about since he had begun working with Stud. Taking a pencil, he started sketching out his dream motorcycle.

As far back as he could remember, he had loved motorcycles. He loved the sounds they made, being able to feel the powerful machine beneath you and know you controlled it, the ability to ride the wind and feel it, like a knife through soft butter, and knowing it wouldn't be the same because you had managed to slip through it at speeds that left other drivers in the dust.

He started the drawing to take his mind off Candi and the conflict she could cause. He was surprised when he looked at the wall clock to see it was almost time to pick up Star and Harley.

Star was in school, and Harley was in the daycare attached to the school.

Flipping the sketchpad closed, he shut down the garage, making it to Harley and Star's school on time.

"Where do you want to grab a bite to eat before dance class, Star? How about you, Harley?"

"You pick, Harley. I'm not as picky as you are. I can eat anything."

Calder grinned, looking into the rearview mirror as Star looked at her brother.

"Can we go to Taco Hut?" He swung his legs in his car seat.

"I don't see why not. That sound good to you, Star?"

Star clapped her hands. "I love Taco Hut. Mama never lets us go."

"Why not?"

"She says Killyama gets sick. But me and Harley don't. Can we go?"

The thought of two sick kids while on his and Crazy Bitch's watch had him deciding against that suggestion.

"I don't think tacos would sit on your stomach well before going to dance. How about we go to Popeyes?"

"We like Popeyes, too. We never get to go there, either."

"What's wrong with Popeyes?"

Jamestown was a small town. They didn't have much to choose from.

"Nothing. Mama is just sick of eating there. It's Fat L— Jane's favorite."

"Then Popeyes it is." He merged into traffic, driving toward the restaurant while listening to the children talk about their day. His eyes went to the back seat intermittently as Star talked about her teacher, her childish face stubbornly set as she told her brother that her teacher didn't like her.

"She made me sit in the back row next to Ricky, and he always steals my pencils and copies me."

"You want me to beat him up for you?" Harley's legs had stopped swinging at his sister's complaint about Ricky.

"He's bigger than you."

"I don't care! You're my sister. I'll ninja him and make him give your pencils back."

"Mama said she will buy me more pencils, so you don't have to do that. But if he keeps pinching me to show him my papers, and if you get bigger, I'll let you."

"He pinches you?" Harley's jaw was set, reminding Calder of Stud.

"Have you told your mom and dad about him pinching you?" Calder asked, parking in front of the restaurant.

"Yes, Mama and Daddy went to the school. Mrs. Holder said I was making it up. Ricky never gets in trouble."

"She didn't move Ricky?"

"No."

He held the door open as they went inside. Instead of ordering, he wanted to drive back to the school and have a talk with Star's teacher himself.

Placing the order, he kept his eye on the children as they found a booth and sat, waiting for him expectantly.

Calder carried the tray of food over, giving the kids their food. As he ate, Calder felt a swelling pride that he had created such a beautiful child. He had screwed up so many aspects of his life, but Star wasn't one of them. He could never regret creating her.

His aunt Katy was wrong. He would never do drugs again. What he couldn't do for himself, he could for Star. The temptations and the lure weren't there anymore, and never would be as long as she was on earth.

When they finished eating, he drove them to Star's dance studio.

He waved to Crazy Bitch as she stood in front of the class.

Lily was corralling the older girls to the other half of the studio. They had combined their classes for the recital.

"Are you going to stay and watch, Uncle Calder?" Star looked up at him with bright eyes.

"Of course. Me and Harley wouldn't miss it." He nudged Harley, who didn't seem happy at his answer, toward a group of chairs on the side of the dance floor.

"You must be Star's uncle Calder."

He recognized the woman as the bus driver from the last time he had watched Star's lesson.

"Yes, I am," he acknowledged.

"I'm Nettie. I drive the bus for the girls. The girls all call me Nettie because I work in the cafeteria at the school and I always have a hairnet in my hair."

He was charmed by the older woman who reached into an oversized purse to pull out a coloring book and crayons, giving them to Harley.

Crazy Bitch and Lily started their lessons by having the girls warm up. Seeing her in the leotard with the bright socks bunched up to hide her monitor, moving fluidly across the dance floor, he promised himself to take her out to the club that weekend so he could feel that sexy body dancing against him.

"Anna-Kate is really great with the girls."

Calder felt her stare as he watched the lesson start. "Yes, she is."

"I don't know what me and Lily would do without her and Norma's help."

Calder turned his attention from Crazy Bitch at the mention of a Norma, realizing she must be talking about Sex Piston. There weren't many who knew her real name. For all he knew, only her own family and Stud knew her name. Then he realized Sex Piston had toned down the use of Crazy Bitch's nickname, therefore, as well as her own not to embarrass Star and Harley.

"I'm sure Anna-Kate gets as much enjoyment out of teaching them to dance as they get from her."

Nettie nodded. "The foster parents love her. It gives them a break, and most of them can't afford the lessons. It also gives the parents a way to see them in a neutral atmosphere."

Calder stared at the women who were also watching, sensing the heartbreak in some of them.

Nettie patted his arm. "It's unfortunate that they have to be separated from their children. That's why Anna-Kate, Lily, and Norma are such a godsend. They are even saving their tip money to help build an extension off the women's shelter. We hope to build ten small apartments, so if the women who are victims of domestic violence have to leave home, they will have a place to stay with their children. So far, we only have two large dormitory rooms with bunk beds for them to stay in. Many of the women don't want their children to stay there, even if we had the room, but sadly, we don't. We're filled to capacity. Our organization services two counties, Treepoint and Jamestown. Those ten apartments will make a big difference. Just think, ten of those girls will be able to return to their mothers."

He didn't have to imagine. He knew the agony of being separated from a child.

"We're having a groundbreaking on Monday. You should come. A few days ago, we were worried we would have to postpone it, since Norma didn't know if she could come up with the twelve thousand she had pledged. I was relieved when she called back the next day to say she would. We have a long way to go in our fundraising, but with them on our side, we'll make it." She beamed, reaching into her bag to hand Harley a baggie of trail mix and a juice box.

"If I can do anything to help, let me know," he offered.

"We're going to need volunteers to help build. You look strong enough to swing a hammer." The wily woman hadn't been randomly talking to him; she was searching for volunteers.

"Count me in." He gave her his cell phone number, planning to get several of the brothers in the Blue Horsemen and Destructors to volunteer. The problem was getting enough funds to build the apartments and furnish them. With Lily involved, it stood to reason The Last Riders would pony up for much of the money.

Crazy Bitch and Lily's lesson lasted an hour. When it was over, Star came rushing over with her juice box and snack that Nettie had given to each of the girls. "How'd I do, Uncle Calder?"

"You danced like a butterfly."

Star giggled. "You're teasing me. I need to practice more. Anna-Kate is teaching me for Daddy's birthday."

Calder swallowed the lump in his throat. "He'll love it."

He had never been jealous of Stud being their father's favorite, or his fans, or being his aunt's favorite, but he was jealous of the dance that his daughter would be giving Stud.

"Something wrong, Uncle Calder? You look sad."

"Do I? I'm not. How can I be sad when I have you and Harley to keep me company tonight?"

"Can we make popcorn and watch *Beauty and the Beast*?"

"Yes. If Anna-Kate doesn't have any, we'll stop at the store on the way to her apartment."

"Whoopie!" Star jumped up, setting her drink down to do a cartwheel. "I'm going to tell Regina. I want her to spend the night, but she can't."

"Why can't she spend the night?"

"I don't know. Never mind. I won't tell her. I'm going to go say bye to her before she leaves on the bus."

"Why can't Star's friend stay?"

Nettie, who was taking the coloring book and crayons from Harley, glanced at him. "Children in foster care aren't permitted to spend the night away."

"That sucks."

"Sadly, I can say that it's for the children's safety. Children aren't always in foster care because of domestic violence. It's sad to say, but it can be because it's safer for some of the children to be away from both parents."

Crazy Bitch had been one of those children. Her father hadn't cared enough to make sure she had been taken care of, too concerned with the stigma of having her. And she had a mother who couldn't take care of herself, much less her own daughter. There were no winners in cases like hers. It was just survival. And she had survived, and now she was on the other side of the coin, volunteering her time and efforts to make sure little girls like she used to be had the opportunity to dance.

Outside, he made sure Star and Harley were strapped into their booster seats before getting behind the wheel.

Crazy Bitch, who was already sitting in the passenger seat, paused as she lifted her bottled water to her lips. "What's that look for? You cheat on me today?"

Confused, his mouth dropped open. "I was just smiling at you. How did you turn that around in your mind to make you think I'm cheating?"

"A man doesn't stare at a woman unless he's guilty of something."

"They do when they're in love."

"Damn."

"What's wrong now?"

"I hate saying I'm sorry."

"Just save your apology for when I really screw up. Then we can call it even."

"That doesn't seem like a fair trade to me."

"It could be worse. I could have cheated," he teased, driving toward her apartment.

"You know, I take it back. I'm not sorry. You're being a d-i-c-k." She had lowered her voice, looking back at Star and Harley. "So, what was the smile about? I know it wasn't because you felt a sudden outpouring of love for me."

"How do you know that?"

She wiggled her eyebrows at him. "You only get emotional when I make you *happy*."

"I met Nettie. She told me what you and Norma are saving your tip money for."

"You call her Norma, it'll be your funeral. And don't tell Stud what it is for. She's holding it over his head as divorce money."

"By the way, I promised Star popcorn and a movie. Do you have popcorn, or do we need to stop?"

"I have it. Did she make you promise to watch *Beauty and the Beast*?"

"Yes. Why?"

"Because I've watched that with her a dozen times already. I'll paint her fingernails and let you two watch it in the living room. Me and Harley can watch *Power Rangers*."

"We can all watch it together. What do you think, Star?"

"Uncle Calder, I really want to watch my movie. Please?"

Crazy Bitch grinned, knowing what he would do next.

"Star, you're the guest. You can do anything you want."

When they arrived at Crazy Bitch's apartment, Calder took Harley outside to toss his football around in the lot behind her apartment building, while Crazy Bitch helped Star practice for Stud's birthday surprise.

He waited until they were in her bedroom and Harley was asleep in her spare bedroom, while Star was happily asleep with her fingernails painted in the same color as Crazy Bitch's on the fold-out couch before telling her about seeing Candi that afternoon.

Reaching for the television remote, Crazy Bitch turned the TV on so Star wouldn't hear what they were discussing if she awoke. "That bitch is going to try to drive a wedge between you and Stud."

"It won't work. If our father and Aunt Katy couldn't, Candi doesn't stand a chance."

"It's different with kids. People get emotional where kids are concerned."

"I'm going to talk to Stud first thing in the morning. Whatever she's planning won't work. I made an appointment with Diamond for tomorrow, too. Hopefully, she can intervene, and Star doesn't need to know before Stud and Sex Piston decide to tell her."

She got to her knees on the bed to glare down at him. "It's not only Stud and Sex Piston's decision. You have a say in it, too." Her voice was low but forceful. "Why do you put yourself last where she is concerned? I love you, but you have a serious self-esteem issue. No matter how much I tell you I love you, or Stud and Star show you how much they love you, you don't consider what your wants and needs are. Why?"

He wanted to look away from her but couldn't. Instead, he focused on the wall past her shoulder, trying to maintain his composure. It took a minute before his voice was steady enough to keep from exposing his emotional turmoil.

"I've been selfish most of my life. I didn't want to deal with my father's badgering to be a racer like Stud. I didn't want anyone but me working on his or Stud's motorcycle, and then my irresponsibility cost him his life. Because I couldn't man up and accept the responsibility for what happened, I did drugs. Then, when I became hooked, I wanted them despite Stud trying to stop me. I wrecked his first marriage. I wanted Candi sexually, and I didn't use a condom because I didn't want to. I wanted you, but I didn't want to drag you into my fucked-up life. Even when I was clean, did I come back and try to make you see I was worth having in your life? No. Because I was still afraid I would backslide. It was Gavin who made me realize I would never go back to that way of life. Ever. I would fucking shoot myself before I'd let another drop of that poison in my body.

"The only thing, and I repeat, the *only* thing I've done right was protecting her from me. Father is just a word. Being a father is another ball game. Any sucker like me can get a woman knocked up, but it's men like Stud who deserve the Father's Day cards and birthday... dances." Calder's voice choked with emotion, his eyes going glassy with unshed tears that he couldn't bear to spill in front of her.

"Hot thang." She lay down on his chest, hugging him close. "Star's not going to love you any less when she finds out she's your daughter. Look at Meri and Keri. They love Sex Piston as much as their own mother. It's not either/or between you and Stud. She'll be able to handle it. I know she'll be fine."

"How do you know? You can't promise me that."

"Yes, I can. You're forgetting the most important part."

"Which is?" He stared down at her doubtfully.

"She's tough. Star's the worst dancer in my class, but she

has the most heart. She gets that from you." She poked a firm finger into his chest. "From you, Calder. That's what she's gotten from you, despite you not being there when she was born, or being there when she took her first steps, her first birthday dances. You might have missed a lot of her firsts, but it's up to you if she saves a dance for you during father-daughter dances, or her sweet sixteen, and her wedding reception. Those are up to you. Her dance card isn't filled yet; it's just waiting for you to put your name on it."

3 0

Calder pulled into the garage. He had dropped Star and Harley off at school, so he hadn't counted on Stud beating him to the garage. He had been mentally preparing himself to talk about Star to Stud. Jesus… each scenario was like a broken record that started and stopped as he would start a pretend-talk in his head. Then he would think of a different way to start until he had given himself a headache. He still had no idea what he was going to say.

Parking the van, he was still deciding the best way to begin when he entered the bay and came to a dead stop.

Candi was in the office with Stud. He could see them through the glass window.

Calder strode through the garage, reading Stud's expression from three feet away. He didn't bother knocking, going inside and bringing the shouting match to an end.

"What are you doing here, Candi?"

"What are *you* doing here? Stud call you?"

Stud sat down on the end of his desk. "How could I have done that? You've been here with me since I opened the door."

"How'd you get here? I didn't see a car outside," Calder asked her.

"I got a taxi. A friend of mine is giving me a car, but he needed it today. What does it matter how I got here?"

"Because if any of the Destructors or Blue Horsemen are giving you rides, we're going to have a problem."

"I'm not seeing anyone you would know. I don't hang out with trash anymore," she venomously struck out at him.

He accepted her insult, because frankly, he didn't care what she thought of him.

His eyes went to Stud, whose cold expression belied the real concern in his eyes. His brother was disturbed by something Candi had said before his arrival.

"What did you need to talk to Stud about so badly that it got your ass out of bed before noon?"

"I don't sleep till noon anymore—prison breaks that habit. And what Stud and I talk about is none of your business."

Calder, seeing a warning look from Stud, instantly knew what the bitch had been doing.

"Have you been threatening him into telling me that Star is my kid?"

He could tell from the surprise Stud couldn't hide that she had.

Shaking his head, Calder said, "Candi, I'm going to give you two minutes to get your ass out of here. Your blackmail wasn't going to work, even if I hadn't come. Stud may have always tried to protect me, but Star is more important than me. He's been what neither of us could be to Star—a parent. Star's the most important thing in my life, has been since I realized she was mine. But you? You don't have an excuse, other than using Star as a pawn, which nearly hurt or killed her if Sex Piston and Killyama hadn't stopped you."

"Stud took my baby away and wouldn't let me see her—"

"Stud took her away because that was the deal when he found out you were pregnant and wanted to abort my baby. Yeah, I knew before you told me yesterday. Aunt Katy told me when I got out of prison. She also told me how much money Stud gave you to get a divorce from you and for you to sign over sole custody to him. You're a greedy bitch who nearly bankrupted him, yet you're still not satisfied? What is she wanting this time?" he posed the question to Stud, ignoring Candi.

"She wants fifty thousand, says she needs to start over, and she wants to see Star."

"No."

"To which part?" Candi asked.

"To all of it. No money, and no, you're not going to see Star. In fact, I'm going to give you an ultimatum. You need to contact your probation officer and find another town to do your probation. You need to leave town as soon as possible."

"What if I don't?"

"I'm not a crackhead anymore, waiting for you to deal out small amounts. I know who you used to sell to. Remember? I waited on my bike when you went inside to make the buys, and then drove you to whoever had you purchase them. The beauty of living in Jamestown is that pretty much everyone lives in the same place. I recognized some of those dealers and buyers at the penitentiary. I don't think you had a better lawyer than I did, and I don't think that it was a coincidence that we all got busted at the same time. You were an informant, and if I let that be known around town, your life won't be worth the cardboard box to bury you in. You should get in touch with your parole officer, and talk to whoever you gave that information to, telling them that your life is in danger, because it is."

"You wouldn't do that." Frightened, she gave him a beseeching look.

"Try me, Candi. Please, try me." He ruthlessly jerked away when she tried to touch him, opening the door. "Get out."

Candi ran out of the office, her high heels *clicking* the concrete as she left.

Calder didn't watch which direction she went, closing the door and turning back to Stud.

"Bro, I'm sorry. I was going to talk to you when you came in this morning. I should have known that bitch wouldn't wait to cause trouble. I made us an appointment to see Diamond. I've been saving for a place to stay. We can use my money to make sure you and Sex Piston don't have to give her visitation—"

"Slow down, Calder. I already knew you knew about Star."

"How?"

"When you and Crazy Bitch came to the house for pizza. Sex Piston and I overheard you two talking about Star."

"Why didn't you say something?"

"Why didn't you?" Stud countered.

Calder rubbed his neck. "I didn't know how. I still don't know what to say to you. How do I say thank you for watching out for my kid, and then tell you that we should tell her? I didn't want to hurt Sex Piston. I know how she is about Star—how you both are. I wanted to make sure I was strong enough not to relapse again. Every day I made through without using, I would tell myself that, if I make it another week without using, then I will talk to you about Star. Then another week would go by, and then another."

"Is that what you want to tell her?"

"Yes. Crazy Bitch said it would hurt worse if she finds out for herself, and that we've been lying to her. I don't want her any more hurt than she has to be. You and Sex…." Calder thought back to last night and realized Crazy Bitch was right. "We should all sit down and discuss the best way to do it and when."

"I agree. I'll call Sex Piston, and then all three of us can go to Diamond's office to talk to her about the best way to handle Candi. You're not going to oust her as an informant, so we need to find the best legal way to stop her from causing trouble."

"And if there isn't?"

Grimly, Stud didn't hesitate. "Then I'll oust her. This time, I won't have to worry about you leaving town, and I don't have to worry about her being pregnant with your child. She comes at me, trying to hurt those I love again... God help her. I will destroy her."

"Stud..." Calder still couldn't find the words to tell his brother how much he appreciated what he had done for him. Not only for Star, but the other past mistakes he had made and didn't know how to atone for. "You deserve a better brother than I have been to you. I'll spend the rest of my life making it up to you, but it'll never equal what you've done for me. I'm sorry about Dad. I'm sorry about Reese—"

"Dad's death wasn't your fault. He started a fight with me before our race, trying to distract me and put me off my game. You tried to tell him you wanted to double-check that tire and he wouldn't listen. He wanted that purse, but more importantly to him, he wanted to beat me. You were smarter than me. I wanted to race badly enough to put up with him; you gave up what you loved instead of letting him destroy the love of it like I did. That's why I gave up racing. Not because of you, but because I didn't love it anymore. And I didn't love Reese. That's why she found someone who could.

"You loved Star, so when you realized she was yours, you didn't make waves by acknowledging it. You've sacrificed your love for her to make me and Sex Piston happy. Calder... I'm not the one who needs repaying. It's us who owes you gratitude. You gave life to my daughter, that beautiful little girl who I have held in my arms and has given me such joy that I will never be able to repay your gift."

Calder broke, his regrets shattered, raining down on him and cleansing his soul.

Stud jerked him to him when he couldn't hold back his own tears any longer, seeing the tears in Calder's eyes. Tears that had been held back too long. Tears for their mother's death, for their father's, for the years he had used drugs as an escape, the years they had been apart. The last ones they shared were of laughter that they were standing in his office, crying like babies, before breaking apart and slapping each other on their shoulders.

"It's a little late, but congratulations on being a father," Stud said, using the sleeve of his T-shirt to wipe his cheeks.

Calder used a rag on the desk to wipe his own, keeping his face impassive. "Thanks. But talking about our girl, we have a problem to solve."

Stud became serious.

Calder's eyes twinkled with laughter, knowing his brother thought he was talking about Star's living arrangement. "We have any work that needs to be done today?"

Stud glanced through his window, toward the empty garage. "No. It looks like you took care of it yesterday. Why?"

"We have four little fuckers—as Crazy Bitch likes to call them—to take care of."

Stud's expression lightened. "Who?"

"Sam, Steven, and Brandon. We should have enough time to take care of them before meeting Diamond."

"What about the fourth one?"

"We have to wait until Monday to take care of that little fucker."

"Why do we have to wait until Monday?"

"Because Ricky is in school now, and our meeting with Diamond gives him a chance to get home."

"Star told you about Ricky?"

"Technically—by the way, that's another favorite word of Crazy Bitch's—Star told Harley."

"Technically, I like that word, too. By the way, I need to use it more often with Sex Piston. Technically." Stud savored the word, letting it roll off his tongue. "We should let Harley deal with little Ricky. Don't you agree?"

"I agree, brother, I agree." Calder reached into his pocket for his bike keys as Stud reach for his and the key to lock the garage.

"You ready?"

Stud locked the office as Calder backed his motorcycle out of the garage bay, where he had stored it while he had been driving Stud's van.

Once both of them were seated on their bikes, Calder looked at Stud. "Do we need to go by the clubhouse to get backup?"

Stud shook his head. "We got this. Let's ride."

The brothers pulled out of the parking lot in unison, neither taking the lead. They were going to defend their girl as one, and as one, they would triumph.

31

"Why are Stud and Calder looking so happy?" Killyama asked, pouring another glass of tequila for the crew as they sat at their usual table at the clubhouse.

"Who knows? Who cares?" Crazy Bitch shot Killyama a dirty look for not topping her glass off like she had the others. "Why you being stingy to me?"

"A couple of reasons. First, you don't handle tequila the way we do, and you're in enough trouble with the law."

"What's the second reason?" Taking the shot and sucking on a lemon, she waited for her answer.

"You're the reason Train isn't sitting here. Did you have to ask him how sore his dick was loud enough for everyone in the club to hear?"

"Inquiring minds want to know." She laughed, pouring herself another shot, despite Killyama trying to take it away.

"No one wants to know." Killyama snatched the bottle back, holding it in a firm grip.

"I do." Fat Louise held her shot glass out for a refill with pathetic eyes.

Seeing Killyama refill the glass, Crazy Bitch made a

mental note to remember that particular expression. It could be useful.

"The only thing you bitches need to know is to throw that potato masher away."

The bitches at the table cracked up, pounding their glass on the table for Killyama to refill their glasses.

"Who's the hottie with Skulls and Sizzle?" Crazy Bitch reached for another lemon, biting down on the tart flesh.

Sex Piston rolled her eyes. "You know Devon Carpenter. His mother is sitting at the table with them."

Crazy Bitch squinted her eyes. "Well, he looks hot from here."

"You don't need any more tequila if you think a seventy-year-old man looks hot when you're fucking Calder." Sex Piston moved her glass away.

"I'm not fucking him right this minute," Crazy Bitch griped, trying to get her glass back. Next time, she would make a pit stop at the liquor store and buy her own tequila before hanging out at the club with her friends.

She was about to fight for her glass back when Calder leaned over her shoulder, prying her hands away from Sex Piston's. "Dance with me."

She willingly released the glass. Standing up, she pointed two fingers at her eyes, then at Sex Piston, before moving away with her boy toy.

Crazy Bitch mentally cracked up at her pun.

The music was loud and obnoxious, just the way she liked it. She fucking loved to dance when she was drunk and horny.

Calder slid his hand to her hip, letting her dance suggestively while keeping her within arm's reach. The fucker was good enough to match her movements, intensifying her hormones.

When the music switched to "Way Down We Go," she

smirked, turning around and sliding down his hard body seductively. Bouncing on her feet when she was crouching to raise slowly back up, she then repeated the movement. She went down again and shook her breasts so they jiggled under her slinky midriff top that ended just below her matching red bra.

Each song melded into another. Crazy Bitch pushed her ass harder back into Calder as they danced to one blaring song.

Smiling, she couldn't help feeling like life was good for once. She had a hot-ass man at her back, and she was surrounded by her bitches, who, by the looks of it, were also planning on fucking their men tonight. All of them were on the dance floor, getting their groove on, when she saw T.A.'s face start to drop when Ginger came up behind her and Bear dancing, trying to garner his attention.

It was obvious Bear had already downed a few too many drinks when he began trying to dance with both women. When his hand landed on Ginger's ass and he began giving more attention to Ginger, a hurt T.A. backed up.

"That bitch!" Crazy Bitch muttered to herself. That was when she saw red, and she could feel everyone in this room was about to be reminded exactly how she had gotten this nickname of hers.

It was like the music had stopped as she moved away from Calder and snatched a bottle of beer out of a brother's hand. She had grabbed it by the neck, flipping it over and making the contents spill onto the floor and shoes of the people dancing nearby. She held it, ready to use it as a lethal weapon.

"Shit." Calder realized too late what she was about to do. Before he could do anything to stop her, Killyama had shoved him back, and the rest of the bitches started backing her up.

Gripping the bottle, she swung it at the head of her target, hoping she just might get lucky and nail the two-timing fucker with one blow.

"Ow! What the fuck?" Bear grabbed the back of his bleeding head, turning to see his attacker. It was clear he was puffed up and ready to fight until he saw her backed up by Sex Piston, Fat Louise, and Killyama. The fight in his eyes was slowly replaced by fright.

The clubhouse went silent, until Ginger was the first one dumb enough to speak when she went to check on Bear's wound. "Why the hell would you do that to him? You poor bab—"

Crazy Bitch grasped the neck of the bottle tighter. The broken bottle was now thankfully fully capable of killing someone.

Reaching out, she grabbed a handful of Ginger's hair, yanking it to expose her throat and placing the jagged edge of the bottle there.

"You ginger-ass, hoeing bitch, give me one good reason not to kill your ass, other than the brothers for your mediocre dick-sucking skills, or so help me God, I'll shove this bottle right into your throat."

Calder had somehow made it up close to her. "Remember the flashing thing on your ankle? I'd say that's one hell of a good fucking reason."

"He's right; let me shove it down that bitch's throat." Sex Piston stepped forward.

"No, you got kids." Killyama glared at a terrified Ginger. "Let me."

"I would offer, but I think one of you has this." Fat Louise didn't step forward.

Bear put his hands up. "Okay, let's all calm down. I didn't do nothin—"

"Shut up, you little fucker!" Crazy Bitch snapped at him,

not knowing if the "little" or the "fucker" part was what hurt his feelings when he cowered back.

Putting the bottle closer to Ginger's stretched-out neck as she pulled her hair even harder, she looked at a now happy T.A. "You want her? I'll give her to you."

"All right. Enough." Calder motioned for the bitches' men to start grabbing up their women while he grabbed the bottle out of Crazy Bitch's hand and started to place it in T.A.'s hand, but then gave it to Dozer instead.

Crazy Bitch then saw Calder grab a wooden bowl of nuts from a nearby table. Spilling them out, he handed the bowl to T.A. "Go fucking crazy."

The men were still struggling to grab their women, while Calder unsuccessfully tried to un-pry Crazy Bitch's fingernails from Ginger's hair. She snapped at him with her flashing pearly whites. It was only when he smacked her on the ass did she finally release the skank's hair.

The asshole swung her over his shoulder. Thankfully, the tequila she had earlier was finally starting to get to her, slowing her crazy-ass down. Otherwise, she would have taken the fucker out for spanking her.

"I wasn't done with her!" She smacked at the big man for taking her away from the fun.

Sex Piston had cold-cocked Bear for trying to pull T.A. off Ginger.

"Why can't they be normal bitches when they get drunk? Most bitches strip, and put on shows or fuck you to death. Ours turn into bloodthirsty psycho's that would make Dexter run for his life," Looney complained, dodging a fist Crazy Bitch aimed at him as he stood innocently watching the commotion. "Who in the hell taught you to fight? I'm going to fuck him up."

"I'm self-taught," she bragged, raining her fists down on

Calder's back. "You deaf? I told you I wasn't done with that two-bit excuse for a woman!"

Calder ignored her struggles. "You wouldn't have been done with her till she left in a body bag and your ass was back in jail."

"Like I said, I wasn't done! Where are you taking me?" Staring down at the floor was fucking with her equilibrium. Either that or the tequila was fucking with her.

"Well, I *was* gonna take you to a room so I could fuck your crazy brains out." He stopped walking down the hallway to open a door. At a "Get out!" he slammed the door, going farther down the hall.

"Oh... you were?" Her body started getting warm, not knowing if it was from the alcohol or his words, but her tongue finally started to sweeten up.

"Yes, and I still am, if you're wondering." Calder kicked in another door then kicked it closed, tossing her down on the bed as he started to strip.

Her mouth watered when she saw how hard he was. "What did it for you? The dancing, or me almost killing Ginger?"

"When you nearly made Bear piss himself."

Calder grabbed a condom then kicked his jeans out of his way.

She shimmied out of her tight black skirt then spread her legs. "Is hot thang ready?"

"Fuck yes. You're not wearing panties."

She wiggled on the bed. "They get in the way."

"Yes, they do." Giving a loud groan, he pulled her to the edge of the bed.

"I thought you deserved a little something-something for taking care of those little fuckers from Eastern."

"Stud and I would have taken care of Sam, too, if we had found him."

"Forget about Sam. You have bigger fish to fry."

"Like what?"

"Like putting that big dick where it can do the most good."

She screamed out in pleasure when he drove into her over and over again. It was hard to get her words out through the hard fucking, but she finally managed.

"I thought I might have turned you off back there with my craziness."

Leaning down, he took her mouth for a hard kiss while he continued what she hoped would be an endless night of fucking. "You might be a crazy bitch, but you're *my* crazy bitch."

32

Crazy Bitch pushed her sunglasses up the bridge of her nose.

"Are you feeling okay?"

She gave Nettie a wane smile. "I'm fine. I must have eaten something bad last night."

Or drank too much, she thought to herself. Every bone in her body was sore, and her stomach was queasy. She and Calder had gone hard. God knew she wasn't complaining about her two-day fuck-fest, but she was still paying the price for the tequila on Saturday night.

Damn, it was disheartening to feel the effects after two days. She remembered when two bottles wouldn't even give her a buzz. Of course, those bottles had been shared with the other bitches, but still, it was a hard pill to swallow.

"Onions do me that way."

The thought of onions made her even queasier. The sun shining down directly on her head had her glad she had grabbed a bottle of water from an ice chest at the ground-breaking ceremony.

Lucky stood on the makeshift stage, which consisted of

Greer Porter's lowered tailgate. Townspeople from Treepoint had driven to Jamestown to the dedication of the extension of the women's shelter.

Nettie sniffed into a tissue she was holding. "I've been waiting for this moment for six years. If my daughter had had a place like this to turn to, she would not be where she is now."

"Is she in the crowd?" Crazy Bitch asked, wishing she had worn a big, floppy hat like Nettie's. Looking around, she didn't see anyone she didn't recognize.

"No. Charlotte is in prison."

She turned her sunglasses toward Nettie. "What'd she do?"

"Her husband was a lunatic. He had been so sweet when they got married. He was the son-in-law I always wanted. After they had my grandson, he became jealous of every man she talked to. He would read her emails, listen to her phone calls. Charlotte had enough when he started becoming violent with her. I begged her to come and stay with me, or one of our friends, but she wouldn't. She was too afraid he would hurt me or one of them."

Her sick stomach grew worse.

"That was before I knew you, Sex Piston, and Lily. She didn't feel like she had a safe place to stay, so she stayed home, took out an order of protection, and filed for divorce. Mike stayed away, other than filing for primary custody. I thought he was handling the divorce well, yet Charlotte kept saying it was all an act. That he kept breaking into her house and her car.

"That night, I called to say good night to her, and the next thing I knew, a friend who lived next to Charlotte called to tell me that she had been arrested for killing Mike and his brother when they had tried to take my grandson."

"How did they send her to prison? It must have been self-defense."

"The gun was Charlotte's. Mike had told his mother that she had told him he could have Spencer that weekend. The sheriff and the Commonwealth Attorney said she had lured Mike to his death and killed his brother to make sure there weren't any witnesses. They even called the gun store owner to testify that Charlotte had said that if Mike came near her house again, she would shoot him."

Crazy Bitch promised herself, the next time someone pissed her off, she wouldn't spout off about shooting them.

"How much time did she get?"

"Fifty years. I'll never be able to hug my daughter again."

"I'm so sorry, Nettie. But surely, you can hug her when you visit."

"Not in the one she's in. It's maximum security. We have to keep a table between us."

Crazy Bitch's heart started pumping so fast she had to drink her water to calm down.

No one was standing near them; most of the crowd had gone to the front to listen to Lucky's speech. She and Nettie were standing in the back, where the ribbon was going to be cut.

"What's the name of the prison she's in?"

"She's in the Kentucky State Penitentiary."

Crazy Bitch cleared her throat. "I have a friend not far from Eddyville. I could go by and visit her."

"Would you? She'd get a kick out of someone else seeing her. I go to visit her once a month. You have to fill out an application online. Just type in that you're Charlotte's cousin. They'll email you back that you're approved. I'm going to see her tomorrow, so wait to apply. I wouldn't want her to deny you're her cousin before you fill it out."

"Just text me when you get outside, and I'll fill it out. How long does it take to get approved?"

"Not long if you don't have a record. If you do, they won't approve you."

Her stomach sank. There was no way she or Calder were getting in by conventional means.

Her mind buzzed, drowning the rest of the speeches and the groundbreaking. How in the hell were she and Calder getting inside to see Charlotte? Sex Piston and Stud wouldn't be leaving the twins anytime soon. They had taken their car away from them, and their phones, and they were grounded until hell froze over. T.A. and Bear had broken up, so she was refusing to play the game. Killyama and Train weren't playing. That left one person in their crew who could get the job done. Fat Louise didn't have a brain in her head, but Cade did.

She sidled back to Nettie as the woman was about to leave. "Now that I think about it, I don't go to Eddyville that often, but Jane is friends with my friend, too. She could go see your daughter. Just tell Charlotte her cousin Jane and her husband will be coming for a visit when they're approved."

"I will. Can you tell them to change some dollar bills into change? They allow visitors to buy food and snacks from the concession area."

"I'll make sure Jane and Cade take good care of Charlotte."

She said a quick goodbye then searched through the crowd to see her friends were watching Stud, Calder, and the rest of the brothers stack wood near the building site.

"Having fun?" Crazy Bitch grinned at Sex Piston as she watched a shirtless Stud carry boards over his shoulder.

"You have no idea." Her eyes roved over Stud's muscular body.

"I believe I do." Crazy Bitch watched Calder carry a

bigger stack across his shoulder. "Damn, I might need to put Rider on my wish list," she said, taking out her phone to snap a picture of him carrying the smallest amount of boards. It was clear The Last Riders had more muscles, but the Destructors had more brawn.

"I don't see Train packing any boards," Crazy Bitch teased Killyama.

"He's passing out water to everyone."

"There are those who can do, and those who can't... pass out water." Crazy Bitch snickered.

The comment set off a catfight that had her sunglasses flying through the air as Killyama tried to twist her arm behind her back to say she was sorry.

Calder started to drop the boards he was carrying, but stopped when Crazy Bitch laughed as Killyama put her in a headlock. The brief fight ended when she saw Moon walk past.

"You win." Crazy Bitch reached for her phone again, taking another photo. Then she quickly shoved it into her pocket when she saw Calder furiously approaching.

"I want to see those pictures tonight. And just so you know, every picture that is a Last Rider is going to piss me off. You get my meaning?"

Damn, Calder was sexy when he was jealous.

She gave him a smart-aleck salute when he went back to the woodpile.

"Yo! Hot thang!"

Calder turned around at her shout. She quickly took a picture, hiding her phone before he could take it away from her.

When he lifted her up into the air, she looked down at him, grinning. The other night, she had thought life was good. She was wrong. It was fucking awesome.

Tugging his hair back to plaster a kiss on his mouth, she thrust her tongue inside in a frenzy of love and need.

Lifting her head, she wiped her lipstick away with her thumb. "You can go now."

He set her back down on her feet, giving her a hard smack on her ass.

"You're making a habit of that!"

"Then behave," he grunted, picking up another pile of lumber.

"Where has my bitch gone?" Sex Piston said mockingly.

"Your bitch is right here," Crazy Bitch said gleefully, pursing her lips to throw an air kiss at Rider, who hurried past her. "Got to keep those suckers on their toes."

"Which one?" Fat Louise put a hand over her mouth when Sex Piston shot her a quelling glance.

"Both Rider and Calder. Remember the good old days when Rider was afraid of me and Killyama? And I have to keep Calder on his toes. I don't want him too sure of me."

"How does letting him get away with spanking you keep him on his toes?" Sex Piston asked.

"Because he thinks I'm letting him get away with it, and then I get"—she reached out a hand, palm up, closing it into a fist—"to crush his nuts like peanuts."

"You didn't forget to use the lube, did you?" Killyama laughed, slapping her on the back.

Crazy Bitch had to catch herself before toppling over in her heels.

"Maybe I did. Maybe I didn't. You'll never know." Crazy Bitch patted her hair. "You might be the lucky bitch, but I'm the most devious."

"Which one am I?" Fat Louise asked innocently.

"The one who is going on a road trip in a couple of days." Crazy Bitch's eyes beamed with pride when the other bitches moved closer.

"You figured out the clue?" Sex Piston looked over her shoulder to make sure no one was in hearing distance.

"Calder and I both did."

"Where are Cade and I going?" Fat Louise's eyes widened when she told her Eddyville.

"Is Greer still here?" Sex Piston looked for the truck that Lucky had been standing on thirty minutes before.

"I waited to tell you until he left," Crazy Bitch informed her.

"Why do I have to go?" Fat Louise bent down to pick up Crazy Bitch's sunglasses, handing them to her.

"You and Cade are the only ones who don't have a police record, and Sex Piston won't want to leave the twins."

"Damn right. I won't unless you're offering to babysit them again?"

"No."

"Come on, Fat Louise. Me and Train will watch the baby," Killyama offered.

"Prisons give me the creeps. What if someone tries to make me their bitch?"

"Tell them you're already taken." Sex Piston slung an arm over Fat Louise's shoulders. "I can take any of those bitches."

"Let's just hope you get approved and none of The Last Riders figure out the frozen clue."

Crazy Bitch noticed one of her fingernails was chipped. Putting her hand in her pocket, she decided it was time to leave.

"I'll see you. I got to go. Tell Calder I'll see him at home."

"What's the rush?" Killyama moved out of her way when she brushed past her.

"I have a chipped fingernail. I have to go home and fix it."

"Heaven help Calder if he sees you with a chipped nail."

"He thinks I'm perfect. I don't want to disillusion him."

"You're too late!" Killyama yelled after her.

Crazy Bitch didn't turn around, walking toward her car to slip inside.

Starting the car, she aimlessly waited for her passenger in the back seat to show himself. He waited until she had turned onto an old road that led to the trash dump before he sat up.

"Took you long enough," she said, looking into the rearview mirror.

"I don't want to be seen talking to you." Lucky stared back at her.

"No one looks at my car. They're afraid it will make them sick. So, what did you need to talk about that you had to sneak into my car?"

"I wanted to talk about why you didn't warn me about Stud and Calder searching for Sam?"

"Because I didn't know. I only found out when Calder came home that night. They thought they were defending me."

"What they accomplished was sending him into hiding so we can't find him."

Crazy Bitch slapped her hand down on the steering wheel. "I texted you as soon as I found out."

"By then, it was too late." Lucky's expression turned ominous. "The drug task force is going to make their move tomorrow morning. Diamond showed the video of the deputy from the realty company to the Commonwealth Attorney this morning. She asked the Commonwealth Attorney to ask for the police camera of the sheriff and the deputy. The sheriff's was on, but the deputy's was off."

"What a surprise." Crazy Bitch turned the air conditioner on higher. She was sweltering. "So, who was the one who planted the drugs if the sheriff had his camera on?"

"We don't know. The sheriff may not have planted the

drugs, but he knew they were there. The video showed he went directly under the mat."

"Stupid bastard."

"Not as stupid as the deputy. He might have remembered to turn off his body camera, but he forgot there's a camera on the ceiling of the cruiser, showing the back seat. His confession that he knew you had stopped at the stop sign was caught on tape."

"Why didn't the sheriff erase it?"

"He planned to, but Diamond had asked the state police to seize the tapes the night you were arrested. He didn't have time."

"If you don't have Sam, then why is the task force going to make some arrests tomorrow?"

"We're hoping Sam is at one of the houses we're going to hit."

She narrowed her eyes at Lucky. "That's not all, is it?"

"I want you out of this mess. I want you to talk to Calder tonight so he can be on guard. When we go back, I want you to drop me off at the Destructors' clubhouse. Stud should be back by then. He can make sure the brothers have your back."

"Aren't you worried about losing some arrests?"

"No. They're already staked out. I came out of retirement to help you. I've done that, and now I will finally be able to get the sheriff. Once we find Sam, most of the danger will be off you. The paperwork leads back to him. Once he's arrested, the town will believe he's the informant, not you."

"He'll know."

"I'm going to offer him a sweet deal."

"Which is?" She hated that the rat bastard would get any kind of deal.

"I'm going to let him live."

329

33

Crazy Bitch lazily blew on her fingernails, admiring the job she had just finished.

Looking at the clock, she reached for her phone. Calder should have been home by now.

She had come home right after dropping Lucky off, and she had actually expected Calder to be there. When he hadn't been, she had texted him. So far, he hadn't returned it.

Pressing his phone number, she stared down at her toenails critically, thinking on working on them. When Calder didn't answer, she called Stud.

She didn't give him time to say hello. "Calder at the clubhouse?"

"No, I haven't seen him since I left him at the ceremony. He's not there?"

Her feet went to her carpeted floor. "Did Sex Piston give him my message that I was going home?"

"Yes. He said that's where he was going."

"Could he have gone to the Blue Horsemen clubhouse?"

"Not without telling you."

"Is Lucky still there?" she asked.

"I haven't seen Lucky."

Terror filled her. "Stud, is Sex Piston with you?"

"No, she's at the house with the kids."

"Where are you in the club?"

"At the bar."

"Go to the office and lock yourself in. *Now*. Don't say anything until you're there."

Silence met her ear, though she could hear Stud's boots on the floor.

"I'm here. What in the fuck is going on?"

"You alone?"

"Yes."

"You got a gun in there?"

"Yes."

"Get it. I'll talk while you're getting it."

Hysteria had her wanting to scream, but Calder and Lucky were in danger. She couldn't let the crazy out until she found them.

"I dropped Lucky off at the club before I came home."

"Why—"

"Shut up and listen. We don't have much time. Someone has a head start on us. He was going to tell you that he was going to arrest several people in town who are involved in selling painkillers. I was the informant. Lucky wanted you to have the brothers to protect me and Calder until he could find Sam. When I dropped him off out back, your van was outside. You didn't see him come in?"

"I parked the van at the club, but I drove my bike to the ceremony. I was going to drive the van home tonight."

"Fuck, we thought you were inside. Lucky said the sheriff didn't plant the drugs in my car, but he knew where the drugs were going to be. Someone from the club must have planted the drugs. The rental car was parked outside. I didn't bother to lock the door."

"So, someone in the club planted drugs on you to get you arrested, and you think they've done something to Lucky?"

"Yes, and Calder. That's why he's not answering. I'm scared shitless. What do we do?"

"You got a gun?"

"In my bedroom."

"Get it. I'll stay on the line until you get it. When I hang up, I'm going to call Killyama. She, Hammer, and Jonas will protect you. Don't answer the door, even if Jesus shows up knocking. I'm going to the Blue Horsemen and will send half the men to Sex Piston, and keep the other half with me."

"Are you going to stay in the office until they get there?"

"No, we don't have to wait. There are twenty men out front. I'm sure the one who took Lucky is gone. If he is, I'll find out which one it is. Who did you report to?"

"Lucky. But he gave me a number in case of an emergency."

"Call it. Then call me back." The call went dead.

She immediately called the number Lucky had made her memorize. It answered on the first ring.

"Hello?"

She recognized the cold voice.

"Shade, I can't find Calder. And Lucky had me drop him off at the Destructor's clubhouse, but he's not there." She held her phone tighter.

"Where are you?"

"At my apartment. Stud is calling Killyama to bring Hammer and Jonas to me."

"I see her and Train pulling out of the parking lot now. Make sure you keep a gun in your hand until they're there." Shade kept his instructions short and clipped.

"I was hoping Lucky was at The Last Riders' clubhouse."

"He's not. I got to go. Stud's on the other line." The phone went dead.

She waited several minutes before calling Stud back, wanting to give him time to talk to Shade. She took the opportunity to lower her blinds.

When she called Stud back and he answered, she could hear a commotion going on in the background.

"What's going on?" she yelled when Stud's voice didn't come over the line.

"It was Bear."

She sat down on the couch, setting the gun down next to her. "Did he say where Calder and Lucky are?"

Crazy Bitch started crying. She had loved Bear like a brother. Many times, he had spent the night on her couch. She had even cried on his shoulder when she had broken up with Joker.

"Not yet. But he will. I'll call you back when I find something out."

She remained on the couch, holding her phone in one hand and her gun in the other.

Calder had wanted her to download an app so she would know where he was all the time, and vice versa, but she had told him no. She hadn't wanted him tracking her movements while she was an informant. She had made a lame excuse, and they hadn't done it.

Crazy Bitch cried harder. She couldn't live without him. Going through the same monotonous existence would drive her crazy for real.

Calder was so gentle. Even when he spanked her, it was like being swatted by a three-year-old. When she had shaved a rat on his head, he had never said anything to her. Even when she had pulverized his dick, he hadn't broken up with her. A man like that would be impossible to replace.

When a knock sounded on the door, she ran toward it,

looking through the peephole. She opened it when she saw it was Killyama and Train.

"Jonas and Hammer aren't with you?" she asked, locking the door when they came inside.

"They're watching the parking lot."

"Stud said it was Bear who must have done something to Lucky and—"

"Sit down, Crazy Bitch."

She had been friends with Killyama a long time, long enough to know she wasn't going to like what the woman was about to say.

"You found Calder?"

"Not yet, but Stud found Lucky."

She shakily sat down on the couch. "Is he alive?" She had grown to like the man since she had begun working with him.

"Barely. Bear slit his throat and stabbed him several times before throwing him down the ravine behind the clubhouse. They don't know if he's going to make it."

Crazy Bitch buried her face in her hands, crying. "This is my fault. If I had just minded my own business, he would have never come out of retirement," she sobbed. "He just had a baby. If he dies, his son will be fatherless because of me. I tried to help because I wanted to find out who kept supplying my mother with pills. It was never worth getting Lucky and Calder killed."

"Lucky isn't dead yet, and neither is Calder." Train took a seat next to her. "And as far as it being worth Lucky's life, he knew the cost of what he was doing. He always has. He doesn't know how to turn a blind eye to what goes on around him, and he admired you for risking your life."

"He told you?" She lowered her hands at his words.

"Yes. He told me and Killyama. He would have never let you do something dangerous without having you watched.

Calder was watched, too. We can't understand how he was taken. I was the one watching him. The last time I saw him, he was going to the bathroom in the shelter. I didn't want to make it obvious I was following him. He didn't come back outside, and I couldn't find him. His bike was still where he parked it in the parking lot of the shelter."

"That's the parking lot that Shade said you were pulling out of. I assumed it was The Last Riders'."

"No. On the way to your apartment, we got a call from Stud that he found Lucky."

"Bear hurt Lucky because he must have known Lucky was going to tell Stud what was going to happen in the morning. But why Calder? It doesn't make sense. He doesn't even know what I've been doing. He would have been in danger if anyone found out I supplied the information for the arrests. But no one has been arrested yet. No one has been burned yet. Could it have been someone on the task force?"

"We're checking them out, but we don't think so. Those agents are highly screened. Not only that, but I know most of them, and I don't think anyone would have taken the chance of ruining their career for a small-town bust. None of those the task force were going to arrest are traffickers. Most of them want their own fix. What little they have left isn't enough to kill a man for."

"Have you eaten? You want me to cook you something?" Killyama offered.

"No, I couldn't eat." She rubbed her arms. "Something happened to him. I feel it." Crazy Bitch bit her lip, trying to hold back her tears.

Killyama sat down on the coffee table in front of her. "Sex Piston called me. Stud won't let her leave the house, though she wants to be here with you. She said, as soon as she can, she'll be here."

Crazy Bitch nodded, her mind on Calder, going back to when she left him at the building site.

"I didn't even say goodbye. I told Sex Piston to tell him I was going home. I'm trying to remember if I told him I loved him this morning when we woke up, and I can't."

"I'm sure you did." Killyama took her cold hand in hers.

Whatever had happened to Calder was bad, so bad she could practically feel him calling for her.

The night was endless as she intermittently walked around her apartment. She found the shirt he had worn last night and took hers off, putting his on, and then changing her leggings to faded jeans.

Going back into the living room, she saw that Train had made coffee. Pouring herself a cup, she sat at the counter, staring at her phone, waiting for it to ring.

"You want to go rest? I'll wake you if we hear anything." Killyama came to stand at the counter next to Train.

"No. I don't want to sleep. I don't want to sleep knowing he could be hurt. I don't want to be asleep and wake up to you telling me he's dead." She choked back her tears. "Calder, Stud, and Sex Piston were going to tell Star she was his daughter tonight. Did you know?"

"I suspected. She looks like Calder."

"Yes, she does. She has his personality, too." A sob escaped her. She put her hand up, smothering it. "I love him... so much. You know, it surprised me how much I love him. I didn't expect to."

"I know you do. Calder knows, too."

"I hope so. I was just kidding with those pictures of Rider and Moon to make him jealous. I like it when he spanks me. No one's ever spanked me before. No one cared enough. My mom didn't care, none of my foster parents, none of the men."

"If you needed a spanking to know I love you, all you had to do was ask."

Killyama's teasing made Crazy Bitch laugh, causing a chain reaction that had Killyama coming around the counter to hold her as she cried into her shoulder.

"We'll find Calder. We'll find him."

34

It was the waiting that was the hardest. The first night of Calder's disappearance was hard. The second was pure hell. Hope waned away hour by hour until there was only a flickering light remaining by the end of the second night.

Crazy Bitch stared down at her notebook through blurry eyes. She had fallen asleep at the counter for four hours during the day, but had woken up when Train's phone had rung. It hadn't been news about Calder. It had been about Lucky. He had survived the night and was in critical but stable condition, and the doctor thought he would make it.

Crazy Bitch thought of a name and added it to her list.

"Whose name did you add?" Sex Piston asked. She had come over that morning after taking the kids to school, telling Stud they would be safe there and could go to her parents' house when school was released. She had bluntly told her husband that she was staying with Crazy Bitch until Calder was found.

"I added Harmon Myers. I remembered he was standing next to Mrs. Carpenter." Crazy Bitch used an ink pen to point at the name. She had come up with the idea to make a

338

list of all the people who had attended the groundbreaking. One of them had to have been the person who had taken Calder.

"Did you put Devon on the list? I saw him there," Fat Louise said.

"I don't think a seventy-year-old man is capable of carrying Calder to his car." T.A. gave her an annoyed look.

"I didn't think he did, but maybe he saw someone go into the shelter with Calder. I saw him standing by the ice chest. He was refilling it."

"I'll write it down. Shade said to write down everything we saw and make a note of everyone we knew. I sent most of the list last night. Right now, I'm trying to figure out if we forgot anyone." She slid down off the stool. "You guys go over it and see if we left anyone out." Stretching, she tried to work the kinks out of her back. She wanted another of cup of coffee, but she was out and Hammer wasn't back from the store yet.

"I didn't put Devon on the list. I didn't see his car. Put him on the list for me, Fat Louise."

"He probably drove his mother's car. It was parked next to mine," Sex Piston said, writing his name down.

"No, he didn't. He parked on the side of the shelter. That's where the ice chest was. He volunteered to bring the water," Fat Louise explained.

"I volunteered to bring the water. How did Devon end up bringing it?"

"Mrs. Carpenter called me at work and said Devon was at the store and wanted to help, so she gave him that job. She was on the committee, so I didn't think anything of it."

"Why does it matter who brought the water?" T.A. sat down on the couch, pulling a cushion by her side to protect herself from Manson scratching her.

"I don't know, but I want to know why he decided to

bring the water. I've cut his hair for years. He's never given me a dime tip, yet suddenly he volunteered to buy bottled water for fifty people?" Crazy Bitch twisted her hair into a knot, going into the kitchen where she kept a hair clip for when she was cooking. She was continuously thinking about Calder's disappearance.

"Call him. I have his mother's phone number." Sex Piston picked up her phone, scrolling through her numbers.

"Give me his name and address. I'll call Shade and get him to check it out." Train took out his phone to type down the number.

"Can someone else do it instead, so Shade can come here?"

"Why?"

"I want to talk to him. How far is he?"

"Not far. He's talking to some members of the task force. I can ask him to come here when he can."

"Do it." Crazy Bitch went to the kitchen counter, taking her notebook away from Sex Piston.

"Did you think of another name?" Sex Piston slid her pencil toward her as she stared down at the names.

She listened to Train talking to Shade, waiting until he finished to reply.

"No. What did Shade say?"

"He's on his way."

Something about the list was bothering her, but she couldn't understand what it was.

"Shade is sending Rider to talk to Devon." Train moved to stand behind Killyama, rubbing her back as she sat at the counter.

"When he's done there, have him go to talk to his mother. She's blind as a bat, but she's a busybody. Maybe she saw something."

"Okay."

A sharp knock sounded on the door. When Train opened the door, Hammer came in, carrying grocery bags.

As one of Killyama's bounty hunter partners, Crazy Bitch had met Hammer several times. She had even thought of doing him a couple of times, but he had backed off after she had tested him with some of her wisecracks.

Calder hadn't backed down. He had kept coming back for more. He had more courage than most men she knew. No man had ever found her sweet spot, and she wasn't talking about the one in her pussy. He had found that inner sanctuary within her that had never been found by anyone before.

It had kept her safe as she had grown up and realized her mother wasn't like other moms. It had kept her safe when she realized her father had a daughter the same age as her. It had kept her safe through numerous foster homes, Joker, so many men she had lost count, and her mother's death. None had found that sweet spot where she could actually be her, not the bitch she portrayed to everyone else. Just her, a not-so-pretty, lame geek who didn't have to lose her temper when she was hurt and strike out at whomever had dealt that hurt.

The smell of fresh coffee brewing was in the air when another knock sounded in the room.

Shade came in as Train opened the door.

Crazy Bitch came around the counter, seeing Shade didn't even look tired as he pushed his sunglasses to his hair.

"I'm glad someone's getting sleep," she said angrily, needing someone to strike out at to alleviate the rage of not being able to find Calder.

"I haven't slept since the night before Calder disappeared." He didn't seem to be upset by her attitude. She even wondered if he was capable of emotions, unless Lily was concerned.

"I'm sorry. You look like you just got of bed."

"I can go days without sleep." He shrugged.

"Have you found anything else about Calder?"

"No. From the moment he went into the shelter, no one has seen him. It's like he dropped off the face of the earth."

Her shoulders slumped in weariness. Discouraged, she wanted—needed—to find something to do to keep her from losing what sanity she had left.

"Can I have some of that coffee?" Shade asked Train as he made himself a cup.

Turning back to her, he stoically stated what had been going on since Calder hadn't come home. "The drug task force took Bear into custody last night. Stud handed what was left of him over when they found Lucky. The Last Riders had already been worried because he didn't show up to pick up the baby after work. We assumed the last place he was, was the groundbreaking ceremony, so we went there and found his and Calder's bikes. That's about the time you called. Then Stud called and said he found Lucky in the ravine outside the club. If Stud hadn't convinced Bear to tell him where he was, his luck would have run out. The doctor said he had minutes to live."

"How did Stud know Bear was involved?" Crazy Bitch shook her head when Train offered her coffee, too disgusted with what Bear had done. She didn't want to burn anyone if she slung it against a wall.

"Stud gathered all the brothers in the room and told them that Lucky was missing and that someone planted the drugs in your car the night of your arrest. Dozer remembered seeing Bear near her car when he pulled into the parking lot from work. Ginger said that Bear was the only one in the clubhouse when she left to go to the liquor store. The brothers had him confessing that he didn't know Lucky was there and that he came in the back door when he was talking on the phone with Sam. Lucky must have heard and tried to leave, but Bear heard him leaving—"

"A chime sounds in the bar when the door is opened and closed," Crazy Bitch said. "It's not very loud. It's from when the club used to be a restaurant. It's old as fuck. Most of the time, we ignore it. He must have come in when Bear was talking and he didn't hear Lucky come in then heard him leaving after he hung up."

"Bear caught him in the parking lot. When he heard the brothers parking in the front, he threw him down the ravine. He thought he was dead."

"Where's he now?"

"Nowhere you can get to him anytime soon." Shade set his coffee down on the counter. "He's sitting on ice, with Sam in the next cell. He was found where Bear said he would be— in a small apartment that Bear had rented so he and Sam could stockpile their products and meet where no one could see they were connected. That's why Stud, Calder, and the task force couldn't find him.

"None of the prescriptions that Sam forged were in Bear's name. They used aliases or used patients' names of the doctor he worked for. Sam worked part-time for another doctor. He and Bear had been raking in the cash until you made waves. That's why they decided to frame you and take you out of the picture. The deputy who stopped you was one of their best clients. Instead of issuing summons, he was a delivery service to their buyers.

"And the sheriff, he was in on it, too. The problem is, when you stack the deck, one misplaced card can topple the rest of the cards down around you. You were the wild card. You sent them all crashing down. The sheriff and two deputies have been removed from duty."

"So where is Calder? Let me see Bear. I'll convince him to tell me—"

Shade shook his head. "Both Sam and Bear say they don't know where Calder is. Bear said he only attacked Lucky because he heard him talking to Sam. He said he had no reason to hurt Calder because neither of them knew about his involvement. I believe him."

"What about Sam?"

"Sam said the only one he wanted to kill was you."

"He could have done something to Calder to get back at me."

"He passed a lie detector test."

She went into her living room to sit down on a chair, burying her face in her hands. "So, the only lead we have is a seventy-year-old man and his ninety-one-year-old mother?"

"That about sums it up." Shade placed his hands on the back of the couch, where T.A. and Fat Louis were sitting, jerking his hands back when Manson swatted at him. "Have you given any thought to the fact that maybe he wanted to disappear?"

She raised her head. "Did you give any thought where Lucky was concerned, or is Calder the exception?" Crazy Bitch said sarcastically.

"We have to look at all the options." He coldly brought up Calder's past. "It wouldn't be the first—"

She stood up, pointing toward the door. "Get the fuck out. Now."

He didn't react to her demand. "I'm not saying I believe it. I asked if you had thought about it."

"No, I didn't think about it," she snapped. "I tend to give the people I love the benefit of the doubt. That's where The Last Riders and the Destructors differ. We're loyal to those we love, while The Last Riders don't know what love is."

"I'm trying to help." Shade's impassiveness was more than she could take.

"Calder has done nothing but help Gavin. He's earned

344

your help. Don't act like you're doing him a fucking favor!" she screamed.

Shade's eyes shot out shards of blue ice. "Do you know why most drowning victims drown?" he asked conversationally.

She had to hiccup back the hysterics that were rising to the surface. "I don't—"

"They panic," he calmly answered before she could. "Take a deep breath, grab a beer, or drink a cup of coffee. Use your heads." Shade stared around the group gathered in her living room and kitchen.

Taking him up on his suggestion, she went to the fridge, taking out a beer. Opening it, she took a drink as Shade walked to the counter to watch her.

"What's this?"

Crazy Bitch took another drink, focusing her mind. She flipped to the first page. "I started a notebook of the clues for our treasure hunt." She flipped another page. "This is everyone we saw during the groundbreaking and where we remembered them standing. That's why Train called you about Devon and his mother."

"Rider talked to Devon. He said he didn't see anything suspicious when he went into the shelter, and he wasn't paying attention when Calder didn't come back. Rider's with Mrs. Carpenter now. He'll call me back when he's finished."

Crazy Bitch flipped another page. "This one, I was going to make a list of people Calder had pissed off and who wanted to hurt him."

Shade looked at her approvingly. "Good call. Why's it blank?"

"Because I can't think of anyone. Calder is pretty laid-back. The only one I can think of who hates him is Candi. She got out of prison last week, and they had an argument."

"What was the fight about?"

345

"It's personal." She might have revealed to Killyama and Train about Star, but she knew she could trust them to keep it to themselves.

"You want me to find him?" he challenged.

Calder's privacy wasn't worth his life. "Star is his kid. Candi was trying to blackmail Stud for money to keep from telling Calder and Star."

"What was Stud's reaction?"

"Stud, Sex Piston, and Calder were going to talk to Star the night he disappeared. Calder also told Candi that if she didn't get out of town, he would spread it around town that she was the informant who got him and several of their buddies arrested."

"Was she?"

"Calder seemed to think she was."

"That's pretty much what Stud said," Shade added.

"If you knew, then why ask?"

"To make sure nothing was left out. Sometimes one little detail can be a matter of life and death. Stud is trying to find Candi. I pulled a few favors and found out who her parole officer is. He didn't want to give out her information, but Knox found out and gave the information to Stud. The apartment she gave was her sister's, and she hasn't seen her since Candi moved out three months ago."

"She's been out that long?" Sex Piston jerked sharply in her chair at the counter.

"Yes. Her sister said she has a boyfriend, and Candi told her she was moving in with him."

"Who's the sucker?" T.A. asked, shoving Mason off the couch.

"Her sister didn't know."

"Is Stud the only one looking for Candi?"

"No, when we got Bear and Sam's lie detector results back, I sent them to Stud. We've already gone to where she told her parole worker she's working. She didn't last a week there. No one can even remember her. They said she mainly spent the time flirting with customers."

"That sounds like her," Crazy Bitch remarked contemptuously.

"Stud sent a couple of the brothers to some of the places where Candi and Calder hung out when they were together. We're hoping one of them might have seen her since she's come back and know where she's at now."

Crazy Bitch had to admit, Stud and The Last Riders weren't leaving any stone unturned.

"I'm sorry I snapped at—"

"It's cool. I've been in your position. It's not easy when you don't know where they are and you can't protect them."

"No, it isn't."

"Where'd Candi work?" Fat Louise went to her candy drawer, taking out a chocolate bar. Everyone watched as she flushed. "Sorry. Thinking about her made me want one."

Shade's lips curled in what Crazy Bitch thought was a smile. "Taco Hut."

"I know why she quit." Killyama leaned against Train tiredly.

"I don't know why you hate it so much." Fat Louise bit off another bite of her candy bar. "You hate the food so bad, you should tell Mrs. Carpenter."

"Fuck... fuck..." Crazy Bitch wanted to hug her friend. "Devon goes there a lot. She says that way, they can keep quality control of the food being served. Not only do they own Taco Hut, but they own rental houses." She was becoming so excited she could barely get the words out. "Shade, call Rider—"

Before she could get the sentence out, Shade's phone rang.

She frantically went to the knife block, taking the kitchen

347

shears out. Running to the couch, she tried to cut her monitor off.

"Stop. You'll have the police coming if you don't. Rider's got the address. Devon has a new tenant who hasn't been paying her rent. Mrs. Carpenter wants her thrown out. Devon doesn't."

"He's her sugar daddy." Crazy Bitch looked wildly at Shade. "Can you get this thing off or not?"

Shade grinned. "What do you think?"

She held her ankle out. "Don't make me ask twice."

35

Crazy Bitch sat in the front seat of Sex Piston's van as she followed Shade. They pulled out of her apartment parking lot, going to the address that Mrs. Carpenter had given Rider. He was going to stay with her to make sure she didn't tip Devon off. Shade had called Razer and Cash to keep Devon from doing the same and find out if he had been the one who had kidnaped Calder.

She didn't know how he had done it, but she was sure he had.

As they passed the street the hospital was on where Lucky was at, Crazy Bitch saw one biker accelerate to ride in front with Shade. Then Moon and five other bikers waited until Sex Piston's van had passed to fall in line, cutting in front of Hammer and Jonas's vehicle.

As they passed the street the Destructors' clubhouse was on, Sex Piston slowed down to a crawl to let the Destructors get in front of them.

They watched as the Destructors accelerated their bikes, weaving among each other until the Destructors were in the lead. Viper and Shade were in front of the van, but the Destructors led the way.

"If I ever hear any of you say you saw me crying, I'll rip your hearts out." Crazy Bitch reached into Sex Piston glove compartment for a baby wipe, knowing she kept a package there for her makeup repairs.

"I don't see anything. You, Train?" Killyama said from the back.

"No, I'm hunched down so no one can see me in this van."

"What's it worth to me to keep my mouth shut?" T.A. asked.

"You get to live."

"Sounds fair. I don't see a thing."

"Fat Louise?"

"You know me; my lips are sealed."

"Can't we go any faster?" Crazy Bitch wanted Sex Piston to put the pedal to the metal.

"You want me to get pulled over? I'm doing sixty in a thirty-five-mile speed limit."

"I'll pay the ticket."

"With what? We gave all our money to the shelter."

"Put your emergency lights on—"

"Too late." The blare of sirens had Sex Piston putting on her blinker to pull off when the police car whizzed past them.

"It's Knox." Crazy Bitch reached for another baby wipe, seeing him pull in front of the Destructors, giving them a police escort.

Without having to worry about getting a ticket anymore, Sex Piston pushed down on the gas pedal, and they flew down the two-lane highway, everyone getting out of their way.

"Damn, Killyama, you might not be the luckiest of us bitches. Diamond might be taking your place."

"Diamond isn't in our crew," Sex Piston snapped.

"She gets me out of all those charges, she will be." Crazy Bitch reached for the door handle, getting ready to jump out when they reached the house.

"We'll talk about it when it happens." Sex Piston cursed as everyone in front of them turned down a tree-lined street. It was a cul-de-sac, and the circle already had several motorcycles parked in front a green one-story house.

As soon as Sex Piston stopped, Crazy Bitch jumped out, running toward the door that stood wide open.

If Candi was responsible for Calder's disappearance, she would kill the woman.

Before she could run inside, Stud came out, his face filled with mixed emotions.

"Does she know where Calder is?" She wanted to brush past him to drag the answer out of Candi herself, but Stud gripped her forearms, holding her in place.

"He's inside. He told us to get the fuck out."

"He's alive?" She fell against his chest, sobbing in relief, despite Stud's bleak expression.

"Yes."

When she would have jerked away from Stud, he jerked her back.

"Didn't you hear what I said? He told us to get the fuck out."

Crazy Bitch remembered when Calder had told her, when she felt the crazy coming over her, to push the red button to stop herself. Mentally, she had to do it several times to keep herself from hurting Stud.

"Stud, I'm going in there to talk to him. You'll have to fucking kill me to stop me. Let. Me. Go!"

Sex Piston placed her hand on Stud's arm. "Let her. Whatever is in there, she needs to see for herself. We'll go with her."

"It isn't pretty," Stud warned, his face contorted in sorrow.

"Let her go." Sex Piston's voice wobbled at her demand.

When Crazy Bitch felt him release her, she didn't hesitate. Going inside, she searched the room for Calder, passing over Candi and the others in the room. None of them were Calder.

Her eyes flew back to Candi, who was sitting on a chair with a slinky grey robe knotted at her waist. She was obviously naked, with her titties barely covered and unconcerned that most of her thighs were showing as she smoked a cigarette.

Candi leaned forward, tapping her cigarette in an ashtray on her coffee table. "Welcome. The more, the merrier," she said waspishly, making a pretense of adjusting the top half of her robe when Crazy Bitch gave her an insulting glare.

"Where is he?"

Candi waved her hand with the cigarette in the direction of a doorway to her left. "In my bedroom. Next time, call before you come over. Calder and I are back together. We'd like time alone right now. Calder would have called Stud in a few days. We've... been busy."

"I bet you have." Crazy Bitch scornfully crossed the room, going to the bedroom. Hearing her friends' footsteps behind her gave her the courage to enter the room.

Not expecting the room to be dark, she had to blink to adjust her eyes. She wrinkled her nose when the stagnant smell of sweat and sex hit her nose.

"Where's the light?" She reached for the wall when she heard Stud tell her it was by her shoulder.

The harsh light had her wanting to turn it off again. Calder was lying on a bed so tumbled the fitted sheet had come off the corners. He jerked when the light came on, his arm protectively hiding his eyes.

"Turn the lights off." His thick voice indicated he was half-asleep, high, or both. "Go… away."

She moved closer to the bed, seeing he was naked, not even bothering to cover himself when she tried to touch his shoulder.

"Leave… me," he slurred. "Go."

"I'm not going anywhere. What about you and me? What about Star?"

He reached out, jerking on her T-shirt. "More… I need… more. Where is… she?"

"Let's go," Sex Piston said to Crazy Bitch. "Don't do this to yourself. Stud and the others can bring him to the clubhouse."

"Not going…" He started fighting her touch. "I need her. Where is she?"

"I'm here, Calder!" Candi yelled from the other room. "Bastards won't let me come in."

Crazy Bitch twisted away when Sex Piston tried to get her to leave. Sitting down on the bed next to him, every memory of her mother played out, taunting her to leave. She hadn't lived through years of living with her mother's addictions to put up with a future filled with the same.

Calder looked as if all the life had been drained out of him, and all that was left was the empty shell of the man she loved with all her heart. She thought of the times she had lost the battle with her craziness, and he had taken it, giving her love pats only when he had been afraid she would get hurt.

In everyone's life, you had to make decisions that would affect your life. Every choice she had made with men, she had failed. Was she just going to sit there and make another one? Give him another chance that she would never give anyone else?

Her eyes welled with tears. Looking at her friends and how they were in their lives, she wanted that for herself.

Every woman did. If they didn't, they were lying to themselves. No one enjoyed being alone, or being with someone who wasn't that special one.

She turned back to Calder, who couldn't look at her and smelled like another woman. That was when she realized her choice had already been made.

"How did you get here?" she asked him.

"Don't... know. Drove awhile. Sleepy..."

His words didn't make sense, but she hadn't expected them to.

Standing up, she walked toward the door.

"Need her. Need..."

Sex Piston, Stud, Killyama, and Train took one glance at her face and backed away as she passed. As she walked into the other room, Shade, Viper, Moon, and Dozer did the same, leaving the path to Candi open.

"Stud, call a fucking ambulance," Crazy Bitch told him.

"If he goes to the hospital, they'll know he broke parole for doing drugs."

"Call them. We have a good lawyer."

Crazy Bitch didn't miss the frightened look that came across Candi's face when she mentioned calling an ambulance.

"How can you care ab—"

Candi's voice broke off when Crazy Bitch grabbed her by the throat.

"You two-bit fucking cunt, I will fucking strangle you to death with my bare hands if you don't tell me what you've done to him!"

None of the men or women tried to stop her as she waited until Candi started to turn blue before loosening her grip.

"I ha-haven't done anything," she gasped out. "I saw him at the ceremon—"

Crazy Bitch tightened her grip again, this time waiting until the slut's eyes nearly rolled backward before loosening it again.

"Dev... hit him... and brought him to me."

Crazy Bitch heartlessly tightened her grip again. "What did you give him?" She gave her enough air to answer.

"Whatever is in the bottom drawer of my nightstand," she sobbed. "I stole them from Dev and his mother."

Crazy Bitch itched to snap her fucking neck. "If you ever come near him again, I'll kill you. You won't be the first fucker's blood I've spilt." Candi tried to nod, but couldn't. "I don't give a frog's fart that you fucked his brains out. I don't care that he smells like your nasty cunt. I don't care that he called out your name when he came. That man is mine. And if his dick rots off or he loses every hair on his head, he'll still be fucking mine." She shook Candi so hard her head banged against the back of her chair.

Letting her go, she gave Knox a warning glare. "Don't let her move."

Seeing him place himself next to Candi, who was holding her throat and crying, Crazy Bitch walked back toward the bedroom.

"Move!" she yelled, sending her friends and the brothers moving out of her way.

Calder had rolled onto his stomach, giving everyone in the room an eyeful of his ass.

She went around the bed to pull out the drawer. "Get me a bag!" she snapped.

When Stud left and returned a minute later with a plastic bag, she threw at least ten different prescription bottles into the sack.

She was about to tie it closed when she noticed one with a brand she recognized. That bitch had to use a seventy-year-old's medication to get a hard-on out of Calder.

She wanted to go back into the other room and shove the whole bottle of pills down the bitch's throat, bottle and all.

Mentally, she pushed that red button in her mind again. Tying the bag closed, she tossed it to Stud. "Give that to the ambulance drivers."

She went to the other side of the bed where Calder was facing, hearing the ambulance sirens grow louder. Kissing his cheek, she rubbed hers against his. "I'm going home to put my monitor back on, and then I'll be at the hospital in a few. I love you, hot thang."

"Crazy Bitch, you need to hide until we can sneak you out," Shade said from the doorway.

She stood up, trying to find a place to hide. Assuming a door in the room was a closet, she started toward it.

"I... need... her."

She had almost reached the door when she heard his whimper.

"An-Anna..."

She turned back toward him.

"A-Anna-Ka... Need... her."

"Breathe, breathe..." she told herself as tears slipped from her eyes, uncaring who saw.

"Crazy Bitch," Shade warned.

"I'm not leaving him." She sat down on the bed, taking Calder's hand. "I'm here, hot thang, I'm here." She lovingly covered his ass.

"I... need... you."

"Baby, you've always needed me, and I've always needed you. You told me you'd catch me if I fall remember? Well now I'm here ready to catch you."

C alder sat on his bed, watching Crazy Bitch unpack his clothes. He fidgeted with the bracelet that had just been snapped onto his wrist, wanting her to leave.

"I can do that. I'm not an invalid."

"You will be if you use that tone of voice with me again."

He jerked his gaze away when she looked over her shoulder at him. Calder couldn't bear to have her look at him.

It was all still a blur to him. The last thing he remembered was coming out of the bathroom to have an elderly man asking him to lift a case of bottled waters out of his truck, and then following him out of a side door to a car with the trunk already open. When he bent to lift the case out, he remembered feeling a sharp pain. He didn't remember anything after that until he woke up in a hospital room with Stud and Crazy Bitch sitting on chairs beside his bed.

He had numbly tried to wrap his mind around what had happened to him the two days he had been under Candi's sick control. That she had conned an old man into kidnapping him was bizarre. That she had also used the promise of sex and marriage to get a rent-free home and money showed that the time she had spent in prison had taught her how to up her game.

"Why didn't you tell me you were an informant?"

Crazy Bitch put his empty suitcase in his closet before turning back toward him. "I was going to the night you disappeared."

Stud had already explained to Calder about the DEA's drug bust and Crazy Bitch's involvement.

"You had plenty of time to tell me before then, like the night me and Stud went looking for Sam."

"You know what happens to informants. I wanted you to stay out of it. I knew you would try to help, and I didn't want you hurt."

"You didn't want me helping because you didn't want me coming into contact with some of my old friends," he accused.

"Maybe," she admitted frankly with a shrug. "Don't bust my chops because I wanted to protect you."

"But you denied me the opportunity to protect *you*."

"I'm used to watching out for myself."

"You didn't mind Lucky watching out for you."

"And how well did that go? He's still in the hospital. He may be going home tomorrow, but the doctors say it will take a couple months for him to fully recover. His nickname is Lucky for a reason." She rolled her eyes.

"You were the lucky one. What if you had gone inside the club with him?"

"Then Bear would have been dead, plain and simple. Bear wouldn't have been able to take both of us on. He just got lucky that Lucky didn't really believe Bear would hurt him. It nearly cost him his life," she mumbled the last part.

"Like you wouldn't have made the same mistake." Feeling

disparaged, Calder jerked to his feet, shoving his hands into his back pockets to keep from shaking her.

She rigidly braced herself as if she could read his mind. "It takes more to earn my trust than sharing a few beers. How do you think I caught on that Sam tried to roofie me?"

Calder blanched, sitting back down on the bed. "You've been roofied before?"

She looked at him as if he had lost his mind. "I had been in and out of foster care since I was three years old; you really don't think all of them were doing it out of the kindness of their hearts, do you? Jeez, I got some swampland I could sell you cheap."

"Who? I want to know—"

"Why? He's dead."

Calder's mouth dropped open in astonishment. "He's the second man you killed?"

She pressed her finger against her forehead then pointed the same finger at him. "Give the man another cigar." She sarcastically gave him a smug grin. "Son of a bitch didn't know what hit him. Of course, he didn't know I had caught on to what he was doing. I switched drinks with him. Poor man." Crazy Bitch clicked her tongue against the roof of her mouth. "Had a heart condition, so they didn't do an autopsy."

"You really are crazy." Calder stared at her in stunned disbelief.

"I've been telling you that all along."

"Yes, you have. You really don't need me to protect you, do you?"

She came to sit beside him, taking his hand. "No, I don't. But that doesn't mean I don't need you. I need you to help me figure out when to push that red button from going crazy, and I'll help you when you need to push yours when you get tempted by drugs."

"I didn't willingly take the drugs Candi gave me. I told

you I didn't need to come here. I spent five days in the hospital."

"It's a safeguard. It's just for a couple weeks."

"I want out." He pulled his hand away from hers as he felt the familiar need clawing at his guts. "I shouldn't have to stay here. The police know Candi and that old man kidnapped me; they said I could go home. If you and Stud hadn't talked me into coming here, I could be at the club."

"Why did you say the club instead of my apartment? Because you know it would be easier there to get what you want?"

"Go home and leave me alone!" he shouted, angry that she had spotted the real reason he wanted out of the rehab center.

Ignoring him, she stood up. "You want me to go to the restaurant next door to get you a burger and fries? I know you must be sick of hospital food. You're probably sick of the food here from when you stayed with Gavin."

"What is it going to take for you to go home and leave me alone? I've told you every day since I woke up, I told you all the way here from Jamestown, and I'm telling you now. How can you even look at me?

"I may not remember the details, but I know bits and pieces. You know I fucked her." He jerkily stood up, unable to look at her. "You know I want whatever she pumped into me so badly that I'm willing to lie to you to get out of here."

"I know." She moved around him so he couldn't see her. "I know how much you love me doesn't compare to how much you want those drugs. That's why I'm here. That's why I'm not leaving—to remind you how much we love each other."

He ran his hands through his hair, wanting to tear it out at her stubbornness. It was easier not to argue. She didn't know how hard it was to want it so badly. She would never know, because she had always been strong. He was weak. He would always be weak.

Lying down on the bed, he pretended she wasn't there. Then, when he heard the door opening, he didn't know what was worse: that she had gotten fed up with him and left, or that the nurse had come in to give him another dose to ease the cravings that were splitting his every nerve ending with a driving need that wouldn't be assuaged until it got what it wanted.

He heard someone walk around the front of his bed. Raising his eyelids, he looked up to see Gavin.

He waited for him to say some of the same bullshit he had told him when he arrived at the rehab center.

Gavin didn't say a word. He didn't have to. He just held out his hand.

One Week Later...

"Cut it off. I can't stand it. Either you do it, or I will." Calder yanked at his hair, unable to stand the pressure of it on his head.

"You love your hair."

Calder irritably tried to yank a lock out.

"Fine. You want it cut, I'll cut it for you." She left his room, coming back five minutes later and motioning for him to take the chair by his window. "I love short hair on men, so it's no skin to cut yours."

As he felt her cut his hair and each lock fell, it felt as if he was losing ten pounds of dead weight.

When she finished, he ran his hand over it, enjoying the feel of the cut.

"Let me see your makeup mirror." He held out his hand for her to give it to him.

"Why? It looks good."

"I want to see."

"Then go look in the one in the bathroom."

"I will, but I want your mirror so I can see the back."

Scowling at him, she didn't reach for her purse. "You think I'm such a bitch that I would shave another rat on the back when you're down?"

Calder didn't drop his hand, waiting for the mirror.

Glowering, she got the mirror, slapping it down onto his palm. "There."

Going in the bathroom, he went to the sink, admiring his haircut until he turned around.

Gritting his teeth, he went back to his room.

The bitch had sneaked out. She had cut off most of his hair, leaving one long strand that looked suspiciously like a long rat tail, and then ran away. Crazy bitch.

"THREE MUSKETEERS."

"What?" Calder asked when he came back from group therapy. "You want a candy bar?"

Crazy Bitch was sitting on his bed, painting her toenails. He wanted to take a nap, yet she had all her shit arranged so he would feel like an ass to make her move.

"Fat Louise and Cade were allowed to visit Charlotte. Fat Louise asked her if Greer had given her a clue to give them. Charlotte didn't know what she was talking about, just kept asking them to get her something to eat. Their time was almost up when Cade figured it out. Fat Louise had asked him to buy her a candy bar for the trip home. They gave one to Charlotte, and she just thanked them, and they left. Well, they left after Cade bought all the Three Musketeers they had in the machine. I feel sorry for the poor fuckers who go to visit her before the vending machine is restocked."

She was laughing so hard that Calder didn't think she was sorry at all.

"When they opened the candy bars, there was a clue inside?" Calder asked, sitting down on the bottom of his bed.

"What do the musketeers guard? They protect the royal family, damsels in distress." Crazy Bitch laughed. "You like this color?" She wiggled the big toe she had just finished painting. "It's called Sinful Red."

He swallowed. "I like it a lot."

"Thought you would."

"So, what about the clue?" Calder watched as she accidentally painted the side of the nailbed.

"The clue *was* Three Musketeers. Fat Louise must have eaten half the candy bars before they were smart enough to figure it out."

She handed him the nail polish and brush. "I hate painting my toes. I always make a mess of them."

He swallowed hard at her helpless, wide-eyed, pleading look that enticed him to take over. "I can do them for you."

"Thanks." She plumped his pillows behind her back. "Make sure you do them right. I'm picky about my toes."

Calder set her foot on his lap. The part of his anatomy that hadn't stirred since he had awoken in the hospital lengthened under his jeans.

"You are?" His fingers started shaking when she pressed her heel down on his growing bulge.

"Hot thang, you have no idea about the things I can do with my toes."

One Month Later...

"ARE YOU READY TO GO?"

Calder locked the sliding glass door then turned to see her waiting by the door, his suitcase already in her hand. It was a sight he would always remember. The woman he loved waiting to leave by his side.

"Almost." Calder went to the wall in front of his bed, grabbing the pictures she had hung there, despite the administrator's protests. They were in a row so he would see them first thing in the morning, and so they were the last things he saw at night. And every single time he had seen them, he had wanted to break. He had wanted to break so many times, and he had. And when he had broken down, falling backward into despair, she had caught him and brought him back.

He lifted Star's picture off the hook, then Crazy Bitch's, and then Stud and Sex Piston's family portrait.

They were all waiting for him in Stud's van, waiting to drive them home.

Tucking his pictures into the outside pocket of his suitcase that he took from her, he let her go first, taking one last look around before turning out the lights.

Holding hands, they walked to Gavin's door, where Calder paused before knocking.

"Are you sure? It's your last chance to change your mind?"

Crazy Bitch grinned. "I'm sure."

Calder knocked, letting her open the door when they heard Gavin tell them to come in.

The friendship they had developed when they had first met had transformed into a bond that had Calder saddened at being released before Gavin.

The man who was staring out the window no longer needed his constant companionship. As close as they had grown, Gavin's personality had undergone a change after seeing Taylor.

When he had met Gavin, he had been helpless, almost childlike, wanting to please and obey those around him, with a conscience that ripped his soul to shreds because of the things the Road Demons had made him do, destroying the intrinsic goodness that had been Gavin. As the drugs had been gradually reduced, his mind had then become a labyrinth he couldn't find his way out of. Then Viper, their father, as well as all The Last Riders, had become gossamer threads, making Gavin feel lost in the cobwebs he couldn't find his way through.

How could he turn to them for understanding when he was afraid they wouldn't accept the acts he had been forced to commit? He couldn't even accept them himself.

Taylor's visit had been like taking a water hose to those cobwebs, taking away his last hope of leading a normal life, decimating what Viper had worked so hard for him to regain —the Gavin they all knew and loved.

Gavin might have gained weight and strength, yet there was now an austere countenance about him that didn't give away what he was thinking or feeling. It was nerve-racking and, with his body getting larger every day, it was becoming frightening. Calder had several friends who were the same size, but with Gavin, it was in the way he moved silently, the way he could touch something as benign as a soda can and a tingle of fear raced up your spine, as if the man had a lethal weapon in his hands.

Calder wasn't a praying man, but he said a prayer each night for Gavin. The man had gone through hell. The traumatic years of abuse and the degradation Gavin had dealt with had taken its toll on him. When he had realized Taylor had irrevocably moved on, it had destroyed something inside him. Calder didn't know if Gavin would ever get it back, but he hoped so.

Crazy Bitch had helped and fought alongside him so he could find his way back. Until Gavin found that person or cause that gave him a worthwhile reason to take one breath after another, he would never be free of his past.

"I thought you two left hours ago?" Gavin closed the book he had been reading.

"We were about to, but Crazy Bitch wanted to ask you something before we did."

"Gavin, I know this is going to sound silly, but do you have a package or box that Greer Porter gave to you?"

Gavin stood, going to his closet and taking a box out. "He told me to give it to the first person who asked. Shade introduced me to him when I first got here. He came back a few weeks ago and asked me to keep it for him. He told me it was a surprise and he didn't want them to see it before the time was right. At first, I told him no." Gavin's forbidding expression showed that he wouldn't be so gullible to anyone who tried to take advantage of him again. "But he said I would know whoever would come to pick it up." He held the box out farther for them to take.

Crazy Bitch shook her head. "It's yours."

"Mine?"

"Yes. It's a present. Go ahead and open it," she urged.

Gavin set the box down on the bed. Tearing the tape off the box, he then tore it open, pulling out three black leather jackets, each with different patches and club names on the back.

"I don't understand."

Crazy Bitch took a step forward. "This jacket is Stud's. As president of the Destructors, he's telling you they will always have your back. In the pocket is a motorcycle key. It belonged to Stud, but now it's yours."

Calder reached for the Blue Horsemen jacket, spreading it out to take the keys out of the pocket. "This is my jacket. As president of the Blue Horsemen and brother, I will always have your back." Calder handed Gavin the key. "This is the key to my motorcycle. It's yours. Stud will put both bikes on a trailer and park them at The Last Riders' clubhouse tomorrow."

Calder then put his hand in Viper's jacket. "You don't need me to tell you that this is Viper's jacket, or that The Last Riders will have your back; you already know that." Calder placed the last key in Gavin's hand. "Viper said he's been riding it for you, but that you need to ride your own bike. They want you to know that it's time to come home."

"You having a good time?" Crazy Bitch grabbed a marshmallow that had been speared by a toothpick, raising it to the lame chocolate fountain Sex Piston had bought online, letting the chocolate dribble over it. Then she raised it to her mouth, bit down, and slid her red lips over the marshmallow, pulling it off the toothpick.

Calder's mind went blank... with lust.

"Excuse me. I need to find Diamond," Knox said, stepping away.

Calder didn't even notice the man leaving, his eyes trained to the strappy black piece that Crazy Bitch was wearing. The fucking thing had more gaps that showed off her skin than it did material. Raking his eyes downward to her shoes that would make a stripper envious, he had to set his paper plate down before he spilled the food on Sex Piston's carpet.

"What were you and Knox talking about?" Crazy Bitch asked.

"He asked how your community service is going. I told him you were diligently doing your time."

"I can deal with the community service. It's the paying for it that sucks. I still miss my car."

"I'm still amazed you managed to sell it to Train, and for so much."

"He didn't complain when I asked how much it was worth not seeing Killyama in it when we go out."

"He didn't appreciate you threatening his wife's safety to get a higher price."

"He didn't say anything to me." She dunked a strawberry into the chocolate fountain.

"No, but he had a lot to say to me."

"What'd you say to him?"

"I told him it's a classic and that, if he restored it, he might get his money back."

She ran a caressing hand down the front of his T-shirt. "A devious man makes me horny. You know, if Train restores it, Killyama will make him give it to her."

"I've learned from the best."

"I'm not in Greer's league, but I'm close." She gave him a luscious smile, reaching for another strawberry. "I only needed enough to pay back for the damages I did to the police car, but it helped with the work I missed."

"I wanted you to take my money, but you refused."

"We're saving for our house; we're not touching that money. I need a backyard for the dog we're going to get."

"The bigger, the better."

"The house or the dog?"

"Both. We need a dog big enough to eat Manson."

"I was thinking of a chihuahua."

"No, Manson would think it was his dinner."

"Then we'll wait until we can afford a bigger house and dog."

"We'd have enough if you hadn't come up with the idea to give Gavin the jackets. You were the first one to figure out that Gavin was the last clue. Most of the teams were stumped on the castle."

"You solved the castle one." She swayed to the music as they watched Star dance with Harley. They were in the living room. The brothers had moved her furniture to the side, making enough room for everyone to dance.

"Are you ever going to tell me how you figured out that Gavin was the answer to the clue for the Three Musketeers? You said it just came to you when we were having lunch with Gavin, but something tells me you knew it much longer. I think you were trying to decide on keeping the jackets and motorcycles before asking me if I would be willing to give them away."

"Those bikes are expensive. I wanted the one Rider gave to Viper to put up. When I told him what I was going to do, I'm glad he gave you the other set to switch out for the one in The Last Riders' jacket pocket."

Calder watched her nibble from the buffet Sex Piston had set out for Stud's birthday, promising himself he would be finished with the one he had been secretly building for her by Christmas.

"So… how did you know Gavin was the answer to the Three Musketeers clue?"

"That was the easiest of the clues. Three jackets belonging to three club presidents: you, Stud, and Viper."

"You're saying that we are the musketeers?"

"Oh, yes." She ran a caressing hand down his chin, running her thumb over the naked flesh of where his goatee used to be. "And what do they all have in common that they were protecting?"

"Gavin."

During his last week at rehab, he had been able to tell something was on her mind. After lunch with Gavin one day, she had told him that she knew the answer to the clue, pretending that she had just realized it. That must have been what was on her mind: deciding to take the prize or give it to Gavin. She had decided to give it away.

It had only taken him a second to agree. He had already planned to let her have it all, anyway.

Calder still believed she had waited to tell him for another reason. She had hoped The Last Riders would win it and let them be the ones to give the prizes to Gavin, taking the temptation away from her.

When Crazy Bitch had called to ask if Viper wanted to switch the bikes, Viper had told them that the closest team to winning was Shade. He and Lily had gone to the penitentiary, too, but it seemed they had been all out of Three Musketeer bars.

She had worked so hard to win, but then had given it away without a backward glance.

Crazy Bitch deserved more than the motorcycle that was in the same disastrous shape as the green car she had suckered Train into buying, but that was all she had now to get back to work.

She had stayed with Peyton during his time in rehab, refusing to leave him in Lexington. Sex Piston had taken what appointments she could, but she had lost her income for several weeks.

There came a time in a man's life when he had to decide how he was going to spend the rest of it, and Calder intended to spend the rest of his with her.

No other woman would have been able to tolerate him touching her after she had gone into that bedroom. From Stud's description, it had turned his stomach.

He had confessed his doubts about wanting to be with her due to Candi's Oscar-worthy performance, making Stud and everyone else believe he had seen her at the groundbreaking and had left with her. That is, everyone but Crazy Bitch.

Not once had he felt recriminations from her, and when he had felt too dirty to touch her, she had taken care of that problem, too.

"What color lipstick are you wearing?"

"Sweet Pink."

"Jesus."

Calder turned to see one of Razer's sons asking Star to dance. "Which one is he?"

"Who?"

Calder frowned. "The little—"

"That's Chance."

"Suit's him. He's taking a chance."

"Chill, papa bear. You have a few years before you have to worry about boys. I don't think he even knows how to tie his own shoes yet. If you keep glowering at him, he'll go crying to his mama."

"I can take Razer." He stared across the room at the man, judging his fighting skills. When he decided it would be an even match, he continued to finish his plate. Besides, he had plans for when he went home. None of them involved nursing another black eye.

"Have I told you today I love you?" She twirled her strawberry into the fondue. Pulling it away, she lifted it toward his mouth.

Calder opened his mouth, letting her place it inside. Before she could move her hand back, he swiped his tongue over one of her fingers that had a drop of chocolate.

"Yes, you have."

"Just checking." She moved closer to him, making room for Killyama and Train to fill their plates.

"How's it going?" Calder greeted Train.

"Good. You?"

"My woman just told me she loved me for the fourth time today. I couldn't be better."

"I heard." Killyama made gagging noises.

"I didn't hear you say it back."

"Give her a good whack for me." Killyama snickered.

"Huh?" Calder looked questioningly at Killyama, who had gotten into a shoving match with Crazy Bitch.

Calder set his plate back down, pulling Crazy Bitch away from Killyama, who had gotten into a weird karate pose and was egging her to "Bring it."

"There are kids around," Calder hissed.

"She started it." Crazy Bitch pulled her top back up that had become dangerously close to spilling her breasts into the fondue she was standing next to.

Killyama dropped her pose, coming back to take her plate from Train. "I was just trying to be helpful. Issues like yours need serious attention."

Calder frowned. Was there something going on with Crazy Bitch that she hadn't wanted to tell him.

"What issues?"

"Bitch, shut your mouth!"

"Like, she thinks nobody loves her because no one spanked her when she was little. I offered to give her a hard whack whenever she wanted."

"You're dead, bitch, fucking dead." Crazy Bitch lowered her voice to a mumble when Lily and Beth gave her disapproving glares.

"She said that?" Calder smothered his laugh when Crazy Bitch turned eyes that were twitching with anger at him.

"She did. She also said you hit like a sissy. You should really buy a paddle and show her how much you love her. Let's go, Train. Sex Piston is saving us chairs. I don't want to miss Star's performance. The sooner it's done, the sooner the kiddies are going upstairs for their sleepover."

Fat Louise shouldered her way between the bickering women. "Poor Lily and Beth. They got saddled with all the kids while we get to par-tay. They don't know what they'll be missing."

Killyama rolled her eyes. "Beth and Lily have been to better parties than Stud's birthday."

"Want to make a bet? We can get rowdy." Fat Louise shimmied her whole plate of food under the fondue.

"No, you'd lose." Killyama gave Train a nudge toward where Sex Piston was sitting. "Calder, don't forget, if it can't kill a fly, it isn't hard enou—" Killyama hurried away when a strawberry came hurling toward her.

"She's still mad at you." Fat Louise stared at Crazy Bitch sympathetically.

"What did Crazy Bitch do to make Killyama mad?" Calder asked, his shoulders shaking.

"She asked Train if his dick was better and texted him a number for a doctor who deals with fertility implants."

Calder winced. "They do that?"

"They must. All the brothers called to see if it was a working number."

"How did the brothers know she had texted Train about it?"

"It was a mass text."

"Jesus." Calder was shaking his head at his girlfriend when Star raised her hands to get Dozer to stop the 60s music Sex Piston had put on for the children to dance to.

"Daddy?" Star called out for Stud.

Calder grinned when Stud went to the middle of the room to stare down at Star. His brother towered over the girl as she stared up at him in hero worship.

The first night he had been released from rehab, he and Crazy Bitch had spent the night at Stud's. Together, they had all told Star the truth.

The pills that Candi had fed him could have killed him;

not only that, but accidents happen. He didn't want life to take him out without her knowing the truth.

Candi was back in prison, where she would be long after Star was grown.

Crazy Bitch was right; sooner or later, she would have found out the truth. It was easier to contain the blast before it happened. Except, there had been no blast. Star had accepted it matter-of-factly. She had always been told Sex Piston wasn't her biological mother, and she was secure enough in their love that, when she had found out that Calder was her biological father, she had just stated that most of her friends had two daddies, some of them had three. Apparently, one of her friends named Riley had three and the mother was working on four.

"Daddy, you sit here." Star took Stud's hand, leading him to one of the chairs that the brothers had moved.

"Papa," Star called out.

Calder froze. She hadn't called him that before.

Crazy Bitch gave him a hard shove in her direction.

When he got closer, her eyes twinkled up at him as she led him to the chair next to Stud's.

Going back to the middle of the room, she turned back to face them. "Daddy, I've been practicing this for your birthday. Papa, the last part is just for you."

Dozer turned the music on, and as a male voice singing "Always and Forever" filled the room, Star danced around the room in moves he had watched her diligently practice for weeks. In the middle of the song, she did big spins. When she danced near Stud, she pulled him to his feet, raising her arms for him to hold her as he danced with her in his arms. When the song ended, she kissed him on his cheek.

"Happy birthday, Daddy."

Calder watched as Stud kissed her back with tears in his eyes. Then the music started playing again, with a female voice singing "One Moment In Time." As the song played, he watched Star dance as if she was dancing on air.

Every breath he had ever taken had led him to this very second—watching her dance for him.

Looking around the room, he met Crazy Bitch's eyes, seeing tears rolling down her cheeks. She had made it possible for him to be Star's father.

When Star twirled around the room and came to a stop in front of him, she took his hand so he would stand. Raising her arms, she waited expectantly for him to pick her up.

Lifting her into his arms, he danced her around the room. Unashamedly, he cried when the song ended much too soon.

Her arms tightened around his shoulders.

"I love you, Papa."

"I love you, too."

Calder buried his face in her hair, smelling the sweet scent and taking a minute to regain his composure before he lowered her back down to the floor.

Sex Piston stood up. "Kids, you can all go upstairs, and Beth and Lily will put a movie on for you."

Calder saw Crazy Bitch coming toward him to where he stood in the middle of the room as the adults shooed the children upstairs.

"Enjoy your dance?"

"Yes, it's something I'll always remember. Thank you for helping her. She looked beautiful."

"That's not the only thing you're going to remember tonight. You ready to get frisky? I told Dozer to play our song when the kids are gone."

The beat that filled the room was very familiar.

"Hot thang! How low can you go?"

Calder started to move, matching her movements with every beat.

"Let's go crazy and find out."

HARLEY LICKED at his tasty blue snow cone while he walked until he finally sat down on the bleachers.

The young boy he had sat down next to looked over at him strangely before he turned his head back to the football game.

His little legs swung back and forth as he continued eating his snow cone. "My name's Harley. What's yours?"

Again, the boy looked over at him, but only for a second, seeming to be bothered that a little boy Harley's age would disrupt his football game with his friends. "Uh… Ricky."

"My sissy Star knows a Ricky in her class." Harley paused for a moment so he could lick a trail of blue that was starting to fall down his hand. "She says he's a meanie who won't leave her alone. Does that mean you're a meanie, too?"

This time when Ricky looked at him, his head didn't turn back to the game. "Are you lost or something, kid?"

"No, my daddy's right there." He pointed one of his little fingers at Stud, who was surrounded by a big group of bikers.

You could hear Ricky gulp, even over the crowd. "Th-That's your d-dad?"

"Uh-huh, and that's my cool uncky Calder." Just like perfect timing, Star had been picked up by Calder and placed on his shoulders. Even though you could see some pissed-off faces in the crowd that now had their views blocked, no one dared to open their mouths.

The young boy now wiped at the beaded sweat that fell down his spikey hair.

"Uncky Calder wanted to teach that meanie face Ricky a lesson when Star came home crying, but Daddy wouldn't let him."

You could hear the exhale of relief, only to be replaced by

fear once more when Harley swung his little legs harder as he continued.

"Daddy said they'd have to wait till he was older to teach him a lesson."

Terrified, Ricky looked at Stud, who was now searching the bleachers until his eyes landed on him and Harley. The sweat coming from his spikey hair now poured down while Stud walked toward them.

"Don't worry; it's not uncky Calder comin' over." Harley smiled, showing his little, blue-stained, sharply pointed teeth. "Daddy won't hurt you till you're a man."

www.ingramcontent.com/pod-product-compliance
Lightning Source LLC
Chambersburg PA
CBHW020237200626
46816CB00001BA/16